The Sanctum

Praise for The Sanctum

Pamela King Cable has created an unforgettable heroine in Neeley McPherson, a remarkable young woman of such courage and spunk that she dares to stand against unspeakable abuse and injustice not only for herself but also for her beloved caretaker, Gideon. Fleeing a horrendous life, Neeley discovers the true meaning of family, forgiveness, and love in a wolf sanctuary, which becomes a central metaphor for the difficult journey we all must undertake to find our way home. Thoroughly enjoyable book!

~ Cassandra King Conroy
Bestselling author of *Moonrise*, *The Same Sweet Girls*,
The Sunday Wife

This coming-of-age tale, *The Sanctum*, brings readers deep into the underbelly of the Carolinas, introducing us to a spunky young woman named Neeley who captures our hearts and breaks them at the same time. When life takes a few bad turns, she hits the road with a friend she is determined to protect from the dangers of violent racism. Tucked in the North Carolina mountains, Neeley comes head-to-head with robed Klansmen while learning the secrets of her family's past. With a circle of compassionate strangers, a first love on the brew, and a pack of wolves in their midst, Neeley discovers the true meaning of family and faith. In this gothic but inspirational tale, Pamela Cable thrills readers with her tight plotline, lyrical scene descriptions, and complex character development. She also leaves us aching for more.

~ Julie Cantrell
New York Times and *USA TODAY* Bestselling author of
Into the Free, *The Feathered Bone*,
When Mountains Move, *Perennials*, *Dog Saves Duck*

Filled with timely questions of race, religion, and belonging, *The Sanctum* is told through the broken yet resilient voice of Neeley McPherson of Summerfield, North Carolina. Emotionally and physically scarred by the immense loss she suffered as a child, Neeley is determined to save Gideon, the beloved elderly African-American man who raised and protected her from the racist hypocrites in her tight-knit community and ultimately saves herself. Its mystique, evocative of *The Secret Life of Bees*, *The Sanctum* is a novel you will find yourself reading out loud simply to hear the cadence of language, and yet is so engrossing, you won't want to stop until you have reached the conclusion, declaring that truth will indeed set you free.

~ Jolina Petersheim
Bestselling author of *The Outcast*, *The Midwife*,
The Alliance, *The Divide*

The Sanctum

A Novel

Pamela King Cable

Published by Gracelyn Rose Publishing
GracelynRose.com

ISBN: 978-1-962754-08-8 print
ISBN: 978-1-962754-09-5 eBook

Interior design: Julie Murkette   Cover: Gracelyn Rose Publishing

The Sanctum is a work of fiction. Names, characters, places and incidents are products of the author's imagination or are used fictitiously. Any resemblance to actual events or locales or persons, living or dead, is entirely coincidental. Any mentioned brand names, places, and trademarks remain the property of their respective owners, bear no association with the author or publisher and are used for fictional purposes only.

Scripture quotations are from *The Authorized King James Version*. Rights in the *Authorized Version* in the United Kingdom are vested in the Crown. Reproduced by permission of the Crown's patentee, Cambridge University Press.

The language used to describe the diverse groups in *The Sanctum* is intended strictly for narrative purposes and to reflect the era in which the story occurs.

10 9 8 7 6 5 4 3 2 1

Printed in the United States of America

Other Books by this Author

The Televenge Trilogy

Andie Oliver is a devout young woman dedicated to God, her husband Joe, and the influential televangelist Calvin Artury—a Godfather in a Mafia of holy men. As Joe immerses himself in the megachurch ministry team, sinking deeper into its corruption, Andie determines to free him from the Reverend's control and far-reaching influence. To uncover murders and long-hidden secrets, she sacrifices everything, including her children. In a valiant fight for her life and the lives of her family, Andie confronts the very definition of sin and shakes the Christian evangelical world to its core. Evading ruthless adversaries who will protect Reverend Artury at all costs, Andie Oliver battles the dark side of televangelism and those who have made a mockery of the church.

Televenge
Book One of the *Televenge* trilogy

Avenge Us All
Book Two of the *Televenge* trilogy

Vengeance Is Mine
Book Three of the *Televenge* trilogy

Southern Fried Women
A collection of Southern gothic short stories

For more information or to purchase, go to:
GracelynRose.com

Praise for Southern Fried Women

Pamela King Cable is one of those infrequent writers who can bring reality to fictional characters so strong that you'd swear you had encountered them in your own life's history. *Southern Fried Women* will leave the reader looking forward to more from this accomplished, imaginative, skilled, and entertaining author!

~ *Midwest Book Review*

If you don't find yourself devouring this delicious book of short stories by Pamela King Cable, then you are not a *Southern Fried Woman* (or Man). After laughing and crying your way through this collection, you will eagerly await new offerings from this talented writer!

~ Cassandra King Conroy
Bestselling author of *Moonrise, The Same Sweet Girls,*
The Sunday Wife

With a clear Southern voice and a remarkable gift of storytelling, Pamela King Cable has crafted a masterful collection of short stories. In themes ranging from flea markets to coal mine strikes, *Southern Fried Women* speaks of the wounds, joys, and sacrifices experienced by women who held strong in the winds of adversity and emerged bruised by miraculously unbroken. Each story is as though provoking as it is beautifully written.

~ Beth Hoffman
New York Times Bestselling author of *Looking for Me,*
Saving CeeCee Huneycutt

For Lilli

Life is either a daring adventure or nothing.
To keep our faces toward change
and behave like free spirits in the presence of fate
is strength undefeatable.

~ Helen Keller

Acknowledgments

Special recognition goes to Elizabeth Sherwen Mahaffey of The Wolf Sanctum in Bakersville, North Carolina, for revealing the true essence of a sanctuary many years ago.

As always, my gratitude goes to Julie Murkette. Having such a priceless friend in my corner is a true blessing. I am eternally thankful for your expertise and for being an unwavering champion of my work.

My heartfelt thanks and abundant love to my sister, Kathy Savoy, and dear friend, Debbie Shircliff, for your vigilant support and keen insight.

To my family and the readers who have been a part of my journey, I am filled with immense gratitude for your steadfast love, support, and prayers.

And to Michael, you are my sanctuary. This book belongs as much to you as it does to me, for without you, it would not have been possible.

> For the strength of the pack is the wolf,
> And the strength of the wolf is the pack.
> ~ Rudyard Kipling

CHAPTER ONE

My parents died on November 13, 1951, my fifth birthday. Some nights, I'd hear the glass shatter and wake in a puddle of sweat and chills. Their faces had started to fade from memory until I discovered two old photographs, creased and sticky with dust, hidden beneath the dining-room hutch.

I wasn't in those snapshots of my parents; both movie-star beautiful. But I had become desperate to remember them, the way they smiled at each other and at me, the way their fingers touched at supper, and even the way their arms filled their sleeves. My father's shaved face, chapped and red from the cold. Momma and me dancing to the wail of Hank Willliams on the radio, her fingers clicking to the beat, eyes closed. The twirl of her stiff petticoat and the gentle swish of her skirt, all while I tried my best to imitate her every move.

The morning my mother died, she had washed two loads of clothes, starched and ironed my father's shirts, and then hung them near the front door, which seemed strange. She couldn't find her black snow boots with the rim of fur on top and the front zipper, which made them easier to pull on over her shoes. I had helped her search, crawling on my belly under the bed beneath the coverlet and sheets into a cave of dust balls and dead flies, finding them entangled on the braided rug. I tossed out her boots.

"Good girl," she said. "Now, let's finish packing while we wait for Daddy, and then we can celebrate your birthday." I remember climbing on a chair, watching her empty dresser drawers, and folding our clothes into two suitcases, a large one and a smaller one. My mother sang, her voice vibrating inside my chest and speaking directly to my heart, *Hey, Good Lookin* . . . But when the last suitcase clicked shut, a fat tornado fell out of a storm brewing inside our house all morning.

My grandfather, whose name was Pudge, had yelled during breakfast. "Your yella-bellied husband ain't movin' in here to take over *my* farm. Get the hell out!"

Well, that was fine with us. That's what I believed we were doing—getting out.

My father had come home on leave, or maybe because somebody wounded him because he walked with a cane and wore a uniform. I think it was an army uniform, but nobody told me about his time in the military or how he got hurt. Any way you looked at it, he came home to rescue us, to take us to our new home. That's what my heart told me.

The vicious thud of Pudge's hobnail boots spiraled up from below and grew louder and louder with each stomp up the steps. He blew into my mother's room, scooped me off the chair, and set me outside the bedroom door. His thick lips broke into a sneer of crooked yellow teeth and foul breath.

The air turned hot when Momma balled her hands on her hips and shouted, "You think we *want* to live with you!? You're not doing to me what you did to my mother. I *never* want to see you again!" When Pudge threw Momma against the wall like a ragdoll, she pounded her fists on his chest as I clung to her leg. Rage, like smoke, billowed through the hallway, and I remember thinking the house was on fire. Words sharp as razors filled the hot air, growing hotter as my mother's hands picked me up and held me close, pressing her lips against my ear. "It's okay, sugar. Get your coat." The fear in her voice sounded like the screech of a rusty hinge.

But as soon as she said it, my father showed up with my coat in his hand and carried me downstairs, hobbling out the front door and then setting me down on the porch. "Get in the car, Neeley, honey," he said.

I pushed and squirmed, trying to get back inside, wanting my mother more than life itself. "Where's Momma?"

"She's coming." He turned me again toward the car. But I stood firm, listening to Pudge pitch our suitcases against the wall, and as I opened the screen door, he shoved my mother forward, sending her flying down the staircase.

My father staggered forward to catch her, his voice shaking the house like thunder. "You touch her again, and I'll kill you!"

Pudge struggled to pull something from his pocket. When the gun appeared in his hand, I recall falling, scraping both knees, wanting to save us from the evil Pudge who yelled foul words again and again. But my father had rushed up the steps in time to knock him backward. That's when the gun fired. The shot hit the second floor's ceiling, transforming what were once bedrooms into abandoned spaces. A hole in the heart of what remained of my shattered family.

My mother pulled me out the door while my father followed us to the car, limping like always, sheltering us with our suitcases in his hands. His fingers moved quick and intent on starting the car, shifting into reverse, and barreling fast out the gravel drive. My mother said we were going somewhere special, and I remember feeling safe in the front seat, nestled between them.

Pulling onto the dirt road, my father smiled and lit a cigarette. "We're free of him, Lizzie. We're free."

I can still picture Momma in her pink dress and matching pearls beneath her gray wool car coat with shiny buttons. She loved pink. The reflection of snow and sunshine outside the car lit up her berry-brown hair. Bobby pins crisscrossed behind her ears, holding back the curls that tumbled down her neck and onto her coat. She removed one of the pins, bit it open, and slipped it into my baby-fine hair to keep it out of my cornflower-blue eyes that matched her own.

My father's pitch-black hair glistened in the daylight. Cut clean off, it stuck out of his head like a teeny bristle brush, and he smelled like the Black Jack gum he shoved into his pocket. Sitting there, I sniffed that licorice scent into my memory of him. Even now, I still remember that smell. He cracked the window, which felt good because I had stripped off my coat and balled it up to sit on. I giggled when he told my mother, "I feel like a roasted pork butt. Lizzie, honey, can you turn down the heat?"

I recall crawling to my mother. She nuzzled my neck and said, "Gimme sugar, birthday girl." She said she loved me and that I had grown *so big*—so big. She almost sang the words. Her fresh laundry smell covered me whole. To this day, I avoid ironing clothes like a severe case of food poisoning. Once, in Home Economics, I was supposed to iron a simple skirt I'd sewn in class. Smelling the yeasty scorched cloth, I broke out in hives and a sweat. The school nurse said I was probably allergic to the starch. At least it got me out of laundry day on the farm.

Swirling snow powdered the car's hood as more sparkled on the road. Minutes later, I scooted off my mother to snuggle close to my father, begging him to let me drive. He lifted me to his lap and placed my little-girl fingers on the wheel. My eyes hovered just above the dashboard.

And then my mother screamed, *"Martin!"*

A horn blew, and my father jerked the steering wheel out of my hands to miss a truck, hurling our car into a spin and turning it over and over. The horrific sound of metal against metal crashed around me, and the crack of glass ended with a bright, bright light—like staring into a flashlight at night. My entire five-year-old body felt like someone had flung me through a barbed-wire fence as fierce pain raked an icy hand across my head, and my mother's scream pierced through the middle of it. I think I fainted because the terrible noises around us stopped. But the snow, smooth as a satin blanket, woke me, and I found myself lying on the ground.

Covered by the cold, I watched big round snowflakes fall through brilliant sunshine while warm blood dripped into my ears. It was then I heard my mother's soft voice repeating my name; the sound of it I'll never forget. Crawling toward the car, I saw my father on a pallet of snow and leaves, twisted in ways I'd never seen a body twist. I couldn't wake him. I found my mother inside the car, and I sat beside her, thigh to thigh. She made small, gentle baby noises, and I knew if I wiped the blood off her arms and neck, she'd open her eyes. If I prayed *Now I Lay Me*, God would wake them both. But they died anyway, and I fell asleep to the blare of sirens and panic and woke up in a hospital bed.

I'm sure I've not slept over three or four hours at a stretch since.

I had no idea who the people were at the funeral. I remember my brown velvet coat and matching hat that covered the thick bandage on my forehead, a ceremony of soldiers saluting, trumpets playing, a folded flag, and guns that fired and fired. The rifle blasts scared me, and I reached for Pudge's hand. That was the moment I knew I couldn't depend on him for comfort, for love, for nothing, because he pushed my hand away and whispered sternly into my ear—"Behave yourself. Do *not* embarrass me. Stop crying, or I'll whip you good when we get home."

I can barely remember myself before the accident—or before Pudge and his Bible belt. Our neighbor lady told me I was a happy baby with rosy cheeks, a friendly sort who never met a stranger. But the memory of my parents dying in the snow struck me at times like the painful wound on my forehead, and I grew pale and quiet.

Pudge took what was left of my parents when he changed my last name from Morrigan to McPherson. I survived, but they buried the two best parts of me under the cold, red dirt in the Sunset View Cemetery, leaving me with horrible guilt and a fierce ache in my heart that I hid from God and everybody. Nobody ripped my parents out of my life but me. I, alone, am responsible.

I'll never forgive myself for this cross I bear.

The wolf that one hears,
is worse than the orc that one fears.

~ J.R.R. Tolkien

CHAPTER TWO

Pudge, our farmhand Gideon, and I lived northwest of Greensboro, North Carolina. Three churches, a school, a filling station, and a general store that sold everything from perfume to postage stamps made up the crossroad town of Summerfield. Sheriff Troyer raised the confederate flag every morning in front of the town hall, a symbol of deep-rooted heritage in the land of Dixie. Old Glory didn't seem to be enough for some folk.

Several generations had passed down the acres and acres of farms around us. Outside our windows, the true meaning of *rural* stared us in the face. Summerfield was the place to live if you liked the odor of horses, the taste of tobacco, and the constant clang of church bells.

Nothing more than a muddy track strewn with pea gravel, our driveway stretched back two hundred feet from a dirt road to our eighty-year-old farmhouse. Horse stalls, a tobacco barn, and a chicken coop sat near fenced pastures, acres of cultivated fields, and weeds poking up through every inch of red McPherson dirt. Over time, the blue house, yellow barn, and green chicken coop faded to the color of uncovered bones and peeled like sunburned skin. A starved farm. Starved of everything that once made it beautiful.

But my grandfather was a well-fed man. His name was Bainbridge, but everybody, including me, called him Pudge. His gobbler neck bulged beneath a stubble-covered jaw, and when he spoke, his smidgen of sooty-gray hair floated around his bald spot and the tops of his ears. I guessed him to be sixty. Or somewhere thereabouts. He'd said too many years of fried potatoes and buttered biscuits hid the body of his youth. I figured the beer joints he haunted most nights didn't help, either.

On my thirteenth birthday—November 13, 1959—I pleaded with Pudge, promising him everything but my soul, to let me to go with my only girlfriend, Jacine, to the dog pound. Her father needed a new hunting dog, and I needed a change of scenery. Pudge said, "I'll see once't I talk to Jacine's daddy." I about chewed off my fingernails before he gave in.

The dogs stood on their hind legs, stomachs caved in and scabby with dull coats like mud-covered cowhide. Trapped in their pens, begging to be let out of prison, the jailbird dogs howled like someone had set their tails on fire. One black dog rose in the dirt on stick-like legs for the coolness of a breeze or the scent of freedom. I dropped to my knees and wrapped my fingers around the slats, allowing the dog to sniff and taste my hands. Looking into that animal's teary eyes, feeling as if someone had hollowed out my heart, my life has never been the same. I believe its spirit slipped into me because, at that moment, I woke up to a world without color.

When Pudge collapsed on his bed that night, I tippy-toed to the back porch and waited for the moon to rise. With a November-smelling wind at my back, I twirled my furry-white rabbit's foot around my finger. Months earlier, Jacine had given me the lucky rabbit's foot that hung from a short key chain. She said as long as I lived with Pudge, I needed all the luck I could get. I carried it everywhere. But the evening of my birthday, out of nowhere and for no good reason, wild dogs started howling at the edge of our farm. They moved into our woods like a car full of old aunts and cussing cousins, fixed on digging up trouble for everybody but me. Those dogs showed up on my Friday, the 13th birthday, like sweet Baby Jesus, a sinless creature born to save us from our sins.

Listening for the next wave of wind to carry the howling to me, I pulled a quilt around my shoulders. Since the cold had silenced the cicadas and tree frogs, the only sound was of trees and bushes swaying in the distance. No hint of anything unusual appeared in the yard. Just the shadows of outbuildings and our barn sketched against the darkening sky.

Gideon joined me, rocking on the swing with a blanket across his lap, eyeing me like I'd gone plum loco for sitting in the cold, staring at the dark.

"They're a noisy bunch," I said. "How many dogs do you think are out there?"

He didn't answer. Gideon rocked back and forth, the rust-covered chains screeching out familiar tunes I'd heard since I was a baby. Not five minutes had passed when he said, "You know, Neeley, wolves howl 'fore they go at your throat."

"They're not wolves; they're dogs. For crying out loud, even *I* know there's a difference."

"How you know? You seen 'em?"

"Wolves and dogs don't sound the same. Do they?"

"I 'spect there's not much difference between 'em. You beat one down enough; it goes wild. Back to its ancient history. Becomes who it was in the beginning."

I believed Gideon and trusted him because his words bore truth and light. He was not just my caretaker but my favorite person in the wide world. Ricky Nelson, Jerry Lee Lewis, and Little Joe Cartwright were my favorites, too, but not because I knew them. I didn't know them at all. That was not the case with Gideon Jackson. It wasn't easy to explain. Ours was a connection only those who had experienced such a relationship could understand.

Pudge picked Gideon from the tobacco fields. During priming season, Gideon had toiled alongside dozens of men, women, and mules, his days filled with the backbreaking labor of harvesting and curing tobacco. Broad shoulders and solid arms testified to twenty-five years of it. He often said that, in his youth, his arms were quite the spectacle, and his long legs, thick and straight as poplar trees, never seemed to tire.

But the hard life had taken its toll. Gideon's hands, knobby and scarred, resembled cast-iron skillets, and he claimed his eyes were going bad because they'd seen too much. Funny-looking freckles covered his flat, wide nose kicked by a few mules, yet every tooth in his head gleamed when he smiled. He had said he was seventy-something, born on or around February 1 in a year known only to God, and in Nashville, where his momma had cooked and kept house for three Tennessee Governors. Gideon professed he was barely a Negro, because his daddy was white. Although, in our world, you're either a Negro or you're not. His hair gave him away. As wiry as a hunk of steel wool, so silver and coarse, I imagined he could cut it to scour rust off the garden tools. At first glance, he did not appear to be the gentle type. But he was.

Gideon lived in a two-room shack attached to our barn. When I was little, he loomed over me, powerful and strong, his energy endless. After a while, his health sputtered and stalled like his truck. His back ached, yet he worked with no days off, shoeing horses, shoveling manure, fixing meals, and bending over backward to care for me the best he could.

Living on my grandfather's farm, he had become my only real friend. Although my heart longed for a family with brothers and sisters and parents, an actual family, somebody other than Pudge McPherson, I would've never guessed that I'd come to care about Gideon more than I cared about anyone. More than I cared about myself.

I'm sure people wondered why a girl like me wanted to hang around an old man who lived in a shack. No doubt they asked, how could a little white schoolgirl think of friendship with an elderly Negro man as anything but strange? To me, it was like the smell of strong coffee. You don't question what it is. You've smelled it all your life. You accept it as coffee, there for the taking. It warms you. You recognize it every morning and know it's waiting for you. Every day. It tastes the same. Every day. It's safe to drink and never fails to comfort your spirit. Gideon was my one sure thing. Every day of my life.

The people in Summerfield talked about Pudge, Gideon, and me. Not that it mattered. Most folks had known Pudge all his life, or somebody in their family did. They knew we were there. A reluctant Negro hired as a farmhand but forced to mother the orphaned granddaughter of a reclusive drunk. I kept myself alive, hiding the true depth of my loneliness and desolation by walking in the shadow of that Negro on the dusty roads of Summerfield amidst the whispers and glares of those who knew. They knew we were there, living on the same farm. After a while, it didn't matter anymore.

The howling stopped long enough for me to assume the dogs had better things to do than entertain us. Gideon's rheumatism had bothered him all day, so he turned in early, shuffling down the path to his shack. Sleepy myself, I headed inside and crawled between my sheets. I lay there, thinking about all kinds of things a brain does when it winds down for the night. But sometimes, if the breath of a dream doesn't catch you soon enough, your mind takes flight, and off you go into the wild blue yonder.

I thought of Jesus raising Lazarus from the dead. Now, I didn't believe in miracles. At least the cheap, dime-store kind, like the miracle of being asked to a dance or a sleepover. And I knew the ground wasn't about to spit out a couple of bodies just for me. But I imagined standing over my parent's tombstones, shouting with a loud voice and enough faith to split their graves wide open. "Arise, Elizabeth and Martin! Come forth!" And they did. Out they came, back to the land of the living.

My father smiled and pulled me into his muscular chest, holding me on his lap, smoothing my hair, while my mother kissed my tear-stained cheeks until they grew raw, whispering my miserable life with Pudge was over. News spread across the globe about the girl who loved her parents so much that she brought them back from the dead.

From then on, my parents taught me how to act like a lady; they showered me with birthday gifts like a lovely necklace, a new bedspread and matching curtains, and pretty pictures to hang on my freshly painted bedroom walls. We shopped for stylish clothes, and they arranged for a doctor to remove the scar on my forehead. My father wore a suit and tie every day, while my mother and I wore coordinated sweater sets to card parties and luncheons at the Greensboro Woman's Club.

I tried imagining what the girls at school got for their birthdays. I would've given my teeth and toes for a sweater set on *my* birthday. And a skirt with pom-poms and a poodle dog sewn on the front. But Pudge, naturally, refused to buy me nice clothes. He preferred to ask the churchwomen for hand-me-downs. Over and over, I endured hurtful remarks at school, such as, "I wonder whose old dress Neeley plans to wear tomorrow?" So, I turned into a loner. I didn't make friends easily. Besides, Pudge never liked Jacine, and it wasn't worth asking if I could invite a friend to supper. I already knew the answer. Feeding Gideon and me was enough of a burden.

Truth be told, I didn't want anybody to see my absolute misery or to meet Pudge. He was far more of an embarrassment than my ugly clothes. And my scar. I was a thorn in his side. He'd said that. Can you believe it? He was mean year-round, especially in the summer when he managed his tobacco pickers from daylight to dusk. I kept my distance. He only smiled when he worked his mules and horses and handfed his two cats from the table. You'd think I'd have pitched my lucky rabbit's foot by then, but I didn't. I held on to it like I held tight to the memories of my parents, hoping something good would come from it.

I will admit I had begged God more than a few times to smite Pudge with the jawbone of an ass as He had done to the Philistines in the Old Testament. But for some reason, God never answered that prayer. So, I stopped calling Pudge, Grandfather. He was anything but grand. He was my mother's father, yet for the life of me, I couldn't see any of her in him. And God only knew what possessed my grandmother to marry the man.

Gideon once said tobacco farming takes its toll on a man's health, moral fiber, and money—that I shouldn't nitpick. He said scabs never got better when you picked at 'em. Still, some scabs needed picking, and some never healed, especially winter scabs. But they were easier to hide under pants, long sleeves, and Pentecostal dresses down to my Baptist ankles.

In the dead of night, jerked from the edge of sleep, I heard the howling pack start again, softly at first, and then, like turning up the volume on the radio, their music swelled in my room like a symphony of cellos and violins. I raised my window to hear the wild dogs clearly, thinking maybe they *were* wolves. The beauty of their howl was unimaginable for mere dogs or even coyotes. It was as if they had lifted my bed and carried it outside while their cries echoed in the air. I felt like a lunatic, my heart pounding, wanting to run to them despite Gideon's warning. My thoughts exploded with stories of humans raised by wolves, and I tossed and turned in the darkness, staring toward the sounds of whatever animal howled at the edge of the woods, praying they'd adopt me.

I also prayed the noise was loud enough to wake Pudge. But I knew he was asleep, and he didn't just sleep. His whole body got sucked into a massive dip in the middle of his mattress, slipping into a coma as if he had drowned, his sweat gluing him to the sheets even in winter. Pudge rattled the windows, his snoring a deafening backfire and clattering like our Allis Chalmers. Nothing opened his eyes in the morning but a couple of earsplitting banty roosters. Those loud-mouthed birds gave me a heart attack at least twice a week.

But then I thought, go ahead, Neeley. Shake the living daylights out of him. What do you care? It'd be a right-smart shame to miss one of those dogs taking a bite out of his throat.

I flipped back the covers and bolted to his bedroom door. Poking at his chest, my finger sunk into his doughy flesh, and then it dawned on me I hadn't thought of what to say. All the scraps of conversation I'd dreamed up to start some worthless discussion with him were words to be examined under a microscope before I opened my mouth. Otherwise, I might find myself knocked flat.

I decided to wake him slow and gentle-like. I'd seen him go berserk if the TV took too long to warm up or if I sneezed one too many times and blamed it on his cats. He'd cuss, fling his arms, and threaten to fetch his Bible belt out of the closet.

Pudge sat up in his underpants, and his underpants smell sat up beside him. I was familiar with his old-man odors: whiskey breath, loud farts, and a constant rotten attitude. But I never knew the degree of his foul moods until he was fully awake.

His crusty eyelashes fluttered, and his pocked face, swollen and tense, looked like his fist when he punched a wall—which he often did. Good sense warned me to apologize and go back to bed, but my excitement whirled and skidded, and I shouted. "Wild dogs! Come on. They're howling."

Pudge's bullet-shaped head wobbled with sleep. Confused and irritated, he frowned while his goose-down hair set off in forty-eleven directions. His tongue tripped over words that slid out the side of his mouth like drool. "Get me my smokes."

I ran to the dining room hutch. Hooking my finger through a brass ring, I opened the drawer where he kept a fresh carton of Lucky Strikes, along with a half pint of Old Crow, a deck of cards covered with naked ladies, a broken pocket watch, and a Bible tract that read, *Are You Born Again?* When I handed him a new cigarette pack, he glared at me like I had three eyeballs.

"What am I supposed to light it with? Goddamn it, Neeley, you're about as useful as bird shit on a door knob."

I tossed him a pack of matches I found on top of his dresser.

"Is the barn on fire?" he asked.

"No, sir."

"Should we head to the storm cellar?"

"No."

"Did you puke?"

"No, sir."

"Then what's so all-fired important you had to wake me in the middle of the goddamn night?" He blew smoke in my face and then yanked his pants off the back of a chair.

"There's lots of dogs. Howling," I said, breathless. "Out in the woods, I promise."

"Yeah?" He stood and zipped up his fly as far as he could reach under his gut, which hung like an inner tube over his pants. His eyes narrowed from the smoke. "Well now, shit fire and save matches—I think I hear Louis Armstrong playing his gold trumpet out by my new Cadillac." The Lucky dangled from his lips, flipping up and down, but Pudge didn't so much as tilt his head toward the window. Instead, he stumbled into the living room, irritated at God and everybody, and fell, butt first, into his squeaky Naugahyde recliner. A chair covered with cat hair and cigarette burns even though his rubber tire ashtray sat smack beside it. "Come here."

I crept through the archway separating the dining room from the living room. As usual, his oily face glared at me sideways beneath bushy raised eyebrows. "What the hell do you think you're doing?" Pudge opened and closed his hands, waiting for my answer. His stubby, pink fists looked like boiled pig feet.

"I—I wanted you to hear the wild dogs. There's a bunch of 'em. Howling near the pasture. By the fence line, I think."

"Wild dogs, huh? I'll call Sheriff Troyer. We'll set traps." He took a long drag off his cigarette. "Packs of dogs, coyotes—good for nothing but dead livestock."

"I don't want you to *kill* them." I should've known better than to wake him. Pudge had no concept of beauty; he never once questioned why wild dogs were howling in his woods.

"Now look," he said, his nostrils growing as large as his eyes, "what do you want me to do, invite 'em to supper? It ain't up to you! You pull me out of bed again, and I promise you—I'll fetch my belt, you got that?"

I nodded, then sulked to my room in the dark. It was my cue to nip it. Nip it in the bud. Neither he nor I talked to each other about the wild dogs again.

Stretched out on top of my covers, Gideon's words tumbled around in my head. Still, I couldn't believe the dogs meant to sink their teeth into me. Then I thought maybe they came to finish what God had started on my fifth birthday. Every stray animal in Guilford County could've stalked me like a lion and pulled me in sixteen different directions, ate my spleen and liver, and drank my blood until I croaked. That didn't bother me. No, sir. Not a bit. Not by a long shot. I'd lived at the edge of Armageddon for a long time.

The toilet flushed, and then Pudge slammed his bedroom door. My brain flew into motion, and my fertile imagination clicked into gear. I was the next contestant on Queen for a Day. I had just spilled my guts, describing my life on Pudge's farm, crying uncontrollably, when Jack Bailey handed me a clean, white handkerchief and told me to dry my tears; the studio audience had applauded the loudest for me. He awarded me a brand-new Hotpoint refrigerator/freezer, a set of brilliant flatware for eight, and a top-of-the-line bear trap. A razor-sharp trap that, when stepped in, slices and dices a man's foot in only minutes. Then, Mister Bailey put a dozen long-stemmed red roses in my arms, a diamond crown on my head, and a red velvet cape around my shoulders. I smiled a beauty pageant smile as one tear slid down my scarless Queen-for-a-Day face. "Just what I always wanted," I said.

CHAPTER THREE

I was six when I buried my only doll in the pasture to keep her safe from the Bible belt. Pudge's Bible belt was thick and cracked and made of brown leather—long enough to reach around his enormous middle. But instead of wearing it, he wrapped it around his King James, a large Bible with his name stamped in gold on the front. Too many times, I'd seen him untie the belt like he'd untie a rope around a deer's neck hung from a tree to bleed out. He'd unwind it and mutter, *Proverbs thirteen and twenty-four, spare the rod and spoil the rotten child.*

Then he'd make me hold the Bible so I wouldn't have the use of my hands to protect myself. But if I dropped it or tried to run, I'd end up with a few more welts added to my legs and backside, which happened only once. That taught me to stand still, count the licks, and be done with it. The licks were never more than my age. So, you'd think when I turned thirteen, I wouldn't want to do anything to piss him off and end up with thirteen cracks across my hindquarters.

I heard him tell our newly ordained minister, the Reverend James W. Cole, that he vowed to mold me into the God-fearing citizen he'd failed to do with my mother. I had no life, just lots of Wayside Baptist that he never attended with me—except once. He drunk drove me to Christmas Eve service in '57.

I might've been a normal kid without Pudge and his stupid vow. I might've volunteered in class more often. I might've bought my lunch and sat with friends in the middle of the cafeteria instead of eating alone out of a paper sack—by the exit door. I might've cared more about my clothes, homework, and the white socks that constantly slipped down into the backs of my shoes. I might've been a straight-A student; I was smart enough. But

I pretended not to care and stayed middle-of-the-road, average, flying solo under everybody's radar. I spoke softly, stepped lightly, and avoided the tiniest speck of attention to keep my tissue paper self from being ripped to shreds and blown away in the wind.

Everybody thought I was doomed. Destined to a hard row to hoe. I'd heard Missus Fiona Troyer talk about me in the church sanctuary, "The girl is gonna end up an old maid, a floozy, or worse. Why Lordy, who wouldn't, raised by two old men, and one of them a Negro. A girl without a mother is like a ship without a sail, a bird without a nest—"

"—Hands without the proper covering," Miss Sue added, tugging on her white gloves.

Pure light trickled through the stained-glass window over Missus Troyer's head, making the colors bleed into each other and spill onto her ugly hat. But that didn't stop her from snickering. "It's a pity the poor girl will never get the proper training she needs. The old man has money to send her to finishing school but wastes every cent on whiskey."

Over the weeks, I had prayed three times a day for a joyful heart, dropped an extra quarter in the offering plate on Sundays, and surrendered my tongue to nothing but kind words. It didn't matter a lick. My heart, like Lot's wife, had turned to stone. Missus Troyer told the entire church membership her opinions of me every chance she got, and I grew more invisible as time passed. Of course, Fiona Troyer made everybody's business—hers.

But I didn't want to be an old maid or a floozy, for crying out loud. Despite what I didn't have, or the people in my life who died, was it too much to ask to be noticed, loved, forgiven, to live like other girls, invited to sleepovers, church socials, and picnics? I'd longed to receive a birthday card, a Valentine, or have somebody request one of my school pictures. Nobody looked twice unless they wanted to stare at my scar.

The fact was—I hated being female. I hated asking Pudge for money to buy girl things like deodorant, a training brassiere, and Noxzema. But when the snow fell, I remembered what it felt like;

my mother's fingers in my curls and her hairbrush's soft pull. My father's hands, strong and able, tying my shoes, helping me into my coat and boots, and pushing me on a tire swing.

Other than what churned in my memory about the tragic accident that had befallen my parents and me, I recalled only bits and pieces of their lives. Whenever I asked Pudge to tell me something about them, to lift the lid off my pot of patchy memories, he'd stomp off, goddamn his way to the toilet or to town, slam doors, and yell, "Shit'n bricks, Neeley. I ain't got time for your dumb-ass questions. Leave it alone, and leave me the hell alone while you're at it!"

Gideon chimed in when he could. "I swear, chile', you is poles apart from every girl the Lawd ever made, asking too many questions, getting Mistah Pudge all riled up. Your momma and daddy, they not sitting up in Heaven blaming you. A little faith can move mountains and that scar, too. Why, God Ahmighty, if He gets a notion, could peel that thing right off."

I rubbed the thick, silvery scar that rippled across my forehead like melted lead. A painful reminder of my past I couldn't escape, it cut upward from my right eyebrow to my hairline, then down and over, ending above my left eyebrow. At first, it was raw and scabby with crisscross stitches, a jagged rip in my skin, turning me into a piece of gossip for those who knew me. Pudge named it when I was seven. After supper one night, he scooted his chair toward me until his face landed a few inches from mine, blocking out the light in the room. He stared at me like I was some kind of freak. Then, he pulled back my hair and closed his tobacco-stained fingers, thick like sausages, around my chin. Stretching my neck upward, he leaned in close, his breath smelling like boiled cabbage, and I gagged. "The Devil's mark," he said, giving my cheek a soft swat.

The heat of his words burned the scar deeper into my skin and across my heart. I stared back at him. At his long, fat face, his crooked nose, his cheek and chin stubble, and the pink hives spreading over his neck and up to his fleshy earlobes. Stinging tears filled my eyes, and my throat hurt like I'd choked on a mouthful of peanuts.

Clearing the table, Gideon waited until Pudge left the room. "Old man is nutin' but a crazy ol' coot," he whispered, patting my head. He said not to pay him any mind—and that my scar looked like the fat little worms he used to bait his hook when the crappie was biting.

But the first thing folks noticed about me before they said a word or looked into my eyes was my scar—they stared at it like it was a disease they could catch. I avoided mirrors, windows, and anything that reflected my face. I never pulled my hair into the popular ponytail, not even during our hot and sultry summers. It hung like a curtain, hiding each side of my head.

Pudge had said that underneath every ponytail is a horse's ass. Because of his crude comment, my hair glowed red as a bad sunburn down to the middle of my back and kinked in a gazillion corkscrews. Still, that wasn't the worst of it. I was born far-sighted. My eyeglasses were rimless. The kind old women wear. The only kind Pudge would buy. I wanted eyeglasses shaped like cat eyes and black with a curve of three diamonds at the points.

I was no raving beauty. Not at all.

Pudge *did* say I inherited my dead grandmother's poor eyesight and red, fuzzy hair. That single tidbit about her became my only glimpse of her appearance. Thanks to Pudge, there were no pictures of Maeve McPherson in the house. Once, in his absence, I ransacked every room, desperate for a trace of my grandmother, my parents, or even a baby picture of myself; any hint of a family other than what I had stored away in my memory. Cobwebbed memory so thick and tangled I sometimes had to pull it off and away from my entire body.

My life had to change, and yet I knew, living in North Carolina, danger arrived in winter. Southerners hole up during cold weather, their spirits frozen as the landscape. Food is tasteless, and the world smells like rusted roofs, heating oil, and car exhaust. Religious conviction freezes on our faces, but our sins are not confessed. I was a child of winter, haunted by the consequences of snow and cold. It was a dreaded time of year, knowing every cold and flu season brought me bad luck and closer to truths too terrible to bear.

But the day I turned thirteen began a new chapter proving that bad luck could turn into good luck, even though it might take time. Even though the proof of good luck is often invisible as a bubble at first. Even though the evidence of things unseen can make you think you've lost your mind.

With the tobacco cash crop running slow in the winter, Pudge bought and sold horses and mules year-round. Everybody in town knew about our sign—MCPHERSON HORSE FARM. He had the words painted across his pee-yellow barn in giant red letters, bigger and bolder than the *Chew Mail Pouch Tobacco* barns I'd seen on a trip to South Carolina to pick up a new horse. Not long after the paint dried, a couple of hoods from the high school climbed the fence and changed it to read MCPHERSON HORSE*'s ass* FARM.

The next day, Pudge walked all over town with a rip up the back of his overalls, running the entire length of his butt crack. He was an absolute fool, showing his underpants to God and everybody in Summerfield, but he wasn't stupid. No, he was not. He did it on purpose! My grandfather was his own best walking advertisement. Pudge never repainted the MCPHERSON HORSE*'s ass* FARM sign. I think he liked it. That vulgar sign fit him to a tee.

It embarrassed me. I hated it. But I'll admit, I loved the horses. Every day after school, I helped Gideon finish work in the house early so we could spend our evenings in the barn. I intended to volunteer at the Oak Ridge Horse Show every spring, except Pudge never allowed it. His mules had taken first place in years past, and he needed me to ensure nobody messed with them. I only wanted to take tickets or work at the concession stand. But no, Pudge forced me to sit in a lawn chair next to long black tails that switched against gnats and flies, shovel mule manure into buckets, and endure *jackass* comments, one after the other, from boys with Brylcreem slathered in their hair, and Skoal cans tucked into their back pockets.

But at least Gideon let me ride the horses around the pasture to where our road dead-ended. Pudge's farm bordered property belonging to Vivian Crumley, our local divorcee. I enjoyed trotting the horse next to her backyard in the summer because she sunbathed in her brassiere and always waved. I didn't know any kids at school with divorced parents. Divorced women like Missus Crumley stuck out like lace panties on a clothesline full of cotton bloomers. Other folks who stuck out in Summerfield were Mister Petree, a retired college professor from Raleigh who never joined a church. Some called him a communist. Then, there were men with no jobs, old people who lived off the government, and the occasional vagrant wandering into town. Pudge called them all *lazy, no-good sonsabitches.*

But Lord help anyone who socialized with the Negroes. Unless your family hired colored help, you stayed away from them *and* the streets they lived on. White people didn't care to stick out in 1959 when it came to Negroes. They wanted no one to discover their flaws or affection toward any person of color, and for that to happen, they lived as nearly like their neighbors as possible. Everybody worked hard to fit in, agree with the majority, and keep their mouths shut.

Everybody but Pudge.

He was clearly drunk one evening after weeks of constant rain wiped out his bottom tobacco field. Hunched over the kitchen table, burbling with 100-proof breath, blaming his bad luck on *niggers and women,* Pudge said the Negro was ignorant and that Jews and Catholics were no better. And then he said educating girls and niggers was as useful as sending cats and coons to college, that if I planned to go, I better find a way to pay for it. He was a stubborn man whose opinions didn't mean a hill of beans to anybody but me.

I struggled to fall sleep each night, rolling from one side of the bed to the other, my tongue pressing hard against my teeth and my pulse pounding in my head. Pudge had a way of creeping up and stealing my hopes and dreams before I could hide them. Knowing I wouldn't dare talk back to defend myself, he made me feel stupid. I had seen college in my future, figuring a better education might help me find my place in the world, but I never considered how to pay for it or that I even had to. I also didn't understand the hostility between the Whites and the Negroes. Had it not been for Gideon, I might have died soon after my parents did.

Gideon nursed me day and night when I was six, down sick with the measles and laid up in bed with a scalding fever. He sang and prayed, his callused hands wiping my forehead with a cool, damp rag. Pudge barely spoke to me back then. My care and upbringing rested solely in Gideon's hands. Well, that was fine with me. But *nobody* warned me about menstruating, so how was I to know what to think when I started bleeding *down there* other than I was about to kick the bucket?

One summer evening, the light had dimmed to crimson when Gideon found me sitting on a pile of firewood, scrunched up behind the tobacco barn, my thighs to my chest. The sun had changed my freckled, fair skin into a blistery burn. I hid my face. Bubbles of snot and tears had mixed with the dirt on my arms and ran down my legs and into my Keds. Lord, I was a *mess.*

When I sheepishly told Gideon why I was crying, he slapped his thigh with his hat and dropped beside me. His face turned from toasty brown to fire-engine red, explaining my infirmity. At least I knew I wasn't rotting from the inside out, and I knew Gideon telling me I was now a full-fledged woman was a chore he would've preferred not to do. After that, everything I learned about my *down-there parts* came from the pamphlet inside a Kotex box.

Okay, so my grandfather ignored me. I could live with that. But the mean things, the cruel things Pudge did, left me boiling with no way to relieve the pressure. My silent state of anger simmered beneath the surface like my bruises, a constant reminder of his violent temper bleeding under my skin. It never went away. Sometimes, I swear I prayed for the ground to swallow me whole. Practicing the virtue of forgiveness, which I was never any good at, seemed like a waste of time living with Pudge.

There was *one* nice thing I remember about Pudge. He'd come in early from the fields during the tobacco harvest, hollering at me to empty his ashtrays. Standing at the kitchen sink, he stripped to the waist. Red dirt and sweat covered him like shoe polish. After scrubbing his hands and arms with a stiff brush and 20 Mule Team Borax, he reached for his metal tumbler of iced tea. It was my daily chore to boil the water, dump in a jelly jar glass of sugar, and a handful of whatever tea bags Gideon bought on sale. You couldn't have paid me to drink a drop of the stuff.

Tired and worn out as his truck tires, Pudge wobbled to the back porch, shirtless, to sit, smoke, and cool off. He said his back and legs hurt, but I had no reason to sit and discuss his pain or even the weather, for that matter. It's not something we did. Instead, I stepped out on the porch, slipped into my flip-flops, and meandered to where he had parked his truck.

I don't know what came over me, but I crawled inside, and that's where he caught me. Sitting on the ripped-up seat, talking to myself, pretending I was Dinah Shore and that I'd driven down the California coast to see the USA in my Chevrolet, imagining the Pacific Ocean was as blue as his truck. It wasn't easy. The worn-out spot where Pudge hung his hand on the wheel lay in my line of sight, and he'd wedged his snot rag between the gearshift and the seat.

When Pudge appeared at the driver's window with his hands jammed behind his overall straps and his comb-over blown straight up from a breeze, I flinched, then yanked the handle to hop out, but I wasn't fast enough. He grabbed hold of the door and blocked me in. Instead of turning into a raving lunatic, he said, "Every woman needs to learn to drive. If I teach you, you can help Gideon haul hay bales to the pasture." He detested helping Gideon. "You think you can do that?"

For a moment, everything got quiet, as if I'd gone deaf and dumb. Of course, I nodded *yes*.

"Then scoot over," he said. "I hope you catch on fast 'cause I'm only showing you once't."

"Yes, sir." My heart raced, my mouth went dry, and my ears itched like before I took a math test.

Pudge chain-smoked and drove around the pasture while I memorized every word he said. When I got behind the wheel, driving came as naturally as walking. "Put in neutral, pull out choke, push in clutch, start the truck, push in choke, put in gear, lift off clutch. I got it!"

But soon, he'd had enough of listening to his gears grind, and we switched places so he could drive back to the house. He avoided looking me in the eye, shifted to a lower gear, and spoke sober and slow for a change. "You can drive Gideon's truck, but only on the property. I'm watching you like a hawk, and if I see you on the road or sitting in *my* truck again, I'll blister you good." He opened the door, stepped out, and then stood there with his hand on the gaping truck door before he flashed a quick smile that ended at the edge of his eyes. "You did fine," he said.

I felt hot and cold at the same time. For the first time in my life, I wanted to say *thank you* and feel him reach out and hug me to his chest, but that didn't happen. Instead, he cleared his throat and blinked hard. Then he turned and walked toward the house. He'd gone halfway when he looked back. "I don't want what happened to your folks to happen to you. You belong here. On this farm. Turn off them truck lights. They'll wear down the battery."

I sat silent, listening to the truck engine tick and the porch steps crack and grumble as Pudge waddled up to go inside.

I didn't get it. If he wanted me there, why did he treat me like horse poop? I supposed that was the 64,000-dollar question. One I wasn't sure I cared to know the answer. I slid out, stood by the truck, and sighed at the notion of living forever on the Horse's ass Farm. Forever was a long time. And yet, Gideon groaned about how quickly time flew and how old he was getting—but as far as I was concerned, I couldn't get older and fly off that farm quick enough.

When I told Gideon I had learned to drive, he didn't take it well. He knew I'd pester him to death for his keys—which I did. But he never once complained. He simply handed them over with a warning, "You get stuck in the mud; don't 'spect me to pull you out." So, I swapped riding horseback for the driver's seat, cruising around the pastures in a green 1945 Ford pickup, missing a front fender and speckled with rust and dents. After years of hauling hay and manure, it probably wasn't worth a chipped nickel.

Still, that old truck was my escape. For an hour, I'd bounce on the seat, pop the clutch, crank up the radio, and sing along with Patti Page and The Everly Brothers, pretending I was on my way to California and had never looked back.

Chapter Four

The morning after my birthday, the air was so cold and quiet that I heard Missus Crumley's front door slam a mile away. My breath swirled into a plume of white frost the whole hour I dug through the tool shed until I found what I was looking for. Walking up the porch steps with a rabbit snare in my hands, I watched Gideon shake his head. "Lawdy," he said. His eyebrows raised, forming deep lines across his forehead. "What're you doing?"

"Figuring out how to trap a wild dog without hurting it. Pudge wants to kill them."

His head rolled back. "Have mercy," he sighed. Gideon pitched a bucket of dirty water off the back porch onto the cold ground. He'd been scrubbing the kitchen linoleum. Steam rose from his forehead where sweat collected in the creases, the bitter air making his eyes water. He wiped his hands on a rag and stared at the small noose in my hand. "Girl, you be lucky not to get the Bible belt again. You lynch some dog and get bit, don't come hollering for me. No, ma'am, you get bit, you jus' live with it. And don't you walk on mah clean floor with them muddy shoes."

He always said stuff like that to me, but I knew better. I knew more about Gideon than I knew about myself. Gideon loved three things.

First, he loved to sing. Every Sunday morning, he'd drop me off at Wayside Baptist before heading to Oak Ridge Missionary Baptist, our local colored church, to sing in their choir. On weekdays, while he nailed shoes on horses, shoveled manure, or cut firewood, I listened to Gideon belt out several verses to songs from the church hymnal. He often strolled up the smooth dirt path to the house, carrying a fifty-pound sack of flour over his shoulder, singing *the sweet by and by*, and ending the song at the bottom porch step on a perfect note.

Second, he loved food—boiled peanuts, sausage biscuits, and pulled pork sandwiches. Easter ham and Christmas turkey. He baked cakes from scratch and cured several ailments with his herbal and honey concoction. He'd said he learned to cook from his momma, which was our blessing because he rolled out the best butter crust pies in the county. Every year, Pudge volunteered Gideon's services during the annual church barbeque to raise money for African missionaries. Folks came for miles and stood in a long line for Gideon's pulled pork.

Third—he loved me. Only *I* knew his heart was as large as his hands and far more tender than his pulled pork. I also knew Gideon had turned down several job offers because of me. Unfortunately, Pudge knew that, too. Keeping me meant keeping Gideon around to do the chores he had no desire to do.

Late that afternoon, I followed my grandfather into the kitchen. "Since Gideon was down with the rheumatism in his back yesterday, we missed my thirteenth birthday. I'd sure love some sweet corn for supper." It had always been my favorite food. Especially boiled in sugar water.

I watched Pudge, hunched over at the kitchen table with a stack of mail. His cats rubbed around his legs, leaving fur balls on his overalls like always. The only noises were purring cats, a rattling furnace, and the swish of Pudge's long-handled knife opening envelopes. But I didn't budge. I stood as close to him as I dared until, finally, he looked at me in his queer way and said, "Where the hell do you expect me to get corn in the middle of the damn winter?"

That's it. That's all Pudge thought to say.

Hurt and resentment surged through my heart up to my throat, raw and painful-like, having nothing to do with my craving for sweet corn. Any granddaughterly feeling I might've hidden inside me went flat as a roadmap right then and there. I never pretended to have the marvelous traits of patience and courage I felt sure my parents had. I had chucked that notion the year before. But I sensed a low growl, as if from a rabid dog. A sound I heard. A sound I imagined had festered for years deep in the pit of my stomach. A burning rage, enough to chew bolts and spit bullets, rolled up into my chest. I thought possibly I'd grown wolf fangs, and I touched my teeth with both hands to make sure I hadn't.

Pudge slumped in his dirty denim coat. "I got more important things to worry about than corn." The last envelope he'd slit open was from his lawyer, Judd Hastings Esquire. "In fact," he continued, "I don't give a shit about your birthday." He turned away to read the letter and rub at a big brown mole on his cheek.

At that moment, my few diluted hopes and dreams got swallowed up like flies near a frog pond.

"I hate you."

The words popped off my tongue like spit. I hesitated, then stepped back as he lifted his head and peered at me over the letter he held to his suddenly red face.

"Let me tell you something, little girl. Every year on your birthday, all I can think about is that you killed my only child. You and your no-account father killed my daughter. My only daughter. Why the hell do you think I'd want to buy you something for that? Huh?"

I think my jaw dropped to my chest. Since when did he care about my mother?

Pudge set his knife on the table and leaned back in his chair. "Well, now, Miss Priss." He spoke in an eerie rhythm—a tone I hadn't heard before. "Gideon told me why he needed extra money last week for groceries—to buy you a box of them *women things*. So, you're a woman now."

I couldn't look at him. I stared at my feet and nodded.

"Well, la-de-da, ain't you special. Your *mammy* suggested I ease up on you. *That's* your birthday present, you thankless child. Instead of belting your britches for your sass, I'm ignoring your smart-aleck remark. Now, go on. Get the hell out of here before I change my mind. Go help Gideon with the horses," he said.

Grabbing my coat, I stormed out, indifferent to the screen door's protest, as I almost tore it off its hinges. It smacked the door jamb behind me. The old porch boards, rotting and sagging like my spirit, creaked beneath my feet, and I collapsed on the wet top step, hugging my knees to my chest. My rabbit snare stared up at me from under the rose trellis. I didn't care about catching a wild dog anymore. It wouldn't have made a bit of a difference. Besides, my snare would've been better used around Pudge's neck. Sitting there, mesmerized by the idea, I felt the first snowflake of winter melt on my cheek.

Snow started falling like God sprinkling powdered sugar over the earth with His fingertips. A dusting so delicate you could flap your arms and watch it blow away. It settled over the pastures and yard in strands of white ribbons along the path to the barn, drawing my attention to Gideon, backing out of his shack and carrying a pie. He had dug into the winter apples that morning and then crawled on his hands and knees—scrubbing floors until he couldn't stand up straight. Guilt wasn't a big enough word, watching him do chores I should've done by myself. But Pudge never let me do anything but help because he said he wasn't paying Gideon to sit around on his big, black ass.

I strolled to the barn, distracted by dancing snow clouds. Shoving aside the huge rolling door, I found a table set with two dishes, two forks, and a napkin for me. Gideon smiled and then poked a knife into the crust to slice the pie.

"I guess that pie is for my birthday."

"Sho' is. It was your birthday yesterday, wasn't it?"

"It was my bad luck birthday."

"Pah. I don't believe in that number thirteen nonsense. Course now, I don't take much to Mistah Pudge's black cat, and I keeps mah distance from sidewalk cracks, but maybe it be time to make your own luck. Maybe you deserve something special for your birthday. A new start. Even if it is a day late."

I shrugged. "My parents were married on October thirty-first, Halloween. I was born the next year, on November thirteenth. My thirteenth birthday was on Friday the thirteenth. Don't you think all of that means something?"

"Nah, missy. I don't," he said.

I slid into his one and only chair and rubbed at the rabbit's foot in my pocket, knowing why I always kept it close. Gideon sliced the pie, grinning like a mule eating berries and briars, his black gums shining like polished rocks. When he handed me a piece and a bottle of Nehi, he smelled like the salty-earth odor of the peanuts he'd boiled that afternoon. Pulling up a straw bale and straddling it, Gideon bowed his head and prayed one of his silent prayers for snacks. Lord knows, the man never ate a morsel but what he prayed over it first.

"Exactly how long *have* you worked here?" I asked when he opened his eyes.

"For long as I can remember. Too long, maybe."

"Were you ever married?"

"Why you want to know? You not think of that 'til now?"

"I suppose so. I never thought of you living anywhere but here."

Gideon sighed. "Never married. Fell in love once, tho'."

"Did she love you back?"

"I believe she did. Yes, she did. But it jus' didn't work out."

"You have any children?"

His grin pulled at my heart. "Nah. You as close to a chile' as I'll ever have."

I snorted and followed it with my sarcastic laugh. "When was the last time you saw a white girl sit at a table with a Negro man, sharing an apple pie?"

Gideon's eyes narrowed as if peering inside my head. "Today, I guess."

I forked a bite into my mouth. "Whether or not Pudge likes it," I said, "he has created our own integrated corner of the world." Chewing and smiling through my next big mouthful, I savored Gideon's buttery crust and could have easily devoured the whole pie.

But he sat quiet for a moment, then looked up, swallowed, and wiped his mouth on his sleeve. Shaking his head, he leaned back, his voice low, grim, matter of fact. "What you know 'bout integration? Don't go talking 'bout that. Not 'round here. Folks stirring up trouble too much as it is lately. Talking 'bout Negro uprising and such. You don't remember, but it shocked the sugar out-a some when Mistah Pudge hired me to be your nanny. Thankfully—after a while, folks gots used to it. Me being an ol' man with no family mah own." He sliced another piece of pie and mumbled. "We was lucky they gots used to it."

Gideon avoided the whispers and stares the best he could. But sometimes, he had to ask for the colored restroom key. Bitter hatred spewed from the mouths of men—as if he should hold his pee. Yet the women nodded a quiet hello in passing when we went for groceries. Something about Gideon dragging me behind him revived their kindness.

He learned to go to town when the men were at work or too busy to notice him, and a lot of the time, it worked like a charm.

I dropped the subject. I knew it boiled down to the tenderness of Gideon's soul. That's what kept him on the farm when most help would've hightailed it. He tolerated Pudge because of me. He wasn't afraid of him. Only of what Pudge was capable of.

The smell of cinnamon and nutmeg filled my nostrils. I was ready to gulp down my next piece. But a surprising ray of evening sun trickled through the window, landing on my pie plate. The first bit of sunlight we'd seen since October. I swallowed a sigh. "A fat lot of good it does me to have another birthday."

"Why you say that?" Gideon took a swig of his Grape Nehi.

"No offense, but I'd rather play records at a sleepover. Except I don't have any girlfriends. We won't even discuss my sad luck with boys."

"Why you let them boys pick on you?"

"I don't. I always push them away or something. Lucas Cooper said he wasn't hard up enough to like me *and* my scar. He's nothing but a knuckle-dragging ape, anyway." My next bite of pie stuck in my throat.

"I'll never know why them boys gots to be so mean," he said.

"It don't matter. I ain't interested in that twerp."

"Now, c'mon. I didn't raise you to talk like that."

"Like what?"

"Like some trashy white woman. Don't say *ain't*. Don't say *twerp*, neither."

I nodded. We finished my belated birthday celebration in silence. I gathered the dishes and forks, then maneuvered the rest of the pie in my other hand, balancing the pan on my hip. "You're my best friend, Gideon. I appreciate all you do for me. Thank you for my party."

He shushed me with a wave of his hand and shoved an elbow into my ribs, shuffling by on his way out to the pasture. He loved me, and it wasn't so peculiar as some might've thought. Thrown together by a sad assortment of life-altering events, we seldom spoke about them. We simply accepted our fate.

Carrying the remnants of my party to the house, I glanced up at the rolling clouds, forming layers of gray above my head, and listened to the howl of wild dogs in the distance.

I woke on Sunday to the whistle of the wind blowing new snow into drifts and of a shovel scraping it off the porch. The sounds of winter filled the biting air. From my window, I saw Gideon blow streamers of hot breath into his palms before traipsing down to the coop to gather eggs. Then, rushing inside, he got busy helping me with breakfast because only Gideon made biscuits to suit Pudge. He had the touch for punching dough, a skill he used while packing my lunch and frying eggs, and I had become his constant shadow, moving behind him from one side of the kitchen to the other.

At that time, though, I began to watch, with increasing interest, the relationship between Gideon and my grandfather.

Before carrying his breakfast to the barn each morning, Gideon paused at the table, a beacon of devotion, and prayed out loud. That morning, my curiosity piqued and I raised my head, noting the deep shadow Gideon's shoulders cast over the table. His eyes, raisin folds of wrinkly skin, were closed in prayer, and his hair shimmered like tinsel strands in the overhead light's soft glow.

Sitting at the other end of the table, my grandfather, a man of few words and even fewer expressions, begrudgingly endured him. Pretending to be the God-fearing man he was not, Pudge wore a mask of indifference. With his eyes fixed on his plate and hands itching to light the cigarette he twirled between his fingers, his lips puckered with annoyance. He was the only person I knew who smoked and ate at the same time.

"Sweet heavenly Jesus," Gideon began, "I thank ya for a new day, a good night's sleep, and this food here on Mistah Pudge table. Bless Mistah Pudge, who bought the food, and those who is mos' fortunate to eat it. Keep our minds stayed upon thee and our bodies fit for thy service and sanctified holy for thy kingdom whenever it do come. Amen." At the end of his prayer, I watched his chin quiver like I'd seen the Pentecostals do at Jacine's church.

Pudge never said a word during mealtime. Not a *thank you, good biscuits,* or *have a nice day.* Nothing. Those words were not part of his vocabulary. He reserved his rare kindness for his few rare friends, who I'd heard call him a *shifty son-of-a-bitch with as much charm as a painted outhouse.*

But on that particular day, Pudge spoke after his first bite of biscuit and drag on his Lucky. "Gideon. Next time you go to the store," he said, then swallowed, "you bring back the correct change. You were three cents short yesterday." Then he simply stuffed more eggs into his mouth. Pudge's fork on the plate sounded like fingernails down a chalkboard. I hated how he had shamed Gideon and didn't bother to raise his head to do it, and I reckoned the next time I set the table, I'd spit on the old man's fork. Maybe his plate, too.

That morning—nobody went to church.

There was no arguing with Pudge. Gideon stared at the floor, embarrassed. I knew how he felt, and he knew I knew. He only nodded, fixed his plate like always, and toted it to the barn. Against every impulse of his heart, he shuffled out to his worn, wooden table and his one chair that Pudge had thrown out because he said the black leather seat reminded him of nigger skin. Gideon ate alone, as usual, inside his shack. A wood stove warmed him during the cold months. But during better weather, he often sat outside on the ground and leaned against a tree with only barn swallows and field mice for company.

After breakfast, Gideon returned to the kitchen to help me with the dishes, and as he stepped inside the back door, I heard him groan. He was not easily riled up, but the words poured out of him like soured milk that day. Rubbing his chin stubble, he ambled over to the sink and whispered something that caused shame to flutter in my belly like the nervous birds trapped in our barn.

"I'm nothing but ol' Mistah Pudge house nigga," he said.

I bit at my lip and said nothing. No matter how hard he tried to avoid it or how much he believed he was doing the right thing by watching over me, no matter how much I hurt hearing it, Gideon was right. Standing in front of that pitted sink, he looked like he'd hit a brick wall, and I watched his jaw grind the words he *didn't* say between his back teeth.

For years, he'd put up with Pudge and the constant humiliation it took to work for him. I guess Gideon never stopped to think about it, or he most certainly would've left town. And probably should have. Instead, he cooked and cleaned, pitched hay, pulled weeds, and picked tomatoes and beans until sweat soaked his body and bug bites covered him from head to foot. Every day but Sunday, he walked the long driveway to the mailbox because Pudge sure never did it and forbade me to do it. For years, Gideon bent his back in the scalding sun and the freezing snow, nursed his own wounds, and neglected his heart to care for me. When did it become a mission instead of a job?

I kept on biting my lip until it throbbed like my pulse and bled. Tears rolled out and over my bottom eyelashes and down my cheeks. How could Pudge talk to Gideon worse than he spoke to his mangy mules? He had done Pudge the biggest favors of his life by raising me and tending the farm, favors Pudge purposely overlooked. I hated my grandfather, and it scared me how much.

I tried to shut out the shame and sorrow of that morning, knowing I was the granddaughter of the man who mistreated Gideon the worst. He had worked hard to stay out of Pudge's way. From dawn to dusk, it consumed his days. Struggling to finish his chores with me at his heels, he said my mouth ran like a house afire. But he never shooed me away, yelled at me to go inside, or told me to hush. He only patted my head and kept on working. I couldn't picture my life without him. Gideon was alone in his world, and God knows, so was I.

⟫⟫⟫

CHAPTER FIVE

Pudge set off for Greensboro at sunrise, leaving me to my own devices. So, I ate in the barn with Gideon that morning, watching him chew his biscuit, fork eggs into his mouth, and pull meat off a pork chop bone with his teeth. I wanted to forget about Pudge and his ridiculous demands.

Gideon had shown me how to make donuts, hang tobacco, and patch a tire. He said he wanted to teach me how to shoe a horse after breakfast, but I had a different idea. "It's deer season," I said.

"Uh-huh."

"You promised to take me deer hunting this year."

"Don't think so. Not today."

"Then when? Pudge is gone all day; we got a woods full of deer. Maybe I'll see the wild dogs while we're out there."

"Why you want to hunt?"

I didn't answer. *No girl can shoot straight, even if her life depends on it.* I'd heard Pudge say it repeatedly, and I was determined to prove him wrong.

"It's a perfect day for it. Please?"

"No."

"Then can I drive your truck around the pasture?"

That's all it took. After a steady half-hour of non-stop begging and the threat of me getting his truck stuck in the mud, Gideon gave in, and we trotted off into the woods to find a patch of ground covered with acorns and apples.

A faint, cold mix of steady rain and snow fell from a persistent gray sky. The hours dragged, sitting in the bushes. I grew sleepy and chilled to the bone and had to pee. Three does bounded by, then stopped to eat from a tangle of wild honeysuckle. Gideon helped me lift the gun. But then, fifty yards ahead of us, we spotted a buck. His antlers sprouted out of his head like small saplings. Gideon wrapped his arms around me from behind and bent his finger over my finger, whispering to wait until I was sure and ready to take the shot.

I looked through the iron sights and watched the buck scrape his branch-like antlers on a small maple tree as if he were scratching a terrible itch. The buck took an occasional glimpse through a shield of brush and bare-naked trees to where I hid behind the gun, undecided about pulling the trigger.

"Now," Gideon whispered, "shoot now."

My hand trembled on the gun, waiting for the perfect moment to slaughter a regal wild buck. I didn't so much as step on a twig or breathe. But to the buck with his nose twitching, I was a scent he somehow suspected. The End of Days. My fingertips tingled as he wheeled around and bolted away, and even though I knew it was too late, I pulled the trigger. The deafening boom and kick from the gun sent my butt to the ground while a white tail flickered in and out of the brush like a flame on a gas stove until it disappeared.

Gideon shook his head, pulling me to my feet and taking the gun from my hand. "You think you a wild Indian or something? Why'd you shoot?"

"Because you told me to," I said, struggling to keep my voice from shaking.

"But you were s'posed to wait for the right moment, and he was hightailing it!"

"I guess I'm a terrible shot."

"You guess?" he grunted.

"I guess I really didn't want to kill him."

"You guessed right on both counts. You didn't want to kill him, and you a bad shot." Gideon set the gun over his shoulder and stomped off in a huff. "I swear. Out here in the cold, wasting half mah day, horses need feeding, gots me too much to do to be messing 'round in the woods, playing hopscotch with a bunch-a deer."

My legs were almost at a run, catching up to him. "Can we try again?"

"No," he hollered back over his shoulder, sounding disgusted enough to spit. "You had a chance, but you didn't take it. When God gives us chances, we best latch on, not push His hand away, 'cause we may not get another. Anyway, you too young. Jus' a bitty girl, playing with guns, Lawd-hep-me. I don't get paid enough for this nonsense."

Gideon didn't say another word about my deer hunting fiasco that day. We never spoke about it again. He was right. I didn't want to kill the deer. But at least I knew I could pull a trigger if I had to, even though I still couldn't shoot straight.

I became a Christian at age twelve while riding a Greensboro bus. For the first time in my life, I traveled to the city without Pudge. He allowed me to go with my Sunday school class during the Easter season to see The Ten Commandments. But my teacher, Miss Warlick, ended up with a terrible headache when our rowdy group arrived at The Carolina Theatre. Naturally, I volunteered to hop a bus to the Woolworths and buy her a tin pack of Bayer aspirin. An adventure like that was seldom dropped into my lap. Miss Warlick handed me a dollar, money for bus fare and the aspirin, and off I went.

The bus lurched along Greene Street, the driver shifting and grinding gears. I rose from my seat and kindly offered it to an elderly Negro woman who had just boarded. "Here, ma'am," I said. "Take my seat."

Three teenage boys sitting at the front turned and stared at me as if I had committed the unforgivable sin. One hollered, "Where you from, carrot top? 'Cuz we don't cater to niggers down here."

He sneered at both of us while the other two threatened to report me to the police. Right then, I prayed for God to send lightning bolts and slay those boys. But as usual, God didn't listen to me. The elderly woman shook her head sadly as she shuffled past me, and I reclaimed my seat, praying again for God to save me from the cruelty, suspicions, and ignorance of my race. "Jesus would've given His seat," I muttered. And that was it. The moment I truly believed. The moment He entered my heart. Right on that bus.

The bus shuddered to a screeching stop back at The Carolina Theatre. When the doors opened, the hot smell of diesel fuel hit me in the face as I stepped off. I felt confused about Miss Warlick. She had taught us Jesus was a white man. "No matter what *others* might say," she said, "always remember He was white."

Her way of teaching made me picture Jesus as the relative who'd gone off to college and returned educated to the hilt, but not show-offy. She said He was a real person: a little boy who got in trouble for getting lost in the temple, a quiet and well-mannered young man who never cussed, played cards, drank liquor, or got fresh with girls. A handsome man who sacrificed himself for the sins of mankind by allowing the Romans to nail Him to a cross. The hard part for me was imagining whether Jesus was white. Or not. Did anybody know for sure?

But I had an in-depth knowledge of segregation and integration. I understood far more than I was supposed to. Gideon had called me an *old soul* because he said I had matured more than the total of my years. I think life's entanglements often force us to grow up faster than we should. The funny thing, though, was how I *learned* about Jim Crow.

The Sunday before Thanksgiving, we closed our hymnals after singing *The Old Rugged Cross* when someone threw open the back doors of the church. Cold air rushed inside, and I scrambled to pull on my coat but stopped mid-sleeve. Forty-some men, clothed in white sheets and pointy hoods, marched two-by-two down the middle aisle and straight up to the choir loft as if it was part of every Sunday service.

Pastor Cole stood behind the pulpit in his dingy white shirt and rumpled pinstripe suit, grinning like a polecat in a berry patch. Then he cocked his head toward Heaven and thanked God for the brown envelope they handed him, an offering for *the cause.* He introduced them as Protectors of Jim Crow laws for a free white society. God's warriors. Knights of the Ku Klux Klan. He said our women and children were now safe from Negro cruelty because of the gallant men who stood behind him.

One man stepped forward. He sneezed as loud as a sick mule and tugged at his pointy hood, which slid sideways, causing his nose to slip out of an eyehole. When he bumped into the pulpit, a few giggles erupted from the congregation. I knew who hid behind that sheet—Eugene Cooper and his muddy boots. At school, I sat behind his son, Lucas, who, like his father, wasn't much for good manners or clean shoes.

Floyd and Farley Whitsett, the twins from Stokesdale, were easily recognizable. Under their hoods, the Whitsett brothers moved their heads in unison, like always. Known for raising pigs and draft horses on the biggest farm in the county, the brothers' potent stink reached me all the way to my pew.

I spied them all—Joe Renny, our local veterinarian, and Mister Blythe, a kind man who owned the feed store. Mister Carter, our postman, and Gus Griffin, our milkman, who sometimes left candy for me with the milk bill. Like working a puzzle, I sat there and figured out each man's identity under his white pointy hood made from a flour sack.

When Mister Cooper finally got his hood on straight, he announced his Klan club was organizing a membership drive and invited all of us to a holiday potluck at the town hall before Christmas.

Pastor Cole thanked the ghost-like men for coming and ended the service by asking them to join us in singing *Victory in Jesus,* which they did before they filed out, two-by-two, the same way they'd marched in.

Now, most Sundays, I kept to myself and waited in the parking lot for Gideon to pick me up after *his* church service ended. But that day, oh Lord, no. I marched to the back of the sanctuary and stood in line to shake Pastor Cole's hand. The Klan club worried me. If they were anything like the clubs in Mississippi I heard about from Mister Chet Huntley and Mister David Brinkley, we were all in a heap of trouble.

Shoot, I'd heard if a Klan member lost his job, or if his wife up and left him, or even if one of his kids fell and skinned a knee, he blamed the Negroes. If their wives needed taken down a peg or two, the Klan blamed the Negroes. And if a Negro man didn't step off the sidewalk for a white woman to pass, Lord help him. The Klan went plum nutty come nightfall, ripping a Negro man's back to shreds and hanging him from a tree at the side of the road for everybody to see.

The Klan burned crosses in colored neighborhoods, threw bricks through windows, and shot at Negroes after dark. Pudge laughed and said it was another form of *coon huntin'*. I didn't think it was funny. Mister Brinkley reported the Klan in Alabama burned barns, crops, and cotton fields. Anything that belonged to Negroes. And why? Out of pure hatred that had incubated in their white families for decades.

On TV and everywhere, Negro catastrophes and uprisings were suddenly all folks talked about. Except for the girls at school. They filled their yakety-yak-don't-talk-back conversations with boys, the latest hairstyles, and Bobby Darin. Until that morning, I had hoped, for Gideon's sake, to never see evidence of the Klan. But now, here it was. In Summerfield, and in the people I knew. Neighbors who looked the other way and allowed the Klan to join their churches and kill Negroes.

Shaking Pastor Cole's hand, I tried asking my question. "Excuse me, Pastor."

"God bless you this morning, little sister," he said, not even looking at me.

"God bless *you*, but—but," I sighed, watching his eyes move on to the lady behind me. I refused to budge. "HOW can the Klan call themselves Christians if they hate Negroes? Doesn't Jesus tell us to *love* our neighbors as we love ourselves?"

Shouting my question so quick and to the point—it surprised him. At first, he smiled, but then his lips twitched with a bit of agitation. Several deacons standing nearby craned their necks my way. Maybe they wanted to hear his answer, too. Pastor Cole tightened his grip on my hand and said, "A little girl like you shouldn't concern herself with anything other than helping her mother at home and getting good grades."

"Well," I said, "I already make good grades, and in case you've forgotten, I don't have a mother. My *mother* is a Negro man."

As he strained to keep his cool, his smile twisted into a scowl, and his face flushed a blotchy red. I had definitely caught him off guard. He let go of my hand and finger-combed his thick, coal-black hair. "My, my," he said. "Maybe the church can help change that." He pulled at the knot in his necktie, and his eyes darted around like flies. "Maybe you ought to have more of a *female* influence—"

"—Female or *white?*"

Unexpectedly, he seemed to recall who I was and where I lived. But the next words that oozed from his mouth were so thick and rich I could've bottled them to pour over my pancakes. "Go home, precious girl. I will talk to your grandfather on your behalf. In the meantime, Jesus will supply your every need."

The Klan and their church visitation spread like an incurable disease. Everybody shared the same opinion about the dangerous Negroes and their new leader, Martin Luther King. They would not take it lying down, sitting up, or standing still; they would not kowtow to colored civil rights, not now, not ever. Not in Mississippi, not in Alabama, and now—not even in North Carolina. Not in any state that flew the flag of Dixie. But what I knew was the men in white sheets gave me the creeps more than any Negro on the street and that I sure as heck wasn't flying under the radar anymore. I couldn't stand the thought of it, but I also knew that life for Gideon was about to get much worse.

The way I understood it, the closer you were to God, the more blessings you'd receive. But there wasn't a lick of truth in that statement.

For my thankless Thanksgiving Day, I woke up aggravated that the sun dared to shine through my window and then realized, to my horror, I couldn't remember the last time I'd felt truly thankful. My mood turned dark, and the morning light had blurred my dream of a fairy godmother changing me into a raving beauty.

I was simply Neeley Rae—a gawky girl with the elastic shot in her underwear and a training brassiere that didn't fit. But that wasn't the worst of it. I suffered from menstrual cramps, two aching bumps on my chest, and a blight of pimples on my chin and nose, forcing me to give up my one pure pleasure in life, Ovaltine, because it had turned my already unsightly face into a canvas of Noxzema dots.

"Geesh," I said after a long exhale. Rolling out of my self-pity bed, I hurried to dress. Gideon needed help with breakfast before church, and feeling sorry for myself was as pointless as stubbing my toe—nobody cared.

Most area churches held special Thanksgiving morning services, with folks having the day off work and school. I wore my usual black jumper, blue blouse, and faded-blue knee socks. My parents had left me with a memento of their death stitched across my forehead, and as a result, I became pretty good at keeping my state-of-mourning look; thank you very much.

After breakfast, I slipped into my coat while Pudge collapsed into his slick recliner with his two cats, Abbott and Costello. They draped themselves over the back of his chair like a fur collar.

Standing in the foyer, waiting for Gideon, I felt the sun's warmth through the beveled glass door. "I'm off to Thanksgiving services," I announced, tucking my Holy Bible under my arm.

Old age odors of gloom and misery reeked from where Pudge slumped, reading the *Greensboro Record.* A brownish film from thousands of cigarettes and nickel cigars coated the wallpaper behind him. I watched him close his newspaper to light yet another Lucky. "You need a coat," he said.

A quick glimpse in the front door reflected the obvious. My shabby coat barely buttoned in front, and the sleeves ended above my wrist bones. What the hello did he expect? It was second hand from the previous winter with patches on the elbows. As my hands smoothed over the wrinkles, I swallowed the bad words inside my mouth.

Pudge flicked cigarette ashes into a beanbag ashtray, but some fell on the floor anyway. "I got an appointment with my lawyer on Saturday in Greensboro. I'll drop you and Gideon off at Woolworths. Newspaper says they're having a sale. You can buy an inexpensive coat."

I didn't know what to say. He needed his head examined if he thought I'd be shoutin' hallelujah grateful. Once a year, Pudge bought me underwear, a pair of school shoes, and snow boots. That was it. Every article in my pitiful wardrobe was hand-me-down, including my socks. I didn't have a clue what possessed him to blow the moths out of his wallet and buy me a coat.

Blue smoke filled the cold air like fog when Gideon's truck jerked and stalled at the front porch. With my hand on the doorknob, I hollered, "I'm staying after church to help my new teacher with the flannel boards," and slammed the door behind me.

Gideon unlatched his truck's hood and fidgeted with the oil stick. A rag hung out of his back pocket. "Shoulda done this yesterday. I'd forget mah head if God hadn't screwed it on so tight."

I stood on the porch, listening to Missus Crumley's disgruntled cows in the pasture and the far-off rumble of a truck approaching in the distance: frequent sounds of rural silence. I'd heard Pudge say too many folks were moving into the area, that the population had gone up some twenty percent at the last census. But Pastor Cole declared Summerfield was a slice of Heaven. I believe he was mistaken. After all, he pounded on his pulpit every Sunday, shouting that more people went to Hell than to Heaven.

I bounced down the steps and reached for the rusted chrome handle on Gideon's truck. I wasn't sure where Heaven was, but it definitely wasn't Summerfield.

CHAPTER SIX

Sometimes, I dreamed about my grandmother, the woman I so strongly resembled, according to those who knew her. Evidence she existed sat in plain sight throughout the house. Her invisible fingerprints covered the delicate teacup collection, gathering dust in the dining room hutch. I imagined her hanging the lace panels on the living room windows and ironing the flowered kitchen curtains. Filling the plastic daisy napkin holder and dusting the picture of Jesus over the TV. Pudge never bought things like that. Collections of unusual ashtrays were the only decoration in *his* life.

But anyone who mentioned Maeve McPherson to me said things like—*My, you look like your beautiful grandmother—you have her hair, Neeley; it just plain gives me the willies.* She was still a ghost to me. Her death was even more of a mystery. I had seen her final resting place next to my parents' graves, but nobody, not even Gideon, told me how she died. What I knew about her could fit inside the cavity in my tooth. So, when I heard they promoted me to Missus Lila Goodeve's class, I about chewed my fingernails to bloody nubs, waiting for that special Thanksgiving Day service to arrive.

My previous Sunday school teacher, Miss Warlick, had let it slip that years ago, my grandmother's closest friend was Missus Lila Goodeve. Shyness had prevented me from speaking with her in the past, but at thirteen years old, I couldn't wait any longer.

After hearing the same sugary-sweet Jesus stories I'd heard since I was six, I approached Missus Goodeve in her blue polky-dot dress and bland face. She sat at the door, nodding goodbye to her students, wishing each of us a *happy Thanksgiving*. I was the last to leave. Her hands folded in her lap, she looked at me and set her mouth into a tight seam. I think she always knew the day would come. She said, of course, she knew my grandmother, that she was pretty with green eyes, and when I asked her how pretty, she pointed her bony finger at me, her breath smelling like coffee and cigarettes, and said, "Pretty like you."

"Well, if you don't mind me asking, how did my grandmother wear her hair?"

"In a finger wave, mostly."

I took a moment and pictured my face with my hair styled in a finger wave. "Did she sing in the choir?"

"She sure did. Maeve loved *Reach Out and Touch the Lord*. As I recall, it was a Pentecostal song, but she always sang it. Hmm. Let me see, how does that song go?" Missus Goodeve rolled her head back, raised her hands in praise position, and opened her mouth to sing—

"—Yes, well," I blurted, "what color exactly were her eyes?"

Missus Goodeve snapped her lips shut, dropped her hands to her lap, and glared at me.

"Um, you said her eyes were green, but were they dark green like pine or light green like tobacco leaves before they turn brown?" I paused, but only for a second. "And what about my grandfather? Do you know him?"

Puffing out her cheeks, my new Sunday school teacher sighed and flapped a church bulletin back and forth like a fan, as if her face were on fire. The air had grown cold with the oncoming winter, so I didn't understand why she needed to cool off. Wisps of stringy hair scattered around her flat, ivory face in the breeze. I almost laughed. She was a butterbean—a butterbean with mousy gray hair.

"Do you know Bainbridge McPherson, my grandfather?"

Missus Goodeve gathered her purse and Bible and pushed herself to her feet. She shot me a bleak, smirky-lipped smile until her words exploded like popcorn on the stove. "Now, I don't believe, even for a moment, that your grandfather had any involvement in her death, if that's what you truly want to know. Your sweet grandmother was a diabetic; she simply bruised easily. Please excuse me, Neeley, dear, I've got a turkey in the oven and a houseful of company. I need to skedaddle on home." With that, she spun around and ran smack into Pastor Cole.

The sunlight streamed through the stained-glass window above his head, casting a red glow and transforming his white shirt into a satiny shade of orange. Both Pastor Cole and Missus Goodeve followed me as I hurried out the side exit. Stepping into Gideon's truck, my eyes filled with hot tears. How could I have not known? My teacher's words settled heavily in my stomach like a plate full of greasy dumplings. I glanced back; they stood in the cold without their coats, watching us as we drove away.

Gideon eyeballed me a couple of times, rolling a toothpick back and forth in his mouth. I finally met his gaze with a blazing one of my own. "I think Pudge killed my grandmother." We rode in silence while I finished my cry. "You think I'm crazy?"

"Nah, missy," he said softly, staring at me and shifting gears.

"You think he killed her?" I asked.

I didn't like Gideon's look one bit. The only way I guessed his thoughts was by the look on his face, which at that moment was all narrow-eyed, like, *why are you asking foolish questions again, Neeley?*

"I think you should leave it be, is what I thinks," he said, finally.

My stomach cramped. I couldn't talk. A lump of despair slid down my throat like castor oil. Forcing my weepy self to change gears before I got sick on the side of the road, I leaned my head against the cool window. I never knew my grandmother had the sugar diabetes, but worse, I'd never considered her life to be as horrible as my own.

Pudge had hit her, hurt her, but did he kill her? I knew what I had to do. I had to confront him and do it soon. From the look on Pastor Cole's face and the vague answers from Missus Goodeve, they were on Pudge's side. I'd take him by surprise. I was no longer afraid. I didn't know why, but I wasn't. Maybe because I was older, a teenager, practically grown. I took a few deep breaths and decided not to mention it to Gideon again. In fact, I changed the subject entirely. Glancing over at Gideon, I studied his face once more and coughed to get his attention.

"I'm going with you to your church from now on."

"I don't think so," he mumbled.

"Maybe I'll wear my Easter hat since you said the ladies at your church wear hats."

"I said no." He shot me a look so swift and curious my next words nearly caught in my throat.

"Why not?"

"Why you want to go?"

"I don't like my church anymore. Am I not allowed in your church?"

Gideon drove while I watched his jaw tighten. "I can't take you, and you know it. It jus' not done."

It was time to shut my mouth and let Gideon drive in peace, but my stubbornness must have gotten the better of me. "Y'all wanted integration last time I heard. Why can't *I* go to *your* church?"

Looking straight ahead, Gideon ignored me. When we turned the corner to the farm, he pitched his toothpick out the window and said, "Since Mistah Pudge don't go to Sunday services, I 'spect he won't know if you miss one. I'll call Deacon Hayes at mah church, see what he thinks." His eyes glistened. "You uppity now? Thinking you know all 'bout right and wrong. You don't know nothing 'bout mah people, what we been through, what we *still* going through."

He parked the truck and sighed, rubbing the back of his neck. "Fine. First Sunday in December is Newcomers Sunday. You wear your hat and whatnot; jus' be ready to go early."

My answers to my grandfather's questions were rarely honest because I was all about keeping him in a decent mood. When we sat in the same room, I only half-listened and said *yes, sir*, and *no, sir*. To argue with him was cause for a whipping. As a result, I agreed with everything he said to shut him up. But those rare conversations only lasted a minute or two until I managed to leave the room. Or until Gideon needed help in the kitchen— then Pudge usually hollered, "Go on, Neeley; don't stand around with your thumbs up your ass. Go help Gideon."

So, after our Thanksgiving Day meal of nothing special, when he asked me why I had inquired about my grandmother; I hesitated and then said, "Because Missus Goodeve commented I looked like her, and one question rolled into the next."

What Pudge said next opened a whole crate full of canned worms. "Lila Goodeve don't know jack shit. You want to know about me or my wife, you ask me."

I sat there thinking I'd asked him six hundred times about my parents and my grandmother, but he shot me down repeatedly. And as far as knowing anything about him, I didn't care to know his age, height, or even his shoe size. I didn't want to know what he did as a boy, if he ever read poetry or comic books, or if he went to college, which I believed that no, he did not. I didn't care who taught *him* to drive or if he had a favorite color. Lord knows he didn't have a favorite anything. Unless it was Jim Beam, Lucky Strikes, and taking the Lord's name in vain. I didn't want to ask him not one detail about his life with my grandmother, the story of their courtship, or how long they were married. I knew all I needed to know about Pudge. He was as dark and gritty as the life-everlasting ring around our bathtub. Why in the hello would I want to know more?

I fought back the acid shooting up into my throat until my tongue felt dry as cardboard. My fangs dropped again, and I shook visibly, but not from fear. Not that time. I had only one question I wanted to ask. "Missus Goodeve said her bruises were from the sugar diabetes."

Scowling at me, he crossed his arms over his chest, his demeanor collapsing as each second clicked by. "That's it? That's all you got? Your only question is whether or not she was a diabetic?"

"No. What I want to know is, how badly did you beat her before you killed her?"

It was a fast pitch, thrown straight at him. But it hung in the air, a carcass dangling from a long rope in a dead tree. For one entire minute, my grandfather froze. And then the branch broke. He lunged for me, kicking up the scent of secrets and knocking his chair to the floor. His hammy hand gripped my upper arm with such force it sent chill bumps to my arms and legs. He yanked me into the dining room like I was a horse he could harness and shouted, "Stay!" Pudge stormed into his bedroom and returned within seconds, unwinding the Bible belt.

His face grew hard, despising and full of new rage, and a vein pulsed in his forehead. He nearly spit at me. "You accuse *me* of killing your grandmother when *you're* the one who put your mother and father into their graves? You ask any more questions to a living soul within one hundred miles of this farm, and you, little girl, will wish you hadn't! You got that!?"

"Yes, sir. I got it." Boy-howdy, did I ever. *One hundred miles.* One hundred miles away from him and the Horse's ass Farm would've felt like flying to Heaven.

Pudge had whipped me with that belt since my fifth birthday, and it never got easier. He shoved the bulky Bible into my arms, and I faced the wall. Smelling his sour sweat, I stood motionless and was determined not to cry. But those last few seconds without pain, before Pudge's strap landed on my butt, I thought of nothing but my grandmother and dug my fingers into the leather cover.

It ended up I was thankful for two things that Thanksgiving Day. For Gideon, and for the mere notion of packing my suitcase, hopping a bus, and traveling one hundred miles in any direction—as long as it was one hundred miles away from Pudge McPherson and the land he stood on.

With every agonizing crack against my backside, I thought of a new way to make him pay. I took my punishment without another word, feeling my pants rip behind my knee, which caused the final blow, the thirteenth lick, to meet my bare skin.

After it was over, I did what I always did. First, I re-wrapped the belt around the Bible and put it back in his closet as part of my punishment, and then bolted outside to the barn and fell into a pile of straw, hiccupping back my sobs. Gideon saw I bit my lip to keep my loose tongue from screaming every curse word inside my head. He walked to the straw mound, bent over, and wiped tears off my cheeks and chin with the bottom of his shirt.

I sighed, then halfway smiled. "I'm okay. I'm getting used to it."

He stood and reached for a jar of bag balm. "Not me. I'll never get used to it. You is stubborn as an ol' mule, Neeley. You confuse boldness for courage. Why you egg him on so?"

"I hate him."

"Don't go talking like that. He already angry with you, and if you say anything else, them licks on your backside be nothing compared to next time."

"He killed my grandmother. I know it."

Gideon crouched down and handed me the jar. "Go inside and put this on. You pray. You pray hard. Asks God to work this out, 'cause it's a boil, and it's gone fester and break, Law, it'll be one mess. You beseech sweet Jesus to heal your heart, get you through knowing 'bout your grandmomma. Otherwise, we both gone find ourselves on the street or worse, now that's fuh sho'!"

I choked back wasted tears. What was the point? Curled up on that bed of straw, I removed my eyeglasses to wipe away tear tracks. The odor of horses and the evening sun seeping through the wide plank walls warmed the barn's insides and was as soothing as bag balm. I didn't even mind the smell of manure. It was a field of daisies compared to the drunk stench of Pudge. In a current of air filled with evening light, dust motes whirled around like a swarm of fireflies. I wanted to remain in the barn for the rest of the night. I hurt. I didn't want to move.

He'd belt-buckled my gangly legs enough that I'd started thinking of whippings as something I had to put up with, like cold weather and math tests and my sneezing fits around cats. But that time, it was different. The look on Gideon's face told me it was different. I staggered to my feet, walking like somebody had hit my body with a ball-peen hammer. Stumbling to the door, I managed a smile at Gideon.

He leaned on a pitchfork and looked at me with pleading eyes. "I can't save you. You gots to stop making him angry 'cause I can't watch him beat on you no more, either."

At sunset, I crept through the back door. Pudge sat at the kitchen table with a bottle of bourbon, pouring himself a shot. He drank it in one gulp and then wiped his lips with his thick hand. "What are you looking at?"

I bowed my head, letting my hair fall over half my face and the scar, and glanced up at him from under my brows, shooting him a look that said, *I'm looking at you, you old nasty hog, stooped over your booze like somebody's about to steal it.* I folded my arms across the front of my jacket and stared at my grandfather, who, in many ways, was a total stranger.

Swallowing pride that nearly gagged me, I hesitated and then opened my mouth. "I'm sorry for what I said. I'd like to go with you and Gideon on Saturday if you still want to buy me a coat."

He paused before he spoke as if he'd rather not. "We'll go after lunch," he said. "Gideon can ride in the truck bed. You're getting too old to be seen sitting close to him in public. Fact is, Pastor Cole called me. Says you need taken down a peg or two. He wants me to think about hiring one of the church ladies to help you cook and clean. Keep Gideon out of the house from now on."

I rolled my eyes in silent reply and backed into the bathroom like *I* was the drunk in the family. How could Hell be worse? I flipped on the light and then closed the door before squatting next to the electric wall heater. I hit the button. It blew directly on my legs, soothing me like a heating pad, taking away my chill bumps. Standing, I leaned on the sink and squinted into the mirror, wiping Pudge's words off my face with a hand towel. Tangled curls hung in my face, and straw stuck to me everywhere. I blinked hard before opening the bag balm jar.

That night, I nestled deeper under my blankets. An unshakable sorrow filled my gut as sleet and rain hammered the window, and gusty winds scattered the last of the autumn leaves around the farm. My nerves gnawed at my stomach until grief became a growth attached to my innards. I'd already seen my share of heartbreak and knew the best way to get through trying times was to pull the covers over my head and sleep.

But I couldn't. Life wasn't getting any easier. Jacine had up and split town with her father, who boarded a train to Pensacola after he left her in Georgia with a relative, or so I was told. I doubted I would ever see her again. Our horses caught a terrible virus the same day Pudge heard tobacco seed was at an all-time high. He had become unbearable, cussing and taking the Lord's name in vain at every turn.

Sleep avoided me until I faced the truth. I had to leave—never look back. Otherwise, they would bury me in the family plot between my parents and my murdered grandmother before my next birthday.

A howl began in the bitter distance, rising and falling with the wind, singing what had become a familiar yet haunting lullaby. Within minutes, I drifted into another restless sleep.

CHAPTER SEVEN

Delicate morning light pressed through my curtains, like sunshine streaming through a prison cell. Shivering, I wriggled my face deep into my pillow and drew up into a ball, making the mistake of moving my legs. My back, thighs, and calves still burned like I had sunbathed in the nude. The rising sun slowly woke me to find frost inside my window, which I scraped off with my fingernail. Yet, the biting cold called for scarves, layered shirts, and trousers. Girls got to wear dungarees to school when the temperature dropped—a welcome change for me because sometimes even a long skirt and knee socks didn't hide bruises.

Then I remembered it was Saturday, two days after Thanksgiving. Cold and snow would have Greensboro in a holiday tizzy. I crawled to the window and popped it open with my fist to see the sugary frost that had coated the farm. A rush of sharp air stole my breath away. White smoke swirled from Missus Crumley's chimney, hinting she might invite me over again to admire her silver Christmas tree. I had mentioned it to Gideon, and he said it was downright sacrilegious, changing God's green trees into aluminum foil. But then, I'd never had a Christmas tree; Pudge didn't allow it, so I reckoned an aluminum one was better than none.

Since Gideon had resumed his regular house duties, I thought maybe, come Saturday, he'd wouldn't have to suffer the drive to Greensboro wrapped like a cocoon. But he did. Pudge actually told him to ride in the truck bed. After lunch, Gideon made a pallet of horse blankets in the back of Pudge's truck. Up in front, the heater warmed the cab where my grandfather and I rode in silence. Toasty. Damn comfortable, in fact.

I looked at Pudge. He'd got all gussied up for his appointment, put on a clean, pressed shirt, and spit-shined boots. Gideon's spit, not his. When we reached Battleground Road, I glanced back at Gideon for the umpteenth time, watching him bury his face in his coat collar. His blankets flapped in the wind while needles of icy sleet blasted him from every angle. He appeared frozen solid.

"What if I rode in the back instead of Gideon?" I asked. "I love the cold."

But Pudge only sped up, ignoring me, and spoke as if I were slow and stupid. "Judd's expecting me at one o'clock. I'll drop you both off at Woolworths. You've got an hour. Be ready to go at two. Don't spend over ten dollars; bring me the correct change."

I sighed and nodded. He had no intention of making life tolerable for Gideon. But I did.

I kept my mouth shut the rest of the way, thinking about the storm that had rolled in the previous evening. It started out as one of those rare winter storms that carried thunder and lightning. I had nursed my fresh welts, praying for God to strike a bolt of vengeance on Pudge, passed out drunk up against the toilet. But I couldn't influence God any better than He controlled Pudge. Then the phone rang.

"Hi-do, Miss McPherson, this is your grandfather's lawyer. He around?"

"He's down with a headache," I said. "Can I take a message?"

"I'm calling to remind Bainbridge of our Saturday appointment. Please tell him to bring any records of your grandmother's last will and testament and her death certificate. You'll make sure he gets that message, won't you, little gal?"

"Yes, sir. I'll tell him."

"Good girl. You have yourself a blessed evening."

I shook my head. Blessed? *Poor Neeley, bless her heart.* I'd heard it said repeatedly among the churchwomen, and it worked no better than my lucky rabbit's foot. I didn't care why Pudge needed a lawyer. Knowing it had something to do with my grandmother rattled me, but I let it go. It didn't matter. I knew the truth. I may have been responsible for my parent's deaths, but I didn't mean to kill them. Though he refused to confess, I believed with every breath in my body that my grandfather murdered my grandmother, probably in cold blood.

I was helpless to do anything about it other than finish what my parents had started. Leave. And that's the moment I knew I had to convince Gideon to go with me.

As car after car sped by, splattering the windshield and Gideon with gray, sooty slush, Pudge casually smoked his Lucky with the window cracked. I wanted to get there and be done with the whole coat-buying ordeal.

I'd stuffed two extra dollars in my pocket Pudge didn't know about—money I'd earned the past summer planting and picking tomatoes and peppers for Missus Crumley while she sunbathed in her brassiere, short-shorts, and her red sling-backs. I'd saved twenty-five dollars. Hidden in a plastic oval change purse and packed inside a shoebox at the back of my closet, it became my escape fund.

After my last encounter with the Bible belt, I'd counted every cent. I didn't know the exact price of bus tickets to California, but as soon as I had saved enough for Gideon and myself, I'd persuade him to go with me. Stand on my head if necessary because I knew I couldn't go without him. So, in my mind, we were already gone. I was no longer Neeley McPherson of Summerfield, North Carolina. I was Neeley Morrigan, citizen of the world, and I was going to buy Gideon a piece of pie and a cup of hot coffee at Woolworths after I bought my coat.

Pudge dropped us off at the corner of South Elm and Sycamore streets. Gideon unwrapped himself and quickly piled the blankets in the truck bed before Pudge sped off to the Jefferson Standard Life Building and his lawyer appointment. The way I saw it, though, he would need Perry Mason, not Mister Esquire.

Gideon looked like a Fudgesicle standing on the sidewalk. Frost clung to his hat and eyebrows. His tattered, dingy-colored coat and pants blended in with the concrete shades of the surrounding buildings.

I pulled a pair of Pudge's old gloves from my pocket. "Here, put these on. They're warm."

Gideon's eyes met mine. "Thank y-you," he said, shivering and moving like the tin man, rusted and creaky, peeling off his cold gloves and tugging on the warm ones. "Let's g-go buy you a c-coat."

Walking into Woolworths, the bell jangled on its metal spring, announcing our arrival. Scents of cheap merchandise, greasy lunch specials, and dime-store dust met me in each aisle. Gideon took a detour at men's hats, while I wandered aimlessly like a rudderless boat.

I ended up in the record department where Annetta Riley, a popular girl in my class who occasionally borrowed my milk money and weighed about as much as a two-cent stamp, pawed through the latest 45s. I couldn't take my eyes off her poodle skirt, saddle shoes, and ponytail swinging back and forth. Moving her hips and singing along with Frankie Avalon, Annetta saw me and waved. Before I knew it, she had whisked me to the Mickey Mouse Club.

"Neeley! Hey, Neeley!"

"Hey," I said, leaning my head to the right, hoping my hair covered my forehead.

Annetta's wad of pink Bazooka got in the way of her tongue when she talked. "I'm Christmas shopping, but I've spent all my money on records."

"Sounds like fun."

"It's a blast. You buy anything?"

"I'm buying a coat."

She gave me a half smile and raised one eyebrow. "Oh. Well. Neato! I better go. I have a piano lesson in an hour. Bye, Neeley."

"Bye."

I stood there, waiting for her to walk around me and out of the department. The idea of piano lessons, sleepovers, and sharing Jerry Lee Lewis records immediately captivated me. I couldn't help but notice how pretty Annetta was with her shiny skin, bright blue eyes, and a silk scarf tied around her glossy black ponytail. I was willing to bet she glowed in the dark. She blew a giant bubble and marched her Mouseketeer self out of the record department as if on parade.

After a quick search, I found Gideon and we continued our coat hunt. Finally, I tapped the shoulder of a man squatting near a bottom shelf, stacking toilet paper.

"Sir, excuse me. Where can I find the coats that are on sale?"

He stood and removed his eyeglasses. His nametag read *Curly Harris, Manager*, and smiled until he saw Gideon standing behind me. "We have a few left; they're on closeout against the back wall." Nodding toward Gideon as if Gideon couldn't speak for himself, he asked, "Is he with you?"

"He's our caretaker. My grandfather drove us in from our farm in Summerfield and dropped us off here to buy a coat."

His lips twisted, and his eyes narrowed. "Fine," he said.

I didn't like his tone. But Gideon tipped his hat and said, "Suh, could you point me to the restroom?"

"Down the stairs to your left. We're renovating our restrooms, so make sure you use the right one. The sign for coloreds may be off the wall. Be sure and ask somebody."

"Sho', 'nuff. I thank you, suh."

Mister Harris only nodded and resumed his squatting position, opening boxes and pricing merchandise.

I walked in the direction of the coats with Gideon close behind. "You warmed up yet?" I asked over my shoulder.

"I'm working on it. I need to find the restroom, tho'—soon as you pick out a coat."

I told Gideon the blue tweed with the brown velvet collar looked like Donna Reed's coat. He didn't care so much. Gideon said it was 50% off, like the sign said, and big enough to grow into, and that he could sew the few covered buttons dangling from loose threads. The coat reminded me of my teacher's coat at school and how her blonde hair looked perfect every day, like the real Donna Reed. It wasn't as pretty as Annetta Riley's coat, but it *was* cheap and warm, and Gideon was right; that made it good enough.

After buying my coat, I crammed the change and receipt into my pocket and led Gideon to the lunch counter. The feeling of a Woolworths sack filled with something new in my hand easily rated up there with an invitation to a party or a sleepover. Exhilarating. Lost in my excitement, talking and not paying attention to where I was walking, I turned a corner too quickly and collided with a shiny silver rack of Timex watches. It tipped forward, but Gideon's quick reflexes saved the day, righting the entire rack before it crashed at my feet. Only two watches fell to the floor.

"Law, girl, you act like you never stepped foot in the Woolworths before. Where're you going?"

"I'm sorry." I helped him hang the watches back on the rack. "I've got a surprise for you. I'm buying you a cup of coffee. Don't worry; it's with my money. It'll warm you up."

I didn't give him a chance to say *no*. I bolted for two chrome stools, one covered in orange vinyl, the other in green, next to a pair of overfed housewives who gulped down the lunch special, which looked like meatloaf. They nearly dropped their forks when they saw Gideon. Fast as a flutter, both women stacked their packages on the seats beside them. I moved to the other end.

A curvy waitress with a poufy hairdo waltzed back and forth on the other side of the counter, tilting a coffeepot, making small talk, and wearing a faded yellow uniform. The same color as the egg and cheese sandwich advertised on the wall above her head.

I stepped up, sat on the stool, then swiveled in my seat to see Gideon standing feet away, shaking his head. "What's wrong?" I asked. "Don't you want pie and coffee? My treat."

"They don't serve Negroes at this counter."

"But you're with me. Sit. Please?"

"They not gone serve me, Neeley, you watch." He sat, but not happily.

The waitress in the cheesy uniform wiggled over to me, cracked her chewing gum, and said, "We don't serve niggras at this counter."

Gideon sighed and shook his head again. "See? What'd I tell ya?"

She pointed to a separate stand-up counter. "He can eat over there."

"Can I eat there, too?" I asked.

"No, you should eat here."

"Can he buy soap and toothpaste in this store?"

"Yes, of course, he can."

"Then why can't he buy coffee at this lunch counter?"

"Wait here, I'll get the manager." She stormed off, shaking her round head and rounder behind.

I dug in my heels, determined to get to the bottom of that stupid nonsense. But Gideon had made a mad dash for the stairs. I ran after him. "What? Don't you want coffee?"

"You be sweet to spend your money on me, but I'm an ol' man, and I gots to use the restroom. Now you go on back, buy yoursef' a piece-a pie. Mistah Pudge coming in ten minutes. There's no time to start a ruckus today."

I sighed and waited for Gideon at the top of the stairs. I'd lost my appetite when I spotted Mister Harris, the Manager, heading my way.

"Where's your colored friend?"

"He needed to use the restroom."

Within seconds, a man hollered at the bottom of the steps. "Hey, nigger! That's the wrong restroom! Why'd you use a Whites Only restroom?"

I flew down the steps with Mister Harris at my heels, only to see Gideon struggling to explain to a man in a painter's hat. "I—I'm sorry, the manager told me to use the right one." A pile of paint cans, lumber, tools, and old restroom signs rested against boxes of new tile on the floor. Construction workers, colored and white, milled around us like spectators at a football game.

Gideon tripped over his tongue, trying to speak over the painter's cuss words. "I—I'm sorry—"

Mister Harris stepped between them. "—I meant for you to use the *correct* restroom, not the restroom on the *right*! And I *told* you, old man, to ask somebody."

I tugged at Gideon's coat. "C'mon, you apologized, let's go."

"Oh, hell, no!" Hollering like we were all deaf, the man with turquoise paint on his white overalls let loose with a mouthful of words that could've curdled the fresh paint on the wall. "I ain't going back in there unless that stinking nigger cleans the stall he used."

"He apologized!" I yelled. But as I pulled on Gideon's coat again, a Timex watch fell from somewhere off his clothes and landed at Mister Harris's feet. "It must've stuck on your sweater," I said as my stomach lurched into my throat.

"Call the police!" The painter yanked off his hat and threw it on the floor. "Damn nigger has the gall to use a Whites Only restroom and steal a watch, too. Call the police, Curly!"

Gideon's hands shook. "Now, now calm down, no such a thing. I didn't steal it. Miz Neeley here, she knocked over the watch rack upstairs in the sto'. She didn't mean to, but we cleaned up the mess, and it be like she say; it must-a hooked on mah clothes. I didn't know it."

The painter made fists with his hands. "You blaming that little girl?"

Mister Harris pulled a wooden chair from a storage closet and unfolded it. "You sit," he said to Gideon. "Don't you move. I'm calling the authorities."

I ran up the stairs after him. "You can't do that. He didn't steal anything!"

"We'll let the police decide, little lady."

When I saw my grandfather's truck pull to the front of the store. I raced back down the steps. The painter had disappeared around the corner, discussing the situation with his painter buddies, so I grabbed Gideon by the arm. "Let's get out of here. *Now!*"

"I can't go!"

"Yes, you can! The coast is clear; they don't know who you are, and Pudge is out front. Do you want him to come in here after us? Let's *go!*"

Gideon saw by the look on my face I didn't want to see him get his neck in a noose. Before I counted to two, we were hightailing it up the steps and out of the Woolworths. Heavy snow fell as Gideon rolled into the truck bed and laid out flat with his hands around his head, holding tight to his hat.

I hopped into the truck cab with Pudge, open-mouthed and out of breath. Slapping a smile on my face, I shouted, "Got my coat, and that light is about to turn red!"

I knew Pudge had little patience for red lights. He gunned the engine and took off, not waiting for Gideon to wrap himself in blankets. I turned around in time to catch a glimpse of the manager bolting out of the store, searching for us up and down the sidewalk. From the look on his face, he had no idea where we had gone. Then it occurred to me I had told Mister Curly Harris we lived on a farm—in Summerfield.

> ... The wolf is gentle-hearted.
> Not noble, not cowardly, just nonfighting.
>
> ~ Lois Crisler

CHAPTER EIGHT

By the next Friday, nearly a week had passed since our unfortunate Woolworths shopping trip, and we hadn't heard a peep from anyone. That evening, I tried to focus on my homework at the kitchen table.

My two-page book report was to include a hand-drawn picture of my subject, a totem pole. Of course, my arm flew up when the teacher asked, "Who would like to do a report on wolves?" But Lucas Cooper passed a spiteful grin over his shoulder, having raised his hand first. So, I flipped through a few encyclopedias and found a photograph of a totem pole crafted by American Indians in the Pacific Northwest. A part of the country I'd never thought of visiting, but suddenly, the place intrigued me. I'd nearly erased a hole in the paper when Gideon peeked over my shoulder, shaping sausage into patties with his skillet-like hands.

"Hmm. You an artist. That's good. Whatever it is."

I blew eraser crumbs to the floor and jabbered on about totem poles, how they keep away evil spirits, and that maybe we should carve one, but the telephone's shrill ring sent nervous birds flittering inside my stomach again. Since the Woolworths incident, I about peed my pants every time Pudge answered the phone, my heart racing and palms sweating.

It rang five times before Pudge finally waddled over to pick it up. "Hey there, Henry," he said. I felt Gideon's tremor. Henry Troyer was our County Sheriff.

"Probably nothing," I said. Up close, the worry lines on Gideon's forehead told a different story. I scooted closer to the living room, where Pudge held the phone to his ear with his shoulder, his hands stroking the cat on his knee. Hidden behind the TV stand next to the window, I hoped to see an evening blue sky. Gideon loved cloudless skies and sunsets. He needed cheering up. But the sky was gray. Cold, merciless gray.

"You bet, not a problem, Henry. Gideon will be here tomorrow." Pudge whispered into the telephone, except it was more of a mumble because Pudge didn't know how to whisper. "Sure, Henry. Ask him any question you want—no—I'll not mention it to either of them."

Questions. That's all he'd do. Ask questions. I'd tell Sheriff Troyer that Gideon didn't mean to pee in the Whites Only restroom, and he certainly didn't steal that damn watch. If I had to, I'd say I stole it. Sheriff Troyer's punishment and the Greensboro Police combined couldn't be any worse than Pudge's Bible belt.

The air bled through the window, and outside, icicles clung to trees and hung from eaves, sleek and sharp like butcher knives. The first actual attack of winter and the first time in my life, the faintest hint of panic showed in Gideon. I tippy-toed back to where he stood, frying sausage at the stove. "They're coming."

"The Greensboro police?"

"No. Henry Troyer. Tomorrow. To ask questions."

"Sweet Baby Jesus." Gideon set his spatula on the counter, shuffled to the window, and stared into his weary eyes. His panicked reflection disturbed me. "Sheriff Troyer belong to the Klan," he said.

I fell into my chair, folded my report, and stuck it into the borrowed encyclopedia. Somehow, I knew I'd never complete the totem pole report.

"Neeley!" Pudge yelled as he wobbled into the kitchen.

My heart stopped. "Yes, sir?"

"You got your list of girlie chores to do tomorrow?"

Pudge had a knack for making me feel like the cigarette ashes he flicked to the floor—disgusting, burned-up pieces of nothing. "I got work to do in the barn. All day."

Pudge raised an eyebrow at Gideon.

"I asked her to help me shoe a couple-a the mares. They stand still when Miz Neeley has hold of 'em."

"Then you two work out in the barn, but don't run off in the truck."

"No, suh," Gideon said. "We be nearby if you need us."

Pudge walked to the door but glanced back. "Fix me a plate and keep it warm. I got to run into town."

"Yes, suh."

I stood at the window and watched Pudge's truck roll down the driveway toward the road. "We need to get out of the county. Maybe the state. Head to California!"

"Let me repeat mahsef', Neeley. It jus' not done. Ol' nigga and little white gal running off. It jus' not done."

I huffed. "Who makes up these rules, anyhow? If Sheriff Troyer brings the Klan out here, they'll kill you, or worse. I've seen them on TV, killing Negroes for spitting on the sidewalk. And they get away with it! Don't confess to anything tomorrow!"

Gideon clutched the dishtowel, his eyes avoiding mine. Clearly, he didn't know what to do any more than I did, nodding his head in silent admission. But I refused to admit anything.

"Now listen," I said, "we're both in trouble for something we didn't do. We need to get far away—as quickly as possible!"

The house felt cramped with the overwhelming smells of sausage, Pudge's dirty laundry, and cat pee. Watching tears form in Gideon's eyes, I only wanted to run, taking him with me. But as persuasive responses to Sheriff Troyer's questions tingled on my tongue, I grew weak in the knees and sick to my stomach. I could *not* let this happen.

Saturday morning, Gideon spread a newspaper on the breakfast table while Pudge spent his usual hour on the toilet. "Martin Luther King's in the paper again," he whispered. "He causing all sorts-a problems for the white folks, 'specially in the South. It gone get worse, 'fore it gets better." He turned the page and then tapped the newspaper. "I been praying. Look." He pointed to an article in the corner he circled with a pencil. It wasn't the first time

I'd known him to pray without ceasing. "Bakersville," he said. "It's where we need to go."

I looked toward the bathroom, then back at Gideon. I nearly fainted. "We're leaving? For real?"

He nodded and smiled a paper-thin smile. Picking up the *Greensboro Record*, he read quietly. "Bakersville, a place of refuge in the North Carolina Mountains, the town is enjoying a surge in building and economic prosperity." He let the newspaper drop to the table. "Mah—sistah—she lives there."

I nearly choked on my Ovaltine. "You have a sister?"

"Uh-huh," he said with another smile that made me jump up and hug him.

"You think we have half a chance, then?"

"I'm praying God gives us a whole one," he said. "'Course they gone accuse me-a kidnapping now." He shook his head. "Law, what Negro man in his right mind takes a little white girl from her grandfather?"

I vibrated with new life and said something I believe as much now as I did then. "One that doesn't want to see her dead before her next birthday."

Gideon picked up his breakfast plate and tipped his hat at me before gripping the doorknob. "True a statement as I ever heard. Looks like you won't be needing your hat tomorrow. Mistah Pudge be thinking we at church, but we get a couple hours down the road. Head to Bakersville."

It was all I could do to hold myself together and not run up to the roof, shouting loud enough to wake the dead. "I'll be ready," I giggled.

Leaning forward, Gideon gave me a comforting smile and spoke quietly. "You clean up, then head to the barn. We gots lots to talk about."

I'd never felt so happy and wound up. I was like a horse let out to run in a pasture full of sweet grass and apple trees. I heard the toilet flush. The idea of an escape sent an electric shock through my whole body. I held the article close to my eyes. "Bakersville, a place of refuge."

Gideon didn't wait around to say grace that morning. Pudge stepped into the kitchen, the stink from the bathroom wafting in after him. *Good Lord, light a match!* I quickly folded the newspaper and stuffed it under my shirt.

"What's wrong with Gideon?" he demanded.

"Nothing a good night's sleep won't cure. He's complaining about his back. It's hurting again." I took my dishes to the sink, my hands jittery. "Better get going; there's lots to take care of in the barn."

Pudge lit a cigarette, plopped his lard butt into his chair, and then buttered his biscuit. It never ceased to amaze me how he could chew, swallow, and puff on a cigarette within seconds. Beneath his labored breath, I heard him say, "His back's gonna hurt a lot worse when those boys get through with him."

With trembling hands, I closed the door softly behind me, wanting nothing more than to watch my grandfather suffer from the same lash he felt sure was coming for Gideon.

⁂

Late that afternoon, I heard the crunch of tires in the driveway. A set of headlights appeared as I meandered out of the barn.

Gideon and I discovered we had about forty-five dollars between us. It was enough for gas and a few meals before reaching Bakersville and hopeful employment. We'd have to sleep in his truck, but we figured we could park in an abandoned barn or shack for the night. If we took enough horse blankets along, I'd be fine, I'd told him. We couldn't wait for spring; it wasn't possible. Gideon said he wasn't wasting any more time hating and regretting, and I said, neither am I. So, when I heard the squeaky brakes stop at the house, I was thankful we'd at least figured out some kind of a plan.

The high-pitched squeal of a rusted-out door hitched open and shut, and the sound of heavy boots stomped up the walk. Sheriff Troyer and his massive stomach that rivaled my grandfather's suddenly stepped around the boxwood. His holster and gun hung heavy on his belt, and he rested his hand on the pistol, his thumb rubbing the smooth handle like a sore place on his hip. Swiftly, his other hand plucked a toothpick from his mouth and pitched it into the snow, a small action that seemed to carry a threat of its own.

"Hidy, little lady. Your granddaddy here?"

I felt my cheeks burn. "Yes, sir. He's inside."

"Mind if I come in and sit a spell?"

"Not at all."

When I led the sheriff inside, Pudge rose from the recliner where he took his sit-up naps. A glossy smear from his mouth into his chin stubble marked a line of drool, and his shirt hung halfway out of his unzipped pants. They shook hands after Pudge zipped his fly and palmed his greasy hair over his bald spot.

"Neeley, run out to the barn. Fetch Gideon."

"If this is about Woolworths, I can tell you what happened," I said.

The sheriff gave Pudge a cold-eyed smile, his gun belt squeaking when he moved. He looked at me as if I were the town idiot. "We need to talk to Mister Jackson. We got us a little matter to clear up."

I stared at Sheriff Troyer's shiny badge. "But—you said—"

Pudge snapped his finger and pointed. "—You're in enough trouble. Do as you're told!"

I bolted out without another word, letting the screen door slam again. Glancing back, I watched my grandfather offer Sheriff Troyer a drink of whiskey.

I fled to the barn with panic behind me at a close clip. It may have been the half-assed smile the sheriff shot at Pudge when he entered the room. Or maybe it was the way he clicked his tongue before he said *Mister Jackson* and then the way he winked at me after he said it. Sure as shootin', something in my gut told me he hadn't come to just ask questions.

There are some things you simply know, like when you feel a storm approaching. The air changes, and you smell rain. A strange current circled my head, shouting, *Think quick, Neeley. Otherwise, y'all got as much chance as a kerosene cat in Hell.*

I considered our options. Escape in Gideon's truck right then and there. Not good. We didn't have enough head start, which would've landed Gideon *and* me in jail.

Let the sheriff take Gideon and hire a lawyer. With what? Our getaway money? My backside still stung from the last whipping, and Pudge was already pissed off I'd not told him about the Woolworths disaster. Yet, the mere thought of Gideon hanging from a tree in the middle of nowhere while Pudge got away with living two sheets to oblivion and beating me in the meantime? No.

I chose a third and final possibility. We needed outside help. Someone with influence. I had to spill my guts to somebody who cared that Gideon was innocent and knew Pudge was responsible for the bruises bound for my backside. It was the only choice possible.

Walking into the house, Gideon handed me his hat and coat. Like a startled horse, he cautiously entered the living room and nodded hello to Sheriff Troyer, whose previously pleasant demeanor had now turned spiteful, a reaction that didn't surprise me. His hard edge of self-importance rang loud and clear as he looked at me and said, "You can stay in the room if you don't interrupt."

Pudge sat smugly in his recliner with Abbott on his lap, while Gideon settled on the chair I dragged in from the kitchen. Standing by the TV, I silently wished my knees would quit knocking.

The sheriff looked at me and pulled a notepad out of his pocket. "You want to sit?"

I stared at the razor sharp part in his polished brown hair. "No thanks, I'll stand."

"Suit yourself," he said. He was as rude as the flick of his wrist. Sinking to the sofa, he spread his legs to make space for his enormous gut. "Mister Jackson, I'm sure you know what this is about. The manager of Woolworths, Mister Curly Harris, has pressed charges against you. You shouldn't have run off the way you did."

He paused, waiting for Gideon to respond with more than a nod. But Gideon didn't.

"All right, here's the deal. I've got orders to bring you in for questioning. We'll keep you at the Summerfield town hall until we're finished. If we find no evidence of a crime, we'll release you. If we suspect you've committed a crime, we will read you your rights, and then the Greensboro police will transport you to the Guilford County Jail, where the court will appoint for you an attorney while you await a fair trial. Do you understand me?"

Gideon's eyes popped wide in surprise but again said nothing.

My scalp felt hot, and I gritted my teeth to keep the cuss words from escaping my mouth. "But you said you'd ask questions—here!"

"Neeley!" Pudge shouted.

"It's okay, Pudge." The sheriff turned to me. "I don't know where you got your information, little gal, but Mister Jackson is not under arrest. We're only taking him to our local town hall to ask questions and read him the complaint. The Greensboro police requested we investigate this, uh, trivial matter, as they called it. Way I see it, a crime is a crime. But if Mister Jackson cooperates, he may be home in time for breakfast tomorrow morning."

He stared at Gideon and pressed his lips together before speaking again. "As sheriff, I am empowered to take certain steps to secure the safety of this family and every family in Guilford County against all those who break our laws. And those steps I am fully prepared to take."

"What steps are you talking about!?" I blurted.

Sheriff Troyer stood, glared at me for a few seconds, and then walked over to Gideon. "You ready?"

Gideon nodded. "I get mah coat and hat."

The sheriff's broad face twisted into another brutal grin. "Sharp nigger you got yourself here, Pudge—so amiable and all. He's a real nice tribute to his race. Like I said, if this is just a wild goose chase, Mister Jackson can sleep in his own bed—tomorrow night." Sheriff Troyer slipped into his coat. "Pudge, thank you for letting me do this peacefully."

"Any time, Henry. I'm always willing to cooperate with the law."

"We know that, Pudge. 'Preciate it."

Gideon looked back at me and nodded. "I see you soon," he said.

I made no sound because I had no breath. I nearly doubled over, straining to draw air. My heart thrummed so hard I thought it might fly out of my chest. On the verge of shattering into pieces, desperate for something solid to hang on to, I groped the kitchen table's edge to steady myself. Pudge followed the sheriff and Gideon to the car. In seconds, as my blood began to boil, my strength returned, and I burst out behind them in a rage. "Take me! I saw what happened."

Sheriff Troyer assisted Gideon into the backseat of the cruiser. I shoved past Pudge and the sheriff, reached inside, and wrapped my arms around Gideon's neck. He gave my back a pat and whispered into my ear. "Truck keys are in mah nightstand."

I nodded.

The sheriff pulled me out of the car, and again Gideon's teary eyes almost crippled me. I ran back inside the house and paced the floor, waiting for Pudge. As his feet hit the back porch, I braced myself for war. "*Why?* Why did you let the sheriff take him?"

Stomping into the kitchen, Pudge's untied boots left mud and slush on the linoleum Gideon had mopped early that morning. He refused to look at me. Instead, he tossed his coat on a kitchen chair and helped himself to a bowl of soup. His nostrils flared. "We don't make the rules; we follow them."

I felt my temper rise in response. "Well, fine. But they're bad rules. They're not fair. Somebody needs to make new ones because Gideon stole nothing, and he got confused because nobody put a sign on that restroom door!"

"It's not for you to question what's fair or what the sheriff does," he said. "You'd best follow the law. Law's not to be disobeyed. Coloreds ain't the same as whites. The sooner you get that through your damn thick skull, the better off you'll be. It's what the law tells us. It's why coloreds don't go to our schools and churches, eat at our tables, piss in our toilets to spread their diseases."

I sunk into the chair Gideon sat in only moments before, feeling the heat his body had left behind, my spirit grieving, waiting for Pudge to get the Bible belt. But he finished his soup, then reached for a shot glass, pouring one after the other until he stumbled to his bed and passed out in his pants and boots.

I shut his bedroom door so I didn't have to hear him snore. Back in my room, I stretched out on the floor, praying to God to save Gideon from the Klan. I cried until my hanky soaked up every ounce of water inside me. Until the wild dogs began their nightly serenade. And I thanked God for sparing my backside that time.

Sometimes, whiskey was a good thing.

A wolf is no less a wolf because he's dressed in sheepskin
and the Devil is no less the Devil
because he's dressed as an angel.

~ Lecrae

CHAPTER NINE

The morning after Sheriff Troyer hauled Gideon away, I crawled out of bed to find Pudge reheating the previous morning's biscuits. "Get out in the coop and gather me some eggs. We better think about how we're gonna get along without Gideon."

"But the Sheriff said—"

"—Gideon ain't coming back. Ever. He broke the law, and he's on his way to jail for it. I've hired Missus Troyer, Sheriff Troyer's wife, to come out here three days a week and help you with the housework. Teach you how to cook and clean proper. I can't afford daily live-in help. Not no more. Anyhow, you're old enough to do some real woman's work 'round this place."

A flippant answer came to mind, but I bit my tongue. "Who's taking care of the farm now?" I asked instead.

"We don't need Gideon. I got enough men on the tobacco payroll to work the horses and mules. Take care of things here. Your place is in the house from now on. You want to be treated like a woman; you start acting like one."

That's why he never wanted me to leave? To be his free live-in maid for the rest of his miserable life? "Gideon worked in your fields for twenty-five years, then took care of me and this farm for another eight, and you can let him go? Just like that?"

Opening a new jelly jar, Pudge's fat hands slipped around the lid as he twisted and grunted. "Just—like—that. Now, get out in the coop like I told you. You got Sunday school in an hour. I'll have to drive you from now on."

Gideon and I were supposed to be on our way to Bakersville. I didn't feel like facing Lila Goodeve and her thick Baptist grin after the beating I took because of her, so I pretended to be sick. That suited Pudge, who promptly went back to bed. Hung over from the night before, he didn't feel like driving me to church, anyway.

Winter was harsh on Pudge. During other seasons, tobacco farming occupied his mind, and he spent most of his days in the fields, watching over his crop and the hired hands who picked it. But in winter, Pudge spent his time choosing among the local beer joints, drinking in front of the TV, or sleeping the day away. No matter the season, he rarely did any of his own work.

One hour rolled into the next. When lunchtime ended, I switched on the radio. Another storm headed our way. I glanced at the clock—two-twenty. No sign of Gideon. All I could do to pass the time was sit by the phone and work my fingers through the knots in my hair.

Suppertime came and went. Neither of us ate. Pudge parked himself in front of the TV with a fresh bottle of Jim Beam until his red-rimmed eyes drooped to a close. By bedtime, my nerves had got the best of me. I was really and truly sick, and Pudge was really and truly drunk. I heard him follow me into my bedroom, but I moved with deliberate slowness, feeling the anger building inside me.

He stopped at the door and slurred his words. "I got to go to the vet tomorrow afternoon and pick up some medicine. My mule is sick," he said. "When you get home from school, stay in the house. Don't leave this house. You got that?"

I nodded, knowing Pudge's prize mule had fought the same virus that had killed one of his horses a few days before. "Sorry 'bout the mule."

He turned to leave.

"But I'm not your prisoner."

He spun back around. "What the hell d'you say?"

"You cooking tomorrow, or am I?" I also knew he'd not considered how his stomach would suffer without Gideon around to fix his meals.

He pointed a beefy finger at me. "You better watch your mouth."

But, like Gideon said, I didn't know when to stop. "Gideon was the only person in this world who cared about me, and you just let him go to jail for nothing!"

Pudge stiffened. "If I weren't so drunk—" The color faded from his lips. He belched. The smell of whiskey and pork rinds nearly strangled me. "I'll take care of your smart-ass mouth tomorrow. You think real hard on that, little girl."

He stumbled out, and again, I heard the creaky bed springs as he rolled onto his mattress. Despite the anger in his voice, the force of his foul breath, and the fear that rose in me like floodwater, I stood against my open bedroom door and listened to his hacking cough, deafening snores, and the lethal explosions of passed gas while he fell asleep in the dark.

I simply loved Mister Jim Beam.

Within the hour, a shiver, born of fear, slid along my spine as I moved to the window and pressed my face to the cold glass. I asked God for mercy and once again felt a chill, like a stranger had entered the house. Outside, lit up by moonlight, two wolves stood in the yard. Their eyes, like fiery darts, locked onto mine. I froze, unable to move, my breath trapped in my throat. But after what felt like an eternity, they suddenly sprinted toward the woods, their departure marked by another eerie howl that pierced the darkness and filled my room like thick, viscous sludge. I've never spoken about them to a living soul—until now.

I was already treading water in Pudge's cesspool, but Gideon going to jail was about to pull me to the bottom. I had to get help, and the only place I knew that offered it free was my church. Wayside Baptist formed committees to take food to funerals or invalids in the hospital. They ministered at the old folks' home and sent money to missionaries in China, Africa, and the Philippines. Every Christmas, my Sunday school class filled shoeboxes with

Bible tracts and homemade cookies and delivered them to families living in tarpaper shacks without running water. After everything I'd done to help with one committee or another, I reckoned someone there could take ten minutes and listen to me.

There had to be a Wayside Baptist member besides me who *didn't* hate Negroes. Once they heard my side of the story, they'd know Gideon was innocent and help me get him out of the town hall or jail if that's where he ended up.

So, on Monday morning, while Pudge spent his regular hour stinking up the bathroom, I called myself off sick from school, and instead of catching the bus as usual, I hid in the one place on the farm Pudge never allowed me to go. Inside Gideon's shack.

From the moment the sheriff drove away with Gideon in the backseat, pure rage threatened to boil every bad word inside my head to the surface. I leaned against the shack wall with my hands behind me, holding onto the last shreds of my self-control and thinking how swear words had no place in Gideon's world, and how he'd scolded me each time I let one slip out. To Gideon, risking Heaven wasn't worth the use of foul language. In my whole life, I never heard him utter a single profanity, and now he was about to be consumed by men who cursed as easily as they spoke their names.

I missed him so badly that the soles of my feet ached. Not wanting to make my presence known by flipping on the lone bulb suspended from the ceiling, I waited until my eyes adjusted to the dim morning light.

Gideon had made his bare-boned shack homey by adding a braided rug for warmth on the cement floor and topping his bed with a worn but clean quilt. He had strung gingham-checked curtains on a rope over his solitary window—curtains most likely donated by the ladies at his church. A tiny wood-burning stove with an oven hugged the wall where pots, pans, and various cooking utensils dangled from hooks nailed into the wall. There was a cracked sink but no Frigidaire. His few clothes hung on wire hangers from a rusted pipe, leading into a second smaller room with a toilet and a round galvanized tub. But the spotless rooms smelled of sweet oil and soap, and I breathed in the scents of him.

He had fashioned pieces of barn siding into a shelf on the area above his bed to hold his books. *Moby Dick*, three volumes by *Mister Mark Twain*, and four church hymnals leaned against a book of essays, *The Souls of Black Folk*, by a name I couldn't pronounce, a *Mister DuBois*. I wondered how often Gideon had read his books by the faint light in his room and why he'd never discussed them with me.

On his nightstand and open to the light, the red ribbon of Gideon's Holy Bible caught my eye. I'd not been much of a Bible reader, but I picked it up. The ribbon had parted the Red Sea scriptures of Exodus. Pages fluttered; some were bent with passages underlined and sermon titles written in the margins. Others were seamless and straight; they hadn't a pencil mark on them.

Gideon's Holy Bible felt nothing like the Bible Pudge shoved into my arms each time he beat on me. There was a comfort in knowing the difference. Something Gideon had taught me when I was ten after a particularly terrible beating, he read me the scriptures of Jesus and the children and about the millstone bound for Pudge's neck. From that moment on, I knew Pudge's Bible and Gideon's differed in more ways than one. Sitting cross-legged on the floor, I ran my hands over the worn leather cover and stared at the clock, watching the hours tick by, hoping for deliverance and a sign that God had not abandoned us.

Hunger pangs gave way to nervous knots, filling my belly like curdled milk. At two-thirty, I stood to peek out the window at the snow-filled sky. Watching Pudge drive away, I drew in a breath. "It's now or never," I said out loud, rooting through Gideon's nightstand drawer for his truck keys. I took my time pulling on my boots and red stocking hat. I didn't want to leave too soon. Driving up behind Pudge would've been the kiss of death.

Gideon's truck started when I pulled the choke and turned the key. I'd never driven on the road before, but I'd had plenty of practice tooling around the pastures the past summer; Pudge's driving lesson had come in handy.

On the road, I talked to God like He had hopped into the truck with me. "God. Sir. It's just You and me here, so how about we make a deal? Nobody has to know." I paused, hoping for some sign He was actually listening. Nothing happened. "Well, fine. No doubt my sinful nature has taken me over, so haul off and wallop me if You've a mind to. But please, Sir, please let me find Gideon before you punish me. I—" I stopped my plea, sighed, and shook my head. I decided to worry about my backslidden condition later and concentrate instead on my plan.

Slowing the truck to a crawl at the Sunset View Cemetery, I peered across acres of gravestones stuck up every which way, like mouths of crooked teeth. Some were new and shiny, planted in freshly turned earth, while others appeared worn and cracked, with the names nearly weathered off. Steering onto the shoulder, I looked off into the distance. The truck tires crunched over gravel, and it started to snow as I rolled the window down.

Morrigan. I barely saw the marker where my parents lay side-by-side under the dirt, next to a thick patch of small trees full of dormant kudzu. Pulling slowly back onto the road, I knew that raising my parents from the dead was one thing, but if I ever saw their graves again, it'd be a bonafide miracle.

I drove past Brittain's General Store and noticed the red and green twinkle lights in the windows reflecting on the wet sidewalk. Three weeks until Christmas—such a tiny sliver of time. I figured, shoot, I'd never whooped it up over the holidays, anyway. And unless they hauled my butt off to reform school, I'd celebrate Christmas some other time.

Sitting at the stoplight in Summerfield at three o'clock on the dot, I tugged at my hat. If anybody had seen me, they might've recognized my red hair and Gideon's green truck. Praying that I blended into the red and green of Christmas, I held my breath, impatient for the light to turn.

Nothing moved but the wind, churning a sky full of gunmetal-gray clouds. To ease my nerves, I tuned in to our local radio station. "Snow comin' tonight, folks. Almanac says it's gonna be a big'un. Mother Nature'll be dumpin' 'bout a foot of the white stuff 'fore midnight." Our weatherman sounded as happy as the kids at school who constantly prayed for snow days. But I prayed it'd hold off until Gideon and I got the hello out of Dodge.

I'd never attended church on a Monday, but I knew the pastor's secretary worked until five o'clock. It surprised me to find the parking lot packed with cars and pickups. Hurrying up the church-house steps like I was late for service, I figured something was happening in the fellowship hall attached to the church's back entrance. When I opened the double doors at the front, it smelled musty, like opening a storm cellar. The stale, dry air felt cool. Before my stinging eyes adjusted to the darkness, I stumbled over a pew leg, groping my way to the altar rail.

At the vestibule door, I watched more cars pull into the lot. It didn't take long to discover what kind of meeting it was. They *wanted* folks to see them parading around the parking lot in their white robes and pointy hoods, slapping each other's backs, and hee-hawing like a bunch of jackasses.

I ducked into a nearby Sunday school room and kicked my backside. I kicked it hard. A church that allowed the Klan to hold meetings wasn't about to help me get a Negro out of jail. Tires squealed, and more cars jammed into the remaining parking spots like it was revival time. A warning blared in my head, and I had a bad feeling. I tried, but I couldn't shake it, and I suddenly realized I wouldn't make it back to the farm before dark to pack our things. It was so unfair. Gideon had done nothing wrong other than his skin not being the right color.

Standing in the Sunday school room's dusky light, I peered out the window for a familiar face. *So many people.* Cars and trucks filled the lots and lined the street, obscuring my view. An uneasy shiver crept up my spine once more. Alone, I scanned the hallway again, finding a small amount of comfort in the silence except for the distant voices in the fellowship hall.

But in seconds, a lump rose from my chest and stuck in my throat when a dozen or so hooded Klan men marched through the vestibule doors, past me, and then down the hallway into the meeting, chanting, "White Power—White Power—White Power," and carrying a large wooden cross above their heads. I couldn't move or think until I smelled the stench of pig on the matching coats of the Whitsett brothers who brought up the rear.

Finally, my feet let loose of the spot they'd frozen in, and I crept down the hall. By the time I peeked into the fellowship hall, the Klan members had pulled off their hoods, revealing a red-eyed meanness and sweat popping off their foreheads like drops of blood.

It disgusted me to watch the ladies from the choir smile and serve potluck from the kitchen pass-through window like it was a social reception. Old man Cutler, our church's oldest father the past Father's Day, lingered near the back. He grabbed his cane and waddled into the hallway when he saw me. "We don't permit children at this meeting, dear," he said. "Who are you looking for?"

I had to think fast. "Oh, well, Pastor Cole," I said, even though he was the last person I wanted to see.

"You mean Catfish Cole?"

"Who?"

"Catfish Cole. Tonight, he is not Pastor Cole, dear girl. He is Catfish Cole, Grand Dragon of the Ku Klux Klan of the Carolinas!"

I couldn't believe what my ears told my brain. "I'll come back. Thanks."

"Probably best you do," he said.

That's when I felt an icy hand on my shoulder and nearly jumped out of my skin.

Backing away from a devil-red robe and pointy hood, I all but fainted. "Your colored man isn't here," Pastor Cole said, lifting the flap that covered his face. His high-pitched evangelist voice always got on my last nerve. "Sheriff Troyer got called out of town on another matter, so I expect the Greensboro police will arrest the niggra at the town hall in the morning. I hear he's got himself in a peck of trouble, stealing merchandise and breaking our laws." His lips curled into his scornful preacher-politician smile.

My hands clenched into fists. "Gideon stole nothing from Pudge the whole time he's worked for him, and he never stole that cheap watch, either!" I didn't care what he called himself; that man was no longer my pastor.

He held his Bible tight against his shiny robe. It gave me the creeps. He had that smirk, that sneer, that all-knowing look Pudge had before he pulled his Bible belt out of the closet. "First, young lady, you should watch your tone in the House of God. And it doesn't matter if it was only one *cheap watch*, as you call it, or a hundred expensive watches." He squeezed his Bible as if trying to drive his words down the back of my throat. "Thou shalt not steal. He *stole*. Stealing is an abomination."

I shook so badly that my eyeglasses jiggled, and I couldn't see straight. "I need to see Gideon. I need to know he's all right."

"He's fine. Take my word for it, little sister."

I stepped back again. "I'm *not* your sister, and I'm *not* taking your word for nothing." I flipped around and started for the exit door.

Pastor Cole hollered after me. "We got a guard on him. He's *not* to see anybody. Greensboro patrol is picking him up, so you best get on home! You understand?"

"Yes, sir!" I shouted back down the hallway. "I understand. I understand you're Catfish Cole. I understand you're not a pastor. You're just some old dragon man and head of the Klan that tortures and murders Negroes for no *damn* good reason. I understand *perfectly!* How's *that* for *tone!?*"

"You get out of here, gal!" he snapped. "A niggra ain't worth a red cent 'less he's dead. I'm calling your granddaddy—"

I didn't hear the rest of what he said. I lit out of there quick, slamming the vestibule door behind me and bolting to the truck. It shot off, eating up the pavement. But by the time I'd gotten a good mile away, I had to shake my fingers loose from the steering wheel. Ahead, the Summerfield traffic light turned red. I braked to stop, double-checked my door locks, and then prayed—out loud. Gideon-style. "Sweet Lord Jesus, please get me and Gideon out of here in one piece."

There was only one thing left to do. Go back, grab our bags, then drive to the town hall and break Gideon out of whatever room they'd locked him in. It wasn't jail, at least. There had to be a way—had to be! I stomped on the gas but let up on the clutch too fast, and the truck stalled. I tried again. The tires squealed, the truck jerked and took off, and I kept praying I'd pull into the driveway before Pudge.

As I drove back to the farm, it snowed—the kind that propels itself sideways and covers the windshield, turning the world into a blinding Ku Klux Klan sheet of *white*.

Wolves prey upon lambs in the dark of night,
but the blood stains remain upon the stones in the valley—
until dawn comes,
and the sun reveals the crime to all.

~ Khalil Gibran

Chapter Ten

On the road to the farm, I hit a pothole and bounced off my seat. Driving too fast, I hit the brakes and swerved sharply into the driveway. The truck fishtailed on loose gravel, getting stuck in mud—a familiar predicament over the past year while driving in the pastures. But I knew how to rock the truck and spin the tires to free it from the rut. In minutes, I was speeding up to the house. No sign of Pudge. I breathed a deep sigh of relief. Parking Gideon's truck in its usual spot by the barn, I hurried inside, leaving the keys in the ignition to avoid misplacing them. There was no time to waste; I had to pack fast.

My relief was brief as headlights pierced through the windows, casting shadows on the walls. There wasn't time to escape to town with our bags. I fled into my room, my heart pounding in my ears, and opened a schoolbook, its pages a thin shield against what I instinctively knew was coming. With any luck, I'd sneak out once Pudge had gone to bed.

It didn't take long to hear him stomp up the porch steps and start pacing the kitchen linoleum, the sound of his boots echoing through the house. Peeking around the corner, I watched him appear clueless about preparing something to eat, pulling out pots and pans and rummaging through the Frigidaire and pantry as if he had never seen them. As if he believed some ghoulish haint lurked behind the cupboard doors. Eventually, he poured a bag of pinto beans into an aluminum pan filled with water and lit the stove. Did he really think they'd taste like Gideon's beans, cooked with salt pork, pepper, and onions and simmered slowly over a low flame?

"Neeley!"

I walked into the kitchen, but my legs wobbled like rubber bands. "Yes, sir?" He'd been to the beer joint. I smelled it.

"My draft mule—" He hesitated like he cared about the mule more than God Almighty. "I got to put him down. Watch these damn beans so they don't burn."

I stood there imagining that's what he did to my grandmother. She probably got sick, and he just picked up his rifle and put her out of her misery.

Moments later, I heard the gun firing—twice. Pudge walked inside the house and set his rifle by the door. That's when the phone rang. Instead of eavesdropping on the conversation, I edged around the wall, slipped into my room, and closed the door behind me.

I knew he was coming for me.

Within minutes, Pudge's boot kicked in my door. I backed up and sat on my bed with a sharp stitch in my side, but it was the icy fear twisted around my heart that stunned me, turning me into stone. I couldn't move. I choked back a scream when he slammed his fist into the door jamb, blocking any escape. "That was Pastor Cole. Get your ass up!"

Clutching the edge of my blanket, I struggled to breathe, taking shallow, rapid gasps. In a single heartbeat, his massive hands flipped up my mattress, spilling me onto the floor. I scurried like a scared kitten into the corner and stared at the door, thinking I should run for it.

The room reeked of whiskey and his unwashed body as he towered over me. "Get your damn ass up off that floor!"

I rose slowly, aching in my legs like I'd pulled my hamstrings. We stared long at each other as if the world were ending around us and I heard my voice yell from far away, *Run!* But I didn't. I couldn't. The chain of profanity that flew out of his mouth nearly burned the eardrums out of my head before he finally shouted, "Don't you move!"

I rubbed my eyes to focus, but sweat poured from my head. My shallow breathing turned into more short, labored gasps, and

I felt numb—a frequent feeling whenever he walked off to fetch his Bible belt. But for the first time, I felt abandoned. As if not a soul in the world cared one iota about me. I bit my lip to hold my tears inside, but they fell like they always did. Terrible hiccups rolled out of me, hurting my throat and shaking my shoulders until I saw my distorted reflection in the window. I hardly recognized myself, and at that moment, I wondered why God hated me so much that I ended up on that farm so completely alone—so utterly heartbroken.

I counted—I counted the seconds it took to crumble to the floor once again. By the time he returned, I had curled into a ball.

My crying didn't stop him. Nothing stopped his fiery fit. Like pulling a weed, Pudge grabbed me by a fistful of hair and yanked me to my feet, jerking back my head. Strings of phlegm flew out of his open mouth, and I smelled words as foul as the rotten molars at the back of his throat as he screamed his intention in my face, speckling my eyeglasses with his spit. "Goddamn you! I'm gonna beat the living shit out of you, you little bitch! How dare you embarrass me! How dare you speak to Pastor Cole like you're some kinda nigger lover!"

My tears flowed thick like blood, slick and salty, finding their way into my mouth. My only shame was that I was defenseless, weak, and had nothing to protect myself. No words, no weapon. Nothing.

His thick, rough hands shoved me around the room. Yelling more foul obscenities and random words that rammed into each other and made no sense. It's terrifying, you know, to watch someone lose their mind.

The leather belt shrieked as he pulled it loose. He shoved the Bible into my arms, then flipped me around and pushed me forward. "Hold it! Don't let go of it for one second!" It shocked me when he yanked my pants down to my ankles. With my left hand clutching the Bible, I desperately held onto my underwear with my right hand to prevent them from falling as well. This was something new; he had never exposed my bare skin like that. Before I knew it, he had flung me across my bed, his Bible at my chest, sandwiched between me and the bedspread.

I hated his voice. Hated the way I must have looked, bent over my bed like that, wanting my mother more than I wanted to live. The belt sliced through the air above my head, coming down and whacking my behind with his muscle behind it. But the sound of that strap was more terrifying than the pain of the first few licks. Fire ran along my thighs, making it difficult to catch my breath as the scorching heat traveled up my back to my head. Soon, all I heard was my heartbeat throbbing in my ears, along with the sharp crack of the belt against my bare legs. My arms went prickly and numb until I no longer felt the Bible beneath me.

The number of licks had nothing to do with my age for that beating. Fueled by his pure hatred of me, he wouldn't stop, and he wouldn't let up. He kept going as if one more strike might stifle whatever dark-eyed demon raged inside him. With the strength I had left, I cried out, *"Grandpa, please, stop!"*

Out of breath, he paused after the nineteenth lick.

From my bleary right eye, I watched him stumble out of my room. It was over.

But in one quick motion, he whirled around and lunged at me, either to empty the last of his fierce rage or to make it an even twenty. I hugged the Bible to brace myself and buried my face in the bedcovers. And then, the electricity surged and cracked and the house lights went off. It scared us both, I think. And yet, as if to defy God, he whacked his belt across my body one last time. The darkness stopped him, though. He staggered out after throwing his belt at me, the heavy metal buckle striking my head. "I'm not through with you! This ain't over!"

It didn't matter. I couldn't move. I stayed motionless on the bed, contemplating my responsibility of re-wrapping his belt around the Bible. But I let them both slide to the rug. The house reeked with his stench, and he had drawn the blinds, making what light I could see as dingy as the air. I tried to breathe steadily, but my body couldn't remember how. Clamping my hand over my mouth, I watched the clock and cried quietly for what seemed like forever, thinking if I watched it long enough—time might stop, and I could die and leave that place peacefully. My trance ended when the phone rang again and the electricity popped back on.

Little by little, I pulled myself up to stand on quivering legs, gently pulling my pants over my welts, and holding my breath. Inching into the kitchen, I listened for Pudge, but he wasn't there. His bedroom door stood open, and I stared at the big dip in his bed, filled with nothing but a pile of blankets twisted around his cats.

That whipping was the worst, but it would be my last because I knew if there ever was a next time—he'd kill me. I didn't want to die, not like that. I wanted to glare at him through my thick eyeglasses, with him knowing I saw my grandmother's blood on his hands. I wanted to stay alive long enough to look him in the eye on his deathbed. Make him wonder if those twelve times a year he beat me were louder than his screams for God to save him as he dropped into Hell. But even more than that, I wanted Gideon.

The dreariness inside the house deepened the pain as I maneuvered into the bathroom and peeked at my reflection in the mirror. My hair looked like it had exploded from my head, and a bruise stained my right cheek, where I had pushed hard on the bottom of my eyeglasses as I lay across my bed. They sat crooked on my face. I turned away. Sitting half on the toilet, half off, my bottom had turned hard and purple, and I felt blood seeping from places on my back and legs.

The stinging ebbed to a bearable level when I heard Pudge walk through the back door, the tired floor creaking under his weight.

"Neeley!"

When I stepped out of the bathroom, he peered at me in the dim light before grabbing my arm and pulling me into the kitchen—how it hurt. "Pastor Cole wants to see me. Seems you got the Klan all pissed off and fired up over Gideon. He's thinking about making an example out of him. I got his truck keys, so you plant yourself in your room and stay there the rest of the night. You hear?"

I couldn't answer. Distracted by a stream of new moonlight shining on the kitchen table, my mind and tongue had gone numb.

"DO YOU HEAR ME!?"

I jumped. "*Yes*—Yes, sir." Fresh tears fell and dropped onto my heart. I drifted away from his voice and toward the sound of the wild dogs howling louder than ever. Closing my eyes, I saw myself at age five, six, and seven, bruises and welts for each year of my life, buried by his voice—*spare the rod and spoil the rotten child.*

Stumbling back to my room, I leaned against my bed, dragging in deep gulps of air. The pain, the throbbing in my legs, it wouldn't let up. The agony of it—my mind has refused to forget to this day. I waited to breathe normal again, and for the unbearable stinging to stop shooting through my thighs, cramping my muscles. Wincing with each breath, I tensed, until the discomfort finally faded.

With great effort, I removed my bloody pants and underwear, and carefully pulled on clean ones, deciding I'd better get my hat and gloves out of Gideon's truck before Pudge found them and whipped me again. I crept through the kitchen, grabbed my coat, and carefully shut the back door. Guided by the muted glow of the house lights and my familiarity with the path, I limped to the barn in the dark, offering up what I believed to be my last prayer.

Inside, Pudge's gelding, Rasputin, snorted from his stall, a gentle reminder that nobody had fed him. "You're on your own," I told the quarter horse as if the animal understood me. Tenderly, I patted his enormous forehead, convinced I'd never see him again. But I gave in and fed him anyway, only to see Gideon from the corner of my eye step into the barn. Startled, I dropped the feed bucket.

Opening his arms, he smiled and I fell into them like a baby taking its first steps. "Glory, hallelujah!" I shouted, feeling my bones melting into one big puddle, and then I noticed his eye, swollen, streaked in red and dark purple bruises. "What happened?"

"After I lef' here, the sheriff rough me up a bit. Try 'n get me to confess to stealing."

"He hit you?"

Gideon eased himself down on a hay bale. "More than once. Happened again early this morning, too. I'd slept all night in a storage room; they'd bound mah hands to a metal chair. Sometime 'fore daybreak, I heard footsteps in the hall and figured it was the deputy and a few workers. Nobody said nothing. You knows how folks keep to themselves early in the morning hours 'fore the sun comes up, like it some unspoken rule to talk. I stared at the light seeping through the bottom-a the door. When it opened, mah eyes blinked from the glare. There were three-a them wearing white shirts stained with liquor and sweat. Them men must've stayed awake all night, drinking and arguing how they gone deal with me. When I asked to use the restroom, that's when they came at me again."

Gideon wiped his brow with the back of his hand. "After 'bout the third punch, one-a them laughed from deep in his throat. It was Mistah Eugene Cooper—yes 'um—man works down at the feed mill. His eyes gave me quite a fright. Cold and dark, like lake water 'fore it freeze. Eyes so blue they almost black."

"Was the sheriff there?"

"Oh, he there, all right. Carried on something awful. Hollered at the side-a mah head. 'You confess, ol' nigga,' he say, 'and I let you go with the Greensboro police peaceful like. You don't, and there's no telling what becomes-a you! I could say you escaped, or worse, that you were never here!' So, I began to pray out loud. You knows I do mah best praying out loud. Two-a them held me by mah arms while the sheriff say, 'C'mon, nigga, God don't pay no mind to thieves and liars. You say you stole that watch!' When I didn't, he came at me again. Hit me in mah eye, see here?" Gideon moved his head toward the light and pointed to his eye like he was proud of it. "Haven't had a shiner like this since Mistah Pudge mule kicked me back in '51."

Hearing his voice soothed me, but his words devastated me, and I remained silent, needing him to tell me everything.

"You knows, Neeley, Bible say God is not dead. That He the same yesterday, today, and always. That He still a God-a miracles. You believe that?"

I exhaled, realizing I'd been holding my breath. "I suppose so. But how did you get out?"

Gideon smiled, thinking about it. "Let me say, I never be a doubting Thomas again, 'cause that's what happened. A miracle. That storage room started shaking a bit at first, and then like we on top of a mine that jus' blew, a horrible sound, like a bomb went off. Supplies fell from the shelves, and the lights sparked— Law, I thought, maybe a pump blew down at the filling station. Them men all took out, wondering what exploded. But it was jus' like the scripture say, *And, behold, the angel-a the Lawd came upon him, and a light shined in the prison: . . . And his chains fell off his hands.* I was still locked in that storage room, but no longer roped to the chair. Not a one-a them men came back, and I heard somebody say sheriff be gone 'til tomorrow. I figured I'd jus' sit there—wait and see what that angel do next."

I believed him. Gideon had never lied to me, and I doubted he had lost his marbles with that punch to his eye. "What exploded?"

"I don't rightly know. Somehow, I don't think I ever will."

The burning muscles in my legs screamed for relief, and I eased myself down beside him. "But you still haven't told me how you got out."

"Deacon Hayes cleans the town hall and whatnot after the white folks go home. Late this evening, he shuffled his suds bucket and mop down the hall and sees me locked in the storage room. He asked the guard to unlock the door to let him grab a few clean rags and then struck up a friendly conversation with that guard who jus' forgot to lock up on his way out. After the guard fell asleep, I walked out and Deacon Hayes gave me a ride back here. 'Magine that. Like ol' Daniel in the lion's den, He delivered me right out from under their noses."

My head spun with sudden and unexpected joy. "But will he get in trouble for it?"

Gideon made a dismissive, wavy motion with his hand. "Deacon Hayes even older than me. What they gone do to him time hasn't already done?"

Hiding a sigh behind my labored smile, I felt my rigid posture collapse. When Gideon put his hand on the side of my face, I inhaled sharply and brushed away tears, puzzled that he knew what Pudge had done to me, yet didn't seem shocked. I wiped my nose on my sleeve and spoke through gritted teeth. "Gideon—" My voice sounded less significant than ever. Faint, tinny, and powerless. Like a high-pitched bird call. "You want to know what I did to piss him off this time? It doesn't matter now. He's gone to see Pastor Cole, I mean Catfish Cole and the Klan. They mean to take you. Pudge has your truck keys. What do we do now?"

His eyes brimming with tears, he stood slowly. Gideon placed his hands on my shoulders, snapped out of his daze, and reared back. "You a mess." I pulled his hand to my cheek again, believing if I held it there long enough, the nightmare would end. "Let's go inside," he said. "Klan meeting broke up hours ago. They all gone home. Them men gots to get up early. Nobody want to fool with an ol' nigga this late. Klan think I can jus' rot in that storage room one more night. Mistah Pudge, he be gone a while, stop off at the church, then you knows he at one beer joint or another." Gideon looked into my eyes, reached out with his thumb, and wiped a tear from my cheek. "Get me a hairbrush," he said. "I'll bring the bag balm."

CHAPTER ELEVEN

Once inside the kitchen, Gideon placed a cold, wet towel on my face. "I 'magine your backside probably more beat up than a run-over 'possum by the side-a the road." He removed my eyeglasses. "Stop fretting, now." His quiet voice reassured me like always. "Don't let the fire go out-a them eyes. You not dead yet. Don't let him steal your hope."

Until that moment, despite the pain of living with a monster, somewhere deep inside myself, I had harbored a hope Pudge would soften, change, see the good in me—but that notion shriveled up and blew away like shredded tissue paper. "Why did God let this happen to you and me?" I asked.

"Don't try 'n figure that out. Rain falls on the bad *and* the good. Being angry with God takes too much time and energy to get over," he said.

I concentrated on holding up my head, for Gideon's sake, and kept my eyes on the flower pattern of the towel he held with his fingertips. I felt blood oozing from the belt cuts on my backside, arms, and legs as Gideon spoke blame for not saving me from Pudge. "I'll never let him do this to you again," he said, remorseful. Clearing his throat, he raised my chin gently with his free hand. "Now, Neeley, you knows I haven't seen your bottom since you was jus' five or six and down sick with the measles. But if you need me to tend to any-a them welts on your backside, you feel free to lift your shirt or pull down them britches. Let me take a look."

When it came to Gideon and his caring for me, there was no fear, hesitation, or concern in the world that his intentions to treat my bruised self would be something I'd have to think about. I carefully raised my shirt a bit. After unfastening a button, I lowered my pants, wincing from the pain of the welts that had bled and stuck to them.

"Law, Neeley. This the *worst* one," Gideon said and sighed.

Painfully, I leaned on the kitchen windowsill and forced my mind outside. More clouds rolled in, almost purple with the heaviness of snow. I kept a lookout for Pudge's truck and held my breath, flinching as Gideon moved his large, black hands against my fair skin, applying cold cloths, bag balm, Mercurochrome, and bandages to my backside.

I believed with every ounce of me that Pudge intended to dig my grave as he did for my grandmother and that Gideon believed it, too. Drenched in sweat, I wanted to call out for my mother, but I knew she couldn't save me. My longing for her pulled at my chest as I silently sobbed in short, gasping breaths. For the moment, I took comfort in Gideon's soft humming, like the words in his head filled him with a plan.

After pulling up my pants, I rinsed blood out of the kitchen sink while Gideon took care of the rest. He smiled, nodding to reassure me, and spoke in his cool, deep voice. Calm and sure, like a doctor. "You need aspirin?"

"Two." I swallowed a couple Bayer with a sticky throat, watching Gideon drag a chair into the bathroom. He motioned for me to sit on the pillow he had placed on the seat.

"It's time to leave this place," he said. "God only knows when you might get a chance to wash your hair again, so let's get it out-a the way." I leaned my head back into the sink while he slowly washed the soreness out of my head. Afterward, he towel-dried it and sang softly. *"There is a balm in Gilead to make the wounded whole; there is a balm in Gilead to heal a sin-sick soul."* Resting my head in his hands, he brushed my hair, pulled it back, and braided it, like when he braided bread, all while singing about the bag balm in Gilead.

The pain in my body withered away as Gideon worked his gentle magic. I closed my eyes until he finished his song, and the familiar sounds of the wild dogs began. "There they go, right on cue. Do you think they're howling at the moon?"

It felt strange when Gideon stepped in front of me. Once again, he gently tilted my chin upward. "Look at me, Neeley. Something you needs to know. I don't hear them wild dogs. You is the only one. Mistah Pudge tole me weeks ago he never heard 'em."

I shuddered, my voice raising as I tried to process what he said. "But—but you said—"

"—I knows what I said." He smiled down at me. "After a while, I reckoned you heard whatever the good Lawd wanted you to hear. He still be the God-a miracles."

Like an old lady with the rheumatism, I leaned on Gideon and ambled back to the barn. Moonlight fell beneath the trees and into nearby pastures while we loaded straw bales, tools, and horse blankets that belonged to Gideon into the truck bed, waiting for Pudge to return. I didn't know how Gideon planned on taking the truck keys from him, but my mind was too tired to think that far.

"Here he comes." Gideon ducked behind the barn door. "You go on. Be brave. Act like you tending to the horses. I'll be up to the house directly."

Icy shards of panic prickled along my skin. "What are you going to do?"

"Don't worry. You jus' go on."

I limped up the path, my mind a crazy mixture of hope and dread.

I knew the sound of his truck door. I heard his footsteps pounding toward me and saw the outline of his beefy body in the dark. "You got shit for brains? Huh? Didn't I tell you to stay in your room!?"

"I—I needed to get the bag balm from the barn."

He grabbed my arm. Fear and nausea hit me like the stomach flu. Almost at a run, we rushed past trees and bushes and sidestepped several mud puddles in the dark. Pulling me toward the house and nearly yanking my arm out of its socket, Pudge fixed his stone-cold eyes on me like a snake on its prey. But Gideon's voice rang inside my head—*Be brave!* Out of breath, Pudge stopped and let loose of my arm. I moved backward up the porch steps in frightening silence, putting a good ten feet between us. Silence so unnerving—it froze in my veins, and I told myself he was either horribly drunk or, God help me, he was crazy sober.

Waiting for him to move, I held my breath, didn't swallow, and barely blinked. Pudge, disheveled and drenched in sweat, struggled up the steps; his bootheels clicking on the rotting boards as moonlight reflected off his bald scalp. His slick body, reeking worse than swamp water, glistened in the dim light. "Gideon escaped," he said, panting like a dog. "They're looking for him. Get in the house."

Fast-moving clouds covered the moon, and darkness blanketed the farm. I stood motionless. Still. Solid. The seconds ticked by. I sucked in a breath. And then I think I lost my mind. "Did you murder my grandmother?" From my open mouth, the words slipped out as simply as a prayer and knocked him sideways. "Answer me!"

He staggered in the dark. "Does it matter? She's dead. *Dead!* Same as your mother and your old man!" He gasped for breath. "Goddamn it! If I have to beat it into you—twice a day—for the rest of your life—I'll teach you to stay the hell out of my business once and for all. Fetch the belt!"

"Fetch it yourself," I said.

Suddenly, the wind shifted, and moonlight broke through the haze, its glow hitting us like a spotlight. In a split second, Pudge unbuckled the belt he had on and yanked it loose, slashing the leather strap through the air. It cracked a hair-width from my face, breaking my pigheaded stare. He never saw Gideon spring from behind the rose trellis, bellowing like a roaring bear. "Don't. Touch. Her!"

Gideon fell hard on Pudge, their weight hitting the decaying porch with a familiar, hollow thud from long ago. Like the day my parents died, Pudge rolled over and pulled a handgun from his pants. I gripped the porch rail as if I were on some wild ride at the county fair. Feeling time collapse, almost stealing my vision, I saw Gideon roll over next. Both moved like the two old men they were, sluggish and hurting, with Pudge struggling to aim the gun in Gideon's direction.

But Gideon reared back and punched Pudge square in the jaw. Pudge's head slammed into the door, drawing my attention to the rifle behind the screen. The same rifle he had used to end the mule's misery. I can't recall moving, as the entire episode unfolded in slow motion. Before I knew it, my hands lifted the cold rifle to my shoulder and tugged on the heavy bolt. Bracing myself, I squinted through its rusted sights and pulled the trigger.

Everything vanished. All that remained was smoke, the lingering scent of fear, and an eerie stillness.

Blood seeped between Pudge's fingers, where his handgun had been, where he held the top of his arm. He struggled to his feet to see where Gideon was and where his gun had landed.

Though I had set my eyes on Pudge, I screamed, "Gideon!"

No answer.

Gripping the rifle so tight my arms ached, I knew I could fire a second shot if I had to.

Pudge bled through his coat while a sneer spread across his face. "It's just a nick," he said, watching my arms shake. "I been bit worse by my mule." He reached into his back pocket for a handkerchief, never taking his eyes off the trembling rifle barrel in my hands. Pudge opened his coat and shirt, then balled up his hanky, placing it on his wound. "You're a fool, Neeley, and a stupid one. Your *mammy* has done run off like the jackass he is. Or maybe that bullet nicked me but killed him. Either way— looks like he left you here to fend for yourself. Don't you worry, though. If he's alive, we'll find that nigger and hang him before sunup."

His evil words went off in me like a powder keg, and I yanked the rifle up hard to my face. I had every intention of killing him, and he knew it. But before I decided whether to shoot him in the head or the heart, Pudge snatched the rifle barrel with his good arm and grabbed my coat with his wounded one, groaning in pain.

That's when the moon appeared like a signal fire in the night. Gideon stood in the snow with the light dancing in his hair. "Put the rifle down and let go-a her," he said, aiming Pudge's handgun straight at him. My grandfather obeyed, setting the rifle on the porch floor and raising both arms. Gideon moved up behind him and shoved the handgun into the back of his skull. "Neeley, move on in the house, and gather the rest-a your things."

Gideon's commanding voice caused me to hesitate, but only briefly. Dashing through the door and into my room, I took a breath to steady my nerves. If we didn't get away right then, at that moment, Pudge would do Lord-knows-what to the both of us.

I dragged down my mother's brown suitcase from the top of my closet, the one she had packed eight years before. In a frenzy, I scooped up my socks, several pairs of white cotton underwear and tossed them in with two pairs of clean dungarees, three shirts, another warm sweater, and my one and only raggedy nightgown. My hands trembled as I rummaged around for my Easter hat, which I quickly packed alongside my hairbrush, toothbrush, and my Donna Reed coat. I crammed it all in, then slammed the latch shut. *What else?*

Ah, my getaway money I'd earned working for Missus Crumley! I pulled out the shoebox from the back of my closet, opened it, and gathered my change purse, the photos of my parents, my lucky rabbit's foot, and a map of North Carolina torn at the creases. After I tucked them safely inside my pockets, I looked one last time at my sparse room, switched off the light, and closed the door. Hurrying to the kitchen, I threw two oranges, a sleeve of Saltines, and a handful of leftover biscuits into a sack, only to hear Gideon's voice drift through the screen door, ordering Pudge to *shush* and *be still*.

As I rushed out to the back porch, Gideon had wrapped his large hand around Pudge's neck, the other hand still holding the gun to his head. My heart raced when Gideon reached inside Pudge's coat for the truck keys. "Neeley, get in mah truck." But I couldn't. I had to stay near him.

Pudge fell to his knees. He was clearly in pain, but he laughed. "What? You think you're gonna get away with this? You think kidnapping, attempted murder, and stealing my guns won't put your sorry nigger ass in a noose? You won't get five miles out of this town."

Pulling my grandfather to his feet, Gideon forced him to walk to the barn and sit on a chair. Handing me the gun, he said, matter-of-fact, "Shoot him if he moves."

I dropped my suitcase. I don't mind saying how good it felt to point my grandfather's gun straight at his head.

Gideon tied Pudge's hands behind his back and to the chair, then secured his ankles to the chair legs. He looked like a pig tied to a spit. Next, Gideon uncorked a whiskey bottle with his teeth, opened Pudge's coat, and poured some of it on the wound and the rest down Pudge's throat. "I'll call Miz Crumley in the morning, asks her to check on you. You jus' nicked. You be fine once the bleeding stops. It shouldn't hurt. Much."

Gideon took the handgun from me and set it, and the rifle, on the barn floor. "I'm not taking these. But I'm taking Neeley. Get her away from you. Take her someplace safe, where nobody beat on her." Gideon snapped his head toward me again. "I said, get in the truck!"

Running out of the barn with my suitcase, I tripped and fell, landing flat on my stomach. Pudge laughed and hollered, "You ain't nothing but a retard! You hear me? A retard! A pain in my ass since the day you were born—"

I looked back, shocked to see Gideon shoving his handkerchief into Pudge's mouth. "—And I peed in your toilet today. *Now* we even."

The fear beat into me that day—Gideon siphoned out and drained it into Pudge tied to a chair he had once thrown away because it reminded him of *nigger skin*. Pure terror spread over my grandfather's face like spilled milk. For the first time in my life, I believe he was truly afraid.

My eyeglasses fogged up as I scooted across the cold seat. "Let's get out of here," I said. A gust of wind blew into the truck, and I stared through bare-limbed trees at the sky, black as a coalmine, the moon a bright beacon on God's hardhat. "Pudge said they're looking for you."

"Hmm?" Gideon's unblinking eyes reflected the moonlight. His voice barely a whisper, he seemed stunned at what he had done.

I reached for his hand. "They know you've escaped. We got to go," I said. "Right now."

Gideon's shoulders heaved with his next breath as his weathered hand seized the wheel, and the other fumbled for the ignition key. He drove us out of Summerfield on the back roads while the tired pickup clutched the pavement and plowed through snow and darkness.

I still sensed my grandfather's cruel hands and smelled his vile whiskey stench. Caught between a violent past and an unknown future, I had no idea how to get where we were going. I only had to trust that Gideon did. What I did know was that I was rolling through the coldest night of my life with a Negro man on the lam, taking me to freedom—to a place in the Blue Ridge Mountains called Bakersville.

CHAPTER TWELVE

My dream of escape had become real. But, like Lot's wife, I looked back. As we sped away from Guilford County, I turned in my seat every five minutes, half-expecting to see a red flashing light, and I thought maybe this was how the Hebrews felt, leaving Egyptian bondage, watching out for Pharaoh to come riding up behind them.

We said nothing for some time. Gaining little heat from the truck or each other, we bumped along on the seat, covered with blankets and blind hope. The police *and* the Klan were hot on our trail, and Gideon knew it in his gut.

Rounding a curve, Gideon slowed to a complete stop at the end of a long line of traffic. Fierce wind gusts knocked the truck around, while ahead, police cruisers hugged both sides of the road, their lights whirling and blinking; it was like looking at a carnival in the distance. My nerves were a live wire, chewing at my insides, and I got warm and had to undo my coat buttons and loosen my scarf. "Do you think it's a roadblock?"

"Don't rightly know."

"What should we do?" I panicked. "Stop, Gideon, let's turn around."

"There's no room; road's too skinny, and we gots oncoming traffic."

Gideon eased to the right until my door and the hubcaps scraped the hard snow wall made by the traffic ahead of us. As we inched closer and closer, I fully expected to be stopped, thrown up against the truck, and handcuffed.

"Get down on the seat," Gideon said. "Cover yousef'. They looking for an ol' man and a young girl. Maybe if they think I'm by mahsef', they let me pass." He shifted his hat to hide his black eye.

I did what Gideon told me to do and hunkered down. Listening to him quote scripture from beneath the blanket, I figured a little divine reinforcement sure couldn't hurt.

"I knows, sweet Jesus, *all these blessings shall come . . . if I hearken to Your voice. I be blessed in the city, and blessed in the field. Blessed be the fruit-a mah body, blessed coming in and blessed gone out.*"

The truck slowed to a crawl. Glued to the seat, I couldn't move a muscle.

"*Mah enemies, You will smite before me: they shall come out against me one way and flee before me seven ways . . .*"

A siren blared and like to scare me to death.

"Yes, Lawd," he said, a little louder. "*You shall command the blessing upon mah storehouse, and in all You set your hand to if I keep Your commandments and walk in Your ways, I be the head, and not the tail; above only, and not beneath . . .*"

I lifted the blanket. Peeking out the window, I spotted two cars overturned in the ditch, tires up and on fire. Ambulance workers carried a body on a stretcher past our truck, and I heard Gideon gasp, "Sweet Baby Jesus, hep them poor folks."

The police paid us not one bit of attention. Riding through the middle of that mess, I caught a chill rattling my teeth. It's one thing to feel like the Hebrews getting the hello out of Egypt, but when God parts the Red Sea right in front of you, pointing the way to the Promised Land, it's entirely something else.

You might think it a tragedy if everything you owned in the wide world fit inside one tiny suitcase, but I didn't mind. In fact, I felt better than I had in months or years, despite looking over my shoulder every few minutes. The truck's speedometer read 40. I watched the land roll by my window, rushing flat with Route 65 and the snow, while the truck jostled my head to sleep on and off. We rode quietly through the late hours, stopping on county roads only to clear drifts from our path. There was nothing else to do. Keeping one eye on the weather and one eye on the green-gilled truck gauges, we exchanged glances every few miles. By the time we navigated our way around Winston-Salem, the truck's movement had rocked me to sleep.

After finding Route 67, we stopped for the night. Gideon hid the truck in the barn of a Negro woman he knew named Ludie. Skin and bones under a frayed housecoat, the woman opened the door to her three-room shack that smelled of boiled collards and salt pork, which she shared as her fireplace warmed the cold right out of me.

Our escape from Pudge reminded me of the Underground Railroad we learned about in school. Although I knew it was not even close to the danger those Civil War Negroes experienced, it thrilled me to take wing in my flight to freedom.

Gideon made me a bed of blankets on the floor by the fire. The flames sent a sweet, gentle light into the room while he laid out on Miss Ludie's broken-down sofa by the front door. We slept in the clothes we had on since I was too tired to root through my frozen suitcase. But my drowsiness did not stop my head from thinking.

I reached into my shirt pocket and pulled out my two most valuable possessions, my lucky rabbit's foot and the pictures of my parents. I stared at the photographs for the longest time, listening to a train whistle in the distance. It was one of the loneliest sounds in the world, especially on winter evenings when the only noise was the wind and an occasional truck gearing down as it headed up a hill. I had always loved a train whistle at night, imagining it had started in a city like Chicago, heading for Apalachicola, carrying coal and livestock and hobos on the lam.

"Gideon?"

"Hmm?"

"Your eye better?"

"It's fine."

I turned over to my stomach; the welts on my legs still burned. "Gideon?"

"Hmm?"

"How come Pudge hated me so much?"

I heard him stir, breathing deep, and sounding sleepy when he finally said, "Jus' 'cause you asks me, don't mean I gots an answer. I 'magine some folks, they mean and nasty from the time they little. Don't rightly know why. I 'spect bad things happened to Mistah Pudge long 'fore he was born, and by the time the sin gots to him, it forced him to be the way he is, 'fore he knew what hit him." He sighed. "Yes 'um, sins of the fathers, that's what it is."

I sucked in a ragged breath, not understanding it, but I hoped that one day I would. At least enough to not remember him as horribly awful as I did at that moment.

We pulled away from Miss Ludie's barn after a frostbit sunrise on Tuesday morning with the sky low and crumpled like dirty goose feathers. It didn't snow again until we reached Boonville, where Gideon drove to a filling station and checked the oil. When he called Missus Crumley, she said she'd be happy to check on Mister McPherson and hoped we had a lovely time Christmas shopping in Chapel Hill.

It was a brilliant lie since Chapel Hill was in the opposite direction of Bakersville. Except Gideon grumbled as he hung up the pay phone. "Don't like lying. Not one bit. But what we gone do? Tell her the truth? Law, I don't even know what that is."

Morning's icy patches made traveling tiresome until I started counting abandoned cars stuck in drifts. Snowplows had shoved mounds of ice and snow against the hillsides. The wind whistled through the truck's drafty windows, and the countryside blurred past in monotonous shades of more gray snow. I ached to see the mountains, a sight I had only seen in picture books and my dreams.

Gideon drove like the elderly man he was—slow—but he held his back straighter and seemed more alert than usual. "We still need to be careful, but I don't think the police be setting up roadblocks this far out," he said. "My guess—they think we in Summerfield, shivering down in some hidey-hole."

Dry snow flew in every direction. A car passed on the other side of the highway, spinning a tail of bright crystals that drifted into the wind and covered our windshield. But Gideon didn't stop or slow down. He kept his eyes on the road and a death grip on the steering wheel as the two-lane rolled under us in tune with the windshield wipers.

The truck's pathetic heater barely worked, and I was thankful that back at Miss Ludie's, I had slipped on two pairs of socks, and then once inside the truck cab, I wrapped my body in a scratchy horsehair blanket. Later that morning, though, I unclipped my rubber boots and kicked them off while Gideon unscrewed the thermos, poured coffee into the lid, and then handed it over. Sipping hot coffee, I watched dozens of roadside pine trees, their boughs heavy with snow, dipping toward the ground before snapping upward once relieved of their loads. At every turn, something new demanded my attention.

"I need a job," I said. "A paying one." Sitting forward with my hands in my pockets and my legs jiggling, nervous-like, I had become impatient to get to Bakersville.

"Where you gone work? Only jobs for thirteen-year-old girls are ironing baskets-a laundry, scrubbing toilets, or watching a houseful-a snotty-nose chil'ren."

"I can do it. You know I can do it. Hard work, I mean."

He shook his head. "Hard work's not all 'bout a payday at the end-a the week. It breaks your back. Wears you out. Makes you old."

I gave him a sideways smirk. "You can't pay for everything now. I have to help."

Gideon shushed me. "You gots a few days 'fore you be some white lady's hired hand."

I sighed loud enough for him to hear me, but Gideon straightened in the seat a little more and looked ahead as if he were eager to get farther from Summerfield.

"Will they arrest us? For what we did to Pudge?" I squeezed my hands tight together.

"Hope not," Gideon said.

"I hope not, too." My eyes welled up. Doubt had crawled inside my suitcase back at Miss Ludie's shack. It had unpacked itself and sat beside me on the seat.

Gideon glanced over and then back at the road. "Sweet Jesus knows the truth. Right now, He our only hope. Time to let God sit in the driver's seat."

❦

As the afternoon wore on, I grew hungry. Gideon pulled into an Esso station and told the colored attendant, "Fill it with regular and check the oil." Then he shut off the truck and said, "I gots to buy extra jus' in case there's no filling stations in the mountains to come by."

The Esso station's peeling white cement-block building sat in weeds and mud with a rusted Chesterfield cigarette sign hanging over the door. *They're Mild and yet they Satisfy.* In front stood one gas pump and a frozen rainwater barrel for washing your windshield. Behind the station's window, a wrinkled woman with no teeth frowned at us, her bottom lip almost touching her nose. She pointed at Gideon. A real sour puss, she talked to a man next to her and stared at our truck with a burning cigarette flipping up and down between her gums.

Gideon opened the truck's hood for the attendant to root for the oil stick. My stomach grumbled. With my breath, I made fog patches on the passenger window, thinking of pancakes and bacon. Pressing my hand against the glass, watching the heat make an imprint, I remembered the Mounds bar Miss Ludie gave me after breakfast. It found its way to my mouth, and I nipped off the chocolate with my teeth, pasting the coconut filling to my tongue.

The heavy hood slammed shut. Sitting back inside the truck, his face slick with sweat, Gideon glanced at something through the rear window. "Smile sweet, chile', we gots us a visitor," he said. I glimpsed a man walking toward us in the rear-view mirror. It was the man inside the filling station talking to the toothless woman, a scrawny guy with a beard. Maybe forty. Filthy coat. Ugly hat.

Gideon rolled the window down. "Yes, suh?"

The man chewed at a fresh wad of tobacco he thumbed into his mouth. "Y'all trying to leave without paying?"

"No, suh," Gideon said. "My money be in the truck, that's all."

"Whereabouts y'all from?" His voice had a prickly edge, and he stared at me with glittery eyes.

"Jus' needed gas and oil," Gideon said.

"That's not what I asked you—"

"—Raleigh, we's from Raleigh."

The man sneered at the truck *and* us, suspicious-like. "I think it's best y'all move on."

"Yes, suh. Need to pay you for the oil and gas first." Gideon stepped out to pay the man.

Extending his right hand to take Gideon's money, he gripped an empty RC Cola bottle by the throat with his left, in which he spit a bullet of brown chew. "Who's the girl?"

I smiled a big toothy grin and waved, acting nonchalant, as if me riding alone in the same truck with a Negro looked normal. "Merry Christmas!" I said, feeling stupid.

Gideon gave me his *shut-up* look. "I'm taking her to her grandmomma's house for the holidays. I work for her folks. They didn't have the bus fare."

"Uh-huh," the man said. "Unless you *need* anything else, you got five minutes. If y'all ain't out of here, I'm calling the cops."

Gideon pursed his lips and nodded. I watched the man in the ugly hat shuffle back inside the Esso building.

Grumbling louder than my empty stomach, Gideon lifted a box of oilcans and extra gasoline into the truck bed. "I *needs* mah head examined; that's what I *need*," he said. "No way a nigga man can get through life without lying to the white folks. Lawd only knows if this bucket-a rust will get us two miles down the road, let alone over the mountains. Needs new brakes, gots more miles on it than Methuselah, can't sell it, who'd want it?"

He clambered back inside and started the engine. I turned around and gazed at the homely-looking filling station, watching it fade into the sky while Gideon drove his crippled truck farther and farther west toward a thick, dark horizon.

A snow-covered black tar road cut through fields and forests. Fidgeting with the radio, I tuned into a news station, but nobody talked about a kidnapped girl from Summerfield. Only another happy weatherman broadcasting forecasts of more snow.

Occasional sunbursts beat through the back window, but worsening weather loomed ahead. I tucked my hair beneath my collar, littered the floorboard with cracker crumbs, and watched for road signs. Every time we stopped, I stuck my head out the window like a mutt, breathing in new scents from places I'd never visited. They mixed with the cold air like peanuts in a Coca-Cola. If I could've gulped it down, I would have. An occasional piece of farm machinery or a dilapidated shack popped up around every bend. Still, it was mostly an endless sweeping scene of tobacco fields, tobacco barns, and cigarette billboards. The unknown road ahead scared me—not as much as going past a church—but pretty close.

I didn't know what it was about churches all of a sudden. Maybe it was because I'd met the Devil at church. The building didn't scare me, only the people inside. There was something about driving past a church and thinking about its frothing, sweaty preacher in the pulpit. It made me quiver, so I sang my favorite song each time I saw one. There's nothing like a Jerry Lee Lewis tune to wash away the pain of life. A rousing chorus of *Great Balls of Fire* is guaranteed to make even the darkest hour brighter.

By suppertime, the blizzard hadn't arrived yet, but by all accounts, it would soon enough. *Snowstorm of the decade,* the weatherman had said. Blizzards reminded me of traveling evangelists, big and blustery, cold and capturing everybody's attention, blowing into town and leaving nothing but a mess for everybody else to clean up after moving on.

Scattered, rolling clouds traveled ahead of us in the evening sky as the land curved and swayed from one long stretch of trees and fields to the next. In frozen furrows of red dirt, dozens of crows picked through the snow, all while we headed toward salvation or damnation. It was still a toss-up.

"You think Hell is hot like we learned in church? A place of fire, worms, and thirsty dead people, wailing and gritting their teeth?"

Gideon moved his shoulders as if his back hurt. "I'm guessing it is."

"Hell could be cold. Outer darkness, isn't that what the Bible calls it? My teacher said it's cold in space. Hell could be dark and cold enough to freeze fingers and toes 'til they all fall off."

"You think?" Gideon asked.

"Sure. Why not?"

That's how our driving conversations went. The farther away we got, the more freedom I felt to daydream—even silly ones like watching the earth's giant tongue taste our old, ripe truck—slurp it, chew it, and swallow it whole.

But most of the time, I helped Gideon keep an eye on the gas and oil gauges while commenting on one thing or another. Things like laundry hanging outside in the bitter cold air, dancing and snapping in the wind. Farmhouses and outbuildings in need of paint and clumped at the end of long driveways. Barns weathered to the faded color of whitewashed trees and rocks. Roadside diners, filling stations, and cows. Black cows and tan cows standing at a fence near the road, clustered together like Negroes and White folks waiting for the bus. I wondered if God meant for animals to be segregated and if farmers stalled their black cows at the back of the barn.

Then it hit me like a road apple. I hadn't asked Gideon about his sister in Bakersville.

"Tell me about your sister."

"Who?"

"Your sister in Bakersville."

He hesitated. "Oh. Well, um, well, she was mah momma's oldest. But Momma, now there was a woman. She worked for the governor, you 'member. Took me with her from time to time. I'd sit on a stool in the governor's kitchen and watch her cook and whatnot. Like living in two worlds, tho'. One a palace, and then, well, I always be grateful for the warm spots mah brothers lef' for me in the bed," he chuckled. "Walls in our house—so thin, winter's bite 'bout froze us to death. Mah teeth still chatter thinking 'bout it. The floors, they creaked each time a body moved. Still, my momma," he sighed, "she kept on. Yes, 'um, she sho' did. My brothers, and me—sharecropped some with Daddy 'til he died. Then, I set out on mah own. Never married. No chil'ren. You knows. Not been back to Tennessee in over fifty years, now. Don't 'magine there be anything lef' to go back to."

I felt relaxed, listening to Gideon's chatter. Leaning back, I took in the sights of the road, the high hills and low valleys, even the small towns. Like a tourist, I enjoyed common and ordinary scenes of normal life. A milkman delivering glass milk containers to a woman in curlers at her doorstep. A boy loading groceries into an old woman's car while her coat flapped in the wind. A mailman stepping over snow drifts. Time lost its grip, and I saw the world through a different lens.

Leaving Pudge was the right decision. What lay ahead for Gideon and me was the start of a new life, a fresh beginning. With every passing mile, I felt the constant rotation of the earth. But unlike a bus that stops to let passengers off, the world rushed forward with no stop in sight. Traveling the rising hills and pushing against the horizon, I became conscious of it and felt its pitch and roll in my stomach. For a little while at least, I cleared my mind of the sorrows that consumed my young life, focusing solely on the road ahead. Misery and despair that had once pumped through my hollowed-out heart surrendered to a small measure of relief, even though Gideon still hadn't told me about his sister.

We ascended slowly into steeper terrain while more snow fell and piled up. By the time we reached North Wilkesboro, I was entranced with the changed scenery. But sometimes, I spied a little house with smoke curling out of its chimney, reminding me of Missus Crumley's.

Having eaten everything I took from Pudge's kitchen, we stopped at a store in Roaring River, making bologna and cheese sandwiches for supper. That was good because a new storm made viewing the road ahead impossible. I felt like we'd slipped through a hole in time—a thought as frightening as the swirling snow around us.

Seeing no house in any direction, Gideon pulled off and drove inside an empty, misplaced-looking barn that sat close to the road. Paintless with a rusted roof full of holes, the barn had partially caved in on one side; the planks moaning and gasping, more from decades of abuse and neglect than anything else. I shivered at the familiarity of it.

Gideon cut the engine and said his head would fall off and land on the truck floor if he didn't lie down soon. I sat there wishing God actually could sit in the driver's seat.

After sipping the last drops of the thermos coffee and nibbling on one more bite of bologna, Gideon filled the tank with our spare gasoline. He then broke open a couple of straw bales, piling them in the truck bed. Gideon handed me most of the blankets and quilts, and I watched him through the rear window as he cocooned himself in the remaining blankets and disappeared into the straw.

Knowing I couldn't hold it until morning, I stepped out of the truck and found my way to a bush outside the barn. After a cold pee in the snow, I made my bed on the cab seat the best I could, worrying about the weather, Gideon's old bones, and the nagging sense that the Klan was right on our heels.

After the joy of the day, I ached with sadness. Nobody knows the sick feeling of homelessness unless they've lived it. Pudge's house wasn't a home, which is why, out of the blue, my thoughts about the farm surprised me. Home didn't exist. I had no concept of what it meant. I'm not sure I ever did. There I was, a girl just past her thirteenth birthday who had lived on the same Summerfield farm all her life and had always been—homeless.

The more I thought about that simple word home, the more complicated it became. It wasn't a word I used. Returning from school or church, I didn't think, *I'm going home, now.* Grocery shopping with Gideon, I had never said it was *time to go home.* No. I had never used the word *home* the way I was supposed to. The way everybody else used it. I couldn't describe, exactly, my destitution. It was like explaining what it felt like for someone to beat you with a belt. It doesn't do any good to tell things like that. Nobody wants to hear another person's tale of woe. The folks I saw in the few remote towns we drove through were in an all-fired hurry to return to their warm *homes* with all their stuff and happy families. Who cared about me other than Gideon? Nobody.

That night, the wind picked up, bumping the truck around and brushing its gentle fingertips over the barn roof. An owl sang in harmony nearby. I rolled to my back, watching my breath in the moonlight, fighting the urge to cry. Soon, my cheeks felt like rocks, and then my nose started running. Desperate for a hanky and having none, I used my coat sleeve—so what? Wasn't anybody around to see me blow snot on it.

Minutes later, wrapped in horse blankets, I fell asleep to the sounds of the wind, the owl, and wild dogs howling across the landscape.

CHAPTER THIRTEEN

Early Wednesday morning, a plop of snow on the windshield startled me from a restless sleep. I sat up only to see the sky painted with pink and blue streaks and strings of cotton ball clouds slowly scraping across the pines. When I pushed the truck door open, it squeaked on its hinges, and a sweet-smelling rush of air whooshed inside. Snowdrifts, some towering as tall as me, had plunked themselves outside the barn. With another push on the door, I unfolded myself from the truck, my feet sinking into snow up to my knees, the cold seeping through my boots. After a quick trip to pee behind another bush, I hurried back to the barn.

Gideon rose in the truck bed, yawned, and rolled his shoulders—his coat and blankets covered with straw. Stretching in the dry, early morning air, he rubbed his arms. The cold woke us quickly as we climbed back inside the truck, hoping it would start and create some quick heat.

"Law, it's cold, and I is ol'-man weary. Driving sho' do make mah back sore," he said. "You do your business already?"

I nodded.

"You stay here," he said. "I be right back."

Waiting for Gideon to do his *morning business*, I closed my eyes, still feeling the road rolling under me—one country mile after another. Two days before, I doubted the truck would carry us as far as it did, but the old Ford had hobbled along the roads like a wounded Confederate soldier finding his way back to the Blue Ridge.

When Gideon returned, his cracked and callused hand rubbed the dash, giving the army-green truck an overdue pat of respect. Pudge had sold it to Gideon the winter I turned eleven but occasionally called it *his truck*, so I was sure he had added truck theft to our list of crimes.

Thankfully, it started, but we had to dig ourselves out of a snow bank with the shovels Gideon was smart enough to bring along. The ancient pickup jostled and jerked its way back onto the washboard country road. But our hunger couldn't wait much longer.

As the sun climbed higher, Gideon turned the truck onto Route 421 and its string of diners and stores. We took a stab at a small restaurant called Pete's Place. Someone had put a sign, COLORED SERVED HERE, in the window—a window iced-over with a frosty design like something you'd see on a Christmas card.

After soaking in the diner's warmth, we washed up in the restrooms, and when the tinny ring of a kitchen bell called the waitress to the pickup window for our order, I smiled and kept on smiling through a stack of toast, two eggs, and five slices of bacon. The friendly waitress filled our thermos with coffee while Gideon paid the bill. We left with a renewed sense of hope. Hope for what? I still wasn't sure. Gideon said we'd make Bakersville by evening if the forecasted blizzard didn't hit. Who knew what was waiting for us once we got there.

Heading northwest, I kept looking behind us now and again; it was a habit I couldn't shake. Mountain fog settled into the low places where the highway crossed drainage ravines, creeks, and small rivers. Passing one church after another, I think Gideon got sick of hearing me belt out another round of *Great Balls of Fire!* Finally, he told me to *shush*. So, I did. I knew Gideon needed to concentrate on the map in his hand and the road beneath us.

But each time we rolled down one hill and climbed out of the dip, a spray of mist and sleet built up on the windshield. Snowy slopes rose into a haze surrounding the mountaintops that looked like the clouds on Mount Sinai in the Ten Commandments movie. I imagined I could hike to the peak without a lick of trouble and find Moses talking to burning bushes.

We crept up and up toward Boone, dodging ice patches. Frozen waterfalls on rock walls captured my attention until I glimpsed several deer nosing for food in heavy snow. I hugged myself. I'd been flat-out exhausted for so long; it was like my head had filled with dense fog. Like I'd been sleepwalking through life. I'd never seen such a strange place.

But even in the mountains, winter stood out as the deadliest of seasons. We passed by snow stained with blood. Crows picked at frozen road-kill for their free meal. More crows flew out of a nearby field and perched the animal's corpse. To the right, giant pines had snapped in half and stood on steep hills with other bare-naked trees. There was so much more to the world than I had known living in Summerfield.

The truck's heater blew a fragile warmth, working on and off. I watched Gideon rub his eyes and neck, drinking more coffee than usual and gripping the wheel until his knuckles turned as white as mine.

To lighten his load, and distract him from worrying so much, I started talking again, non-stop, until I think he tuned me out. "Someday, I want to cut down my own Christmas tree, don't you? I bet it's like Christmas here year-round. Isn't the horizon beautiful? Almost like Heaven, don't you think?"

In truth, under all the daydreaming, I expected to see Pudge hiding around every corner. Even the thought of it frightened me. And I knew Gideon didn't enjoy the idea of a new place to live or starting over. He'd already started over more than once, he'd said. Knowing a jail sentence waited for you, or worse—being beaten by the Klan and hung from a tree—it can ruin your new home as a place to start over. I had a feeling Gideon didn't see the horizon as anything but just another spot he had to get to.

For me, each time I opened the truck door to run to the nearest bush and pee, the cold bit off a little more pleasure of my escape to a new life.

At nightfall, the road turned from pavement to gravel seconds after I heard a loud explosion. The steering wheel vibrated in Gideon's hand as he slowed the truck to the side of the road and stopped. We sat and stared in silence.

"What happened?"

"Flat tire, I 'spect."

"Maybe somebody will stop and help us."

"Out here? And what do you think they do in these parts to a Negro man with a little white girl in his truck? They don't know us. Who we are. Where we's from."

I tried to calm his panic. "Well, so far, I don't think you're on the Most Wanted List. What about your sister? Couldn't we get in touch with her now?"

"You see a phone booth out here? Neeley, I jus' gone get out and fix the flat. We sit here, we freeze to death." Gideon opened the door, and I felt the temperature drop. I'd never felt mountain cold before. I handed Gideon my wool scarf to wrap around his face and over his hat.

"I'm gone need your help."

Bowing my head against the howling wind, I steadied the spare tire on the road while Gideon tugged at the flat. The wind sang through tree branches, and it looked as if God had doused the world in snow like I had never seen, living in the flatter farmland of North Carolina. Gideon worked in almost no light, as neither of us was smart enough to throw a flashlight in the truck. But as I mulled over our stupidity, another truck pulled alongside; its headlights, if nothing else, were a godsend.

Gideon stood and shielded his eyes with his hand. "We gots comp'ny!"

The man came into view like a bird fighting against a headwind to get back to its nest. Tall and broad-shouldered, he walked toward us with his mouth covered and his large pointy nose appearing as a beak. "Whatchoo people doing out here in this weather?" He had left his truck's headlights on. I felt confident he meant to help.

"Gots us a flat. Jus' need to fix it. That's all," Gideon yelled.

"You need a hand?" The wind whipped the man's scarf about his face, and he fought to catch it before it blew off entirely. His coat flowed the length of his long legs down to his boots. I'd never seen a coat like it.

"Thank you, suh. I'd be mos' grateful." Gideon nodded and smiled at the man as if God had handed us a blessing straight from

His right hand. He turned to me. "Get in the truck. Keep warm if you can."

"I can help!" I shouted.

"It's okay. The faster I change this here tire, the faster we get moving again."

The stranger had returned to his truck and loaded his arms with an extra jack and tools. I cracked the window to listen and make sure he wasn't the police or Klan or anybody like that. In no time, the man and Gideon had secured the spare tire on the truck.

"Thank you, kindly," Gideon shouted. "Can I pay you for your help?"

"Absolutely not. Where you folks headed?"

"Bakersville, is it far from here?"

"Far enough. You sure you want to drive Route 19 in this weather?"

"I'm not sho'. Where're we now?"

"You're in Valle Crucis."

"Where?"

"Valle Crucis. It means Valley of the Cross. There's a store about a mile from here. Mast General Store. Straight down thataway. You can warm up there and get a bite to eat."

"Thank you again, suh."

"You're welcome. Tell the folks at the store Father Skiles sent you."

Gideon nodded at the tall, white man in the long dark coat, who called himself a Father. The man approached my window and lightly tapped on the glass. I rolled it down completely. He removed his glove and placed his large hand on my head. "May God bless and be with you, Neeley."

"Thank you!" I shouted, trying to make myself heard over the howling wind.

Gideon's tools clattered in the truck bed. When he opened the door and slid in beside me, I crawled onto the seat, knelt, and wrapped my blanket around his shoulders, my hands trembling with urgency to warm him as quickly as possible. When I turned around, the man's truck had disappeared. That's when it struck me like a lightning bolt. *How did he know my name?*

"Did you tell him my name?"

Shivering, Gideon simply shook his head in response to my question, his lips too numb to form words.

"He knew my name. He called me Neeley."

Gideon glanced at the sky, and seemed to concentrate on the worsening weather and the cold inside his bones. He started the engine, and the battered truck rattled along the frozen road. Sliding downhill on ice patches, Gideon managed to turn the truck into the small gravel lot in front of a whitewashed general store that read *Mast* above the door. The blistering blizzard, with its swirling snow and biting wind, was upon us.

"Maybe we should call your sister. Tell her we're on our way."

Gideon lowered his chin to his chest and shrugged. "I don't have a sistah."

I sat stunned. Gideon had lied to me. I knew he lived in a shitty world. A world of pride and prejudice; that was a given. But there was no reason to lie to *me*. He had not meant for our choice to run to put us in danger, but it did. The present looked bleak, and I was even less sure about our future.

"Why'd you tell me you did?"

"To gives you a little security. Make you feel better 'bout Bakersville instead of your dream of California. I'm sorry."

"But—but why this place? Why Bakersville?"

"Neeley. Listen to me. All I can say is I feel something bigger than the both-a us. It's leading me to Bakersville. Do you trust me, chile'?"

I nodded. I did trust him. Everything Gideon did, he did for me. I knew that.

"Alrighty, then. Let's see if we can get us some hot coffee inside."

Mast General Store smelled like wood smoke, bacon, coffee, and chickens, all rolled into one giant aroma. The sign over the cash register read, *From cradles to caskets, if you can't buy it here, you don't need it.* Two elderly men sat in rocking chairs near a pot-bellied stove, playing checkers with pop-bottle caps. Gideon and I stood in the grocery section, and I asked for a half-pound of sliced cheese and bologna and a loaf of bread. I looked behind me. The store did indeed appear to have everything a person needed in life. I soon felt my feet warming up as I leaned against a chin-high metal box of cooling green bottles. Coca-Cola and Nehi, mainly. A wooden case of empties sat next to it, chipped and dusty. I counted thirteen bottles.

Gideon pulled a dollar and some change out of his pocket and pointed to the pickle barrel. "Throw in one of them pickles, if you don't mind. And I needs to buy a flashlight," he said.

The man behind the counter seemed friendly enough. His face had crinkles, like a wad of paper he'd tried to smooth out, but his eyes sparkled, and he smiled when he asked, "Where you folks from?" It was another one of those nosy questions.

"Guilford County," I said. I wasn't lying, but I wasn't giving him more than that.

"How'd you end up here?" he asked.

Gideon shuffled from one foot to the other. "On our way to a—a funeral. Had us a flat tire 'bout a mile up the road. A man stopped to help. Said his name was Father Skiles."

"You say, Father Skiles?"

"Yes, suh. A kind man."

"Only Father Skiles around here I heard tell of died way back in 1862. He built and pastored the old Episcopal Church down the road a piece."

Gideon raised his eyebrows. "I s'pose I heard the man wrong, then. Wind was blowing something fierce."

"I think I'll look around," I said. Gideon heard him right. I heard him, too. Father Skiles knew my name; he blessed me. Something strange was happening. I couldn't figure it out. I didn't want to try. Instead, I spied a peanut machine. I slipped a penny into the slot, turned the metal crank, and a handful of oily, salted peanuts rolled out. I threw all of them into my mouth at once and wiped my hands on my pants. Crunching my peanuts, I wandered into an adjacent room from where the men playing checkers sat warmed by the stove's heat and the familiar tunes of the Grand Ole Opry playing on a staticky radio.

A plump, smiling woman in a tight-fitting get-up stepped out from behind several bolts of cloth and bumped into me. She smelled sweet, though, like Lily of the Valley—a perfume bottle I once held to my nose at the general store back in Summerfield.

"I'm sorry, sugar," she said.

I stared at her orangey-red lipstick and her teased-up beehive hairdo—blonde and hard as a horse's hoof; she'd probably won a beauty contest in her youth—she was that pretty, like an overweight Marilyn Monroe, only without the mole on her face. Her pointy breasts jiggled under her sweater set when she click-clacked across the wooden floor in high heels.

"Did you find what you're looking for?" she asked, staring at my hair like it was a nest for rats.

"Yes, ma'am." I tried to flatten my matted curls behind my ears, but it was useless. At the very least, there was kindness in her eyes, the same kindness I saw in the man's eyes behind the grocery counter, like she'd give me the sweater off her back if I asked for it.

"Where's your momma, sugar?"

"She's not here."

"Can't blame her for not wanting to get out in this weather. She at home?"

"No. I don't have one. A mother, I mean."

The woman turned her head a little and sighed. "Passed away?"

"Years ago. I was little."

She gave me a warm smile. "My momma died from the cancer. Was your momma sick?"

"No."

After straightening the merchandise, waiting for more information than I was willing to give, she stuck her hand inside her sweater to adjust her brassiere or slip strap; I couldn't tell which. "Are y'all from 'round here?"

I was getting unusually perturbed with nosy questions. When I said nothing, she fluffed her platinum hair with painted fingernails that matched her lipsticked lips. "Cat got your tongue?"

I shook my head.

When she glanced at her wristwatch, I stared at her dark roots. "We're closing early 'cause of the storm," she said.

"We won't be long."

"You with that colored man that came in?"

"Yes, ma'am. He works on our farm."

She gave me another perfumy smile. "Restrooms are in the back," she pointed out. "If y'all need one. The colored restroom is outside. I'm sorry about that. It's store policy."

I didn't give a flip about store policy. Gideon and I needed more than a restroom. We needed warm baths, real beds, and something to eat besides bologna and cheese. I paid little attention to the rest of what she had to say, watching her long eyelashes flutter when she talked. I had never cared about lipstick, perfume, and stockings with seams up the back, but there it is. Life can surely change you.

"You eat your supper yet?"

"Not yet. Sandwiches and coffee as soon as my friend pays."

She touched my arm. "Are y'all in some kind of trouble? Don't mean to pry, but my momma always said I had a second sight about folks in trouble. My name's Sheila. What's yours?"

"Patsy. Patsy Cline, and we're fine. Thanks." It was the only name I thought of besides my own. It seemed everybody had to lie now and then to keep folks from knowing your business. "I have to get going. Nice to meet you."

"Nice to meet *you*, Patsy Cline."

When I couldn't find Gideon in the store, I bolted to the door with Sheila trailing behind like a hound on a scent. In the howling wind through slanting snow, I heard only the faint sound of her voice. "You sure y'all want to travel in this storm? Roads are nigh to impassable, sugar—"

I didn't look back.

Gideon had started the truck. "Where you been?" he asked as I slid onto the seat. He handed me a sandwich and the coffee thermos. "I been waiting ten minutes."

"Sorry, some lady sidetracked me. She was pretty. Did you buy a flashlight?"

"Only one they had lef'. Gots to get moving. I don't like the look-a this snow. If we's lucky, we might get to Bakersville by seven o'clock. If we's lucky. Yes, suh, we's gone let God sit in the driver's seat."

It's not that I doubted God's ability to drive the truck, but I slipped my hand inside my pocket, seeking the comfort of my lucky rabbit's foot. It was still there.

CHAPTER FOURTEEN

The road from Valle Crucis toward Bakersville had turned into a stretch of solid ice and wound around the mountains like a water snake on the Haw River. A bitter wind whipped the truck from side to side as Gideon struggled to keep it from falling off the world's edge. Stopping to check the map, he shivered and rubbed his hands together. "I think if we can jus' get to Bakersville, we'll find you a motel and a warm bed until this storm passes."

Snow flew around us from every direction, and I tried not to worry as darkness slid down the mountain. The truck inched along, spinning its tires and then jolting forward. It had been an hour since we left Mast General store. We needed gas again, and it seemed we were climbing higher with every mile behind us. Not a car passed in the opposite direction, and there were no lights from houses along the way. Not that we could see them, even if we tried.

"We'll get mighty cold if this truck runs out of gas," Gideon said. Having no way to turn around and go back, he shifted into a low gear and drove like he was pedaling up the next hill. Blowing snow and a monstrous wind seemed bound and determined to stop us in our tracks. The dark night, split by our two brave headlights, kept Gideon driving at a slow crawl around each hairpin curve of the winding, narrow two-lane. But the old truck crept forward like a blind man feeling his way against the unknown.

Gideon peered through the windshield. Watching his fierce grip on the wheel, I thought his bones might break. In his desperation to keep us from sliding over the cliff outside my door, he prayed, "Lawd, help us—"

—an abrupt, loud hissing noise disrupted his prayer and intensified our panic. But without warning, the snow let up, and Gideon increased his speed. As he clutched the wheel, we skidded around the next curve. "It's all I can do to keep the truck on the road!" he shouted, his words nearly drowned out by the beat of the windshield wipers, the truck's hiss, and the wind's deafening roar.

The road bent again, sharply to the right, but out of nowhere, a deer leaped into our headlights' beam and flipped up and over the truck's hood, crashing against the windshield. I screamed as we slammed into the poor thing. Instantly, the windshield clouded over in a spider web of cracked glass as Gideon fought to keep the truck from swerving off the road—but the truck swerved anyway. We crashed through a barrier of rhododendrons, propelling us into the air and down the steep mountain slope. I clung onto the dashboard for dear life, but my rear end flew completely off the seat.

Gideon frantically pumped the brakes. "Wheels are locked!" The truck rushed and slid along the long, icy drop-off, flinging me into the door, my head hitting the roof from the bounce and jolt as we soared farther down, crashing over small saplings, rocks, and brush until we finally landed in a dark stream not yet frozen solid. The deer's blood washed away when the truck broke through thin ice, sending water over the hood and steam sizzling around the engine.

The truck was dead. But we weren't.

Squeaking out a whimper, I rubbed the top of my head, suddenly aware of a gaping hole in the windshield over the steering wheel. The impact had thrown Gideon forward, his head hitting the glass. Blood spilled over his cheek. I watched him pry his fingers from the wheel and then reach for me. "Oh. Sweet Jesus. Neeley. I'm—I'm so sorry, *you hurt?*"

"You think God's in the driver's seat now?" I swallowed the next bitter remark on the tip of my tongue. "Sorry," I said. "I'm fine. But your forehead's bleeding." Panic again seized me by the throat, but fear slipped into the truck cab like another unwelcome hitchhiker. In a flash, I did what Gideon had trained me to do. I prayed. I pulled my boots over my shoes and prayed. I prayed hard.

"You hurt anywhere else?" I asked.

Gideon didn't answer. His shaky hands rooted through the glove box for the flashlight he bought back at the Mast Store, before handing me a quilt. "It's gone get cold quick. But looks like the snow has eased up somewhat. At least down in this gully."

I tucked the quilt tight around my legs. Gideon opened the truck door and searched the darkness. "The stream is only a few inches deep." A noise behind us showed a pair of eyes and the flash of a white tail. More deer. Gideon wiped the blood from his face and pulled a stocking cap over his wounded forehead, then stuck his regular hat on top of that. "We have to find shelter or—"

"—We'll freeze to death." I might have been only thirteen, but I wasn't stupid.

"Put on your gloves and wrap that quilt 'round your shoulders," he said.

Right then, I was thankful for my long, thick hair since I had given my scarf to Gideon.

"You ready?" he asked, looking over his shoulder at me.

"Ready."

We stepped out into freezing air that hurt my nose, breathing it in, but strangely, the snow and even the wind had nearly stopped. A hard crust lay on the deeper snow, and the moon appeared behind broken clouds, making purple shadows behind the trees. The temperature dropped in nudges that rolled down my spine. Gideon locked the truck before grabbing his small canvas bag and my suitcase. I couldn't imagine why. He shone the flashlight on the front tires and the bumper that had sunk into the creek bed, resting in about a foot of icy water. A harsh cold stung my cheeks.

The stream, crusted with ice, flowed fast in the middle. We walked across and headed uphill, hoping to find help. At first, I clung to Gideon like a tick on a toad, but he shook me loose. Standing still and surveying a wall of bushes and briars, he found a path. I figured my clinging to him only slowed us down, so I let him walk ahead of me, forging our way along the uneven trail.

"It's hard to see, even with the flashlight." I hollered, determined not to panic.

Trudging up the next snowy slope and trying to talk, Gideon's breath became shallow. "We walk—by faith—not—by sight."

I stopped.

"What about smell? Can we walk by smell?"

Smoke. It crept up my nostrils like the aroma of cinnamon. "Where there's smoke, there may be help," I shouted. Gideon sniffed the air, smelling it, too. Together, we followed the scent of burning wood while ghostly mountain noises surrounded us: the rustle of leaves, the snap of twigs, and the snort and cough of deer. At least, I hoped it was deer.

Between cracks in the clouds, sudden moonlight made the passage visible. Seeking footholds to climb, I reckoned it made no sense to return to the truck. It wouldn't do for shelter, as we had no protection from the wind or a way to produce heat. And we sure as heck couldn't climb that steep rise to the road. We needed help. The smoke was our only hope. Step by step, slipping up one slope and easing down the next, Gideon helped me as much as he could. My leg muscles burned, and I pulled the quilt tighter around my shoulders, refusing to cry. My heart pounded against my ribs, and I sucked in each breath from the thin, freezing air as if it were my last. But I kept moving, squinting my eyes against branches that reached out, slapped at my face, and snatched clumps of my hair.

Gideon stopped. "Quiet. Listen. A widow maker," he said.

I heard it. A mournful and eerie sound, like an un-tuned string on a fiddle or a dulcimer. It screeched behind me, sending chill bumps on top of chill bumps to my hairline. Gideon swept the flashlight back and forth up in the tree branches until the light shone on a large tree limb, heavy-laden with snow, which suddenly snapped and fell on top of my fresh footprints with a thud. I blinked. I'd passed under it only moments before. "That was close," I said.

Gideon nodded. "Let's rest." He searched my eyes, straightened, and blew out hard through his nostrils like a horse. "You cold?"

"Just my face and fingers."

"You want to know the secret to outsmart the cold?" he asked, still breathing hard.

"Sure."

"The secret is don't stiffen up or turn your back on it," he said. "It's nature's challenge. Challenge it right back. Bend into it, as you might lean into a warm headwind blowing up from the south. Winter's cold is like the bitter things you can't dodge in life. Might as well get used to it."

My teeth chattered, and I nodded, too cold to bend or lean into anything. We walked on, our eyes fixed on a path that abruptly disappeared. I wanted to be like the animals and insects that burrow into snow, hibernating in caves and tunnels until spring. But we pressed forward, making our way over frozen dirt and broken rock, up the side of the next hill of rhododendrons and ancient pine trees where leftover snow fell like parade confetti. Tears froze on my cheeks, and my cold, gloved fist rubbed at my wet nose, which ran constantly.

Moving at a good clip, we dodged more pine boughs that grabbed at our coats and clothes. Catching occasional dollops of snow on the back of my neck, I stopped midway up the next steep hill. My feet felt like anvils at the end of my legs that had become numb.

Bending over to catch my breath, my hands on my thighs, I felt the rabbit's foot in my pants pocket pressing against me. I wanted to pitch it. Instead, I rested against a large boulder, getting a good look at Gideon's worn-out overalls, the bristle of his overgrown beard, and his torn coat stained with blood. I imagined we looked like a couple of war refugees.

But I still smelled the smoke. The moonlight and our flashlight were enough to keep us from bumping into trees, and I was thankful for one more thing—a break in the weather. Occasional stiff breezes had replaced the fierce wind, and the blowing snow had all but stopped.

Gideon motioned for me to follow him as he squeezed through a hedge, closing his eyes and squinting up his face against the scratch and snag of briars. Encouraged by the stronger smell of burning embers, we breathed in the scent that came and went, dragging us behind it.

"Can you make it up that hill?" he asked. I nodded, stepping in his tracks. Every dozen steps or so, he stopped and let the smoke guide him while I watched the sky darken. We had moved farther into the forest, walking on patches of leaf litter and snow. I'd always been told to stay clear of the woods because it's unsafe, especially at night; losing your way is too easy. And yet, what choice did we have? We ended up lost, anyway.

Gideon's strength amazed me as he carried our bags with one arm and often reached for me with the other. But my thighs continued to burn with the strain. Maneuvering up and around more pine and a bunch of bushes Gideon said were mountain laurel—I think he kept talking to make sure I stayed near him. Melted snow had soaked my neck, and the rough ground made it almost impossible to take another step after hours of sniffing for smoke and pushing forward. I dropped farther and farther behind. My strength lagged. Gideon's stride was too long, his pace too quick, and I was too tired.

"I can't!" I shouted.

He waited for me to catch up, but I had stopped. Outside, my skin was blistered cold, my lips chapped and burning, but sweat poured down my back under my clothes like it was a hot day in August. Thirsty, I scooped up a handful of snow and bit into it.

Gideon stumbled back toward me. "What?"

"I can't do it. Please. Not one more step."

"Smoke jus' over that hill," he gestured with his head. "We almost there."

"Almost? Almost where? Where the heck are we?" I sunk to my knees. It felt blissful to be off my feet.

Gideon let me rest, but only for a minute. "C'mon. We gots to keep moving. I can't carry you, and I can't leaves you here, so c'mon."

I didn't want to, but I stood. The crisp air moved me forward, and the stars and a sporadic glimpse of the moon gave me a slight sense of peace. They were bigger than I remembered, and I forced myself to walk on, wrestling the next breeze for the smell of smoke.

As we reached the top of the next knoll, Gideon gazed up at the stars. "Thank ya, Jesus." Trudging toward the white smoke rising into view, we grew breathless, fighting against sudden new wind gusts whistling through the branches. Overhead, an owl screeched, and more limbs fell, scraping against each other and dropping pieces of themselves as we arrived at an ancient fence, stopping us in our tracks. The split-rail fence stretched the length of a field that bordered the woods we had only moments before walked out of. But something else drew Gideon's head up as snowflakes gently landed on his face and shoulders, his eyes scanning the heavens.

He looked back at me, tossing our bags over the fence. "Do you hear that?"

"Hear what?"

Gideon paused, his eyes fixed on the distant field to our left. It was in that moment I heard them—the soft, quivering growls that sent shivers of panic straight to my hairline.

As the moon slipped out of its blanket of clouds, I saw the wolf stepping toward us. I was halfway over the fence but got snagged on a nail; I couldn't break free. In one swift move, Gideon leaped and grabbed me, tearing my coat and hurling me to the other side, positioning himself between the wolf and me.

"Have mercy," Gideon whispered. "There's two of 'em."

There we stood in deep mountain snow when yet another wolf, distorted but visible, appeared in the moonlight. I had never traveled so far from civilization. It occurred to me that no one in the world knew where we were. *I* didn't even know where we were.

To my surprise, the wolf closest to us stopped and sniffed the air. Then it turned and sprinted back into the woods, kicking up snow, with the second wolf following close behind. I heard Gideon breathe a deep sigh of relief. I didn't understand what had just happened, but I had no doubt we were too cold and exhausted to stand there and discuss it.

Frosted moonlight dappled the land around us, and as we turned and marched across the field, an outline of what had to be a smokehouse appeared in the distance. I got bogged down again and stumbled, plunging face-first into a deep drift, but Gideon pulled me up and helped me stand. Despite my wobbly legs and the welts that still burned on my backside, I pushed myself forward one slow-going step at a time.

The moon banked slowly, throwing a white path across a snow-covered road that curved and ended at a massive cabin. But we came to a complete halt. There, a few feet in front of us, a totem pole jutted high into the air. A totem pole like I had seen in the encyclopedia. It towered next to another fence line surrounding what appeared to be a farm. The giant pole dripped with ice and snow, guarding the narrow road like a warrior from a long-gone wilderness.

"I thought you said those things don't exist 'round here."

"Huh?" I couldn't take my eyes off of it. "Oh. Yeah. They don't. Well, except for this one, of course."

Gideon stared at the bird-like face in front of him. From the bottom up, I counted six faces. A man, a bear, a deer, an eagle with wings spread wide, and what appeared to be a frog—but on the top, someone had carved the most magnificent wolf's head with eyes that stared down at us. By its appearance, it seemed protective, not vicious. What struck me, though, and gave me mountain-high chill bumps was the crown of thorns on its head.

"We best get to that cabin," Gideon said. A ragged culvert ran along the road—like a moat around a castle, leading us to a wrought-iron gate with words scrolled across the top.

Gideon laid his hand on my shoulder. "The Sanctum," he said. "What you s'pose that mean?"

"Sanctuary," I said, my voice barely above a whisper. "It means sanctuary." We passed between two imposing stone pillars and pushed open the heavy, unlocked gates. "Have you ever seen a cabin like that?" I asked.

Gideon shook his head. "I never seen a cabin that big in all my born days." He tucked his bag under his arm and then lifted my suitcase with a grunt. "Want to know what I think?"

My gaze turned toward him, and I smiled at his wide grin. "What?"

"I think God's still in the driver's seat."

CHAPTER FIFTEEN

Making our way to the small wood-clad outbuilding, the moon had climbed higher, casting a faint shadow on the snow around it. White smoke swirled into the air, carrying with it the distinct scents of earth, wood smoke, and bacon. My stomach grumbled in response; only my manners kept me from breaking inside and slicing off a piece of ham.

And then in the moonlight, I noticed rows of tall pens descending down the hillside. As we cautiously inched forward, I saw what resembled large dogs inside them. I wanted a closer look, but Gideon swiftly grabbed my coat and yanked me to a stop.

"Look at that." He pointed, his thick arm trembling.

For the moment, they appeared like long-legged ghosts, silent and vague.

"Those are wolves," Gideon said. "Look at all those wolves. What people live out here and keep wolves instead of horses or cattle, you wonder?"

The wolves knew we were there; they paced back and forth, whining in their pens. I handed Gideon my suitcase, which I had taken from him to lighten his load. "Why don't you stay here, near the smokehouse? I think I have a better chance of getting us some help."

I started walking toward the cabin, but Gideon took hold of my arm and pulled me backward. "How? What you gone say?"

"I don't know. I'll come up with something," I whispered.

Gideon sighed and sat on my suitcase. "Law, we's a bunch-a lying fools."

"Through no choice of our own. We have to survive. Somehow. You think they keep any black bear in those pens, too?" I asked as my teeth chattered.

"I 'spect so," Gideon said, grasping my coat again.

The cold pressed its icy hand on my bare forehead. *Lambs to the slaughter.* Still, I had to try. The notion of wolves and bears pushed me toward the door. "I'm going."

"That'd be best. I'll wait here 'til you find out if these white folks're friendly."

"What makes you think they're white?"

"Girl, no Negro in his right mind keeps wolves and own a place like this."

My whispering turned into frustration, spoken out loud. "If we'd have gone to California, like I wanted to—"

"—Jus' go on, quit your bellyaching, and knock on the door," he said, his hand still clenching my coat like his life depended on it.

"Then let go and quit trying to talk us both into it."

Finally, Gideon released me. "Holler loud if you get into trouble."

Hope and a faint light glowed through the large windows. Standing in the middle of the settlement, recalling stories of mountain people and their peculiar ways, I brushed off my coat and tried, at least, to look presentable. I felt like one of the wolves that stood at the edge of Pudge's farm, camouflaged by the trees. I no longer believed they were wild dogs. They were wolves and had followed me to the mountains and farm I found myself on.

I held my breath, I held my heart, and I stepped into the dark toward the enormous cabin with its hewn logs and tin roof. My feet, heavy with packed snow and numb from the cold, climbed the steps to the largest and sturdiest front porch I'd ever laid eyes on. The wood hardly creaked from my weight. As quietly as possible, I moved to the window.

In the firelight of a large room stood a tall, lanky man with thick, straw-colored hair falling to his shoulders. I was sure he'd never heard of a ducktail or Brylcreem. The moon brightened in the yard, and I hesitated after walking to the door. I opened the screen door and paused again, but desperation positioned my knuckles, and I knocked. No answer. I studied the heavy wooden door and its sturdy lock. A second attempt brought the sound of a man's voice and the click of a gun behind me.

"Who the Sam Hill are you?"

I didn't move. "My name's Neeley. Please, sir. We had an accident a ways back. Our truck slid off the road and wrecked in a creek bed." I felt the cold steel of the gun on my neck.

"Your truck? You say you slid off the road?"

I nodded.

"Most don't survive accidents over mountain ledges. You from Boone?"

"No, sir. From Guilford County. I'm traveling with my—my caretaker. I'm sorry to disturb you, but we're freezing and need a place for the night." I suddenly got a little too brave for my britches. "Look, mister, I'm hungry, and I'm tired, I'm cold, and I *really* have to pee." I turned around and stared down the barrel of a .22 shotgun, but it was not the gun that stunned me. It was the sight of the man behind it.

Two thin braids wound with brass wires fell below his shoulders. The light from the house showed him to be older than Gideon, but equally as large. His eyes were small and heavy-lidded, his cheekbones high and flat, and he had a white man's pointed nose, but he wasn't white. Deep lines had etched across his weathered skin, from one side of his face to the other, rugged and craggy, like a quartz rock. His clothes and the long feather swaying by his ear, testified to his ancestors who probably sat Indian-style in teepees, smoking long pipes and dancing around bonfires, waving tomahawks. At least that's what I'd seen on TV.

He glanced at my scarred forehead. The gun lowered as I stared into the strange man's face. "Do you know the Buchanans from Bakersville?" he asked.

"No, sir. Are we near Bakersville?"

"Six miles out. Somebody else with you, you said?"

"Yes, sir. Mister Gideon Jackson. My caretaker. My friend. He's near the smokehouse."

"Gideon. Sword of the Lord," he said.

I smiled. "That's from the Bible."

"Why did he not come with you?" The Indian man viewed me with mistrust.

"He's a Negro."

It surprised me when a woman walked up the steps, seemingly from nowhere, with her hands in her coat pockets. "Can we help you?" Dark eyes stared at me through tussled black hair that had fallen over her face. Pushing wayward strands off her forehead, she couldn't have been over twenty-six or twenty-seven. In the moonlight, her rosy, pink cheeks glowed from the cold, or maybe it was her natural blush; I wasn't sure. But as I stood there staring at her, a sudden gust of swirling snow collected on her eyelashes.

She spoke in a rush. "She's just a child, Hotah. Let her in." Her voice was strained, like she'd just climbed over the same mountain I did. Then she looked at my face, flinching slightly with a slight twitch of her head. Nothing I wasn't used to. Shaking off the snow, she turned and stepped through the door ahead of me.

The Indian behind me spoke into my ear. "Your friend is welcome. But if you are a Buchanan, I'll shoot first and ask questions later."

"I understand. Just need to get warm, Mister—"

"—Hotah. Only Hotah."

I stood inside the doorway, snow-covered and shivering. "You live here?"

He didn't answer.

I felt like I'd fallen asleep and awakened on that new show, Bonanza, but it wasn't the Ponderosa. It was better. I moved into the warmth of the huge room, its fire drawing me like a moth to a flame. Nothing prepared me as I peered into every corner. The ceiling towered as high as a church sanctuary and the fireplace was so gigantic I could stand in it. Years of smoke and heat had cracked and split the mantel, turning it the color of tarnished brass. Bearskins and quilts overflowed on a barn-like loft railing above me. A chandelier as big as a car, made entirely of antlers, hung from the ceiling. The air inside the room stirred my hunger. It smelled slightly like supper—a leftover fragrance as pungent as the aroma of freshly made bread.

The man with the straw-blonde hair I'd seen earlier through the window approached me. Although he hunched his shoulders, bracing himself against wind gusts from the open door, he was handsome, with a face that belonged on a cigarette commercial. Even I could see that. His hair fell over his forehead, and the curls behind his ears battled each other for room down his long neck, only to spread out once they reached his shoulders. He had a nick in his ear, which surprised me. Handsome men sure weren't born that way.

"Hello there," he said. "Who's this to come calling in the middle of a blizzard?"

Blizzard? I had crossed the threshold but turned around only to hear wind-whipped trees. The mountains were gone. The world had transformed into a sea of wind and snow. In the few minutes it took to walk from the smokehouse to inside the cabin, the land, once again, had pulled a white sheet to its chin. The sudden change in the weather left me bewildered, my senses struggling to understand yet another strange occurrence since leaving Summerfield.

The pretty woman smiled. "I found her on the porch, Baylor. Like a lost pup."

"Come in, get out of the cold. Welcome." His words were a balm to my chilled bones, instantly dispelling any wariness I had. "You met my wife, Sidabee. I'm Baylor MacLennan." He helped his wife off with her coat, his actions radiating warmth. "Hotah, bring some blankets."

"Sida—what?" I asked, my teeth still chattering. I didn't hear what he had called her; I was too busy staring at the eyeglasses she had slipped on. A pair of big blue eyes studied me through pointy frames with tiny rhinestones set in the outside corners— rhinestones that matched the ones in her barrette, holding back a mass of curls from her face. She had ringlets like mine, but so black they reflected greens and blues, like dragonfly wings. A gold chain fell down to her relatively small breasts. A gold band hung from the chain. Her frosty eyes flickered from my head to my feet and back up. I felt a jolt of disapproval in her review of me, which made me stop smiling. Five-foot nothing, her graceful arms touched her husband's shoulder in a way I'd never seen a woman touch a man in public.

"My mother named me after my grandmother, Sidabella, an Irish immigrant," she said matter-of-factly. "My grandmother kept bees, so that's how I got stuck with Sidabee."

"I like it," I said, surrendering to her unexpected smile. As the cold evaporated off my face, I watched her as she bent over to remove her boots. I imagined someone that pretty would take pains with her looks, go shopping for party dresses, serve on church committees, and host bridge club. I pictured her serving Coca-Cola in iced glasses along with crustless pimento cheese and cucumber sandwiches, placing them on big porcelain trays draped with damp tea towels.

But a gush of wind against the door turned my thoughts to Gideon, where they should've been all along. I had to get him out of the cold. "My friend, Gideon Jackson, he's still outside. Please, can someone bring him in? I'm Neeley, by the way. Neeley Morrigan." When we left Summerfield, I had decided to never use the McPherson name again. The name I was born with, Neeley Morrigan, sounded beautiful, flowing off my tongue. But after I said it, Sidabee drew in a sharp breath. Her head snapped up, her eyes glaring into mine. She didn't say a word except to raise an eyebrow. Her stylish glasses slid down her nose, and she nudged them up again. I worried from the look she gave me that she had read my name and Gideon's in the paper or heard it on the radio.

"Go sit by the fire," Baylor said, grinning at me, then at his wife. "I'll find your friend. He won't be able to see his way to the cabin in this storm. Hope the wolves haven't found him first."

I smiled, unsure I'd heard him correctly. "Thank you, Mister and Missus MacLennan."

Sidabee's unspeaking eyes delayed her response. "Baylor and Sidabee will do fine, Neeley, is it?"

Feeling my puckered scar tighten across my forehead, I wasn't sure my first warm and fuzzy impressions of her were correct. "Yes, ma'am," I said.

An Indian woman sat by the fire next to Hotah. Tall and slender, without many curves, she smiled with a nod as Sidabee introduced her as Hotah's wife, Aiyanna. Her hair shone with a midnight hue, intertwined with snowy white strands, and intricately braided with leather strings and beads that gracefully hung to her waist.

When I got a better look at her smooth face, I noticed fine lines etched around her eyes, giving her the appearance of being older than she initially appeared, but the rest of her skin glowed a coffee-with-cream color. The set of her jaw seemed both bold and meek. She reminded me of a delicate bird, right down to the slight hook of her nose and her small, dark eyes sparkling in the room's firelight.

After Baylor found Gideon shivering by the smokehouse and escorted him inside, I immediately shared that we were on our way to Tennessee for my grandmother's funeral. Until, of course, our truck fell down the mountain. Which was half-way true. Gideon, still recovering from the cold, inched toward the fire and sat on a log near the hearth, resting his forearms on his knees. As he thawed out, I took in the room's entirety, my eyes darting from one detail to another, trying to piece together the story of this place.

At first, the cabin was shocking, with its high ceiling and straight floors. They had filled the expansive room from end to end with antique-looking pieces of heavy wooden furniture polished to a high shine, including a dining room table with seating for *twelve* people. They had also arranged several ample leather chairs, cushioned in dark browns and reds, with plenty of room to move about. Butter-soft sofas, long enough to seat four people a piece, faced each other in front of the fire, and a live Christmas tree twinkled beside a grand piano, its top brushing a massive wooden beam in the ceiling.

Someone had used large flat-head nails to hammer down the wide-plank floors like those in a barn, except the wood was shiny and clean. The log walls held warmth from the fire, and plants in various odd-shaped pots, some big and some just clippings, sat everywhere. Sudden comforting scents of pine from the Christmas tree and the faint aroma of wood smoke filled the air. Framed charcoal drawings behind glass and stuffed animal heads lined the walls—deer like the one we rammed with our truck. They stared at me from every angle. Rich embroidered draperies framed each of the large windows, allowing winter's evening shadows to dance through the cabin in ribbons of muted colors.

Despite the majestic fireplace's admirable effort, I couldn't get rid of my chill bumps. Having removed our wet hats, boots, and coats, I had settled on a comfy chair in what Baylor called the *great room*. It was indeed a great, *big* room.

Feeling my eyelids droop like two heavy feed bags, I shook myself awake. I still had more to see. Drawn to the antler chandelier above us, I smiled, imagining the streams of yellow light as a caramel waterfall. It cast a warm, golden glow throughout the room. Two large glass doors at the back led to a screened-in room, which looked like a porch. Aside from where I sat, a room full of books splintered off to the right with walls painted a warm tomato soup red. I suspected someone hand carved the elaborate wooden statues sitting on several tables. More framed artwork hung on a wall near a staircase that climbed to the loft on the second floor. I had never seen a loft without hay in it before. A strip of berry-colored carpet ran down the center of the wide staircase, and as I looked around one last time, there wasn't a TV in sight.

Quickly, the beauty of the cabin stirred me wide awake. I nodded another hesitant smile to Aiyanna, the Indian woman. She was actually sort of handsome, the opposite of her stone-faced husband. She returned my smile, and I kept wishing Hotah would smile—or speak. But he only stared with a fierceness that circled my head and said, *I know where you came from, who you are, and what you did.*

I wanted to cry then, but I didn't. I kept thinking, what if he *did* know me, know how much I hated my grandfather and that I'd left him hog-tied to a chair in a cold barn? The sight of Hotah and his wife sitting there, chatting in a language all their own, filled me with more sorrow, and I wished we had tied Pudge inside his house.

I watched Gideon retreat into himself, disappearing to a place that was unfamiliar to me but had become a part of him that I learned to accept. When his mind was occupied with thoughts, Gideon seldom spoke. I assumed he was devising our next plan.

Sidabee entered the room carrying a tray of sandwiches and coffee. Though she wasn't much taller than me, she carried herself as if she were. She smelled of cookies and spring flowers, and her youthful, unpainted face was flawless, even with a slightly crooked nose. At the very least, she'd found a good-looking man who liked a girl with glasses. Thin as a zipper, the veins showing in her bony arms, Sidabee never sat still. It seemed her thoughts raced, eyeing us closely and possibly reviewing her options of what to do about us. She talked in hurried half-sentences, mentioning something about sleeping arrangements, but I only caught snippets of her jumbled words as she darted in and out of the room like a starling, serving food and drinks to everybody.

I took a sip from a blue ceramic mug and instantly knew it would be my favorite mug if I lived in that house. The coffee warmed me fast and tasted good, creamed and sugared a bit on the heavy side. But as I swallowed the last bite of a sandwich into my blissfully full stomach, I noticed a change in Gideon's expression. He seemed aware of something that I was not. His eyes darted toward Baylor, Sidabee, and Hotah, as if awakening from a trance. Finally, his gaze settled on me.

Sidabee poured more coffee into my deep mug. "The phones are out because of the storm. We have sporadic phone coverage up here, I'm afraid. Hotah can take you both to Bakersville tomorrow to call your family; let them know you're okay. I'm sorry to hear about your grandmother, Neeley."

Before I had a chance to speak, Gideon broke in. "Well, see, uh, Neeley, her grandmomma already done been planted in the ground, bless her sweet soul, and we already done missed the funeral. Neeley's parents passed away a while back, and she, well, she an orphan now, and mah truck, I guess it gone now, too. I'm afraid we stuck in Bakersville 'til I can find me a job and save enough to buy another truck to get us back home to her, uh, her uncle, but he, he in the hospital. He gots the cancer. Yes, suh, he be rotting from the inside out, jus' like a potato. Nobody lef' to take care-a Miz Neeley, 'cept me."

Baylor and Sidabee shook their heads and raised their eyebrows at once. I guessed their kindhearted manners were typical of them, listening to sad and unfortunate stories like Gideon's. I shook my head, too. Out of pure astonishment. I peeled off my eyeglasses and shot Gideon a look that said, *are you out of your mind?* I sat stunned at the whopper he'd told. He deserved a trophy, or at least applause. I wanted to hug him. My skin prickled clear down to my toenails. It seemed Gideon's determination to make a new life for us both was worth one more lie.

"Well, now," Baylor said. "I think it's getting on toward my bedtime. Sidabee can show you to your rooms. And Mister Jackson, I think we have enough to do around here; you can help Hotah in the barn. We can't pay much, but it's a job."

Sidabee almost dropped her coffee tray. "Baylor, I—"

"—Neeley can help out wherever we need her." Baylor looked hard at his wife.

I smiled at everybody in the room. "That'd be great, thanks."

Gideon ran his hand over his new white beard. "Yes, suh, I thank ya. That's mighty fine. But if you don't mind me asking, why you keep them wolves out there in the yard?"

Baylor laughed. "I guess it is strange, isn't it? This is a wolf sanctuary, Mister Jackson. We own other livestock; that's the reason we house the wolves in large pens. Those wolves would've starved to death, or become sick, or shot dead had we not taken them in. Wolves need sanctuary, like any of God's creatures, like you or me, a place where someone can recognize their needs and provide for them. We take the wolves in, feed them, keep them safe, give them a good life until they die."

I'd never heard of a wolf sanctuary. "But if they're not sick now, why can't you let them loose in the woods?" I asked.

"Wolves living in the wild survive about seven years if they're lucky. Our wolves will live up to twelve or thirteen years. Some longer. The sad truth is, sanctuary wolves have forgotten how to survive in the wild, and besides, these mountains are full of happy hunters who shoot them for the nice bounty paid on a dead one."

My toes curled inside my worn shoes, and I was plum worn out, but I had to hear more. "But aren't wolves dangerous?"

"Hotah, I'll let you answer that. Hand out work details for tomorrow. I'm off to bed. Mister Jackson, Aiyanna can give you something to help with the cut on your head and your bruised eye. Good night, everybody."

Turning my attention to Hotah, I waited anxiously to hear him speak more than a few words.

"My name, Hotah, it means gray wolf," he said, his voice carrying a sense of the unknown. He paused, swallowing hard before continuing. "There is more to a wolf than what meets the human eye. Wolves are social, intelligent, and fiercely devoted creatures, protecting their pack and attacking only when necessary. A wolf's purpose is to ensure its family's survival. A man knows when the spirit of the wolf possesses him. If a wolf is your totem, you have the gift of cunning and the ability to outwit those who wish you harm. Wisdom, intuition, protection, and spiritual guidance—these are gifts of the wolf. The MacLennans are from a Scottish clan with the wolf as their totem."

Hotah's head snapped toward the window. He then shifted his attention back to me, silently questioning if I had heard the howling outside. I had. But I knew Gideon hadn't. Judging by the way his eyes closed, Gideon was nearly asleep. I smiled at Hotah, trying to ease the tension in the room, but felt Sidabee's eyes on me like a heating pad. She had finally seated herself in Baylor's chair. With her small, bare hands, she gripped the edge of the stained wooden arms so tight that her knuckles looked like small white stones.

Hotah rose from his chair by the fire. "Tomorrow, we will bring our house wolves inside. Mister Jackson?"

Gideon stirred. "Yes, suh?"

"Work starts at dawn, Mister Jackson."

CHAPTER SIXTEEN

We followed Sidabee through the back of the cabin, where the ceilings were not as high, and entered a spacious kitchen. She led Gideon to a sizeable pantry-like room, filled with the scent of spices and leather. Covered in a wedding ring quilt of deep reds and blues, the half-bed made me sleepy with the promise of rest. They had set another comfy chair with a matching footstool between the bed and a floor lamp. A nightstand, a small closet, and a shelf filled with books caused Gideon's eyes to light up. I could tell he liked it.

"This is a screened-in porch with sliding walls that seal tight in winter. Baylor's invention," she mentioned. "We use this room for storage and guests, and during the hot summer nights of canning season, we sometimes sleep out here," Sidabee explained. "Aiyanna has prepared the bed for you, Gideon. The room should stay warm, but we'll keep the fire going in the kitchen tonight."

In the kitchen, of all places, a smaller chocolate-brown sofa, draped with soft yellow and blue plaid blankets, sat in front of the fireplace. I imagined napping there, warmed by the blazing fire and the aroma of Gideon's apple pie baking. Happy curtains in a sunflower print hung from each of the six large windows. Sparkly blue linoleum, worn thin in front of the sink, matched the blue and white dishes behind glass cupboard doors. Someone tied gold and green Christmas ribbons around pine branches and candles and decorated the mantle. But it was the elaborate plaque over the stone fireplace that drew my attention. *The Pioneer's Creed: The Cowards Never Started. The Weak Died Along the Way. Only the Strong Survived.* Gideon and I read it at the same time and then looked at each other. It startled me, but it also gave me a sense of the people who lived here. Time would tell whether either of us was of pioneer stock.

In a calm but serious tone, Sidabee said, "Gideon, you may use any bathroom in our home you wish, but the closest one to your room is the bathhouse at the end of that hallway." She pointed, and I merely stared at her. These were strange folks— different—better than any bunch of people I'd ever met.

"Thank ya, ma'am," Gideon said.

He nodded his typical good night to me, and I nodded back. Leaving Gideon in his room, I followed Sidabee, climbing the stairs to the loft where someone had painted the wide plank floor a soft willow green and the ceiling a yummy white, like vanilla ice cream. A large hand-braided rug covered the hardwood. Carved curlicues fancied up the headboard of a pine bed tucked into the corner and decked out with all sorts of flowery pillows. When the tips of my fingers brushed over the quilt folded at the footboard, my whole body wanted to fall into it the way I like to fall backward into snowdrifts.

"This quilt," I said. "It's very pretty."

"It's a life quilt, made from pieces of Baylor's clothes from when he was a baby," Sidabee explained. She walked to a window, drawing the curtains together. "For your privacy," she added.

I nodded, but I couldn't take my eyes off the curtains. They matched the bedspread.

"I had Hotah bring your suitcase up here. I hope this will do," she said.

Tongue-tied, I nodded for the gazillionth time. Swallowing a yawn, I looked around the rest of the room. More framed art-work hung on the log walls, and to my further amazement, a small rocking chair and a cherry-wood wardrobe as big as Missus Crumley's Frigidaire back in Summerfield hugged the wall oppo-site the bed near the window.

Sidabee rubbed her watery blue eyes behind her eyeglasses. "You should call your uncle in the hospital; find out how he is and tell him where you are. Hotah can take you to Bakersville tomorrow to use the phone."

"Oh, I think he's too sick to talk to me," I said, hoping the lie wasn't too obvious.

"Then, call and ask the floor nurse how he is. She'll at least deliver your message; tell him you're okay."

"Well, I don't exactly know what hospital he's in." I looked away, feeling a wave of self-disgust wash over me. In that moment, the weight of my dishonesty crushed me and I despised myself for the lies I had spun. Everything Gideon and I had said was a bald-faced lie.

Sidabee cleared her throat. "I understand. Good night, Neeley."

"Good night," I said.

After she left, I lay on the bed listening to the remnants of adult conversation until the house grew creaky quiet. I didn't want Baylor and Sidabee to discover the truth about Gideon and me. That we were on the lam from the law *and* the Klan. I didn't want them to turn us in. I didn't want to tell them about my beatings; I wanted—to feel wanted, like I belonged somewhere. With bedtime routines and dentist appointments—and piano lessons. To feel like I no longer lived a life of fear and loneliness. I reasoned there were people in the world who found better lives every day. Normal lives. Safe lives. Maybe I could, too.

It felt like I had traveled for months. Gideon had said something was leading him, and I believed him. But everything familiar to my life, absolutely everything, had become unfamiliar. The Sanctum was as foreign to me as Lake Gitchegumee. The only Indians I'd seen were the ones on TV, like Tonto on The Lone Ranger. To me, Indians had always seemed dirty, ignorant, and uncivilized. But Hotah and his wife were none of those. That's when I knew I'd thought about Indians the way Pudge thought about Negroes. Despite my pride in not being prejudiced, I uncovered some of it buried deep inside me. I felt sick. I needed air.

Struggling to sit, tangled in the sheets, I fell back under the thick covers more than once until I wiggle-wormed out of bed backward on my stomach. The first thing my feet landed on were my scuffed-up, clip-on boots, which someone had brought upstairs. Leaning against a pink and red rose-covered chair, those black-rubber boots looked like a couple of skunks at a garden party. My torn, damp coat and red stocking cap lay drying next to a thick, patchwork quilt that hung over the banister, and my mother's old cardboard suitcase rested against the Frigidaire wardrobe. Pocked and peeling, that suitcase had seen its last days after dragging it up and down snow-covered mountains. Everything about me, everything I brought, looked dreadful in that fancy loft room.

Sleepy, I climbed back into bed, sinking into my pillow again. I felt for my rabbit's foot on the nightstand. Wrapping the chain around my finger, I held the lucky charm in my palm, thinking maybe I should keep it.

The Sanctum. Picturing the words scrolled across the iron gate near the totem pole, I drifted into sleep as strange and wonderful voices whispered odd-sounding words into my ear.

Morning's weak light seeped into the sleepy cabin. The strange silence of my surroundings woke me gently, but the distant howl of a wolf jolted me awake. I didn't know where I was. Confusion washed over me as I glanced around the pretty room, bathed in daylight. For a fleeting moment, I thought I had died in the truck crash and landed in my heavenly mansion.

Curled under my covers, my mind cleared, and I heard Gideon and Hotah talking in the great room. Reality set in.

A bird pecked at the window, and the aroma of fresh coffee drifted into the loft. The cabin and all its diversions made it impossible to stay in bed. Draping a shawl over my shoulders, I approached the cold glass for my first glimpse of The Sanctum in daylight, but my reflection confronted me. Wild hair fell in knotted strands from our trek over the mountain, and an ugly bruise on my cheek matched the unsightly scar on my forehead— Lordy, I was a fright. Yet I knew the bruise would heal in time, unlike my scar. Nobody asked about the bruise, so I figured they assumed it was from the truck accident.

Returning to the bed, I smoothed back the covers and tried to arrange the pillows neatly. Although the loft lacked a door, I positioned myself in a corner where nobody could see me lifting my ratty nightgown to inspect the back of my thighs. My legs throbbed and tingled with that sick-tight feeling, the lingering effects inflicted by the deep bite of the Bible belt. Scabs had formed behind my knees and on my calves, evidence of the pain I had endured for each year of my young life.

How often had Gideon told me, "Stop picking those scabs, or you'll scar, and unless you gots faith for a miracle, scars last forever." I dropped the hem of my nightgown when I heard someone's stocking feet padding up the stairs. It was the Indian woman, Aiyanna, in pink washcloth slippers. Her thin, long legs moved beneath her wool skirt like the legs of a deer. I imagined her dancing around huge bonfires with women named Pocahontas, Hiawatha, and Sacagawea.

"Excuse me, Miss Neeley." Aiyanna leaned her handsome face toward me, her silver earrings shaped like feathers dangling down her slender neck. "Good morning, sleep well?"

"Yes, ma'am."

Leveling her dark eyes first on my ratty gown, and then on my made bed, she smiled. That early in the morning, she already smelled like warm bread and the faint odor of nutmeg. "Breakfast is in fifteen minutes. I'd like to personally welcome you to The Sanctum."

I felt like a stray pup in the presence of a great Indian Princess. But if Sidabee was a starling, Aiyanna was a wren with earthy-brown eyes. Cold air had pinked up her cheekbones, and her curious face sparkled like the star on the Christmas tree in the great room.

"Thank you," I said softly, watching her descend the stairs. Although I felt restless in this strange place I had woken up in, I repeated its name out loud: "Sanctum." The word felt foreign on my tongue, echoing in the vastness of the unfamiliar space around me.

But it whispered back. *Sanctuary.*

As soon as my toes moved off the braided rug and touched the cold hardwood floor, I realized I'd forgotten to pack my flip-flops. I had never owned a pair of slippers or house shoes. "Goodness, these floors're freezing," I said through gritted teeth. I also had never stepped foot in a house with more than one bathroom, but I soon discovered the cabin had five. One of them, a toilet and a sink in a tiny closet in the loft, was where I did my morning business, washed up for breakfast, attempted to fix my hair, and shivered into my clothes.

I tippy-toed downstairs and entered the kitchen, where Aiyanna set a plate of food in front of me, as though serving me was her sole purpose in life. Steaming eggs, sausage and biscuits, and hot black coffee that burned my tongue—but that breakfast, I swear, tasted like manna from Heaven. I ate like a weasel in a chicken coop.

Sidabee shuffled in like she was eighty, her sleep-worn face offering a nod to Aiyanna and me. "Good morning," she said, all formal-like, as though waking wasn't something she did easily. She gathered her inky-black curls and slowly tied them into a ponytail, an act that appeared to keep a barrier between us. She dodged my stare as she poured her coffee, making it painfully clear I was still an outsider in her home.

I looked away, too, feeling the urge to disappear, but a pressure cooker whistling on the stove caught my attention. Gideon once said some meals take all day to prepare. Aiyanna, working at a butcher-block table near the fire, hummed a strange tune as she pounded at a piece of red meat. Beads of sweat popped out on her forehead in the warm kitchen, and her toffee-colored arms looked buttered. "Mister Jackson is working with Hotah this morning, killing chickens." She grinned and winked at me. "So. Do you like venison?"

"Um, I don't think so. But this sausage sure is good."

Aiyanna hesitated, then fell into laughter as thick as the blackstrap molasses I spooned onto my biscuit. She eyed my plate. "That's deer sausage you're gobbling down."

"Oh." I giggled. "Then I'm sure I'll love venison." I smiled while chewing on my deer sausage, thinking maybe Gideon could show off a little and fix my favorite meal. I easily snapped my fingers when I ate Gideon's fried chicken. It was never greasy, always tender and juicy on the inside, with crisp outsides. Everybody would love it so much that they might want to keep us around longer, so I asked, "Are Hotah and Gideon killing chickens for supper?"

Sidabee's eyes tapered to slits of blue. She fell into the chair opposite me and straightened, pulling a hanky from her robe pocket. Then she yanked off her eyeglasses, huffed hot breath on them, and rubbed slow circles into the lenses while her eyes stared into mine.

"We have sixteen wolves," she said. "In the winter, each wolf devours fifty to sixty pounds of meat weekly. Chicken is the cheapest. That long building you see way back near the woods, surrounded by a double fence—it's a chicken coop. It smells to high heaven in the summer when the wind blows this way. It costs a lot of money to run this farm."

"I guess this isn't a chicken sanctum, then?" I froze with my biscuit in my mouth, waiting for Sidabee to give me a smile. But she didn't. There wasn't even a hint of one. Her face remained stone cold and serious. The biscuit thickened at the back of my throat, and I choked and coughed as soon as the words had cleared my lips. I wanted to bite them back and I felt stupid and embarrassed, kidding with her, hoping to see her at least grin a little.

Sidabee only stood and stepped to the window, drinking her coffee, gazing outside, and hiding secrets behind her eyes. Whatever was bothering her, she toted it like a mule pulling a wagonload of tobacco, heavy and burdensome. "So, Neeley," she said, "would you like to meet the wolves this morning?" Thankfully, she didn't seem to pay much attention to my comment.

"Yes, ma'am. I sure would." I finished my breakfast in silence, the room growing so quiet I heard the air move between the pounding blows of Aiyanna's wooden meat hammer.

After breakfast, I browsed through what I finally realized was a library where a tall wooden ladder rolled back and forth against ceiling-high shelves of books. The room towered with various topics—law, history, horticulture. I discovered Treasure Island, Little Women, and a collection of National Geographic magazines, but nothing else piqued my interest. Someone had nicked and scratched a mahogany desk and cluttered it with pens, pencils, and a smiling picture of Sidabee. The wall behind the desk displayed several diplomas, some from Tennessee State University and others with the title *Attorney at Law* at the top and Baylor's name at the bottom.

Suddenly there she stood, close enough for me to smell her lavender perfume and minty breath. Dressed in brown tweed slacks that zipped up the side, a sweater set, and tan leather boots, Sidabee had found me running my fingers down a shelf of books. Her gold chain sparkled around her neck, and her charcoal-crusted fingers held her folded eyeglasses. I thought maybe she was a famous artist who sold paintings in those hoity-toity art galleries and was upset with me because I didn't recognize her. My gut told me she'd been popular with a close circle of friends in school. I felt her forceful pull, like a magnet to metal, and more than anything, I wanted to attach myself to her—be her closest and dearest friend.

"My husband is a lawyer," she said.

I pictured a tall building with several floors and an elevator, like the Jefferson Standard Life Building in Greensboro, where Judd Hastings Esquire had spent hours with Pudge. "Where's his office?"

"You're looking at it. Baylor isn't here, though. He was due in court at nine."

"Oh." I couldn't quite figure her out. At times, I believed she liked me, and then, seconds later, she glared at me with a sour puss look on her face. "This is the biggest house I've ever seen," I said.

"Well, then. Follow me. I'll give you the complete tour." Sidabee flew from room to room like the starling I imagined her to be. I peeked into three large bedrooms off a long hallway, connecting the great room to the kitchen, each filled with quilt-covered beds and fireplaces and smelling of furniture polish and smoke. Lace panels allowed light to sift through every window. Baskets of scented pinecones sat on the dressers. Carved, fancy mirrors and more paintings lined the hallway's log walls.

"The original cabin was built in 1808 by Baylor's great-great-grandpap. It burned down—twice, but Baylor's father and Hotah rebuilt it to what it is today. He and Aiyanna have lived in this house since before Baylor was born," she said.

We returned to the great room, and I listened to her voice fade like I'd turned down the volume on a radio. Everything appeared different in daylight. I took in the leather furniture again, noticing the brass tacks down the front and sides, how the patterned draperies brushed the floors, and the way every painting seemed to tell a story of life on The Sanctum, all signed by *S. MacLennan*. I knew the answer to my next question but asked it anyway, for the sake of conversation. Pointing to a charcoal sketch of two wolves romping in a field, I asked, "Who's the artist?"

"I am. I dabble at it," she said.

I ran my fingers across the bottom of the carved frame, imagining myself in the field with the wolves. "I feel like I'm there. Your drawings are like photographs. I like to draw. I drew a totem pole once—for a school project."

Sidabee's eyes widened. "You must draw something for me. You're welcome to use my paper and pencils. Aiyanna can show you where I keep them." She sat by the window, her attention seemingly fixed on an object outside. I glanced down at the top of her blue-black hair, plaited in a thick braid down her back with soft curls framing her face. "Creating art through painting and sketching that captures the beauty of this place—it's more than a hobby for me," she said. "It's a way to find peace and calm in a chaotic world."

Uncomfortable, I changed the subject. "So. Do y'all have a TV?"

She pointed to a large cupboard. "It's behind those doors." I couldn't believe it. She smiled at me. But then she turned her head and stared out the window again. I tried to imagine what she was looking at. Nothing appeared unusual. The morning sun trickled through cracks in the clouds; the blizzard had moved east. A lone turkey vulture flew overhead, and I watched its shadow skip and roll over the snow like a Saturday morning cartoon.

It seemed Sidabee stared at nothing and spoke as if I were a ghost she could see through. Her voice held scarcely a hint of sound. "Aiyanna says if you hold your head just right, standing out by the totem pole, the Cherokee whisper many secrets as the snow swirls across the fields."

I smiled as if I believed her. "Have you heard them?"

She slid her gaze sideways, then jumped to her feet and threw her coat around her shoulders. "No. But maybe you will while you're here. Hotah will finish your tour outside before driving you to town."

My heart sank. I didn't want to go to Bakersville, to find a phone, to call an uncle that didn't exist.

CHAPTER SEVENTEEN

Sidabee called out before we reached the barn. "Hotah!"

She pushed aside a giant sliding door on runners, uncovering an enormous cavern of workshops, tools, and endless rows of chicken feed sacks. I spied Gideon, dripping with sweat, stacking straw bales against the wall.

Sidabee pointed. "We stall our horses in a barn and pastures a mile down that way, away from the wolves," she explained. "We keep goats, sheep, and milk cows there, as well. Baylor employs Blossom, Hotah and Aiyanna's daughter, to oversee our small herd of beef cattle and hogs in the next county. We grow vegetables there, too. Aiyanna dedicates a great deal of time in the warmer months fighting rabbits, birds, and deer for possession of the gardens. We are self-sufficient here on The Sanctum."

I struggled to imagine all the pieces of the farm as Sidabee described it. "This place is like working a giant jigsaw puzzle. I've never seen a place like it."

Hotah turned the corner and chuckled. "Ah, Little Red Bird. Not much experience with wolves, then?"

"No, sir," I replied, shocked at his smile and at the name he had called me. "Gideon and I live on a tobacco farm."

My new revelation appeared to bother Sidabee. Her brimming good mood ended. "There's work to be done inside. Hotah, you'll drive them to Bakersville?"

"Of course," he answered.

"Good. See you at supper, Neeley? Gideon?"

"Yes, ma'am."

"Yes, 'um," Gideon replied.

Sidabee nodded sharply. I watched her turn, her heels and elbows moving in sync, rushing back to the cabin as if it were on fire.

Hotah stood inside the barn, shedding his coat, and rolling his sleeves to his elbows, revealing bare skin covered with old, new, and fresh scars. "Look at my arms, Little Red Bird. This is your first lesson. Although these wolves no longer roam the mountains, they are still wild animals. They love to play, and their claws are sharp. But not as sharp as their teeth. If you believe *my* arms look bad, ask to see Baylor's. Only Sidabee, Baylor, and I can enter the pens to feed or administer medicine. Never, never stick your arms, hands, or fingers inside a wolf's pen. Do you understand?"

"Yes."

"Wolves are not dogs. Do not compare the intelligence of a wolf to a dog. It is like comparing Einstein to Howdy Doody."

Gideon and I followed Hotah out of the barn. Arriving at the first pen, Hotah held up his large hand. We all stopped in our tracks. "As you see, we build their pens high and surround them with ground wire so they cannot dig themselves out. Look at their knobby feet; notice their size, how big they are compared to a dog's paws. Wolves in the wild can jump a nine—or ten-foot fence, but our more domesticated wolves cannot."

As I walked in Hotah's shadow, a surge of excitement mixed with unease coursed through me. My eyes were fixed on the majestic wolves ahead. Their sleek fur shimmered in golden sunlight, making them appear larger than I had first imagined. Some, though, seemed rather scrawny and fragile, their spindly legs and visible ribs telling of their struggle for survival. Approaching the next pen, I glanced behind me, only to see Gideon trailing at a safe distance, his eyes wide, his move slow and cautious.

Hotah, raising his arms in reverence, became my teacher that day, introducing me to his wolves and wolf-pack politics. "The pens cover a vast area, each a home to a pair of wolves. The intricacies of Washington politics pale to the dynamics within a wolf pack. That's why we maintain a two-wolf system. Elvis, the wolf you see there, is one of our esteemed house wolves. He bears the marks of age, yet his training and character embody wisdom and gentleness."

Hotah's gaze locked with mine. "But I have seen him devour a chicken in a few bites. Do not underestimate him; he weighs one hundred thirty-five pounds. Give him time to familiarize himself with you. He is the largest alpha male." The wolf leaped up at the fence, his front paws clinging to the wire high above my head. Hotah spoke to him in hushed tones, words I didn't understand. But the wolf's eyes startled me as they were level with my own, a silent communication passing between us.

"Two-Toes is the other male in that pen. He is also a house wolf but smaller than Elvis. You will see he has only two toes on his front right paw. Gnawing off half of his foot to escape a hunter's trap, he came to us more dead than alive. Despite his suffering, Two-Toes is well-mannered. He is Baylor's favorite." With the most beautiful colors mixed into his fur and broad face, the disfigured wolf never took his dark eyes off me, as if trying to convey his harrowing journey to The Sanctum without words.

Pointing to each wolf, Hotah called out their names like Santy-Claus calling out his reindeer in The Night Before Christmas story. He ambled to a different pen and allowed a wolf named Belle to nuzzle his fingers through the wire. "I can do this because she trusts me. Now you come. I will show you what happens when a wolf does not know you." I crept toward the wolf and heard Belle's low growl, an alarm behind her teeth; her eyes flashed with warning, and I stepped back.

Gideon lagged behind as Hotah walked on and continued his lesson. "You know the cry of the wolf. You have heard it," he said to me.

"How do you know that?" I asked, motioning for Gideon to catch up.

Hotah didn't answer. He moved silently and slowly down the hill toward a pen with two massive black and gray wolves. He paused, his back to us, and spoke with a heavy heart: "The Blue Ridge, once a sight to behold, has lost its allure. Man's greed, his desire to kill the wolf for sport, has marred its beauty."

"Yes, sir," I agreed. "Except I've not had a chance to see much of it."

"You will," Hotah responded. His words laced with an air of mystery, coaxed a smile to my lips. Unbeknownst to Gideon, I had already fallen for this place. Its rugged beauty and the untamed spirit of the wolves had captured my heart.

"What's that doing here?" I pointed to an ancient, broken-down pickup truck with no tires. It was a stark contrast to the natural beauty of the mountains, a jarring reminder of human presence. Tangled in dead kudzu, hidden under scrappy pines and a large elm tree, it rusted away in an open-air grave next to the pens.

"It was Baylor's father's truck. Craig MacLennan drove it until he died. Baylor cannot bring himself to bury it. The bees use it now."

"Oh." It seemed nothing went to waste. Even a rusted-out truck with no tires.

Hotah walked purposefully to the wolf pen and poked the metal hook from its eye, moving the door slightly open and slipping through alone. "Watch and learn," he instructed as he stepped toward two wolves he had called Raven and Blackfoot.

Behind me, Gideon placed his hands on my shoulders, whispering into my ear. "I'm not sure them wolves would like me much. I think I'll go up to the cabin and see if the Missus needs me to chop that wood near the kitchen." Nodding at him with a wry smile, I knew Gideon wanted nothing to do with the wolves. But I wanted to know them as well as Sidabee knew them. It was my heart's newest desire.

With a gentle hand, Hotah calmed the wolf. Raven sniffed the air and pawed at the dirt. "Yes, you know you're in for a treat," Hotah murmured. "You are eager to meet our visitor and perhaps eye a chicken or two," he added. He rubbed the wolf's thick fur that circled her neck and attached a leather strap to a halter he had slipped over her body. Blackfoot relaxed on a bed of straw, looked at Hotah, and yawned. He wasn't interested, it seemed to me.

"Raven is behaving. She thinks she is giving me what I want," Hotah explained. "But all the while, I am giving her what *she* wants. The feeling of freedom she once knew. This halter is for your safety, Little Red Bird. Once she knows you, we will not need it. Raven and a few others are more social; their wildness is gone. It is a sad thing."

"Does she understand you?"

"She understands more than you and I together," Hotah said, leading Raven from the pen.

"Maybe she senses I know little about wolves."

Repeating the wisdom his ancestors had probably passed down to him, Hotah said, "That is correct. Most animals possess a strong intuition of the good or bad inside their caretakers. Pay attention to how a man's horse or dog reacts to him. It will tell you about his character."

"Yes, sir." That explained why Pudge never rode his horses. He said they bucked him off. Countless times, a mule kicked him, bit him, or stomped on his foot. Dogs hated him, which is why we never owned one. Only his cats had tolerated him. I wanted Raven to like me and tried hard to remain calm. But I nearly peed my pants when she walked over and sniffed my leg.

Hotah made strange clicks and noises inside his throat and delivered a low whistle the wolf seemed to recognize. "Raven is going to have pups." He bent down, giving her belly a little pat, and she sprang forward, ready to run. Hotah unleashed the wolf. It was a frigid, snowy day, but we followed her the best we could. Before I knew it, the wolf had circled back and pulled Hotah's gloves out of his pocket, running with them in her mouth as if trying to get him to play. "She does that to me every time. Smart wolf, huh?"

I nodded. It stunned me when Hotah shared my smile.

Raven dropped the gloves and dashed across deep grass and snow. Watching the wolf reminded me of my restlessness since arriving, and I mentioned it to Hotah.

"Those who hold the truth sometimes bear a terrible weight," he said, then whistled again for the wolf.

Tilting my head back and inhaling deeply, I leaned into a breeze blowing up through the trees, carrying the scent of pine and meat from the smokehouse. The cold crept into my bones, but I accepted it as a challenge. Hotah was like a Magic 8-ball.

I couldn't shake him without him telling me surprising truths about myself.

The obedient wolf slowed to a brisk walk, turned, and sprinted back toward us. "Good girl," Hotah said, smiling again at Raven. Moving at a fast pace, I struggled to keep up. Hotah's gait was as long as his morning shadow. "One thing you must remember," he said, "the peace here is sometimes hard maintained. Danger and tragedy have often claimed the Blue Ridge, where the law was slow to go. Often, we must keep our own peace."

While Hotah took time to warn me not to wander far, I kept thinking; what fool would cause trouble on The Sanctum? Besides the protection from its sixteen wolves, the mountains rose around it, guarding the land on all sides as if determined to create a fortress for God Himself.

We stopped to catch our breath, beholding a small but breathtaking slice of North Carolina. It resembled one of Sidabee's paintings: rolling hills and steep mountains cloaked in ice, snow, and bare trees—shades of black, gray, and blue, paying homage to winter. I grew colder, staring at it.

Hotah drew a deep breath, his voice tinged with sorrow. "Though I was born twenty years before the turn of the century, to my people, the Cherokee, it feels like the Trail of Tears happened yesterday. The pain and loss, the wounds, are still raw to some. These days, it is the land developers who punish us. The Appalachian forests shrink more every year, a constant reminder of our ongoing battle to preserve our heritage."

I had heard about the Trail of Tears. Suddenly sad for Hotah and his people, I followed him in silence back to the wolf pens, aware of Raven at my heels. But the wolf started circling me before Hotah opened the pen for her to enter. "Stand still, Little Red Bird."

He didn't need to worry. My feet had frozen to the ground where I stood. The wolf's circle grew smaller and smaller until she rubbed against my hips, allowing me to float my fingertips down her soft back. Overcome with a sense of peace, a connection to something greater than myself, I don't remember how long I stood like that, the wolf tramping down snow until it became nothing but mud and grass around me.

After Hotah secured Raven safely in her pen, he rested his hand on my shoulder as we walked back to the barn. "In all my days, I have never encountered a wolf encircling a grieving spirit, a soul in mourning. My father spoke of it, but today was the first I witnessed it. You are no ordinary child, Little Red Bird. You are a special girl. Special indeed."

I didn't know what Hotah meant, exactly. All I knew was my love affair with wolves had just begun.

Later that morning, as Hotah drove Gideon and me to Bakersville, I learned more about The Sanctum. I learned animals that wander into a wolf pen die quickly. Barn cats, rabbits, squirrels, or even coyotes didn't live long there, which was why they built the chicken coop almost a half-mile from the cabin and surrounded it with a ton of wire, in case a wolf got loose.

I learned the MacLennan name meant Son of the Wolf and that they were Baptists. Both sides of Baylor's family came from Scotland. Proud, stubborn, and resourceful, they had fought to keep their mountaintop for over ninety years, Hotah had said. Baylor's father and grandfather not only built The Sanctum but also started the wolf sanctuary and farmed the land with Hotah and Aiyanna, whom I wasn't sure had a last name.

I sat quietly in the truck cab between Hotah and Gideon, thinking about how little I knew of American Indians, their culture, and their religion. "Are you saved, Hotah?" I asked. "Are you a Christian?" I thought everybody in America was either Christian, Catholic, or Jewish.

"Aiyanna's father was a Baptist Minister who fell in love with a Cherokee woman. We have read your Holy Scriptures and believe the teachings. But we also hold true to the traditions of our people. We have learned to mix the two, as you will see on Sunday."

This puzzled me. "Where *is* your church? Do you have lots of members?"

"There are few of us. We worship on The Sanctum. There is no better place."

Hotah and Gideon's conversation moved on to the latest Chevy and Ford trucks, the best manure to spread on plowed fields, and Reverend King's recent civil rights speeches. "Change gone come," Gideon said, "but not as soon as they think."

"True enough, my brother." Hotah said.

It sounded like the two had formed the friendship I wanted with Sidabee. Though Hotah was not a Negro, he had more in common with Gideon than I did as a white person. Needing to know more, I butted in again. "I've heard wolves howling every night for weeks. Gideon doesn't hear them. Why do you suppose that is?"

Hotah slowed his truck, and I watched his dark eyes glow. "Wolves are mysterious animals," he said. "They have been known to possess great powers and sometimes carry out the wishes of the dead."

I gave Hotah a nervous laugh. "Well, I'm sorry. I don't believe in howling ghosts."

But then he said, "Ghosts do not howl like wolves. However, they may have sent them for your protection."

His words hit me like a whack to my head. "My parents sent the wolves?"

"I do not know. Many find that hard to believe. People do not accept wolves in this world, as they are from another time long ago, difficult to imagine. I presume that is why you are drawn to them, Little Red Bird. But it is also why you must learn from them."

Driving toward a large brick house, situated on a wide hill amidst towering oak and chestnut trees, Hotah pointed with his crooked finger and raised an eyebrow. "Do you see that house?"

Hotah slowed the truck to a crawl, and out of the corner of my eye, I caught sight of a wolf's fleeting shadow. As we passed the house, I spun around and peered out the truck's rear window, hoping for another glimpse of the wolf. But there, I saw a woman wearing a high-necked blouse and a wide bell skirt to her feet. An old-fashioned bonnet covered a ton of ringlets that fell to her shoulders. She seemed to glide along the ground near the garden gate while cutting and gathering roses, creating a dreamlike appearance. When she lifted her head, her eyes met mine, and she gave me a nod and a smile, and as she did, the scene turned misty, its edges fading away. I shivered, turning back to stare wide-eyed at the road ahead through the windshield.

Hotah went on. "Once, I spotted a gray wolf through the iron gate that leads to that house, the Hollis House. I sensed that soon, the house would perish, and its inhabitants would meet a similar fate, scattering like leaves in the wind. The wolf knew it, too. This land was his first. Afterward, I kept a close watch on the house. In time, they carried the father out in a coffin. The family mourned and left town. Then, someone bought the place, hacking it into apartments and adding wheelchair ramps for the elderly. Staff members roamed the property in white jackets like wingless angels. But the wolf remained a nuisance until the management summoned the sheriff and men from town. Armed with rifles like soldiers, they hunted down and killed the gray wolf. There are those who insist the grounds still echo with the wolf's nocturnal cries. After all, it was his land first. And people still carry out the coffins of the dead."

Gideon clutched my hand. "I tole you—God is leading us. You jus' leave it at that."

"That is right, my friend. God is mysterious. His ways are not to be questioned," said Hotah. "But look, we are in Bakersville. It is time to phone your sick uncle, huh?"

Bakersville looked nothing like Summerfield. It sat smack-dab in the middle of mountain ranges, and from looking at a map, it hovered close to the state's edge. Although it was early December, golden light softened the entire town. Hotah said that Sidabee had called it—a painter's light. But the road into Bakersville was narrow and curvy. The same road swerved out of town, turning its back on the rest of North Carolina, heading uphill and across the state line. Hotah said tourists had to travel over the Blue Ridge before reaching Tennessee's Great Smoky Mountain ranges.

The few residents seemed peculiar and unpredictable. Some said hello, but most only went about their business. Hotah said they were small-minded folk, not open to the pastoral words of the Reverend King. It didn't surprise me when Hotah said Bakersville churches did not allow Negroes or American Indians to join their membership; that the Baptist church was the biggest bigot in town.

As we crossed the street to the hardware store, Hotah said it was because Mister Dirk Buchanan ran that church into the ground. That he was a banker and land developer who pestered Baylor every chance he got, wanting to buy The Sanctum and turn it into a rich people's resort. Mister Buchanan, Hotah said, took advantage of the fact that the townspeople didn't understand the wolf sanctuary, telling everybody Baylor collected and bred wolves. Wolves that broke out of their pens, ran the countryside, and terrorized livestock and small children.

Right about then, I wished we had brought Pudge's guns. I wanted to pull that Mister Buchanan aside and shoot some sense into him.

CHAPTER EIGHTEEN

The hardware store smelled of chewing tobacco and steel pipes. My eyes scanned the inside for the telephone. I had no desire to call every Guilford County hospital and speak to nurses who would not understand what I was talking about while Hotah listened to every word. But he only gestured to the back of the store. "The office is that way. Collin O'Donnell owns this establishment. He is Baylor's friend and is expecting you. Use his telephone to call your uncle. Gideon and I will load supplies into the truck. If you need help, ask Collin."

I looked at Gideon, who spread his hands regretfully and shrugged. The two disappeared down an aisle of saw blades and sandpaper, leaving me alone in the dimly lit store. Glued to the floor, I stared out the grimy windows at traffic moving on the street, listening to car horns and barking dogs that sounded mad at the world. Snow drifted inside like feathers when a customer walked in, stomping his boots on the worn wooden floors to remove the slush.

"Are you Neeley?" I turned to the voice behind me.

His overalls looked like the ones Pudge wore. It was the first thing I noticed about him. He was tall and thin, with his pant legs tucked into his boots and his faded blue shirt sleeves rolled to his elbows. His hair color, the pale ivory of raw milk, only emphasized the flyaway cowlick at his hairline, and he smiled with bright green eyes. Since he knew Baylor, I assumed he was a decent man who didn't pay any mind to Mister Buchanan, his lies, or his bigoted church.

I cleared my throat. "I'm her." I caught a whiff of his aftershave when he shook my hand.

"Pleased to meet ya. I'm Collin. Baylor's a customer and a good friend." He only glanced at my forehead as if the scar weren't anything he hadn't seen before. "How d'you like The Sanctum?" he asked.

Feeling uncomfortably out of place, my cheeks hard and cold, I rubbed melted snow off my eyeglasses. "Very much, thank you, Mister O'Donnell."

He smiled again. "Call me Collin. Phone's 'round the corner." He pointed. "Over there. Just pick up the receiver and ask the operator to help ya. I don't suppose your uncle will accept a collect call in the hospital, so don't worry 'bout the charges. Baylor'll take care of it."

"Thanks." A sick sensation boiled up in my belly as Collin followed me. I walked to the small counter where a heavy black telephone sat near a coffee can filled with pens and pencils. Flipping through a telephone book, I didn't know how to get out of it. My mind raced with uncertainty. Mister O'Donnell glanced at me as I picked up the receiver and gave me a nod along with a strange half-smile. Thankfully, a woman with blue-tinted hair stepped inside the office and said a customer needed his help in the store.

Left alone, it occurred to me I shouldn't make the call at all, but then it wouldn't show up on the telephone bill for Baylor to pay. Concentrating on what to do, I knew I had to call somebody. And then I asked myself, what harm would it do to call Pudge? *These people won't know the difference between his phone number and a hospital's.* At least I'd find out if he were hunting us or possibly didn't give a damn, which I hoped was the case.

It certainly wasn't because I *wanted* to talk to him. Then again, maybe I did. Perhaps I wanted to rub it in—laugh at him the way he'd laughed at me. Call him the monster he was.

I picked up the receiver and dialed zero hard enough to hurt my finger. "Operator, I'd like to make a long-distance call. Mayfair 8-4148 in Summerfield, North Carolina."

But then my legs nearly gave out. I teetered a bit, pulled a metal stool to the counter, and sat, clenching my jaw and fists, thinking the pain from my nails biting into my skin might bring me to my senses and I'd hang up before he answered the phone. Sighing loud and long, I hoped it would smother the sinking feeling that dragged on my softening heart. It didn't.

The phone rang twice.

"Hello." A woman's voice caused my stomach juices to hurl into my throat. I bent over at the waist and put my head between my knees.

"Hello!" the woman said again.

I sat back up straight and swallowed hard. "Is Pudge McPherson there?"

"Neeley? Is that you? Oh, Neeley—where are you, honey?"

My nausea settled. Somewhat. "Who is this?"

"Fiona Troyer, Sheriff Troyer's wife. I'm taking care of your grandfather; he's been shot. Land sakes, you should *know*. That colored man, Gideon, shot him. Have you gotten away? Where'd he take you, Neeley? The whole town is looking for you. That Negro's in a boatload of trouble kidnapping you like that. Where are you, dear?"

I drew in a long, shaky breath. "May I talk to my grandfather, please, ma'am?" It never ceased to amaze me how that woman managed to position herself at the center of everybody's problems. A smoldering rage in the pit of my stomach made me forget about the nerves raking my insides.

"Well. Hold on. I'll get him to the phone."

I heard shuffling noises and odd muffled voices, as if Pudge's house were full of people. "Neeley? Where the hell are you!?"

"Gideon did *not* shoot you or kidnap me, and you know it. I left because I had to get away from *you!*"

"Tell me where you are, do you hear me!? Get your ass home this instant! Or I'll—"

"—You'll what, Pudge? Get the Bible belt? Those days are over. Do you hear *me*? They're over."

"Don't you dare sass me, you little bitch! The police and everybody are out looking for you. I got me a nasty infection from the bullet wound. I put down another mule today, and I haven't had a decent meal in over a week! You best get on the next bus home if you know what's good for you, and if that nigger knows what's good for him, he'll turn himself in before Sheriff Troyer and his boys find him. *And you know what I mean!*"

"I know *exactly* what you mean!"

"Then get your ass home this *instant!*" His crusty voice popped and cracked as if he'd just swallowed a mouthful of soda crackers.

"Quit yelling, Pudge! I need to ask you something."

His sigh met my ears across the miles. "You called to ask me a goddamn question?"

"Yes." I took another deep breath. "I was wondering. Did you mean it when you called me a retard?"

"Where the hell are you!?"

My lower lip trembled, and I felt my temper rise.

"Answer me!" he shouted.

"You answer me first! Why do you hate me?"

"Jesus H. Christ, tell me where you are this minute!"

"I need to know. Did you—" My words burned in my throat. "Did you—"

"—Goddamn it, Neeley, spit it out!"

"Okay! Did you *ever* love me?"

Taking the Lord's name in vain never stopped in Pudge's world. "I'll tell you what I love; I love that your fanny's gonna sting from now until next year when I find you—"

"—I told you, Pudge, those days are over." And just like that, I replaced the receiver back on the hook.

I had my answer.

I sat for a moment, staring at a wall calendar. Miss December 1959 had dressed in a Santy-Claus hat and a short, racy red-velvet costume with a white fur collar that dipped down around her bulging breasts. Her red get-up matched her high heels, nail polish, and lipstick. Bent at the waist, she held her index finger to her lips as if she'd not heard a thing. "So big damn deal," I said to her. "The call wasn't to any uncle, so what?"

Once again, I sighed deeply and thumbed tears from my eyes. I knew what I had done. I had just lit a fire under a monster.

Leaving the office, I turned the corner and collided with Collin. His voice broke the silence, "Everything okay?"

I managed a quick nod, my eyes drawn to his gentle face. But in the next instant, the door burst open, sending an icy chill to coil around my legs. A pair of muddy boots thundered on the wooden floor not twenty feet from me. I glared at a familiar face—Eugene Cooper, from the Summerfield Klan. The Devil had arrived, dragging Farley Whitsett in his wake.

Farley looked out of place without his twin brother beside him. As the door closed behind them, the wind rattled the store's thin windows, and I spun around so fast that my vision blurred. Collin rushed past me to greet his customers, but I had ducked behind a stack of ladders, closing my eyes and giving thanks that Gideon and Hotah had left me alone in the store.

I peered around the corner. They hadn't seen me, so I sent another prayer of thanks. Collin's eyes crinkled when he smiled and said, "Can I help you fellas find anything?"

"You bet! Got any kerosene?" Mister Cooper's small square frame did not match his thunderous voice. It was as if he wanted his presence known to every soul in town at once.

Collin nodded toward the door. "Outside in the alley. How much y'all need?"

Mister Cooper stuck a cigarette in his mouth. "Oh, 'bout two gallons." He took out a match, lit up, and turned to Mister Whitsett. "That sound right, Farley?"

Mister Whitsett might've agreed had he not been engrossed in the manure spreader on sale.

Collin wrote out their bill with a steady hand. "You two new in town?"

Both men then casually craned their necks down one aisle after another, and I ducked farther back into my hiding place. Mister Cooper's voice boomed across the store like our principal's over the morning loudspeaker. "We're passing through. You ain't seen a young red-headed girl and a strange Negro in town lately, have ya?"

Peeking between the slats, I watched Collin shake his head. "Nah. Can't say I have. Not many strangers in these parts. Might want to check over in Burnsville or Asheville."

"Heading that way," Mister Cooper said. And then he pulled a slip of paper from his coat pocket and leaned over the counter and closer to Collin, and judging by the way Collin's eyebrows popped up, it surprised him. "You'll call this number if you see anybody like that, won't ya? I mean, 'less you and the good folks in Bakersville cater to the Negro cause."

Again, Collin's eyes crinkled. "I'll be sure to keep an eye out." Collin stuffed the paper into his shirt pocket. "Now, if you follow me, I'll get you that kerosene."

I waited inside until my knees stopped knocking. Watching their truck drive away, I questioned if the God of miracles had just jumped out of our driver's seat.

Behind the store, Gideon and Hotah had waited patiently in the truck. Climbing into the truck cab, I felt a wave of relief wash over me when no one questioned the success of my telephone mission. Anxious to leave town, I kept the Summerfield Klan incident to myself. Pudge had warned me they were on our trail, but I didn't expect to run smack into two of them in Bakersville.

As Hotah put the key in the ignition, a man's face appeared at the truck window. Somewhere in his fifties, his sagging right eye seemed stuck in a half-wink. With the cleft in his chin, he looked like Kirk Douglas with a crew cut. A golden *Jesus Saves* tie clip held a pale green necktie against the starched-white shirt stretched tight across his broad chest. A shirt that looked too new and unwrinkled to be anything but expensive.

Hotah didn't move a muscle and stared straight ahead.

Finally, the well-dressed stranger squared his shoulders and tapped sharply on the glass.

Gideon pulled his hat down to cover his eyes. "Man wants to talk to ya, Hotah."

Hotah opened the window, but only a smidgen. "Go to Hell," he said.

The man chuckled. "Been there twice, actually. New York City. You heard of it?" The scent of the Teaberry gum he chewed like a steak drifted through the window. I didn't like how his lips quivered when he smiled. "Seems to me, Baylor being a lawyer and all, he ought to know what happens when a man can't pay back his loans. Law says a man with Baylor's assets might have to sell off some of his valuable timberland to pay his bills. Why don't you talk to him about it?"

"Manmade laws don't apply to things not made by man," Hotah said. If the meek were supposed to inherit the earth, I was certain Hotah would end up with only a handful of dirt. Meek, he was not.

And then the man fixed his eyes on me. Gideon slid down in the seat and stared in the other direction.

"Who are your friends?"

"Visitors." Hotah shifted the truck into reverse but not before the charmingly hostile man in one quick motion flashed his white teeth, tipped an invisible hat to me, and hollered into the truck—

"—Hotah, tell Baylor tourism is looking up. Asheville reported record numbers. Bakersville needs some of that action—"

"—Like I said, Buchanan, go to Hell."

Hotah pealed out like a teenager in his dad's Buick and sped out of town while I held tight to the dashboard and hoped Eugene Cooper and Farley Whitsett had not spoken to Mister Buchanan on *their* way out of town. If Mister Buchanan ever discovered our identities, he'd call Sheriff Troyer or worse—Pudge. The law would incarcerate Gideon and drag me back to Summerfield faster than a bootlegger hauling white lightning over the Blue Ridge.

On the drive back to The Sanctum, Hotah talked about the current phase of the moon and the names of local flowers and birds. But I only half-listened. Instead, I stared out the window at massive-trunked trees standing powerful and alone and groups of reedy, young dogwoods bending and dancing in the wind. From the brown farmland of the Piedmont, we had escaped into a new life split open with blue mountains and the possibility of calling it home. But I also realized that even in this promising place where Gideon and I had landed, the threat of catastrophe loomed large.

I pulled on my gloves, a futile attempt to ward off the chilling introduction to Mister Buchanan and running into the Klan. Pushing down on the woolly spaces between each finger, I wanted to think of anything other than my haunting past still clinging to me like cat fur on a wool coat.

Arriving back at the farm, my eyelids felt heavy, and suddenly all I wanted was to sink into the soft, warm bed in the loft. Gideon had said if Hotah didn't need him after they unloaded the truck, he'd like to head to the cabin to rest a bit before supper. He looked as tired as I felt, his shoulders slumped and his eyes droopy. Hotah, always the silent observer, had a way of understanding without words, and I appreciated his quiet presence, a soothing balm to my restlessness and Gideon's weary body.

I stood at the top of the hill where Baylor parked his Jeep, captivated by the view and thinking about the difference between the majestic scene I was staring at and the ancient, rusted truck beside the wolves' pens. But for the rest of it, where earth met heaven, there was nothing but a ridge-crested skyline and the soft whisper of snow.

As the cold burned my cheeks, I wrapped my scarf around my face, and caught my first glimpse of a smaller cabin off in the distance, football fields away, positioned between the shoulder blades of a valley and nestled into the rise of the next mountain. A thin smoke spiral rose from the chimney. Eager to learn more about The Sanctum and its inhabitants, I pointed to the cabin and asked, "Who lives there?"

Hotah followed my stare. "Sometimes hunters rent it from Baylor during deer season."

"Can we walk there?"

"No."

I looked at him, my face registering a big question mark.

"That cabin is—it is off limits." He stumbled for words for the first time since I'd met him. "They are not up here to receive company. Hunting season on this mountain can be dangerous. It is best you and Gideon stick close to the immediate property."

"Okay." I understood, but I wasn't sure I believed him.

An enormous boulder jutted out of a nearby snowdrift, beckoning me. I trudged through knee-high snow, determined to climb to the top for a better view of the cabin. As I reached its highest point, I spotted an odd-looking stone, nestled like a hidden treasure in a Cracker Jack box. Shaped like an arrow tip, with delicate specks of pink and blue at its core, it fascinated me, even though I couldn't fathom its purpose. When I finally scooted off the boulder, I eagerly shared my find with Hotah.

"An arrowhead," he declared.

I almost dropped it. The idea of holding something that potentially killed a deer or a human felt unsettling. Yet, strangely, I found the stone comforting, like grasping a bouquet of spring flowers or sheltering beneath an umbrella in the rain. I carefully tucked it into my coat pocket, determined to keep it always. The arrowhead, a relic of a past I was only beginning to understand, was more than a mere object. It served as a connection to The Sanctum, a symbol of Hotah's history and culture.

As we watched storm clouds crisscross in confusion, a ray of sunlight pierced through a keyhole in the clouds. Brilliant shafts of light radiated outward, casting a golden glow upon the backs of the clouds. Hotah's gaze lifted, and I shivered at the horizon reflected in his hawk-like eyes. The sun's powerful beams reached the earth, sweeping over the valley like searchlights. Hotah raised both arms to the sky. "On these mountains, God is everywhere," he said. "The Great Creator loves to show off."

I giggled. "I can't believe Baylor and Sidabee own over a thousand acres."

"God owns it," he said.

"Of course God owns it. Why wouldn't He? The beauty here— it takes my breath away." Up in the air, an eagle tore through the clouds, gliding on a current toward blue sky and sunshine. "And I suppose He would want us to appreciate it," I said with a sigh.

Hotah gave me a strange look. *"He speaks through the mouths of babes that we might still the enemy and the avenger."* Before I asked him what he meant, he had walked halfway to the barn.

On my way back to the cabin, I felt for my arrowhead to show it to Gideon, but it was gone. I'd already lost it.

CHAPTER NINETEEN

I found Gideon sitting on the bed in his room. He had to be dead-dog-tired, shielding me from Pudge all those years, being the old, weather-beaten farmhand he was. We were an odd combination; I'll give you that.

"Hey. It's suppertime."

He raised his head and looked at me standing in the doorway. "You doing all right? I haven't had time to talk to you since we arrived."

"I'm fine, I reckon." The words hurt coming out—like I'd bit my tongue.

"You called your grandfather, didn't you?"

I let out a long sigh. "Yes, but I wish I hadn't. He's saying *you* shot him and then kidnapped me. The police *and* the Klan are looking for us. Course, we knew they would."

Gideon looked plain sad. Sad and tired. "Are you angry with me?" he asked.

"What for? Because you spent all day with Hotah? That's your job now as long as we're here. It ain't no reason for me to be angry."

"What'd I tell you 'bout that trash talk? Don't say *ain't*."

"Sorry. You pick who you want to talk to; it's fine."

Gideon shook his head. "Never knew you had a jealous bone. I need to keep mahsef' busy. Can't be sitting 'round thinking 'bout things."

"I'm not jealous. I need to talk to you sometimes, that's all."

He smiled. "I s'pose I'll have to remember that. I jus' don't feel comfortable 'round them wolves. They're bringing two of 'em into the house tonight. I might have to turn in early. You understand?"

"Sure." I hung around for a moment, listening to Aiyanna pull plates and silverware out of the cabinet to set the table. "I should go help with supper."

"Me, too," he said. Gideon didn't look quite as old in the soft light of his room.

"There's something different about this farm," I said. "Something not—normal."

He nodded. "It's been one strange thing after another since we lef'. You feel it here?"

"I do. I feel like my parents are near me." I paused and rubbed the back of my neck. "What if they didn't die, and they're living in Bakersville or somewhere close by? Maybe Pudge blackmailed them."

"Neeley. You stop. They dead, and you know it. But I have to say, a lot 'bout this place don't sit right with me. Odd things gone on here. They seem like fine folk, but you let me know where you go off. So's I don't worry."

"You do the same." I looked down at him, his elbows resting on his thighs, the way he always sat when deep in thought, his head bent to the floor. "Gideon?"

"Hmm?"

"You still think God's in the driver's seat?"

"We gone find out soon, I 'spect."

The root cellar door creaked as it scraped across the cold, damp concrete floor. Aiyanna had sent me to a cobwebby corner of the cellar to retrieve home-canned jars of green beans, pickles, and stewed tomatoes while Gideon sliced bread, set out plates and glasses, and poured cider. Aiyanna served pickle and cheese plates, deer steak smothered in onions and gravy, and mashed potatoes on unchipped blue dishes of various sizes.

We clasped hands and Baylor bowed his head. "Bless this food, Lord, and this family who are about to receive Your sustenance.

Make us grateful for what You have given. Help us not to ask for what we cannot have, and make us mindful of those less fortunate while we sit at this table with all of Your generous bounty.”

I had said *amen* and piled steak and potatoes onto my plate, which steamed up my eyeglasses, when I saw Sidabee creep into the kitchen, pulling a smile from somewhere. Standing proper and pale in a dark wool dress pulled tight across her hips, she scanned the table and slid into a chair, propping up her head with her hands.

“You feeling better?” Aiyanna asked her.

Her mouth opened, and I thought she might say something, but the long sigh that escaped her lips spoke volumes. She simply shook her head, her eyes downcast.

“Go on, then. Go lie down. I’ve got Neeley and Gideon to help. Go to bed.”

As Sidabee reached for a slice of bread, her hand trembled slightly. It was an excuse. I knew it. I forked my pickle in half, scraping the plate. Watching her stumble back to her room left a bitter taste in my mouth. She didn’t even want to eat with me.

After Aiyanna and I finished washing the supper dishes, we settled down to watch the TV stored in its special cupboard. While it took its sweet time to warm up, I stretched out on the floor sketching with one of Sidabee’s charcoal pencils, trying to capture the essence of Gideon’s boot. Mister Chet Huntley and Mister David Brinkley appeared on the snowy screen, reporting on the presidential race between Mister Nixon and Mister Kennedy. Reverend King was always making headlines. Mister Brinkley showed the Reverend delivering a speech on nonviolence at the Southern Christian Leadership Conference, which seemed to hold great importance to Gideon and Hotah who spoke quietly about it during the commercials. I figured Hotah and Aiyanna clung to every hope the Negroes held onto. Prejudice was prejudice against any race.

Sidabee entered the room in a white terrycloth bathrobe and slippers, exchanging a knowing nod with Aiyanna—a silent understanding only *they* knew. Aiyanna stood and switched off the TV. "That's enough," she declared. "Perhaps only the armies of God can fix this world, and even then, maybe not."

Looking more refreshed than she had during supper, Sidabee poured herself a steaming mug of tea. With a slight lip smile, she glanced over my shoulder at my drawings. "Very impressive," she commented, her voice a mixture of indifference and forced politeness that was getting on my last nerve. Nestled on the sofa, she toed off her house shoes, conveying a feeling starkly different from her words.

I rose to my knees as I heard the glass doors to the screened-in room open behind us. Baylor entered with two wolves on leashes. The wolves sniffed the air, as if they knew Gideon and I were there.

Gideon announced, "If y'all don't mind, I'm off to bed. Daylight comes early here." I was sure everybody sensed his fear of wolves, but no one mentioned it.

My friendly wave of goodnight made Gideon smile. "Goodnight, Neeley," he replied and then left the room.

Baylor unleashed the wolves, but they didn't move until Hotah held up his hand. "Come," he commanded. And they did. Obediently, they trotted over to him, their presence filling the room as part of The Sanctum's reason to exist. I yearned to pet them, to feel their massive heads and thick fur, and somehow convey my sorrow for the circumstances that had brought them to The Sanctum. Circumstances that mirrored my own.

"They are our dearest and oldest wolves," said Aiyanna, running her hand down their backs.

"How old?" I asked.

Sidabee's eyes rolled to a close, and her hands clasped together so tightly her knuckles went white again. "They're both around thirteen." She had remained quiet all evening. At least she answered me.

"I'm thirteen. But *I'm* not old."

Baylor sat next to Sidabee and patted her leg as if he preferred to explain. "In wolf years, they're almost eighty."

The ancient wolf named Elvis whined. Apparently too tired to stand around and wait for Aiyanna to rub his neck again, he flopped next to her at the fire and onto a wolf-hairy blanket—his front paws crossed as he curled at her feet, his head resting on her shoes. As his weighty body of skin and fur relaxed, his dark eyes held tight on me.

I edged toward the sofa across from Baylor and Sidabee, my heart pounding with excitement. "Can I . . . can I pet them?"

At the sound of my voice, Two-Toes lifted his huge head and stepped closer to me, placing his gray muzzle into my hands.

Aiyanna laughed. "Looks like he answered your question."

His fur tickled my palms and brushed against my legs. My pity—no, my compassion for that wolf burned to my fingertips. I sat with Two-Toes at my side, my hands stroking his thick coat, while everybody made small talk about one thing and another, but watching the wolf closely.

Within the hour, I felt somewhat drowsy. I had sunk into the cool leather sofa when Sidabee suggested I make myself more comfortable by removing my shoes, my eyeglasses, and stretching out. So, I did. Yet, Two-Toes didn't budge. He stayed beside me, as if guarding my every move. I assumed Two-Toe's behavior was unusual, because each time I glanced at Hotah, his eyes were fixed on the wolf.

I listened to Baylor talk about the weather patterns in the skies, the winter's frost, and the past summer's drought—the worst the area had seen in years. He had an elegant way with words and a seemingly bottomless bucket of tales to tell. A constant, steady hum of words and stories of the mountains and the people who lived on them. The only other sounds were the crackle of firewood, someone's subtle shift in a chair, and an occasional gust of winter wind. No one interrupted as Baylor kept on talking, slowly and in a rhythm that nearly put me to sleep. But somehow I knew, the attention was focused on the wolf—and me, and not on Baylor's next account of life in the Blue Ridge.

And then, in a second that altered the course of my life, Two-Toes brought his face inches from mine. I saw myself in his eyes—eyes as gray and somber as the sky that day. His stare was like a hard frost, so cold I felt scorched. Baylor, sensing the gravity of the moment, stood in concern, but Hotah, with a knowing look, motioned for him to wait.

Two-Toes began licking from my chin to my forehead. He licked and licked for the longest time as if God Himself were washing my face, and I didn't know if it was divine stupidity or reckless faith that caused me to close my eyes, remain still, and let that wolf lick to his heart's content. I felt everybody watching cautiously, possibly moved by what was happening. But I wasn't afraid as I lay there, remembering something Gideon had told me; that faith was the little bird that sings when the dawn is still dark. Long ago, darkness had covered my world like a permanent nightfall, and I had been singing and believing my life had to improve. That night had to end, and the sun had to come out.

When Two-Toes stopped licking, I sat and buried my face in his fur, feeling strange combinations of joy, relief, wonder—love, even gratitude. Emotions I hadn't experienced in a *really* long time. As if in response, Two-Toes laid his big hairy head over my shoulder—a wolf hug. His hot breath trickled through my hair onto my neck. Moments later, I gently pushed away and looked at Baylor, my face wet with tears and wolf saliva. And then, just like that, the wolf walked away and dropped next to Elvis in front of the fire.

But Aiyanna stood, staggered across the room, and eased herself down beside me. Her wrinkles blossomed like flowers around her eyes and smile. She gently lifted my hair away from my forehead and began caressing my entire face with trembling hands. "Glory be. Great Spirit from Heaven above. Your scar, Little Red Bird. Your scar. Is gone."

I grabbed my eyeglasses, bolted to the closest mirror, and stared at my face. On wobbly legs, I pulled and tugged at my hair, thinking maybe the scar had slid off to the side or something. Baylor appeared in the mirror behind me and wrapped his muscular arms around my shoulders, his blue eyes shimmering through his tears. I began to weep and shiver uncontrollably into his chest because from the time my parents died, not a single soul had hugged me.

Hotah stood and stoked the fire, and the room grew warm with affection. But Sidabee sat there with a gleam in her eyes, matching the rhinestones on her eyeglasses. Her shaky hands set her cup and saucer on the table beside her. Tilting her head, she smiled soberly and pushed her glasses back on her nose. Still, she had nothing to say.

I gazed back into the mirror, struggling to keep some kind of composure but failing miserably. "How—how does this happen? It's a miracle!" My chin quivered. The torment of wearing a horrid scar, of being branded for eight years, surged within me and burst out like a torrent. For the longest time, I sobbed quietly until painful hiccups shook my shoulders.

"He stretches out the north over the void and hangs the earth upon nothing. What you call miraculous is not above or beyond the natural order of things. The way the Creator turns the world in a sky of miracles, there is no ending of what can be," said Hotah.

My logical thirteen-year-old mind couldn't comprehend a life *with* miracles or a sky *without* an end. My wildest imagination could not fathom the smallest journey of unexplored skies, or a world where miracles occurred daily, like on The Sanctum. A river of tears had finally found its way to a joyous ocean, existing even in someone like me.

I crawled into bed, praying I had not dreamed the miracle and pinching myself to ensure I was fully awake. And then it occurred to me that not one of them asked how I got the scar to begin with. They were peculiar people, quiet, revealing little about their lives and asking only a few questions about mine.

Plumping my pillow, I hoped wolves existed in Heaven and decided to use my faith for more miracles. I needed to win Sidabee over. I had waded into the River of Life, seeking one thing above all else—a life. No Pudge McPherson, no Sheriff Troyer, no Ku Klux Klan, nobody lurking around the corner ready to throw Gideon and me in jail. Faith might move mountains, but it could also make a mountain stay put. A mountain of a thousand acres where a girl and her adopted grandfather could disappear and live out their days in sanctuary.

The following morning, the second my alarm clock rang, I opened my eyes, threw back the covers, and dashed to the mirror. I didn't bother changing out of my nightgown or brushing my teeth; I flew down the loft steps and into Aiyanna's outstretched arms, who was obviously waiting for me. Pulling me into her soft bosom, she smiled another comforting smile.

"It's still gone!" I gasped, my chest heaving. I couldn't believe it. "It wasn't a dream."

Aiyanna's smiles came often and easily. That morning was no different. "Of course not, Little Red Bird. When God gives you a gift, He doesn't take it back."

"You mean He's not an—um, He won't let my scar come back?" I bit my tongue to prevent myself from blurting out something about an Indian giver. I regretted using those hurtful words I had said in school and wished I could take them back.

"It's gone forever," she assured me. In that moment, Aiyanna's eyes shimmered like sunlight on a pecan tree. "Someone is waiting for you. He wants to witness your miracle. Show him what God has done."

Gideon knew, of course. Someone had told him, because he gently lifted my chin and smiled so wide that I saw every tooth in his head. His joy was infectious, spreading through the room like a warm breeze, causing fat tears to drip down my cheeks. "God works in mysterious ways," he chuckled through his own tears. "I guess I should make friends with those wolves." And then, something he had never done before, Gideon kissed my forehead.

CHAPTER TWENTY

Aiyanna told me Sidabee had gone into town and would be away until after supper. Despite my miracle, I still felt Sidabee's annoyance with Gideon and me. I'd lived with Pudge's rejection all my life; I didn't need *hers*.

It was a sore spot.

But as a wee bitty girl, I had learned to mind my Ps and Qs. Gideon made sure of that. So, since I was only a guest, I kept quiet and spent the day either helping Aiyanna with her chores or drawing at the kitchen table. Picture after picture, until powdery black charcoal coated my fingers. Big grinning cartoon faces, Hotah, Aiyanna, Baylor, the wolves, and even Sidabee and the cabin flowed onto the paper. I had etched The Sanctum on the pages of my mind and allowed each picture to flow through my fingers. I drew away the day until aromas of pan-seared trout, roasted potatoes, and bread pudding pulled me into the kitchen.

Aiyanna's evening meals were mere samples of her constant kindness. She made them special—like her. And there was always dessert and candles. Sometimes, she lit them, sometimes not. We filled the silence with lively conversation, each smile and word finding a place in my heart. The night before, our topics ranged from the new filling station in Bakersville, Willie Mays and his upcoming season, to adding Hawaii and Alaska as new stars on our flags. These suppers were the highlight of my day, imagining myself as part of an actual family. After cleaning the kitchen, I always watched Sidabee, hoping she might find a reason to speak to me. Instead, she usually headed for bed, and Baylor brought in logs for a fresh fire in the great room hearth—the nights already growing colder.

But that evening, after supper, I helped Gideon finish his barn chores until my shoes were so caked with mud that walking became challenging. Each step squished along the path as I trudged back to the cabin, parked my muddied shoes at the door, and padded up the steps to the loft in search of my boots. As I did, I overheard Sidabee and Baylor entering the great room below, deep in conversation. The thing about a loft bedroom— it's impossible not to overhear the discussions below, whether one intends to or not. Curious, I sank quietly to the floor to listen.

"They're down at the barn," said Sidabee.

Baylor cleared his throat. "You sure?"

"I'm sure. And I'm sure it's all a big lie. There's no way you'll be able to pay them enough to buy a truck. That'll take years. You can, however, offer to drive them home."

"I'm aware of that," Baylor said. "But I sense, and so does Hotah, that they're in a serious predicament. I believe there's no home to return to. They need sanctuary, like the wolves. We wouldn't turn out a wolf, and we won't turn *them* out. Besides, nobody is going to take in a white girl and a Negro man together, not even out of Christian charity. Nobody but us. There's something special about her. Did you not witness her miracle? That scar—"

"—How do we know that was an actual scar? I've heard people do amazing things for attention and sympathy—"

"—Sidabee! You, of all people, should know better."

The room grew quiet except for Elvis moving and stretching on the floor below. I pressed my stomach to the rug beneath me, wishing I could disappear.

Sidabee paced the room, her footsteps loud on the wood planks. "What makes you think we can put a roof over their heads without finding out why they're in trouble, if that's the case? You're a lawyer; can't you convince Gideon to tell you the truth? Or call somebody?"

I heard Baylor walk to the mantel and light a match for his cigar. "Who do we call? The authorities will do God knows what to Gideon and send Neeley back to where she's obviously trying to get away from. Gideon loves that little girl. He's seems determined to protect her from something. Or someone. Sidabee, dog-gone-it, you know it's her. You *know* it. No thirteen-year-old should *ever* discover how much they can endure. I doubt much has changed in Summerfield."

"If it's *not* her, won't somebody be searching for them? Her uncle, perhaps."

"Uncle? I thought you didn't believe that story." Baylor chuckled. "We'll find out what's going on soon enough. Gideon will tell us in time. We can't push him."

They had dropped their voices to a whisper then, so I scooted to the loft's edge, wanting to hear them clearly.

"I'm right about this, Sidabee. There's a good reason Gideon risked great peril to bring her here. I think you know what that is."

Sidabee stomped across the floor again. "I'm still not convinced, and until I am, don't ask me to like this arrangement. And I won't talk to her about it. She'll just lie through her teeth."

The smoke from Baylor's cigar rose to where I lay stuck on the hard pine beneath me.

"Fine. But attacking Gideon right now with a bunch of questions isn't the answer. It will only cause him to flee, taking Neeley with him. I won't do it, and neither will you."

"Baylor, *if* she's the real Neeley Morrigan, she could've led that evil man here. You know what that means to us."

My head spun in confusion. The shock of their words hit me like the stingers you get when you smack your elbow wrong. Who were these people? A nauseating wave rolled through my stomach. I wanted to rush down the steps, explain why we had run for our lives, and ask her how she knew my grandfather—but my body refused to move.

"I want to wait until after Christmas," Baylor said. "We'll keep the peace here until the holidays are over."

Sidabee snickered. "This is probably all a coincidence. For all we know, they may be con artists; Neeley Morrigan may not even be her real name. That might not even be her real hair color!"

"Sidabee! *Seriously, stop!*"

"Well, it might not. Con artists do strange things to get what they want."

"And what is it you think they want? Stop imagining the worst. Like Hotah says, the Great Spirit will uncover all truths. God will reveal it in His time." Baylor sighed as loud as I ever heard him, a sigh that floated all the way to the loft. "I'm going to bed. You?"

"Go on, I'll take Elvis out."

Somebody switched off the lamps. Forgetting about my boots or returning to the barn, I climbed into bed, mortified that Baylor and Sidabee were upset by our lies and living in their home, but also relieved nobody was reporting us to the police. I had until Christmas was over. A short time to live the life I had always wanted.

As I stared at Sidabee's framed drawings on the wall beside my bed, a slow resentment rose inside me, much like yeast bread in a hot oven. I had eagerly sought her approval, and it didn't matter a lick. She called me a con artist. A liar. My scar—how could she say that about my scar!? *Who do you think you are, Sidabee MacLennan? Miss Smarty-Pants. I'll bet nobody ever whipped you with a belt in your life. How dare you sit in judgment of me?* That's what I thought, flinging a pillow at her drawing, knocking it off-center on its nail.

Still. How did she know Pudge? She had called him evil. But all of Summerfield knew that. As far as I knew, his vile and sinful reputation might have become legendary from sea to shining sea. That fact wouldn't have surprised me in the least. The kids at school, my Sunday school teacher, and even the Klan pastor knew Pudge was evil. *Everybody* seemed to know, except for God.

Unable to stop my relentless bitterness, I soaked my pillow with fresh tears. Closing my eyes, I saw myself as a helpless baby, crawling toward my mother. The ache of missing her had often felt unbearable. I longed for her touch, her voice, and the sound of her heartbeat as I pressed my tiny baby head against her chest. Like a reopened wound, infected and bleeding, the pain of losing her never faded. There was no comfort in the world. No safe place, after all. My scar had disappeared, but my shattered heart— kept on beating.

In the days that followed, despite strange looks from Sidabee, The Sanctum greeted me with one amazement after another. I began waking early to watch the flame of sunrise over the mountains. The sight softened the sting I felt as a fugitive, escaping to a remote part of the state, far from where Pudge buried my parents. Wanting them remained constant, but Gideon took me to the Blue Ridge for a reason. A reason nobody knew or cared to speak about. Well, fine. Why should I feel guilty about the suitcase of lies we unpacked? Recalling my old, miserable self, living on the Horse's ass Farm; I felt destitute again, but only for the moment. Living on The Sanctum awakened me to something more valuable than the cattle on a thousand hills, and I wanted more of it.

Gideon and I spoke every day, but he never mentioned us moving on, and I sure as hello wasn't about to bring it up. I needed to believe he had found his place, working with Hotah. At least he smiled more than ever. As an advance on his pay, Hotah and Aiyanna bought him new clothes, a coat, and shiny brown boots—boots he spit-polished every night before bed.

For myself, it took only a litter of wolf pups to deepen my attachment to the place.

Aiyanna mentioned she didn't know any girls my age who were interested in wolves. That most folks viewed saving wolves from a hunter's gun as a dirty job—dirty, I didn't mind. They were no worse than Pudge's mules. Besides, there was no one I wanted to impress except Sidabee, and that was proving increasingly difficult.

From my loft room, I looked out at the wolves resting in their pens. Hotah had allowed me to enter Raven's pen to see her pups, but only with him standing at my side. I had hoped that I could visit her alone when the wolf knew me well enough.

As I stood by the window, Gideon's throaty laughter was unmistakable. Yet, it was the unexpected sounds of Hotah drifting into the loft that stunned me, realizing—I had never heard the man laugh.

I took the steps two at a time, heading to the kitchen to ask Aiyanna what was happening, but ran smack into Sidabee at the bottom. Her hair had fallen from its usual loose braid. A mass of springy curls toppled over her forehead and down to her shoulders. That morning, it seemed darker than usual. She had stained her jeans with mud, and the neck of her shirt gaped open—torn by a wolf in its haste to eat chicken, no doubt. Sidabee's eyes flashed with annoyance; her face appeared thinner, and her lips, usually full, appeared tight together in a straight line. "Whoa, what's the hurry?"

"Something's funny outside," I said. "Gideon and Hotah got the giggles."

She smiled halfway. "You need a bath today. Tomorrow is church. How about we tackle that after lunch?"

I frowned from the inside out. "I took a bath two days ago."

"Don't argue with me, young lady."

With her hands on my shoulders, I waited impatiently through her pause, as if she didn't know what to say next.

"By the way, do you like pink?" she asked. "I have a pink dress I can cut down for you. In fact, I'll try it on and see what you think. Baylor says it looks like a dress Lucy would wear shopping with Ethel," she said and chuckled. "But I like it, and you might, too, once I fix it to fit you."

"Sure. Fine. Thanks."

She gave me a quick nod, and I watched her walk to her bedroom. Why couldn't I possess such beauty? I was straight up and down with skinny arms and bony knees. I longed for curves like Sidabee's. Curves that drove men to the brink of insanity. Baylor rarely embraced her in front of anyone, but the few glimpses I caught warmed me in ways I had never experienced before. It didn't matter that she didn't like me; I still yearned to be her. To fall in love with a handsome young admirer, to be held—kissed even. I thought about it a lot.

Once, I'd crept down to the kitchen at midnight for a glass of water. But instead of walking through the great room, I went the other way. Through the downstairs hallway, past the row of bedrooms. Tippy-toeing past Sidabee and Baylor's door, I heard her moan. Not painfully, but quietly. A pleasant moan. I recalled the girls at school saying that some were already *doing it*— whatever that meant. I supposed they were right, though. In the animal kingdom, the pleasure of sex was only for males, but not in the human kingdom. It was for men *and* women. At least, it seemed so. Otherwise, what was the point?

Listening to Gideon laugh again, I wandered into the kitchen only to hear Aiyanna chuckling along with the men outside. She lifted her apron off a brass hook and slipped it over her head like you'd harness a mule to a tobacco wagon. I began to giggle, too—non-stop while I fixed my toast and Ovaltine. Aiyanna shot me one of her grins. Dusted in flour to her elbows, she measured cups into a dough bowl.

"Can I help?" I asked. But before Aiyanna answered, another round of laughter erupted outside the cabin. "Gosh, what's so funny?"

"Hotah prays every morning in the Cherokee tongue and smokes," she said. "This morning, Mister Jackson partook of the pipe. He's delighted your scar is gone."

"But what's so funny?"

"Weeping may endure for the night, but joy comes in the morning. The Great Spirit sent extra joy today." Aiyanna's eyes shone as if hugging an incredible secret.

"A pipe makes them laugh like that?"

Aiyanna smiled. "It's not an ordinary pipe. The Cherokee have guarded the power of that pipe for decades, fearful that others may disrespect it. Hotah felt Mister Jackson needed a rest from his sadness, so they prayed to Wakan Tanka, using the pipe in their meditation and prayer. And the joy came. The joy of the Lord," she said. "It is our strength." Aiyanna's mouth curved into an unconscious smile that time. "Your face is beautiful this morning, Little Red Bird."

"Thank you," I said, laughing and wiping crumbs from my mouth. "Thank you for making Gideon happy." I couldn't stop my giggles. "It's contagious." I carried my dishes to the sink. "Unless you need me, I'm off to see the pups."

"Don't go near those pens without one of us with you," Aiyanna said.

"I'm not afraid. The wolves know me."

Aiyanna schooled her face into a stern frown, shaking her head, her long braids swinging about her shoulders. "Tomorrow is church. You need to help set up chairs in the barn. Leave the pups alone. Stay away from the wolves."

"I won't touch them; I only want to see them. The wolves won't hurt me."

"You talk tough for only knowing them a short time, but you won't be so tough if one of those wolves hurts you."

I shrugged at Aiyanna as if she were worrying about nothing; after all, Two-Toes had licked off my scar. But deep down, I knew I was inviting trouble, except my stubbornness left no room for caution. Determined to slip in and out of Raven's pen unnoticed, I wanted Sidabee to see my bravery so I could proudly say to her—*See, I can handle myself around a wolf.*

Confident, I stepped outside. The wind picked up, shaking the windows and gutters, rolling across metal roofs, and creating a terrible racket. Patches of low-lying gray clouds threatened more bad weather. Crows perched on power lines, cawing out as if to repeat Aiyanna's warning, while a swarm of starlings darkened the sky near the barn. But I trekked across the yard, my boots squeaking against the snow. I pretended I wasn't nervous, and while Gideon and Hotah continued laughing near the cabin, I walked to Raven's pen and stared at the latch for a long moment. My fingers trembled slightly, and then I opened it.

Blackfoot stood watching from his pen. Head lowered, his shoulder blades made peaks in his spiky fur. When the pups were born, Hotah moved Blackfoot to a smaller pen beside Raven's. He had seemed standoffish around me, but Raven's acceptance made up for it. I ached to press my face into her fur, to fall over her thick neck and wrap my arms around her as she allowed me to do on two occasions with Hotah standing nearby. The wolves tasted, saw, heard, and smelled divine things I'd never know. I ached to follow her over the snow-covered hills for as long as our legs would carry us, then curl into a ball and sleep next to her and her babies.

Wearing only a light jacket over my sweater, I shivered from the cold and my nerves, and clasped my hands prayerfully across my chest. Raven stood where her two pups lay, snug inside the large plywood doghouse within the pen. A sudden streak of winter sunlight fell through the trees and shifted, shining down on Raven and her pups as if searching for and finding the only beauty worth its brilliance.

Dewy-eyed and defenseless, far from wolf-like, I took a step towards the light encircling her. And then I watched her lips curl into a snarl, baring sharp, yellowed fangs. Though she stood feet away, there was no mistaking the meaning of her growl. I stepped backward, but it was too late. She rushed at me like a blast of wind, knocking me flat on my back, my head hitting a rock and sending stars to shoot across my eyes. Blood dripped into my ear, but I didn't move. From the corner of my bloody eye, I saw Blackfoot in the other pen go berserk, howling and jumping against the wire, which must have caused Hotah and Gideon to come running. I lay frozen in the mud with Raven's front paws crushing my chest, her teeth inches from my neck, and her fierce growl warning me not to move. It was hard to breathe.

I heard Hotah. "Lay still, Little Red Bird!" Once again, nobody had to tell me that.

Aiyanna's voice shouted in the distance, "I didn't believe her. I didn't believe she'd do it!"

The wolf's hot, stinking breath covered my face like a thick blanket. I recalled Hotah's words about wolves seizing the nose or rump of their prey first, so I instinctively stayed on my back and shielded my face with my hands. After all the beatings from Pudge, believing he was out to kill me, I had never experienced the fear of death until that very moment.

I felt a rope scratch against me as someone tossed it. It landed slack on me, but quickly tightened around Raven's throat, pulling her off my body. Within seconds, Gideon scooped me up in his arms and carried me out of the pen, cradling me in the snow. In horror, I saw what I had done, as Hotah fought to keep Raven from pulling and thrashing back and forth like a fish at the end of a line.

Moments later, Sidabee appeared, racing from the cabin without her coat, stumbling through the mud as she rushed into the pen, her pink Lucy dress billowing behind her. She shouted, "Hyar! Settle!" But the wolf relentlessly fought against Hotah, swiping at his face, her heavy body jerking at the end of the rope. Sidabee screamed, "Gideon! Fetch Baylor! He's in the smokehouse!"

Gideon took off, and Aiyanna knelt beside me in the snow, her arms tight around my shoulders as I buried my face in her chest. *Sorry* wasn't a big enough word for my shame. I needed to invent another word for the overwhelming regret seeping from my pores. I had pretended to know about wolves but, in truth, I knew nothing at all.

When Baylor arrived, he pulled a needle from his coat pocket, like the doctor used on me when I was eight and battling whooping cough. Hotah had finally locked the wolf inside his powerful legs as Sidabee threw a burlap bag over Raven's head. Baylor quickly injected the wolf with something that put her to sleep, or at least that's what it looked like; that Raven had passed out from the drug.

Sidabee tugged on the rope looped around Raven's neck. The Lucy dress she had put on for me was soaked in blood, ripped and torn open on the bodice and skirt. When Baylor finally cut away the rope, the only sounds were my sobs, Aiyanna's wailing, and Hotah collapsing to his knees like a big bull in the mud.

Gideon squeezed my arms, turning me to him. "Let me look at your head." He pulled up my hair. "You be all right, you jus' shaken. That's a tiny cut, a goose-egg bump. You be fine, tho'. You be fine," he said, hugging me to his chest as I never remembered him doing. Ever.

Sidabee staggered over to where I sat hunched in the snow. Glaring at me with red eyes, she screamed hurtful words. Pudge's words. "You stupid fool! What have we told you, time and time again!? Stay away from the wolves! Why did you come here!?"

"*Sidabee!*" Baylor yelled.

I shuddered.

Her eyes smoldered with rage and fire. Turning sharply, she bolted back to the cabin.

Aiyanna moved fast inside the pen to help Hotah and Baylor move the wolf to the barn.

Gideon raised my chin with his hand. "Look up." An eagle screamed over our heads. I'd not get a whipping for what I did, but I deserved one. The eagle agreed.

"You knew better," Gideon said. "You was tole not to go near the wolves alone."

"I only—I only wanted to see—to see the pups," I sobbed.

Aiyanna stumbled toward me with the bloody rope in her hands. She stopped to gaze up at the majestic bird flying overhead, and as if part of a ceremonial ritual, she brought her head back down and chanted something in her language I didn't understand. Maintaining eye contact with the totem pole at the other end of the yard, Aiyanna spoke words that would haunt me for the rest of my days. "She was still weak from giving birth. Now—she is dead."

My world spiraled down a tunnel and went black.

CHAPTER TWENTY-ONE

The Joy of the Lord Day was short-lived as I awoke to find my filthy and wretched self lying on a braided rug in the screened-in room. Gideon sat by my side, lightly wiping blood and dried mud off my face with a cool cloth. "You fainted. How you feeling?" he asked.

I couldn't find the words to respond.

"They gone bury that wolf. Miz Sidabee thinks you should be there. You hungry?"

"No." The notion of food sickened me. I couldn't believe I had fainted dead away. I was stupid and foolish; Sidabee was right. I had been utterly useless to The Sanctum. All I wanted was to disappear into a corner where no one would notice me, to evaporate into the cold air. But instead, I forced myself to sit up and sip the hot tea that Aiyanna had brought out to me.

I couldn't face anyone until that afternoon, when I reluctantly shoved my arms into my coat and followed a silent Hotah to the shed by the totem pole. We gathered shovels and picks before returning to the barn, where he had placed the wolf in a wheelbarrow. I followed Hotah as he rolled it down a path toward a small cemetery.

A place where there was no earthly reason to build a painted stone wall, one crumbled and peeled near a clearing. Just beyond the wall, the graves of the MacLennan family members rested together, along with three nameless crosses beneath a line of poplar and maple trees. Beyond that, large rocks marked the graves of wolves that had died on The Sanctum.

Hotah handed me a shovel, and together, we dug a hole. The partially frozen ground made the digging difficult as sweat and tears tracked through the dirt on my face, but I didn't care. I kept digging as if my life depended on it.

Hotah had carefully wrapped Raven in burlap. After gently placing her in the shallow grave, he chanted loudly, in a way I had never heard before. It was a prayer, I believed, for the soul of the wolf, weaving together sorrowful words, cries, and songs. The intensity of his prayer branded itself into my memory. Though I wanted to cover my ears, I stood there, consumed by grief. Raven had circled me when we first met, and I had assumed the grief circle was because of *my* past, what *I* had lived through, not for what was to come. But somehow, Hotah had known. His boulder-like face and piercing eyes met mine once he had finished his prayers.

"I'm truly sorry," I whispered.

"You will bottle-feed those pups," he said. "You alone will care for them until they are old enough to eat meat."

"Yes, of course."

Hotah placed his massive hand on top of my head. "A hard lesson, huh, Little Red Bird?"

I nodded. Together, we walked back to the cabin on a path previously marked by a wolf. Its tracks, each one the size of a coffee saucer, appeared fresh. I couldn't make myself look at them. In my misery, I fixated instead on the evergreen needles, fallen twigs, and pinecones scattered across the snow-covered ground.

The day passed in a blur, my mind a void, much like the TV screen at midnight when the announcer signs off and the National Anthem plays. I retreated into myself, seeking refuge in the silence. By evening, I realized I had missed both lunch and supper, having spent hours perched on a log pile outside the kitchen door, lost in my thoughts.

A colossal, blotchy moon rose through the fringe of trees on the ridgeline like another searchlight looking for something in the pastures. It fascinated me that people gazed at that same moon hundreds of years before. Brittle stars lit the night sky in a tapestry flung across the heavens, illuminating the yard so brightly that I could've easily read a book or walked without fear of stumbling into a hole. I yearned for a future as clear as that night sky.

"Folks tend to bury the shame in their heads, often searching for ways to survive the best they can."

I turned to see Baylor sitting on a log behind me, leaning back, lacing his hands behind his head, his fingers in his wavy hair, his coat open to the December chill. Cold never seemed to bother him. I froze constantly, as if living in an endless winter. But I didn't feel the need to agree with him out loud. His words rang true enough.

"How are you?" he asked. "You doing okay?"

"All right, I reckon."

The silence between us didn't last long. "I love this time of day," he said. "Just after the sun goes down, it's so forgiving, so merciful. Yes, I believe it's where the heart finds peace."

I sat staring at the darkening sky, spotting constellations like a connect-the-dots picture. All the stars appeared pluckable—like the dew-glazed berries I picked every spring. I didn't move from my spot on the log pile; instead, I surrendered to it and made a Jiminy Cricket wish. I picked out a star and wished I could stop time—to go no further than that moment. The undeniable fact was that I alone killed the wolf as I had killed my parents. I didn't want to make any more foolish mistakes, and what better way than to stop the clock?

"Would you stop time if you could?" I asked.

"Well, now. That's an interesting question." Baylor thought for a moment. "I'm afraid I enjoy the passing of time. Sooner or later, winter always comes to these mountains and stays a while, as does spring, summer, fall, and winter again. Living on The Sanctum, I have no desire to deny the fact that the cycle of seasons is the definition of time passing; even though each season's death brings me closer to my own. The world's need to stop time or turn back the clock seems foolish. Up here, where every day is new, I can't imagine choosing to forego tomorrow. Growing older is a small price for a front-row seat here on this mountain. It's never the same performance twice," he said. "But, I suppose in the dull routine of a manmade world, time becomes a punishment, an enemy to be outfoxed, conquered—denied."

"Lordy. You sure sound like a lawyer."

Baylor laughed. "Yeah, Sidabee says I talk too much."

"Can I ask you another question?"

"Sure. Shoot."

"Why don't you and Sidabee have any kids?"

After a deep sigh, a look of tired sadness passed over his face. Baylor's straw-like hair shone in the moonlight, and his silky voice had grown tender when he finally spoke. "We'd love to have children." He paused a moment. "Sidabee and I have lost three babies. Miscarriages."

"I'm sorry." Although I wasn't exactly sure what a miscarriage was, I wasn't about to ask. Once again, I'd stuck a nasty foot in my big mouth. "Is that what those crosses are, out by that wall?"

"Yes." Baylor smiled. "I see you notice things around here."

"Do you believe in Heaven?" I asked.

"I do. How about you?"

"Gideon says the Apostle Peter will greet us at the Pearly Gates."

"Really? Pearly Gates, huh?"

"He says we'll cross over the River of Life, walk on streets of gold, and sing the Hallelujah Chorus with the angels."

"Sounds like Gideon raised you right."

"Yeah." I leaned back and rested my elbows on another log, thinking that perhaps I didn't possess the faith I thought I did. I had always felt suspicious of God. Staring at the stars again, I said something that I had never said aloud—something no *saved* person *could* say: "I'm not sure I believe in God."

Baylor sighed deep and long. "Well." He leaned forward and placed his hand on my shoulder. "It's okay, Neeley. I'm sure He definitely believes in you."

Neither of us spoke after that.

The kitchen door opened, and Gideon walked outside. "I gots a little feller here, says he's hungry." I stood, wiped my hands on my pants, and reached for the wolf pup Gideon handed me. Its tiny grunts and growls broke my heart. The weight of his mother's knobby paws left a burning imprint on my chest, adding to the guilt. My face grew warm. He nuzzled my cheek with his fur still smelling of wood shavings.

"Where's his sister?" I asked.

"Hotah has her inside. He gots the bottles ready," Gideon chuckled. "Mercy me, look at that pup. He 'bout as big as a salt lick after a couple-a deer get through with it."

Baylor stood and rubbed the wolf pup's ears. "I almost forgot. Neeley, as soon as you feed those pups and put them to bed, Sidabee wants you to bathe."

I hadn't washed off the mud since earlier that day and after what happened, I sure as hello didn't want to go to church the next morning. The dirt on my inside matched the dirt on my outside. Clearly, God had written my backslidden condition on my heart, and it would no doubt be obvious to the barn church members.

"Baylor!" Aiyanna's voice called out from the kitchen. "Bring in some wood for the fire."

"Excuse me, folks, duty calls." Baylor walked back inside, lugging two mammoth logs under his long arms.

Gideon turned to me, looking like a bird dog on point. "Hoowee. I'll tell you what. You smell like wet wool. I raised you to be clean, not stink like an outhouse. You'd think a thirteen-year-old girl'd be smart enough to remember to take a bath."

I smiled, cuddling the pup to my chin. "The cleanliness next to godliness thing, again?"

"I s'pose you'd never take a bath, lessen I tell ya."

"I hate baths on cold nights. My hair freezes."

Gideon shook his head at me like he always did when I was being hardheaded. "Water's nice 'n hot here. Might even want to take a scrub brush to your soul a bit. I heard what you said to Mistah Baylor. Law, girl, I raised you better 'n that. You not lost as some ol' goose in a snowstorm. You saved and sanctified holy. Washed in the blood. Baptized in the river when you was jus' a bitty thing." He sighed. "Maybe time to renew, tho'. Get clean, inside and out. I want you gussied up for church. Wear that hat you brought. It makes your eyes shine. We be sitting together in church first time ever. You make me proud, now, hear? These people, they loves you already."

"Sidabee doesn't."

"Now, Miz Sidabee, she gots her problems. You be patient with her. I 'spect she come 'round soon enough. Go on now. Feed them pups, Momma Wolf, then get in the tub."

After feeding, burping, and cuddling the baby wolves, I headed to the bathhouse, a sizeable steam-filled room behind the kitchen where Sidabee and Aiyanna washed and hung laundry in winter. A huge metal tub with feet like an eagle sat on a sparkling, clean concrete floor. Aiyanna had filled the tub from its copper faucets and left me alone.

First, I checked my scarless forehead. Looking into a mirror for more than a few seconds was a new experience. Next, I peeled off my dirty clothes, and in one quick leap, I lowered my bare-naked self into the steaming water. "It's too hot," I said.

Walking back into the bathhouse, Aiyanna overheard my bellyaching. "We'll have *you* for supper tomorrow," she giggled. Placing a folded towel, washcloth, and shampoo bottle on a nearby chair, she moved to the back of the tub as I grabbed the washcloth, not sure whether to put it over my *down there* part or my budding breasts. Even though the soap bubbles and water covered me, I wasn't used to exposing my blush of womanhood. I liked my privacy.

But Aiyanna paid me no mind. The creases at the edge of her eyes grew deeper, smiling and ignoring my discomfort. I loved the softness of her, the delicate ripple of her muscles when she moved, and even the tender way she poured cold shampoo onto my head. The hair on her neck looked silky soft, like a baby chick. When she dug her fingernails into my scalp, I figured she meant serious business, so I shut my eyes tight, hoping she'd avoid the new goose-egg bump.

I shivered. "Feels good."

"Don't forget to clean your ears and between your toes when I'm done."

"Yes, ma'am."

It felt strange having someone fuss over me. "Let me wash your neck and back," Aiyanna said. I leaned forward, pulling my knees up to my chest. "You have anything—" her voice broke off in mid-sentence. I heard her quick intake of breath, and her arms stiffened. She stopped scrubbing and got quiet. Then she started talking again. "You have anything pretty to wear tomorrow?"

"Sidabee planned to fix her pink dress to fit me, but I don't think so now."

"I have a dress for you. My daughter, Blossom, she's about your size. I'll lay it on your bed."

I traced tracks of water drops down the side of the tub with my fingers, batted at the bubbles, and then lathered my face. "Rather wear pants," I mumbled through soapy lips. For years, I'd not allowed anyone see the welts and bruises on my legs, which I believed Aiyanna couldn't possibly see under all the soap suds.

"Nothing wrong with a girl looking like a girl."

I splashed water on my face. "Who says you must wear a dress to look like a girl?"

Aiyanna sighed and wrung out the washcloth. "I have a granddaughter, Sara. She, too, refuses to wear a dress."

"Sidabee said you have grandchildren."

"Two. You'll meet Jesse and Sara at church tomorrow. Now, you look wringer-washed and ready to hang out with the sheets. You can finish without me, yes?"

I nodded.

Washing and rinsing with my usual lack of grace, I splashed more water on my face, landing droplets on the floor. Then, with my big toe blocking the spigot, I soaked away the grime and some clinging guilt. When my fingers wrinkled like raisins, I pulled the tub's stopper and stood to towel off, careful to dab at my backside wounds, still healing. After grabbing a robe and wrapping my wet hair in a blue towel, I sniffed the air, smelling the aroma of fresh-baked cookies drifting through the cabin.

Rushing to the loft stairs, I didn't get far. Sidabee's voice echoed from her room. "Neeley, I laid a pair of my pajamas on your bed. If you want, I'll comb out your hair."

Her attempt at kindness surprised me. But the memory of my mother's words broke through a time barrier, touching my face, caressing my heart. I had forgotten the sound of her voice until that moment.

Neeley, come let me comb out your hair. To hold back the tears, I walked up the steps to my loft bed with my eyes shut.

Outside the door to Sidabee's bedroom, Aiyanna stood guard, waiting for me. She took hold of my arm and pulled me away. "She'll join us later. Let's go sit by the fire."

"But—she said she would comb out my hair. Is she still angry with me?"

"Sidabee needs a few moments. Come."

I didn't understand. Sidabee confused me, but it wasn't the first time.

My hair, a wild tangle of curls, fell in cold strands down my back over flannel pajamas that hung loose and baggy but soft and warm against my skin. Aiyanna tossed her graying braid across her shoulder and took her usual chair beside the fire. She held tight to a dog-eared photo. Her eyes reflected not only the firelight, but a sadness I couldn't quite grasp. I pulled my legs up in the chair beside her, watching her rub her fingers across the glossy snapshot. It was old, the edges curled, and a deep crease ran down the middle. I didn't ask about the photo, which appeared to be of two small children. Gideon had often said it was rude to pester people with personal questions. They need to stay—personal. It seemed to be one of those times.

I had so much to learn about this family of Indians, wolves, and Scottish Baptists who had buried three babies in their backyard.

Baylor walked in with the wolves. They trotted to us, turning their short, rounded ears and asking silent questions with their small, intelligent eyes. Two-Toes and Elvis plopped on the floor by Hotah, who had sat to my left. Gideon shuffled in, carrying a tray of mugs, a pot of coffee, and freshly-baked ginger cookies. He no longer cowered in his room when the wolves sat in the great room but he still kept his distance. Sitting there, we were a unique blend—strange-looking, but the makings of a family in my mind.

The sweetness of our voices mingling near the fire sent an odd, heady sensation through me. I leaned back and closed my eyes, thinking about the Hollis House, the antebellum mansion turned old folks' home we had driven past earlier that week. Recalling the shadowy image of the woman in the odd clothes gathering roses out of the garden, I sat forward in my chair as pinpricks invaded the back of my neck. "Roses don't grow in winter."

"What?" Gideon didn't appear surprised I'd been talking to myself.

"Hotah," I said, "is there more to tell about the Hollis House?"

Hotah placed his mug and saucer on the table by his chair and raised his brow, glancing at Aiyanna. "There is."

Aiyanna nodded, and Hotah began. "Mister Buchanan began his effort to turn Bakersville into a tourist trap several years ago. He and his Baptist Historical Society screwed a brass plaque into the front door of the Hollis House, declaring it a historic site. The plaque reads, built in 1836 by Major Gerald Hollis for his bride, Cora. Back then, the military used the house as a checkpoint. A gathering place for militia, designated by the government, to move the Cherokee to a reservation. The Trail of Tears."

Watching Hotah tell his Hollis House story was like watching The Ten Commandments movie. I couldn't take my eyes off him.

"I have it on good authority," he said, "that Cora Hollis grew deep-red roses by the front gate." That's when I shivered so hard that Gideon handed me a blanket to wrap around my shoulders. "She could prick her finger on a thorn and foretell a pregnancy by how her blood fell on the ground. Upon laying a hand over a sick man's heart, she saw the hour of his death. Cora Hollis predicted fires, floods, and blizzards, and a month before soldiers marched across the Tennessee state line to remove the Cherokee from their homes, she told the Major that liquor would kill him right soon if he did not stop drinking and did he want her to raise their child alone?"

I needed clarification. "Cora was going to have a baby?"

"Yes, Little Red Bird. Cora was with child as her husband prepared to leave. But the Major, a man more in love with his whiskey than his woman, did not heed his wife's forewarning. Instead, Major Hollis mounted his horse and laughed at his fussy wife. 'You can entertain the world with your fortune-telling,' he said, 'but I have grown weary of it.'"

"One night, Cora awoke out of a sound sleep. She did not know it, but the Major had drunkenly walked through the soldier's camp, wearing nothing but a feather in his hair. His lieutenant mistook him for a Cherokee and shot him in the heart. Cora had heard the shot from that small caliber gun in her sleep."

"Cora lost her husband on the 'journey to relocate savages,' as he had called it. I have often lamented Major Hollis did not suffer instead by my own hands. Major Hollis broke the Cherokee circle of life. For that, he left no legacy, nothing to prove he existed but this story, an old house, and a grave of bones. After the Major's death, Cora refused to wear black and spilled no tears for her husband. Instead, she commissioned his headstone to read *Gerald Hollis, God have mercy on your soul.* Eight small words."

"But nobody knew until she confessed it on her deathbed that her mother was a Negro. So, they buried her in the slave cemetery behind the Hollis house instead of beside her husband. I think she preferred it, anyway. Her spirit lingers over her grave like a lover's perfume. I have smelled it."

"You see, Little Red Bird, Cora was the mother of Abigail and the grandmother of Olivia. Olivia married a Cherokee Chief. They had a son and called him Howling Wolf. Major Hollis, who led us away on the Trail of Tears, was the direct ancestor of a man who led many of us back again—Howling Wolf. Howling Wolf was my father. He closed the circle. Today, the folks in Bakersville and those living inside the Hollis House deny that the Trail of Tears still flows through the plumbing during thunderstorms. It drips from the faucets and downspouts—in blood. Blood-red tears."

"Is that true?" I shouted, trying to swallow my cookie without choking.

Gideon's hands held tight to the arms of his chair. "Hotah, that true?" he repeated.

Sidabee walked in with a hairbrush in her hand. "Telling stories again, Hotah?"

"Ah, The Hollis House story," he nodded.

"My favorite," she said and smiled.

Sidabee motioned for me to sit in front of her. I closed my eyes and let her pull and jerk the hairbrush through my tangles. My head swayed back and forth as she worked through it. We relaxed by the crackling fire, drinking coffee to help shut out the bitter cold. Gideon chuckled at himself for believing Hotah's *wild stories*, as he called them. Somehow, I didn't think they were so wild.

Gideon then wiped his mouth with a napkin. "Cora reminds me-a my great ancestor, Eufah. A story my momma tole me when I was long 'bout ten years old."

"Tell us," said Hotah.

Gideon sipped his coffee, winking first at me. "Seems Eufah was a slave for a Virginia plantation owner—man named Henry. Henry Lee. Large tobacco plantation. Momma said Eufah had the gift. That she could dip her hand in well water and tell when the first snow come. Henry Lee used her gift to prepare for drought, hurricanes, blight, and whatnot. With Eufah being the plantation midwife, she could lay her ear on a woman's belly and tell if the chile' be a boy or a girl."

"But one day, as her ear pressed on the belly-a Miz Anne, the plantation owner's wife, the good Lawd spoke, telling Eufah the boy chile' in Miz Anne was destined to command an army who'd fight to continue slavery for future generations. Eufah delivered the baby on a cold January day in 1807. Henry named his baby boy Robert. Robert E. Lee."

"Soon afterward, Eufah was whupped for a clothesline full-a bed sheets what fell into the snow. The family sold her to a plantation near Biloxi, where slaves went to die. Harsh times. God came to Eufah in a dream and tole her to take her own chile' to freedom, not to go to Biloxi. So, she up an' lef' in the middle-a the night with her chile' and her faith. Eufah fed special herbs to her baby to keep it quiet as she crept through the woods with the hounds at her feet. She hid in cold, dark caves along the way, trusting folks who could've turned her in."

Gideon stopped and sighed. The quiet room flickered in the firelight. "But Eufah, she heard the voice-a the Lawd again, guiding her north, saying, *He make a way where there be no way*. Momma tole me Eufah worked with the Underground Railroad 'til her death. Anyway, that's how I remember the story, and my momma saying, 'He will make a way where there be no way.'" Gideon stared into the fire, the flames reflecting in his eyes.

Hotah laid his massive hand on Gideon's shoulder. "We're not so different, Gideon, you and I. Our people walked different paths, but their suffering is much the same."

It felt strange that Gideon had never told me the story. I figured it was more of a painful memory to him than a story.

The Christmas tree lights twinkled, reminding me of the stars I admired as I sat on the woodpile only an hour before. I thought about Christmas then and that I should ask someone to take me to town to do a little shopping and make a few new memories for Hotah and Gideon—good ones. This strange and wonderful family deserved a happy Christmas. The holidays had never excited me, not until that evening.

Suddenly, Baylor glanced up. We all heard the soft scratching at the door. "Just the wind," I said, not wanting to leave our warm fire to let in an icy blast.

Baylor stood. I didn't like the seriousness of his face. "Somebody's out there." His long legs carried him to the front door in three seconds flat. Pulling it open, he then stuck his head outside, peering through the darkness with the moon still bright in the sky. "Who's there?" Nothing answered but the wind, its icy fingers rushing inside to brush against our skin, its whoosh of air so sharp and frigid I saw it snatch his breath away. I wrapped a blanket tight around my body. Baylor called out again. Shaking his head, he stepped back into the room to shut out the cold fast seeping through my pajamas when we heard it again, the sound echoing through the silent night.

Sidabee dashed to the door. "Baylor, there's something out there."

"It's nothing," he said, confused. But he turned and opened the door again. Taking a deep breath, he shouted. "Hello-o-o?

Anybody out there?" He stepped forward. "A wolf! Hurry, come see." All of us at once rushed to the front porch.

A single wolf appeared on a small hill, not fifty feet away, the moon illuminating its shape.

"Raven," Hotah declared. "She has come to bid us farewell."

How Hotah knew that remains a mystery to me. But I had learned Hotah and Aiyanna only spoke the truth. I will always remember the breathtaking sight of Raven, pacing back and forth in the moonlight, as I stood motionless, asking her forgiveness for what I had done. It was only when I saw Baylor salute her that I felt Gideon's hands on my shoulders.

I lost sight of the wolf as she sprinted across the snow, disappearing into the trees. Hotah ambled out into the yard, singing and chanting his peculiar songs. Aiyanna's body swayed fluidly, in time with her husband's chant. In the gentle light from the cabin, I noticed tears filling Sidabee's eyes, and I asked her, "What is Hotah doing?"

"He's wishing her a good death," she said without so much as a glance my way.

When you see me loyal to my family, then you see the wolf.
~ Robin Hobb

CHAPTER TWENTY-TWO

From my loft room on Sunday morning, I gazed outside at six-foot drifts crafted into sharp-edged snow cliffs, hanging over the road that followed the fence line like a grosgrain ribbon. In some places, the snow created a lip deep enough to stand beneath, like a cave.

I tried putting my mind in a snow cave. I had grown weary from overthinking—not sleeping through the night, resulting in headaches throughout the day. Restless, I couldn't watch two minutes of *Queen for a Day* when ordinarily every woman's pathetic story glued me to the TV like a bear's paw on a honeycomb. I'd lost my appetite, poking around in my plate until the food was cold. Truth be told, I wanted to bulldoze through Sidabee's moody behavior—ask her how they knew my grandfather. But the fear of knowing the truth stopped me. I wanted to know, but then I didn't. My head was in a spin about it. And I was afraid if Gideon discovered they knew Pudge, he'd hightail it off The Sanctum first chance, taking me with him.

I sat to my favorite breakfast of glazed donuts fried in a cast-iron skillet. Aiyanna asked me to set up a few more chairs for Sunday service, which I barely heard. I yawned, nodded, and nibbled at a donut before handing Gideon an extra napkin, which he tucked into his collar to keep the crumbs off his new Sunday shirt.

Gideon laid his fork on his plate. "We been eating at the same table for days. Sho' do feel good. We should go to church this morning with a thankful heart."

At the mention of the word *church*, I yawned again, propping my elbows on the table in a decidedly unladylike way, dropping my chin into my hands, and half-closing my eyes, mumbling through the first few lines of my favorite song—"*. . . great balls of fire!*"

Gideon gave me a *stop-that-or-else* look. "C'mon now. No need to sing that honky tonk song, 'specially on a Sunday morning. You afraid?"

I shrugged.

"I gots a feeling this be a different kind-a church. It's not what we used to, but you might like it." Gideon edged his chair a little closer to the kitchen fire. "You do as Miz Aiyanna say do. Head on out to the shed by that totem pole, gather a few extra chairs. Do it after you eat; it'll wake you up."

"You still want me to wear my hat?"

He swallowed the last of his coffee. "Sho' do."

I rested my head in the crook of my arm. The journey to freedom had left me exhausted.

I buttoned my coat to my neck and shoved my gloved hands into my pockets, thinking what a winter wimp I was. Although the snow looked as hard as a rock, it crumbled at the slightest touch. It curved into crevasses to my hip and thighs and puddled near the trees like whipped egg whites in a pottery crock. Strolling past a row of tall pines leading to the shed, I had no desire for Sunday school. Good Lord. I had church every dang day. Why'd I need more of it?

Aiyanna dished out scripture each morning, along with breakfast. Hotah prayed, chanted, or smoked his spirit pipe nearly all the time. And Gideon had sung more hymns the last few days than I'd heard in my entire thirteen years. *Blessed assurance, Jesus is mine, oh what a foretaste of glory divine. I once was lost, but now I'm found, was blind, but now I see!* "Geesh!"

As I passed the totem pole, a light fog rolled in. A pale young girl with long black braids shivered in snow that blanketed the ground where she stood, her body barely visible against the shed's newly unpeeled log walls. Once painted white, the shed appeared brown and wooly, more like a giant groundhog squatting in a field than a building. I had been inside the shed before, following Hotah through the metal door to gather shovels the day we buried the wolf. But someone had changed the door into deerskin, pulled and tied around a stick frame, a change that sent a shiver down my spine.

At first, I thought the girl might be Aiyanna's granddaughter, arriving early for church. Her clothes looked like the Thanksgiving Day costumes my eighth-grade class made for our play. Wearing a long leather dress and strange-looking boots, she clung to a bearskin draped over her shoulders, much like the one hanging over the loft railing in the cabin. Straddling a rough and woody tree root poking up through the snow, I hoped not to startle her, but I needed to see her up close. "Are you here for church?" I asked, approaching her. But that was when she faded as if disappearing behind a muslin veil. Only her footprints remained in the snow—the silent proof of her. Panic and questions swirled around my head, making me dizzy and weak in the knees, and I grabbed hold of a nearby tree to steady myself. Somehow, I managed to stumble back past the now metal shed to the plowed drive.

As if waking from a dream, I heard Baylor and Hotah call out to one another. Their voices drew me back to the cabin like church bells. My heart beat faster than my legs could carry me, and I felt watched, but not by living eyes. In five minutes my legs got me back to the cabin, when normally, a morning stroll to the shed took the better part of twenty—odd how that works. It wouldn't have surprised me to discover the entire mountain was crawling with Cherokee ghosts. Feeling like a sweaty mess stepping inside the great room, I had seen enough strange events in the past few weeks to last me a lifetime, but this was plain creepy.

My Easter hat didn't exactly match my Donna Reed coat, but it was close enough. Pulling on the lined wool dress that Aiyanna gave me, I was thankful when it fell to my ankles. It wasn't a poodle skirt with pom-poms, but I liked the white eyelet collar and the rope belt with beads at the end—and that it covered my legs. As it turned out, I didn't have to worry about my worn-out shoes because Sidabee had polished a spare pair of her leather boots and laid them in the loft with a note. *I think we're the same size. You can have these.* I felt the warmth of her feet inside them. A beautiful deep red color, the boots fit perfectly.

Aiyanna met me at the bottom step and gently took hold of my arm above the elbow, leading me toward a mirror in a way that made me feel loved and girlie. After removing my hat, she brushed back my hair, skillfully braided it, and tied a red-velvet ribbon at the end. With her hands on my shoulders, she adjusted my posture, tugged at my dress, removed a few stray hairs, and altered my too-long sleeves without uttering a word. Standing in front of me, Aiyanna replaced my hat. "You look as pretty as—" She paused and cleared her throat. "Is something bothering you, Little Red Bird?"

I shrugged. "I didn't get the chairs like you asked. I saw something this morning. Out by the shed."

"What did you see?"

"Nobody would believe me."

She smiled one of her slow, knowing smiles. "The snow reveals many secrets near the totem pole—but only to the pure in heart." Her breathing grew quiet behind her smile. "Every now and again—" She stopped, then dropped her voice to a whisper. "Every now and again, God pulls back the curtain of time, allowing us to see the past or the future. Do not alarm yourself, Little Red Bird. If the ancestors are reaching out to you, it is only for your protection." Aiyanna turned me toward the door and lightly tapped my backside. "Go feed your soul this morning. Collin will gather more chairs if we need them."

Shoulders back, spine straight, I marched toward the barn church, thinking about what Aiyanna said, hoping I wasn't losing my mind. I didn't understand why I couldn't have grown up normal—sitting on the front porch with girlfriends, drinking one ice-cold Coca-Cola after another, and dancing all night to Buddy Holly records until the mosquitoes drove us indoors. I wished my problems were no more serious than overdue library books, pimples on my nose, or an empty box of Kotex.

Baylor leaned against the barn, talking to a bald man wearing one rimless spectacle on his large eye. The man's jowls worked to and fro as he shouted his words with a chuckle deep in his throat. "When you gonna let me haul that truck of your daddy's to my landfill? It's an eyesore out by those pens, Baylor."

"Virgil, I can't move my father's truck off The Sanctum. He'd roll over in his grave."

When I strode up to Baylor, he appeared in shock at the new, cleaned-up me. "Virgil, this is the pretty young lady I told you about. She's come to stay with us for a while. This is Neeley. Neeley, this is Doctor Shelton."

A wide, solid stump of a man, the doctor wore a three-piece brown suit and a paisley tie. His good eye twinkled when he talked. "Neeley, what a beautiful name."

"Thank you. Nice to meet you."

Baylor grinned. "Doctor Shelton is our local doctor. He's de-livered most every baby around these parts for twenty-five years."

I smiled, wondering if Doctor Shelton had delivered Sidabee's dead babies. In that case, maybe he wasn't much of a doctor.

"Do you know what you want to be when you grow up, Neeley?" he asked, lifting one white, spiking eyebrow.

It was the first time anyone had asked me that question. "No. I'm afraid I don't."

He flapped his Bible beneath his armpit. "I do believe you have time to sort that out. Doesn't she, Baylor?"

While I lingered near the door, hesitant to go inside to my first barn church service, Doctor Shelton's conversation with Baylor, who couldn't get a word in edge-wise, drew me in like flies to cake crumbs.

"Well, hell, Baylor, you should've seen 'em. Them pretty-boy bankers and developers rushed up here last week like baby pigs fighting over the same tit, a bunch of low-lifes in new clothes, offering me a right-smart amount of money for my land, each one outbidding the other. Liars, every one of 'em. Improving the land, bah!"

Baylor only nodded and agreed. The good doctor barely took a breath. "They weren't so amiable when I fired my rifle at their feet. Sounded like squawkin' chickens, flying back down the road." Doctor Shelton's belly shook like Jell-O when he laughed.

"From the git-go, all those low-lifes wanted was to turn the mountains around Bakersville into another theme park! Lord knows it happened to them poor folks over in Asheville and Boone and before that in Nashville and Gatlinburg. Developers robbing people of their land just to build hotels and swimming pools—who got all the profit? Sure wasn't the Indians. The only red faces you see now in those fancy resort towns are those getting their pictures taken with tourists and selling trinkets on street corners. On their own dad-gum property!"

It surprised me when Baylor managed to slip in a few words. "I agree, Virgil."

"Well," the doctor said in a huff. "Ain't gonna happen here. No, sir. Don't matter how much them boys offer me for it. My mountain is not for sale. Especially to a bigot like Buchanan. Not my fault the man lives in town on a skimpy ribbon of real estate."

I decided I liked Doctor Shelton. I liked him a lot.

Stepping inside the barn, I walked to where I saw Gideon stacking wood outside on the other side of the barn. Flames shot from a nearby fire pit into the air, and I almost choked on the thick smoke. In the distant field, a line of straight bare trees in heaps of gray-crusted snow appeared as Indians walking toward the fire. I blinked and shook my head vigorously, desperate to avoid seeing more ghosts. Flakes of ash from the fire danced in the morning mist like gnats, but I stood close to the door where the aroma of sage, heavy and sweet, filled the barn.

Church folk trickled in, their noses red and eyes watery from the cold. Bits of conversation sprung up here and there. Yearning for Sunday to end, I longed to shed my church clothes, the trappings of religious conviction, and return to the comfort of drawing the afternoon away.

Three elderly Negro women in matching fancy hats, covered in ribbons and all sorts of doodads, strolled up to Baylor and Doctor Shelton, shook their hands, then glided over to me.

"I'm Hadassa, and these are my sistahs, Jule and Robeena. We live over that ridge a piece. Love your hat, chile'."

"Thank you, ma'am. I'm Neeley."

Miss Jule leaned in and raised her eyebrows. "What'd you say, honey?"

"You got to excuse my sistah, she deaf." Miss Hadassa turned to her sister and shouted, "She said she's Neeley!"

Miss Jule smiled and said, "Oh, honey, you is. You is skinny. Skinny as a bean pole."

But Miss Robeena made me giggle, the way she eyed Gideon up and down like he was suddenly the catch of the county. "Who that man?" she asked and pointed.

"Gideon. He's my friend." I blew out an exasperated breath, admiring their plastic clip-on earrings that had pulled their taffy-like earlobes out of shape. Earrings that matched their lipstick and circles of rouge on their bark-brown cheeks. Once we had made our acquaintance, they moved in Gideon's direction. I smiled, thinking attraction to a man hits a woman at any age.

A few feet to my right, a young woman with a ponytail the color of bottled honey sat on a straw bale stacked against the wall. She wore a long skirt and boots and had nursing mother breasts—I knew that because one leaked through her blouse.

The baby she held made sucking motions with its mouth. I figured that was normal. I mean, what else do babies do other than eat and poop? Eyes scrunched tight, the infant's squeaky noises absorbed me. Wrapped in a quilt, it was a living, breathing miracle. Fresh and sweet as a basket of clean sheets in a barn that smelled nothing like a nursery, the baby stirred and shoved its fist into its mouth. Wavy hair clung to its small head, black, unlike its mother. The woman snuggled her infant, lifting the tiny face up to her own, kissing its soft, round cheek.

Prickles shot down my arms. Having no control over my feet, I stepped closer and touched its incredibly small hand. The baby gripped my finger and hung on, and I marveled how those tiny hands might one day write a poem, play the piano, or drive to California.

"Do you like babies?" asked the woman.

"I do," I said, studying the wee face.

Sidabee strode up behind me in a slim wool coat over a linen dress that buttoned up the front; I had seen her meticulously ironing it earlier. "Neeley, this is my friend Lydia. Collin O'Donnell's wife. You met Collin in town at the hardware store."

"Oh. Nice to meet you and—"

"—This little guy is William," Lydia said. "My pleasure meeting *you*, Neeley. Sidabee, how are you?"

I had no place amidst their baby conversation. I turned to see a girl about my age with dark, chin-length hair and seemingly unmanageable bangs that fell into her eyes. She sure didn't dress up for church. She had rolled up her jeans at the bottom, and her white socks fell over her penny loafers. A plaid flannel shirt did a poor job covering her wrinkled white T-shirt, and she had unbuttoned her heavy wool coat. But the charm bracelet around her wrist jingled as she moved.

"I'm Sara," she said. "Hotah is my grandfather."

"I'm Neeley."

"You ever attend church in a barn before?"

"No. First time."

"It's not so bad, really. We'll have church in the barn, then pass the feather by the fire."

"Pass the feather?"

Brushing wisps of hair from her cheeks, Sara giggled. "You'll see. Church is best in summer. I freeze out here in the winter. I think you've already met Doc Shelton. Over there's Eleanor, Doc Shelton's wife." She nodded toward a tall, big-boned, seventyish woman in a long tweed coat, old lady shoes, curly silver hair, and a hat that matched her coat. The woman stood in the center of the room, smiling and chatting with another woman.

"Come meet my mother," Sara said, walking over to join them, so I followed.

The lady called Eleanor, her cheeks pink from cold, towered a good head taller than her doctor husband. She thrust out her gloved hand. "Neeley, we've been talking about you."

I grasped it. "Ma'am."

Sara slipped her arm around the other woman. "This is my mom."

"Hello, Neeley. I'm Blossom. My father and mother told me all about you."

Blossom's long, black braids and the beads around her neck gave her away as Hotah and Aiyanna's daughter. She clutched a tan leather jacket close around her neck. It looked as though time had rounded her edges and softened her skin, but her smile was every bit like Aiyanna's.

"Hello," I said, embarrassed, as usual. "I believe I'm wearing one of your dresses."

"I'm glad to see *somebody* wear it," she said, eyeing Sara.

I knew I was blushing because a boy had walked into our circle. There was no time to run. I pretended not to notice and looked away, unwilling to meet his eyes. I wasn't comfortable around boys, so I gazed up and over everybody's heads, searching for a streak of blue sky outside the door.

"Are you Neeley?" he asked in a perfect Southern accent. He dangled his hat from his fingertips, studying my face with his soft, dark blue eyes, which made my insides feel feathery. He wasn't as tall as Missus Shelton, but he stood at least a foot over me. "You look like someone I know," he said.

Blossom looked at her forward son. "You say that to every girl."

"That's because, Mother, I know about every girl on this mountain."

Sara poked him in the ribs. "Yeah, but they don't know you."

Frustration showed on his face. He turned to me and said, "I'm Jesse. Jesse Blackwater. Sara's unpopular brother. Aiyanna and Hotah are—"

"—your grandparents," I said.

"True." He smiled. "I'm studying to be a doctor. I want to take over Doc Shelton's practice when he retires; I assist him on his rounds. And I want to someday raise Christmas trees. What about you? My grandmother says you're an artist, like Sidabee."

"No. I mean, I'm not very good."

Doctor Shelton's wife corrected me with a smile. "I've seen your drawings, dear. You're on your way."

I blushed again; compliments were new to me.

Jesse's eyes widened. "I think Baylor is ready to start the service." He invited me to walk with him, but I didn't move. I stood there instead, gawking at him like an idiot, admiring the way someone had trimmed his hair, leaving it overlong on top, causing a wavy lock to fall forward in a curl over his broad forehead, flattering his rather square jaw. Jesse was abnormally handsome for his age. Elvis Presley-handsome. It was simply wrong; a boy who looked like that and, amazingly, wanted to speak to *me*. I found myself a little off balance. The intensity of his eyes made me uncomfortable, as if he had discovered all my secrets. He motioned again for me to walk beside him. I couldn't believe it when my feet actually moved forward.

"Do you live close by?" I asked, as if talking to boys came as naturally as painting my nails or powdering my nose.

"Yes," he said and nodded. "But we're originally from Monroe, over in Robeson County. You know the Lumbee tribe?"

"No, sorry. I—I'm afraid I know very little about—about—"

"—American Indians? I can teach you."

I felt the blood rush to my neck. "All right." I knew my face glowed like a Christmas bulb but thankfully, Jesse didn't seem to notice.

"My father hailed from the Lumbee tribe," he said. "Catfish Cole organized a Klan rally last year near Monroe. But we fought back, and those chicken-shits ran. We blasted them out of town. They cried and carried on like babies." He paused, his eyes welled with tears. It surprised me. "One of those hooded ghosts from Hell shot and killed my father. That's why my mother, sister, and I moved here, to live near my grandparents."

The name Catfish Cole struck at my heart. That same man was hunting Gideon and me, and if he found us, he'd for sure kill off every non-white person on the mountain. At that moment, I wanted to grab Gideon and leave. I had that pukey feeling you get in your stomach when something bad happens.

"You okay?" he asked. "I guess I tend to ramble on."

Sara jumped in between us. "Hey, quiet. Baylor's starting."

But Jesse didn't look at Baylor. He stared at me long enough that Sara and her mother exchanged looks, although he seemed neither embarrassed nor intimidated by them. "I have to help my grandfather," he said. I watched him walk away.

Sara whispered into my ear. "He's fifteen, but he's not all that cute."

"I didn't say he was."

I recognized tall, lanky Collin from the hardware store, arranging chairs in a semi-circle facing a large canvas draped with a colorful blanket. I looked for Gideon and found him sitting a clear distance from Miss Robeena and her sisters. He had removed his coat and waved to me, his eyes beaming as if I were the prettiest girl in the room.

I excused myself from Sara and made my way to the chair next to him. I'd never seen Gideon so dressed up. Wearing a bleached white shirt, starched and crisp, and a borrowed blue tie, he surprised me. I thought of him as handsome for the first time and almost cried. "I like your boots," I said.

"I like your hat."

"You brought your hymnal."

He nodded and grinned. "You bring a Bible?"

"It's Aiyanna's. You singing this morning?"

"Miz Sidabee wants me to."

"You don't need your hymnal to sing."

"It feels good, tho'. Holding it. Sitting in church again. Seeing your pretty hat."

And then I did. I cried.

Gideon handed me a hanky. "You a woman now. Start carrying one-a these."

CHAPTER TWENTY-THREE

Baylor stood at a simple wooden podium, facing his small congregation. He welcomed Gideon and me as visitors, then opened his Bible and read, *"I will lift up mine eyes unto the hills, from whence cometh my help. My help cometh from the Lord, which made Heaven and earth. He will not suffer thy foot to be moved: He that keepeth thee will not slumber."*

Praying out loud with no uppityness, Baylor talked to God like Gideon did. In his normal voice, like God sat in the barn with us, not off in space somewhere. "Dear Father, give us strength to carry our burdens and the wisdom to know when to lay them at Your feet. Make us instruments of Your peace and strong in every battle. For we know there is power in Christ's shed blood. Turn our enemies away and make us victorious. Bring peace to this mountain, the peace that passes understanding. Now and forever and ever. Amen."

The blood-washed congregation, some twenty-five people, pursed their lips and said, "Oh yes, amen, and let it be so." Once that wound down a bit, Baylor turned to his wife. "Sidabee, please lead us in song this morning."

She stood and lifted her face to the rafters as a calm breeze blew inside the barn. I knew the difference between soprano and alto, and she blended them beautifully in her powerful voice. Sounding nothing like the women at Wayside Baptist—Sidabee sang her heart out. Perhaps because she clearly meant every word, her emotions pouring out with each note.

After Sidabee sang, the barn church congregation stood and opened their hymnal if they had one. Singing with deep-bellied, gut-grabbing, and heart-wrenching voices, they belted out the words as if their next catastrophe stared them straight in the face. The mournful tones moved me. Gospel comfort like I'd never heard, each song descended like doves in the dry winter air. I stood on the rim of their burdensome valley and dug my heels into the dirt, determined to ignore the river of conviction pouring over me.

But then Gideon stood and sang a duo with Sidabee, easing my grief and heaviness. *Go, Tell it on the Mountain*, a Christmas song. I couldn't have been any prouder if Gideon was my real grandfather.

After the song ended, Hotah moved to the podium. Clean-shaven as usual, his thin braids neatly trimmed both sides of his head, and several strands of colorful beads hung around his neck. Decked out in a red plaid shirt, bolo tie, and a leather jacket over spotless, pressed overalls, Hotah nodded and spoke, his booming voice unmistakable with genuine emotion. "I thought today, in honor of our guests, I will tell the Cherokee legend of The Wild Christ. Here, in our sacred church, we tell it now and again," he said. "We must repeat this story often, passing it down to all generations."

Blossom lifted her hand. "That's right, Daddy. Tell it." It had become clear that Hotah and his family loved a well-told tale.

The small congregation quieted as Baylor and Collin uncovered a large painting of a white wolf. It was all very dramatic, and despite my resistance, I found myself caught up in the excitement of the moment and in Hotah's impending message.

I stared at the painting, as did everybody. From where I sat, the wolf looked directly into my eyes. Sidabee had painted a crown of thorns on its head, like the one carved on the totem pole wolf. The words underneath read, The American Indian Christian Church of Bakersville.

Gideon touched my sleeve, and I turned to watch two plump tears course down his cheeks. I worried he had become ill. I was grateful when Aiyanna slipped up behind us and placed her hands on Gideon's shoulders. It seemed to calm him. Still, I didn't understand why he got so choked up when Hotah uncovered that painting.

The room grew quiet, like the hush during a heavy snowfall. Hotah spoke slowly. "As you know, Sidabee's new painting, The

Wild Christ, will hang inside the church house we will one day build on this mountain." More *amens* erupted from the group.

Hotah continued. "In the old days, a Cherokee Medicine Man lived in a cave high in the rugged cliffs of Roan Mountain. He told stories around campfires like ours, such as how the Cherokee danced and sang the songs the bear had taught them. They sang for good hunting and a good harvest. At the darkest hour, as the drums beat louder, the elders invited every man, woman, and child to dance in the circle."

"One day, a stranger walked into the village. He knew their language, and the people invited him to dance. The Cherokee had never witnessed a man like him, for he did not look as they looked. But he danced and chanted their sacred songs, knowing their words and customs, as if he were one of them. The tribe called him Unalii, or friend, and trusted the man as he blessed their children, healed their sicknesses, and raised their dead. They had seen him walk on raging river water during a storm, feed the entire tribe during a harsh winter with one loaf of bread and two fish, and he taught them to love all men as he had loved them. When they asked his name, he said, 'My name is Jesus, the Christ,' and that he was God who came down to live in their midst. Then he told the Cherokee that his Spirit Father in Heaven required that he travel across a great ocean to die on a wooden cross for the salvation of all men from their sin."

"From *all* sin!" shouted Aiyanna.

"The tribe wept many tears, begging him not to leave. But Unalii told them he would send a sign that he had risen from the dead and would watch over them from the Heavens. The Cherokee grieved when the man left. But many moons later, a wolf appeared in their village. A white wolf with a crown of thorns on its head. The wolf stayed among the Cherokee for three days, but the thorns had burrowed deep, causing blood to run into its fur."

"After three days, the wolf disappeared. The Cherokee called him The Wild Christ, believing he was a sign sent by Unalii, or Wakan Tanka, as they then called him. Many years passed. White men came and read to the Cherokee from their holy scriptures that, indeed, Jesus the Christ had died on a cross. That soldiers had placed a crown of thorns upon his head. This confirmed to the Cherokee what they already knew—that The Wild Christ, the white wolf, was their sign from God."

I watched Robeena raise both hands above her head. "Preach, Hotah."

Hotah walked toward the painting. "The Cherokee tolerated the white men because of their relationship with the Christ. Until one day, out of greed, white soldiers attacked the village, killing many of them. They stole their land to build a soldiers fort. But the medicine man escaped and hid in a mountain cave until he returned much later to what was left of his people. Some Cherokee no longer believed in The Wild Christ, but many kept the legend deep within their hearts."

Hotah then looked at Gideon. "You see, Gideon Jackson, we indeed have much in common. I will pray to the Great Spirit for your civil rights, and maybe in the months to come, God will bless the Cherokee with a few of their own." It appeared as if Hotah had finished, but he paused instead. "Those taking their first steps into the deep, dark waters of this life on The Sanctum will do well to remember the story, for it is The Wild Christ who protects us all."

I cleared my throat and laced my fingers together. I couldn't move, swallow, or breathe. Inside, I tried to decide whether I was thrilled or scared stiff at the idea.

Hotah then stamped his feet like a faith healer. "It's time to pass the feather, and then we dance!"

We pulled our chairs outside the barn to sit before the fire. I found Jesse beating on a drum as big as a tree stump while Doctor Shelton, his ears tinged red and his face split by a huge smile, played his fiddle. As the worshippers at the fire quieted down, all of us varying in backgrounds, passed a feather around the circle and asked our Creator for favors. Baylor asked for a few more miles on his beat-up Jeep. Aiyanna asked for an abundance of corn and tomatoes come summer. Holding the feather, each person prayed aloud for a favor, a wish, or a plea that seemed close to their heart. Even Gideon asked for a new truck.

For lack of anything better to say, I asked for warmer weather. I had a list of favors to ask God, but I felt reasonably confident He already knew them, and I sure as heck wasn't about to share them with people I'd just met. Then I handed the feather to Sidabee, who closed her eyes and prayed silently.

As the music resumed, Hotah seamlessly took the drum from Jesse without missing a beat. Now free to join in, Jesse raised each knee in turn and spun slowly to the rhythm of the drum, performing a dance that seemed second nature to him.

Collin played his fiddle with such force that it seemed he might saw the thing in half. Sidabee swayed near her friend Lydia, who held her baby to her chest and danced. I smiled, watching the baby's tiny head bounce on his mother's shoulder. Moments later, Sidabee whispered something into Jesse's ear. He stopped dancing, and looked at me with a smile that reignited the fluttering sensation in my stomach. But somehow, knowing I was confused, Jesse walked over and sat next to me.

"We worship with song and dance and a big drum," he said. "Some folks here were raised in traditional church congregations, and for reasons known only to them, they are now more content in this prayer circle. Many of us, including Sidabee and Baylor, have a lifelong mistrust of white folks and their denominations. As far as we know, our circle is the only one of its kind in Appalachia, giving us a sense of belonging. I suppose it's an alternative for people who don't feel comfortable as a Methodist or Baptist. Most of those churches don't want us, anyway."

I watched the barn church members move around the fire, caught up in what appeared to be a new form of worship. Some moved only their feet, while others, like the doctor's wife, lifted their hands into the air and twirled.

Jesse started talking again. "People should be free to worship their own way," he said, smiling at Hotah. "My grandfather, whose heritage is Sioux and Cherokee, created the circle many years ago, using prayer and dance to minister to the few American Indians in this part of the Blue Ridge. We have better attendance in the summer. Sometimes, Grandfather prays before we dance, turning to the four corners and offering tobacco and thanks. First, to the east for the rising sun, then to the south for the warm breath of the Creator. To the west for the brilliance of the sunset and to the north for the cold, quiet months of rest. But we always pass the prayer feather."

I looked at Gideon, who only watched from his seat in the yard, nodding his head to the drum beat. The small congregation chanted verses peppered with words and phrases from a language I assumed was Cherokee.

"Beautiful," Jesse said, pointing toward the sun breaking through the clouds. The light spilled over the nearby pasture, resembling mountain waterfalls. I smelled Jesse's sweat and felt his voice vibrating against my hair, his breath tickling my ear. The blushing heat on my cheeks, ever-present since I met him, was impossible to hide. Leaning as far away from him as possible without tipping over, my attempt to appear unimpressed failed. Jesse only moved closer. "Our dance is a sacred thing," he said. "We're actually dancing in praise to God. The scriptures say, *Let them praise His name in the dance*— well, we're one family, dancing before our Creator. We love good people for who they are—inside."

"I never knew Christians worshipped like this," I admitted, amazed at the tingling beneath my skin that had started with The Wild Christ story. Hotah's Sunday message kept repeating itself inside my brain, mesmerizing me, opening my heart to different ways of worship, and furthering my belief in miracles.

Jesse laughed. "The idea of God in the flesh aligns perfectly with American Indian beliefs. We don't try to figure it out; we simply accept it," he explained, and I found myself nodding at him, actually understanding his meaning.

As the drum ceremony came to a close, Jesse excused himself, walked over to where his grandmother danced in the circle, and whispered into her ear. Aiyanna turned to me and smiled. She tossed the feather into my hands like a bridal bouquet. "For you," she said. "To always remember this day."

I had to admit, from the time Hotah told me about the barn church, I worried they might worship like the Nazarenes or the Pentecostals, where people had fits in the pews, rolled on the floor, moaned, hollered, and hissed like the snakes they handled. I was thankful it wasn't anything like that, but I never closed my eyes that day in prayer, staring instead every chance I got at the light on Jesse's face.

I had waited to feel like that all my life.

When the drums finally stopped, Hotah asked Gideon to sing a closing song. He stood straight and tall, taller and straighter than ever. His voice carried across the fields like smoke. *Precious Lord, take my hand . . .* Nothing the barn church members said or did was more precious to me than Gideon. Saturated to the bone with religious conviction, I finally asked God to wipe my black heart clean.

Standing on the cabin's front porch, Sidabee and I waved goodbye to the last of the congregation leaving that day. Without a word spoken between us, we watched the taillights of cars and pickup trucks drive away, making fresh tracks in the dry snow.

Finally, she spoke. "Glad that's over," she said, as if she'd just come from the dentist. Stepping to the door to go inside, Sidabee's ho-hum attitude confused me. I opened it for her to walk in first, then listened for the screen door to rattle into place, closing the heavy storm door behind it. Desperate for any kind of attention from her, I conjured a question with no thought of her answer. "Did you ever attend a regular church?"

She eyed me carefully. "I did. Then I quit when I was not much older than you. The pastor came by a few times, but he was easy to get rid of. After the feel-sorry-for-Sidabee calls and visits stopped, I disappeared off the church radar."

"What do you mean?" Following her down the hallway, I wanted to ask about her life, her other church, her parents, but she looked as pale and limp as a worn-out rag doll. Opening her bedroom door, she said, "I'm exhausted," her voice trembling.

"Please help Aiyanna with lunch. I need to rest. That service took a lot out of me."

"Sure. If there's anything else I can do—"

"—Just help Aiyanna this afternoon," she interrupted, her tone sharp and irritating.

She closed the door in my face, leaving me standing there like a fool. I had about given up. It didn't take a genius to figure out Sidabee didn't like me. She had tried—like when she combed out my hair. But hoping to win her over had proved fruitless. It was my heart's desire to live forever on The Sanctum, but not if I wasn't wanted.

Hotah stood by the fireplace, stabbing at the logs with a poker. The embers of the near-dying fire hissed and popped, growing into the heat of a full blaze.

Baylor collapsed into his favorite chair. In his lap lay a well-worn Bible and a TV Guide. He fished a cigar from his front shirt pocket, then bit the tip and lit it. He drew on the cigar until the room smelled sweet and ripe with spice and tobacco. "How'd you like the service, Neeley?"

"I liked it pretty much. Gideon enjoyed it, I think. It's different. Probably takes time to get used to. Do you know where Gideon is?"

"He'll be in shortly. He said he wanted to pray about a few things before lunch."

I stiffened momentarily, then gave Baylor and Hotah a delicate shrug. "I'll go help Aiyanna, then." It bothered me that Gideon had broken down and cried in front of everybody. Still, I decided some things, like a man's uncontrollable crying, were better left unexplained.

Sitting in the kitchen, slicing bread for sandwiches, I hoped to someday become an artist like Sidabee, as Doctor Shelton's wife said. But Two-Toes nudged me, sweeping away my daydream. I loved the gray hairs surrounding his muzzle. Although gentle as a pup, the wolf had grown old in human *and* canine years. Watching him wander the kitchen, I thought perhaps he was looking for something. He stopped, sniffed the air, and then spread out on his bed. Dropping his chin on his paws, Two-Toes never took his eyes off me as I helped Aiyanna prepare lunch. I was grateful for that sweet wolf who had licked off my scar. And I was thankful for how he made me smile, but I had the strangest feeling he was desperate to tell me something.

During lunch, Gideon was surprisingly a mouthful of smiles and teeth, gnawing on neck bones and shoveling enormous spoonfuls of Aiyanna's ham and beans into himself. Needing to feed the wolf pups, I excused myself and headed to the back door.

"Girl, you think this is shirt-sleeve weather? Get your coat," Gideon said.

Aiyanna put down her fork. "Were you in the same winter air I was in today?"

I grabbed my coat off the hook. *Who do these people think they are, my parents?* With that thought, I backed against the wall, slid to the floor, and hugged my knees. No matter how hard I worked at it, missing the mother and father I briefly knew remained hidden beneath a thin veil, only to have that veil blown away by a few misplaced words. I sobbed right there on the blue linoleum. "Why doesn't Sidabee like me?" I cried. "I'm so sorry about Raven, about anything I've done to make her angry." The words had taken days to work their way into my throat and out of my mouth.

Gideon gently lifted and carried me to the kitchen sofa. The past few weeks' events, sewn into my tattered, small life quilt, unraveled like the frayed edges of an old blanket. With my eyes closed, I felt the warmth of his large, compassionate hand move across my cheek and over my head, moving strands of curls off my glasses and tucking them behind my ear without touching my skin. "You sleep; you been through enough. This my fault."

I opened my eyes. His pitiful look threatened to consume me, filling me with a sadness I couldn't bear, and I struggled free from the confines of the small sofa. "I'm alright," I insisted.

Baylor poked his head into the kitchen. "Listen to Gideon. Take the day to rest. And as for Sidabee, please find it in your heart to forgive her," he sighed. "She's with child and worried. She doesn't want to go through losing another baby."

Gideon placed his comforting hand on Baylor's shoulder. "I will pray for you and Miz Sidabee."

"Thank you, Gideon. Please—Neeley." Baylor's attempt to smile failed. It seemed his pain wouldn't allow it. "Sidabee has been through some tough times. I don't expect you to understand—"

"—I do. I understand tough times. I'm sorry."

In the end, we blamed everything on Sidabee's pregnancy—my sorrow, her bad moods—because it seemed expecting a baby made a woman do strange things.

The following evening, dry snow shimmered beneath the moonlight. The ground's snowpack had melted during the day, only to refreeze as the sun set over the mountains. After bottle-feeding the pups, I trudged back from the barn with an icy crust crunching under my feet as my breath formed white plumes in the frigid moonlit air. Bone-tired, I dragged myself up the hill.

Most nights, I enjoyed my free time. When the TV worked, it kept my mind occupied. But The Sanctum's real gift to me was one of wonder. I learned that wonder isn't something you earn or purchase—it's an accepted gift. You can't buy a box of wonder at the store. It's not something you touch or wear, like a coat. You must clear some space in your heart and mind to receive it. Like the gift of salvation, it's that simple.

Standing on the mountaintop with the moon directly above me, its brilliance was almost blinding. I closed my eyes and tilted my face upward, allowing moonbeams to caress my cheeks, nose, and lips, and I wondered if the Christmas Angel wished me peace and goodwill and how, despite Sidabee's coldness toward me, I felt a sense of belonging on The Sanctum, as if I were supposed to live there forever.

Hearing soft flute music, I stumbled up the back steps to the cabin and found Hotah and Aiyanna on the porch, bundled in blankets. Aiyanna's fingers moved up and down over her wooden flute while Hotah smoked and gazed at the moon. The music stopped, and I awkwardly searched for words that didn't make me sound silly or stupid. "Um—see you in the morning, then."

Hotah raised his hand to halt me in my tracks. "A full moon over the glow of a city is one more light in a sea of manmade brilliance," he said. "The moon's existence is lost and quickly forgotten, devoured by buildings and billboards. When we reduce the moon to only another light in the sky, when it is unheralded, and no longer needed to keep the night demons at bay, we have made man's creation superior to God's. If you understand that, Little Red Bird, if you believe the power of the Creator is superior to any other, then you may consider The Sanctum—yours."

It was Aiyanna and Hotah's way of telling me I had a new home—if I wanted it. Hotah turned toward the howling wolves in their pens. In that moment, every wolf claimed the night sky. I couldn't help but smile. Until that day, I had liked Aiyanna and Hotah just fine, but that night, I fell deeply in love with both of them.

"By the way," I said, "Do you two have a last name?"

"Smith," Hotah said.

CHAPTER TWENTY-FOUR

The next night, I excused myself early. It was my time of the month, and the cramping sent me to bed early. Strolling past Sidabee's gallery wall, I looked at each picture differently than when I first arrived. The drawings told the MacLennan's story like a diary. I especially liked the ones of Baylor on his annual deer hunt, as if someone had hired Sidabee to document it. The drawings portrayed her husband stalking deer or other wild game, and I imagined her pouring her soul into each one. Although I prayed for Sidabee and her unborn baby all the way up the stairs, her coldness still drove me nuts.

Gideon had told me to be patient. Aiyanna and Hotah carried on as if her mood swings were her usual behavior. But she acted differently around me than she did with everybody else. It was *me* she disliked, and I knew it. Maybe she *was* grieving for her dead babies, but she didn't talk about her pain. Around me, she remained quiet and polite, sipping her tea and clenching her fists in her lap. I often watched as she stared out a window, distracting herself as though straining to halt a flood of overwhelming thoughts. Sometimes, there was a random gesture or a clouded glance, and sometimes, her thin, silly laugh wasn't laughter at all but a dire attempt to stop her tears.

Slipping under the thick down of quilts and comforters, I pushed Sidabee out of my mind by listening to the cabin settle for the night. Like a horse falling asleep, first, there were the heaves and sighs, and then the trembles and twitches, and finally, a roll of air that pushed into each room, swaying the draperies, creaking around the wooden floors and walls and up the fireplaces. Baylor had explained it as the logs nestling into the ground. Or as Hotah, our resident storyteller, had called it—the groan of spirits who had lived on the land long before us, settling in for the night. It didn't take long for the spirits to quiet down. Within minutes, my heavy eyelids closed.

I lay completely still, deciding not to try so hard to make Sidabee like me. I reminded myself that you can't force love. You either do or you don't. I knew something about that.

At sunrise, I warmed my hands around my favorite blue mug filled with steaming coffee. Bundled in one of Aiyanna's colorful blankets, I sat in my usual spot, the top porch step. The air, brisk and alive with promise, tasted sweet on my tongue as I watched the eastern sky blaze in shades of lavender. It only magnified the sweeping golden rays that rose from the backs of distant blue ridges. The brush stroke of God, Sidabee called it. There wasn't anything more restful and peaceful than the mountains at dawn. At times, I wanted to climb the Blue Ridge as badly as I wanted to climb into my father's lap.

"It's almost Christmas," Gideon said with a coffee mug in his hands, too. "That's some view. Think folks who live on these mountains ever grow tired of it?"

"I sure never would," I said. "The thought of leaving this place and settling elsewhere—" I trailed off, unable to complete the sentence.

"You mean like back to Summerfield?" Gideon asked.

With my coffee halfway to my lips, I couldn't answer. I didn't want to think about it.

He looked down at his coffee and then raised a hand to scratch along his jaw. He chuckled when he said, "I been forgetting to shave."

"You look like a mountain man," I teased, noting his scuffed boots, the new denim overalls Aiyanna had already patched, and his old coat that needed patches over the patches. The white stubble on his cheeks, chin, and upper lip made him appear older than his years. "Too late," I jested. "You already look like a Hatfield. Although, I think you'll need a longer beard."

Gideon drained his cup. "Time to get busy. I gots to save money for that truck."

My lower lip quivered. "I can't go back."

"Neeley—"

"—I won't go back. They'll put you in jail, and I'll be in Hell—"

"—Stop. Nothing gone happen—I didn't haul you here to let you go back there. This place needs you. This cabin jus' a pile-a logs without you in it. These people—"

"Breakfast!" Aiyanna's voice called out.

"Well. Best go in. Let's talk later," Gideon said.

I wasn't sure I'd heard him right. Were we on the same page about leaving The Sanctum? The page that read *the end*?

We savored Aiyanna's breakfast of thinly sliced ham layered between cheesy eggs on steaming buttery biscuits. Using the blue-flowered dishes at every meal, she reserved the linen tablecloths, napkins, and the Depression glass from the real Depression for suppers at the fancy dining table in the great room, which happened only once—on Baylor's birthday.

Sidabee opened a Ball jar of the past summer's canned peaches and poured cream on top for breakfast dessert. I couldn't help but notice the changes in my body. My once-skinny arms and legs had plumped out, and my pimples had vanished—due to good eating and fresh mountain air, Aiyanna had said.

Instead of wearing his lawyer suit and tie that morning, Baylor sat for breakfast in blue jeans, one of his plaid flannel shirts, and a white T-shirt that showed at the neck. Clean-shaven and with his hair slicked back, he drank the last of his coffee, then lit a cigar. Plucking it from his mouth, he blew a stream of smoke toward the ceiling. "I saw Dirk Buchanan yesterday," he said.

Aiyanna stood at the sink rinsing dishes while Sidabee and I cleared what was left of breakfast, but only Aiyanna responded. "What's that man up to?"

Baylor spread a newspaper over the table, his eyes focused on cleaning his rifle. "He told me there was a young woman killed last week ten miles outside of town. Maisie Wilder. You may know her, Sidabee. She worked in Bertie Gentry's gift shop. Buchanan said there were no footprints in the snow, but her husband swore he didn't do it. They say she split-cracked her skull, but they didn't find a weapon, just that awful head wound. And—he said she'd been scalped."

I think my chin dropped to my chest because Baylor smiled and said, "Not to worry, Neeley, these rumors happen occasionally. Anyway, Buchanan made a point to tell me an Indian murdered her. 'No white man could've done it,' he said. I asked him if she had other bruises on her body. 'Black and blue from head to toe,' he said. 'Some dirty savage roughed her up, scalped her, then threw her off her own back porch, near as the law can tell.' That's what Buchanan said, and it seems he's told the same story to everyone from here to Boone."

Leaning hard against the Hoosier cabinet and drying a bowl, I recalled Velda Mosser back in Summerfield. The entire town thought she was down sick with some female problem, so I volunteered to deliver one of Gideon's pies because we lived on the same road as Velda and Edgar Mosser. Everybody had said it was a match made in Heaven that became a living Hell. I found her sitting on her porch steps, hugging her knees, rocking and crying, dabbing at her cheeks with the hem of her faded housedress. She looked at me with her puffy face, eyes black and bruised, claiming she tripped over her laundry basket, although the next week, they threw Mister Mosser in jail for putting his wife in the hospital. My Sunday school class had special prayer for Velda a few days before she died.

Sidabee tossed her apron on the counter. "I'll say one thing for Dirk Buchanan. He's one determined man. He's got two boys. You'd think he'd want to set a better example than spreading dirt all over town," she said and sighed. "Gideon baked pies yesterday. Maybe we can take one to the bereaved family."

Baylor closed one eye and looked down his gun's barrel with the other. "Uh-huh."

I dried the last bowl and put it away, then stood quietly at Baylor's elbow, watching him work a skinny brush through the tiny parts of his gun.

I think he sensed my concern because he shot me another comforting smile. "Like I said, that kind of talk travels faster than a speeding bullet around here," he winked. "Gets tongues to wagging and gives folks the gossip they need to spice up their mundane lives. Buchanan would like to run every American Indian and Negro out of North Carolina. There will always be a Dirk Buchanan to circulate lies and rumors, get people scared, and lynch an innocent man because his skin isn't white. It happened a lot when I was a boy," Baylor said. "If the Indians or the Negroes didn't walk the straight and narrow, there was always a group of vigilantes ready to string them up."

That morning, the sky had grown dark enough to switch on the lamps inside the cabin. Hotah looked up briefly; warm lamplight glowed on his weathered face. He sat at the opposite end of the table with Gideon, mending several broken leashes for Elvis and Two-Toes. Touching the solid leather, I marveled at its softness in my hands.

"A storm is coming," Hotah said.

Gideon held a metal ring as Hotah threaded a leather strap through it. "Must be. I feel heat on mah face, cold on mah back, and the air seems a bit unsettled." I knew Gideon didn't want to talk about lynching.

"Ah," Hotah said. "My wife has taught you about weather. That is good."

In the dim light, Gideon's teeth glowed like polished bones behind his wide grin. "Don't think that makes me a TV weatherman, Hotah. But can you 'magine that?" He chuckled. "A Negro weatherman."

Hotah flashed Gideon his typical quick smile. He was often a mixture of hot and cold with a touch of wildness. It was Hotah's quiet nature that smoothed off his rough edges. Yet I knew Hotah couldn't smile and talk about Dirk Buchanan at the same time any more than he could speak Chinese. Pulling another leather strap across the table, his mind seemed to plunge forward like a wild colt through a wire fence. "The storm I speak about, my friend, does not produce rain or snow but bloodshed."

I shivered at the glint in Hotah's eyes. One minute, my heart begged to remain on The Sanctum forever; the next minute, my head filled with questions and fear of the unknown. My emotions seesawed. I couldn't stop them. I wanted to know more about Mister Buchanan. "Baylor, I heard you and Doctor Shelton talking before church on Sunday. About the land developers."

Sidabee laid a log on the kitchen hearth. After brushing the debris from her hands, she grabbed her sweater from the back of the sofa and pulled it on, thrusting her arms in angrily. "Tell her, Baylor. Tell Gideon and Neeley; they need to know in case those bastards show up here again."

Baylor grew quiet, either thinking hard about what to say to me or surprised at his wife for saying, *bastards.*

"Tell me what?" I asked, squeezing into the chair next to Baylor.

"Well, Neeley," he said. "There's a group of men in town determined to build resorts for rich folks. Dirk Buchanan is one of them."

"Hotah has mentioned that. But why?"

"To become wealthy themselves. Money is their god. They believe folks who live in the flatlands and the cities want vacations—the country experience, only with tennis courts and swimming pools. Mountain views for their golf courses, and to be pampered in resorts with views of the Blue Ridge," Baylor said.

"I don't understand. What does that have to do with this place?" I asked.

Sidabee sat on the kitchen sofa, crossed her legs, and kicked off her black heels. "Here's the deal. Dirk Buchanan's deal. His sweet-talking tongue has disarmed a lot of folks who suddenly found themselves in a real pickle. He not only works for the bank, but he's also in cahoots with developers bent on buying up land and houses, and one by one, they're forcing the sale of farms."

"Do they want your land? The Sanctum?"

Baylor nodded. "Bakersville is experiencing a construction boom. Folks love the beauty of these mountains, and some want to capitalize on it. They want a hotbed of activity. Enterprise and opportunity. Bit by bit, they want it all. One at a time, small businesses are opening in downtown Bakersville. New places to eat that advertise the Blue Ridge Parkway on their placemats. Souvenir shops that sell cheap trinkets and tomfoolery. A new feed and seed store with two gas pumps opened last week, charging as much as forty-five cents for a gallon of gas."

"What do they want to do to your cabin?"

"Buchanan wants to turn it into a lodge," Sidabee answered.

"*Our* house? I—I mean, your house?"

Sidabee smiled. "Yes. But Hotah and Aiyanna have lived here a very long time. This is their home. Not the reservation. And—and they want us to kill off the wolves."

Suddenly, I sat ramrod straight. "Kill the wolves?"

"Every last one of them," Sidabee said. "Folks in town are afraid to come here. They don't realize what we do and why we want to save them. They don't understand. They don't *want* to understand." She heaved herself from the sofa and crossed the room to stare at one of her drawings hanging on the wall. "Some folks have sold off pieces of their land out of desperation, but that's not something we plan to do. This is our home. I don't want it developed."

I joined her. "I know," I whispered.

"Then we'll fight them," Baylor said. I turned around to see him smile at his wife. He was my newest favorite person, a giant of hope and optimism.

From the day Pastor Cole, also known as Catfish Cole, opened the church doors to the Klan, my whole world was wrapped up in skin pigment and prejudice. I was sick of it. Why couldn't people get along? Bogged down with it all, I was willing to bet if you skinned a Negro, a White, a Chinese, and an Indian, then mixed up the bodies, nobody could tell which was which. So, when Sidabee asked if I'd like to ride into Bakersville with her and do a little Christmas shopping, I was ready. Ready to forget about skin pigment and have a little fun. She suggested I take care of the pups, then we'd head to town.

The wolf pups knew my smell and rooted for milk before I was ready.

I had named them Soot and Cierra. Soot looked like I had dipped him in a bucket of ashes; Hotah had said he might be a black wolf with golden eyes when fully grown. The ring around Cierra's neck reminded me of her mother. Hotah approved of the names, so they stuck. After a short time, my arms bore tiny scratches, initiating me as their caretaker. I asked Hotah if I could raise the pups to be house wolves, like Elvis and Two-Toes, but I got a lecture instead.

"Once, when I was a boy," he said, "I found a wolf pup sleeping against its dead mother, killed by a farmer's bullet. I begged my mother to allow me to raise the wolf pup like a dog. For a while, the pup licked my hand, slept in my bed, followed me around, chased the cat, and did things dogs do. But one day, it stopped playing. It remembered it was a wolf, not a dog. It gazed off into the woods, and a few days later, it was gone. Never came back."

"Why?" I asked.

"The Cherokee say, you cannot tame a wild animal because it always remembers its past and will return to it. We cannot leave Elvis and Two-Toes alone inside the cabin or outside without a leash for more than a day. Many have tried to train a wolf as they do their dog, which is why the moment the wolf kills their cat and tears up the sofa, they end up here on The Sanctum. A wolf is a wild animal forever, Little Red Bird."

So that was the end of that.

After feeding and watching the pups sniff and explore their den, I ambled to the barn in bright sunlight. By the time I stepped inside, I was blind in the darkness. Standing still with one hand pressed against the plank wall, I waited for my eyes to adjust, feeling the cold wind push into the crack of an opening behind me.

Finding the sink, I cupped my hands beneath the faucet to wash them and caught the scent of freshly cut lumber—a smell of Gideon mending the fence back in Summerfield. He liked to fix things. Make things. A lifetime of hard work showed in his hands. Gnarled and cracked, Gideon's hands repaired the broken better than new, and if it was wood, metal, or grew in the dirt, they made things beautiful. Breathing in the smell of sawdust stirred old memories inside my nose that had never faded.

I ducked into a dim and dusty room stacked with wood and stone. Hotah and Gideon, bent over at the waist, worked on a new totem pole. Wood shavings and grit rolled under my feet. For a moment, the sharp glare of an eagle pinned me to the spot like prey. But the faces of a wolf and a deer pulled me farther inside, trapping me with how Hotah had painted their eyes, life-like and haunting.

Gideon's red bandanna covered his nose and mouth to keep out the dust. Working a fine sandpaper across the forehead of a bear, he hummed his favorite Christmas song, *Good King Wenceslas*, and broke into a grin behind his bandana when he spotted me. I immediately felt the pull of the totem pole, its spirit that whispered we were all connected somehow.

Hotah had changed his hair to a single long braid twisted down his back, nearly to his waist. His dark brown eyes hid his thoughts, as usual. I never knew what he was thinking. However, I was thankful he didn't pass on his craggy looks or quiet nature to his grandson. Perched over a small cabinet with glass doors, Hotah wiped at his hands with a rag that smelled like turpentine. He barely acknowledged me, using the rag to get in between his fingers. "You come to help?" he asked.

I stared at Hotah's face, wondering how to say the words out loud: "I'm going Christmas shopping with Sidabee." My insides were about to burst with happiness.

"Humph," he grunted.

I couldn't stop smiling. My fingertips lingered over the smooth wood carving of the giant bird nearest me. "So the Cherokee carved these poles, too?"

"No. My people did not make them. Pacific Northwest tribes made totem poles. But I always held an interest. If they keep evil spirits away from Alaskan tribes, they might work for an old Cherokee. But you did not see this pole. It is a present for Sidabee and Baylor."

"Okay," I giggled.

Gideon stopped humming long enough to ask Hotah a question about the shape of the bear's head, and I grabbed the opportunity to slip out and run to the cabin. I didn't want Sidabee to have to wait for me, and I needed to change my clothes. A trip to town with someone like Sidabee—*Lordy*, I almost peed my pants getting ready. The only person I'd ever gone shopping with in my whole life was Gideon, and that wasn't always fun.

Before Sidabee even stepped into the great room, I was captivated by the sound of her bootheels and the scent of her perfume. Her entrance was a spectacle, and clearly, she belonged on the cover of Life magazine. Sidabee's fashionably red lips and rose-colored cheeks stood out against her stylish modern outfit—a tight, off-white skirt, red blouse, and pearls, all complemented by a chignon and a green paisley silk scarf.

Struggling to find my voice, I felt self-conscious in my holey sweater and threadbare dungarees. Embarrassed, I stumbled over my words. "I—I didn't dress up. Is what I'm wearing okay—I mean acceptable?"

"You look fine," she said and smiled. "I felt like dressing festive today."

As we stepped outside, I pushed my arms into the cold lining of my coat sleeves, aching for something *festive* to wear, too. The biting cold air seared my cheeks and instantly froze inside my nose.

Despite Baylor's heroic efforts to shovel the stone path, I trudged through knee-deep sunlit snow, lifting my feet high and reaching Sidabee's Buick in a matter of minutes. Suddenly, we were off, two women embarking on a thrilling shopping adventure. It was the most exhilarating day of my life.

Engulfed by the leather seats, I sat quietly, and stared out the window. Glancing behind me, I noticed she had placed a pile of framed sketches and paintings on the backseat.

"I sell my work at the mercantile here and in Boone—oh, and at Bertie Gentry's gift shop, so I brought them along, in case you're wondering."

"You get paid a lot?"

Her eyes smiled through her sunglasses. "Enough," she said.

Driving through town, we passed people milling about the sidewalks, a woman with a small child in her arms, and an elderly man with two tiny, leashed rat-like dogs, one on each side. I almost laughed. Only an hour before, I had walked into a wolf pen. I was living large on The Sanctum and didn't care who knew it.

As we rode along Main Street, a few people noticed Sidabee and waved. They hurried past, turning their collars against the biting wind while she politely waved back. Sidabee's felt gloves and leather boots that matched her long creamy-white wool coat painted a picture of a winter princess. And I—in my faded sweater, knitted hat, and worn coat—looked like her peasant handmaiden.

But then her eyes lit up. "Gideon says you like sweet corn."

"I do. I like it a lot."

"You know, every spring, we plant acres of corn. A good amount of it is sweet corn. Sometimes, we roast it on an open fire. Aiyanna and Blossom freeze a ton during harvest. Hot, yellow corn, sweet and salty, with melted butter that covers your fingers. Mmmm. I could eat it until I pop."

"Me too," I said, grinning from ear to ear.

"I told Aiyanna to cook up a big pot for supper."

"For real?"

She nodded, and we giggled like two schoolgirls anticipating a Christmas feast. Blissfully happy and fully alive, I felt a new warmth from her, a shared joy erasing all shadows from my heart, at least for that moment. Sitting next to Sidabee, I wished for the day to last forever.

After five stores and a pile of brightly wrapped packages, Sidabee bought me a Milky Way and a root beer at the new filling station before driving home.

I suddenly longed to tell her every little detail I knew about myself. Stay up all night, both of us in our pajamas, sipping hot chocolate, painting our nails, and humming along to our favorite songs on the radio. I wanted to compare our church experiences, confide in her about my dead parents, my murdered grandmother, my bittersweet school memories, my encounter with the Klan, my driving skills, the Woolworths incident, every detail of our escape, and all about Pudge. I wanted to lay bare every good and bad part of my life.

But it occurred to me she had shared little about herself. I knew more about Hotah, Aiyanna, their daughter, grandchildren, and about Baylor and his family than I knew about her. Sidabee remained a mystery. It seemed Gideon had cracked her shell a bit, but beyond her love for drawing, fondness for sweet corn, and the heart-wrenching fact that she had lost three babies and was expecting again—a piece of information I got from Baylor—I knew nothing about her.

So I ignored her sad eyes, which periodically glanced my way. I stayed quiet, enjoyed the ride home, and decided not to ruin the day by asking questions I figured she never wanted to answer anyway.

CHAPTER TWENTY-FIVE

As Sidabee drove past the totem pole, I looked out the passenger window to see our burst of winter sun turn into gray skies dotted with heavy clouds. The day had drifted toward night, and I hadn't even noticed. Sidabee parked her Buick by the barn, and I followed her to the cabin as our shadows broadened behind us. Quarter-sized snowflakes started settling on my shoulders and hat. Fresh snow covered the old, swirling around me in the wind. I wasn't confident I'd ever get used to cold mountain weather, but my lightheartedness had not deserted me. With bags of Christmas presents under both arms, my heart leaped, looking forward to the holiday.

I thought it strange, though, when Sidabee headed toward the front door instead of our usual hike up the back. But by the time we arrived at the porch, I understood why. From the sidewalk, I noticed an envelope tacked to the door. Sidabee quickly removed it as one would a tick from their skin, shoving it into her pocket while hurrying me into the house.

We stood on the rug while she toed off her boots and shrugged out of her coat, leaving her gloves on. I noticed her shivering, reading the letter, though perhaps not solely from the cold. When she clicked on the radio, the smoky voice of Kitty Wells filled the room.

Massaging her temples, Sidabee slumped into a nearby chair. "Damn them." Her deep sigh fluttered into the air and tugged at my heart. "He'll never stop."

"What's wrong?" I asked, leaning down to catch her eye.

Sidabee looked up at me with watery eyes. "It's Buchanan. After having ruthlessly stolen Baylor's clients for months, they've called in our loans; we're hanging on by a thread."

Until then, she had offered me only simple conversation, but that day, Sidabee opened up for the first time. Wide open. It shocked me even more when she said, "Here, read it," as if she wanted the whole world to know her business.

I took the letter from her trembling hand and read it—twice, then shook my head in disbelief. The rush of uncertainty and fear I'd battled for days attacked with a vengeance. "They're giving you thirty days to come up with eighty thousand dollars? What on earth will you do?"

Rubbing her arms and biting at her lower lip, Sidabee hid her thoughts—until she heard what I had spoken out loud. Swiftly, she jerked the paper out of my hand. "Oh, Neeley, I'm sorry. I'm sorry to involve you. Look, Hotah has started the fire already. Baylor will be home soon and handle this matter; he always does."

Sidabee flew into the kitchen, and I followed her. "Let's make supper," she said. "Aiyanna must be helping Hotah with the wolves since you and I went to town." After glancing at the wall clock, she slipped on an apron, emptied potatoes from the bin into a bowl, and sat at the table. "They'll all be hungry, so we'll make meatloaf and mashed potatoes—along with that corn." She lifted her chin and forced a smile.

I sat beside her, curling a leg beneath me, giving in to the mounting nervous tension since discovering the envelope on the door. Biting my nails, I couldn't help but notice Sidabee's quick peek at her watch every few minutes while whacking at the potatoes.

"I'm struggling with how to tell Baylor about this," she said.

Seizing the knife from Sidabee, I took over before she cut herself. I wanted to show my sympathy, but the right words cowered behind my inability to trust her sudden show of friendship.

It surprised me when Sidabee mixed up a meatloaf the size of a football. Even more surprising was when she lifted my hand out of the potato bowl, and held it. "I always dreamed of a house full of children. Children who felt loved and safe—no matter what," she confessed. "That was the—" she paused, swallowing her tears, "—the deepest desire of my heart."

I squeezed her hand. "Baylor told me you're expecting."

"Yes, but I'm scared. I've already lost three. Of course, Aiyanna chants and prays over me every morning. She swears this time it'll work."

I smiled, hoping to comfort her. "If anybody can reach Heaven, I believe Aiyanna can."

"Yes, I believe that, too," she whispered.

Sidabee's gaze fell to the chain around her neck, looping through a gold wedding band she wore even with her pearls. "I can't wear gold. I'm allergic. When I married Baylor, he said, 'I want you to wear your wedding ring around your beautiful neck, so everyone will know you're mine.'"

"I always wondered why you wore it like that."

She lifted the chain slowly from her blouse and rose from the chair. Her voice cracked under the weight of her stress. "Baylor said we can adopt children. 'Sidabee,' he says, 'we'll go to the other side of the world and buy 'em if we have to,' but now, if we lose The Sanctum—"

I stood and reached for her, wrapping my arms tightly around her waist. She was as small at her middle as a dried cornstalk. I cared about her and wanted her to know how much. "Baylor's a good man. And you're talking like you've already lost your baby. If God can cause a wolf to lick off my scar, he can grow that baby inside you, good and strong."

Sidabee lifted her head off my shoulder, her eyes glistening with unshed tears. "You're pretty smart for a young girl," she said and sniffed, making me blush.

Outside, the wind howled like the wolves, and there was something else. A car. Its headlights swept across us through the kitchen windows as the driver turned the corner and parked by the back porch. My throat went dry, my heart pounding in my chest. Sidabee's stare snapped to me, her eyes wide with anticipation. Drawing in a steadying breath, she patted the back of my hand. "It's Baylor. He's home."

I retreated to my room. I felt it best to leave them alone. But I stood at the top of the stairs, peeking around the corner because they had walked into the great room, and I wanted to see their every move from the shadows in the loft. I knew honing in on a private conversation was wrong, but I couldn't help it.

In a flurry of snow, Baylor stomped inside, shaking the cold from his coat and carrying his boots to the great room to set them by the fire. I didn't have to see him do it—it's what he always did. But from where I stood, I watched him shed his wet coat and fold it over his arm, looking at Sidabee and smiling.

"You're home early," I heard her say, keeping her tone neutral.

"Yep."

As *she* did every evening, Sidabee moved gracefully toward him to hang his coat.

"I've got it," he said, brushing past her to the closet.

It must have startled her as much as it did me. She dropped her arm, tugging at the sleeves of her blouse, and came right out with it. "Buchanan was here today. He's giving us thirty days," she said, her voice a mix of fear and defiance. She reached into her pocket and handed him the note.

Baylor squared his shoulders in his neatly pressed blue suit and ran a hand over his already smooth hair. "I know."

"You know?"

He sank into his favorite chair. "As luck would have it, I overheard him speaking with one of my colleagues at the courthouse. It was the day Gideon and Neeley arrived," he said, pausing to chuckle. "It hit me pretty hard. I never thought Buchanan would go through with it, and I've been unable to discuss it with you."

In silence, Baylor tapped his fingers on an end table, lost in thought, before repositioning himself in his chair. "I've worked all these years like a bull in a harness to keep this land intact. Wolves or no wolves, The Sanctum is as much about our survival as theirs. All of this," his arm swept out in a grand gesture, "I've sweated from dawn to dusk, like my parents. I've spilled blood. I've given my heart and soul to this place. My dreams. My youth. And now—" His deep and desperate sigh floated into the loft where I hid in the shadows. "—And now they want to take it away from us, bulldoze it, and build a resort."

"Never!" Sidabee cried. I had heard the pain swimming in Baylor's voice, and I think Sidabee did, too. "Baylor, we'll fight, tooth and nail if need be. Fight to keep this piece of earth. Like you said, Baylor. Fight!"

His face went still as a stump before he swung his head away from her.

I think she took a deep breath to muster her strength before stepping closer to him. Pounding her breast with her fist, emphasizing each word, she said, "The Sanctum gave me my life. It gave me purpose, a family, and hope for a future. It gave me—you. Losing it would be too great a loss!"

"Do you mean that?" Baylor's voice broke, wiping at tears.

Reaching out to clutch his hand, Sidabee swept a long look around the cabin, followed by words I'll never forget: "With everything I am."

Like the change of scenery in a play, evening light cast a sudden eerie glow in the great room below, and my gut wanted to know where Sidabee came from, how she met Baylor, and how she ended up on his farm.

Baylor jumped to his feet. They stood forehead-to-forehead, silently appreciating each other, I think. His arms embraced her, pulling her close. "I know this land like every flaw, curve, and fold on your body. I can't stand the thought of losing it any more than the thought of losing you." She rested her head on his chest, staying that way a few moments. I'd never seen anything like it. He sighed heavily, her name slipping through his lips. "Sidabee—"

He had probably sheltered her from bad news their entire marriage. But he clearly could not bear this alone. And whether he liked it or not, I was there to bear it, too.

Pulling his wife to his chest again, Baylor squeezed the letter in his fist and shouted, "Abba Father! Our trust is in You." Drawing back his hand, he threw the paper into the air. "We're not selling. *The Lord is my light and my salvation; Whom shall I fear? The Lord is the strength of my life; Of whom shall I be afraid?*" That's when I watched the letter hurtle toward the fire, and I assume into the flame. That was also the exact moment I knew I'd never leave. For better or worse, wild Indians couldn't drag me away.

At dawn on Christmas Eve, a gentle overnight snowfall had settled on the lawn, the fields, and the trees. Everything that was familiar to me had transformed into a captivating strangeness. From my frostbitten window, I stood admiring the billions of tiny diamond-chip sparkles crusted on the snow, reflecting all colors of the rainbow. Shades of royal purple, parrot green, Carolina blue, flashes of flame orange, and flamingo pink. Pinpricks of color in nature's finest needlepoint blanket. Hotah's giant thermometer near the barn read 10 degrees, and the air was motionless and dry.

It was a Christmas card Christmas.

But years before, Pudge had shattered my belief in Santy-Claus. As I reached out to touch my first-ever Christmas stocking, an iron grip on my wrist stopped me. Sidabee had filled it with tiny, wrapped presents, warning me to keep my hands off until Christmas morning. That didn't stop me from staring at it. The stocking hung from the great room mantel, decked out in pine branches with tall beeswax candles, red velvet ribbon, and holly berries. I sat cross-legged in front of the crackling fire, fixated on the long red and white-striped sock filled to the brim with candy and gifts, almost causing my eyes to cross.

After lunch, I found myself at the window, captivated by the sight of Sidabee strolling toward the barn. Something magical about her fascinated me to no end. Wrapped in Baylor's coat, she paused at a garden bench overlooking the wolf pens. Two-Toes approached and gently nudged her arm, aware she carried treats in her pocket. The silly truth was I had followed the sound of Sidabee's voice for days, aching to be near her. Except for our shopping trip day, she remained guarded and spoke little. Although she *did* smile more often, and that was enough to keep me from coming unglued around her.

Baylor, on the other hand, never stopped talking. We spent our evenings after supper working on jigsaw puzzles. He introduced me to Monopoly and Scrabble, and The Red Skelton Show on Tuesday nights with a bowl of popcorn between us. But Sidabee's glare at Baylor when he announced my school lessons would begin immediately after Christmas clearly indicated he had crossed a line. A line she obviously drew the day Gideon and I arrived. She didn't know it yet, but I wasn't going anywhere. Not after they'd pulled me into their problems with Mister Buchanan.

Suddenly, the sun drew my gaze away from Sidabee. It had broken free of its hiding place, turning the sky into a polished blue hue, like the lapis stone Aiyanna sometimes wore around her neck. There wasn't a single cloud to hold in the earth's warmth. The bitter cold painted a picture of chickadees huddled in old woodpecker holes or buried up to their bills in abandoned squirrel nests. I assured myself that nobody would expect to encounter a hostile land developer on a day as beautiful as this. The hill, curving down to the wolves, stood as the highest pinnacle for miles, plunging steeply into the edge of thick underbrush and woods guarding The Sanctum—protecting us from the outside world.

I padded to Gideon's room in my socks, where he sat in his comfy chair, his legs crossed, reading the newspaper. "Are you looking forward to tonight?" I asked. "Sidabee said we'll open presents before the guests arrive—except for the ones in my stocking. They're making me wait until Christmas morning to open those." I knew full well that presents were as new to him as they were to me. He'd spent the morning baking pies and appeared to need a nap.

"Wouldn't miss it. Ah, thanks for reminding me, tho'. I gots to fetch that ham out the smokehouse." He worked his fingers through the patchwork of bristled hair on his chin, rubbed his droopy eyes, and then picked up his hat. Gideon started for the back door, whacking the hat against his leg to loosen the dust as he always did before shoving it on his head. I wasn't sure if he was only tired, or feeling poorly, or something else was bothering him. Or maybe, we shared the same odd feeling of celebrating Christmas Eve with a house full of people, including the entire barn church congregation.

I recalled the Christmas after my parents died. In his usual nasty manner, Pudge informed me he didn't believe in squandering money on frivolous gifts. So, when the clock struck five that evening, and I tore into boxes wrapped with glossy red paper and green satin ribbons to find new pajamas, a sweater set, and a pair of fleece-lined slippers from Sidabee and Baylor, I found it impossible to hold back my tears.

The next gift I ripped open was a necklace from Hotah and Aiyanna. The necklace was the most spectacular piece of jewelry I had ever owned—the *only* piece I had ever owned. The arrowhead, which I assumed was lost forever, hung from the center of a beaded chain. Hotah's sharp eye had found it hidden in the snow. The beads Aiyanna had carefully strung around it reflected another delicate shade of blue, like a fallen piece of the winter sky. It was like holding a miracle in my hand. My tears never stopped until I opened a gift from Gideon.

Along with baking my favorite pie—apple—he gave me a Timex watch, which made me laugh. "Bought it at the mercantile in Bakersville," he said and winked.

Nobody understood the irony of it except Gideon and me, and neither of us offered to explain my laughter. It was my favorite gift.

I sat for a while by the tree and held my Christmas presents to my chest. I truly believed the worst was behind me. But the best part of that holiday was shopping for gifts with the money I'd earned from sweeping out the barn, polishing furniture, and helping Aiyanna in the kitchen. As I carefully selected each one, what churned in my gut was a mixture of delight and delusion. *What, exactly, do people want for Christmas?* Never in my life had I bought a present for anybody. *Will they like what I give them?* The joy of giving was a learned experience. I had enough money to buy a new leather wallet for Gideon, warm socks for Hotah, a fancy hair comb for Aiyanna, a book of Longfellow's poems for Baylor, and sweet-smelling dusting powder for Sidabee. My first actual Christmas purchases—I knew I would live on the thrill of watching them open those gifts for years to come.

After the flurry of gift-opening, I followed Aiyanna into the kitchen, my heart still singing, *'Tis the season to be jolly*, because I genuinely was. I was as jolly and joyful as I'd ever been. From the kitchen window, I watched windswept snow dance against the blackness of the open barn doors across the yard. Catching the reflection of Elvis behind me, growling softly in his dreams on a braided rug in front of the stove and refusing to move, I giggled. Aiyanna had to pirouette around him as she lifted her ham from the oven. Slow-cooked for hours, the top had caramelized, and the whole ham fell from the bone in mouth-watering chunks.

But it wasn't a Christmas carol I sang next. What popped into my head was the Carter family singing on the radio. I'd heard the song many times, but the meaning never registered until that Christmas Eve. *Oh, this is like Heaven to me. Yes, this is like Heaven to me. I've crossed over Jordan to Canaan's fair land, and this is like Heaven to me.* It captured the contentment I felt in the warm kitchen, with the aroma of the ham filling the air—a moment of pure bliss, a glimpse of Heaven on earth.

The church folk arrived at six, bringing with them the anticipation of a Christmas like I had never known. We had extended the dining table in the great room to seat twenty people, setting it with what looked to be God's own wedding china. Crystal glasses, white linen napkins, real silver silverware, a bowl of red and green apples polished to a glossy sheen, and tiny dishes of nuts and hard candy—I nearly fainted dead away in the excitement of it all. Wearing my new sweater set, watch, and necklace, I placed my hand on my heart once again to make sure I hadn't died and landed in Heaven after all.

It was, by far, the grandest supper of my life. Ham with pineapple, sweet potatoes, yeast rolls with butter, sweet corn at my request, beans and squash casseroles, and Jell-O molds filled with fruit, nuts, and little chunks of cream cheese. Hadassa and her sisters brought deviled eggs and macaroni and cheese, and Doctor Shelton's wife carried in Tupperware containers full of banana pudding and cut-out Christmas cookies. Blossom's caramel cake put a smile on even Hotah's face.

But the real winners were Gideon's apple and pecan pies. I ate until my gut threatened to burst through my pants, and I must've said *Merry Christmas* a thousand times.

After supper, Jesse, Sara, and I played Monopoly until Doctor Shelton, a dead ringer for Santa Claus in his costume, sat at the piano. He pounded out his favorite Christmas carols with such sidesplitting theatrics the entire room shook with laughter, mine included. I laughed until my ribs felt kicked in. And then I watched as Baylor slid one arm around Sidabee's waist, and she gazed up at him with a smile that sent a warm blush across my cheeks.

"Here, have some cider." Jesse passed me a glass from a nearby table. A knot formed in my throat, an indescribable mix of feelings. As I surveyed the room, soaking in the moment, I felt a surprising new sense of belonging. I never expected to feel like that. Everywhere I turned, people were happy. And so was I.

It was Christmas.

All was calm.

All was bright.

CHAPTER TWENTY-SIX

Once the guests had gone home, I admitted to a stomachache, and Gideon suggested we get some fresh air. His mind was working overtime again.

As we walked the snow-packed gravel drive toward the totem pole, our breaths forming misty clouds in the chilly air, Gideon shuffled along with his head hanging low and his hands buried deep in his pockets. It was easier to match his pace since my legs had grown stronger. I kept an eye on the sky, hoping to discover the Christmas Star of Bethlehem, picturing it as a celestial body more enormous than the moon.

Imagining myself as a Heavenly Host Angel, I devised a new message to deliver to the wise men and those abiding over their flocks. *Well, people of the world, no tidings of great joy for you this year! I never said peace on earth and goodwill toward white men only!*

But that's when Gideon's boots crunched to a halt in the snow. I figured he was out of breath, but he dropped a bombshell on me instead.

"You happy here?"

"You know I am. Are you?"

"I'm happy that you're happy." He walked a few more steps and stopped again. "Neeley, I gots something to tell you. I gots to go."

His words hung in the air, heavy with their implications. I was too stunned to move, to speak, to even understand what he was saying. All I could do was blink and breathe. Gideon had blindsided me completely.

"It's for the best. They gone find us, eventually. They already looking in this area. Mistah Baylor done tole me jus' today, somebody asking 'round town, sniffing out information about a little white girl and an ol' colored man, wondering if anybody like that show up lately."

My defiant nature took over, obliterating any trace of reason. "I refuse to listen to this!" I plunged my hands deep into my pockets, rushing ahead of Gideon, determined to drown out his words or at least force him into silence.

But he followed me. "You know somebody gone tell we out here on The Sanctum. Listen to me now. You belong here. Mistah Pudge won't fight Baylor for you. It's me he wants."

I spun around, walking backward to confront him. "How can you be so sure? How do you know he won't drag me away from here? Huh? You can't go! You can't abandon me. I won't let you!" Suddenly, my feet refused to budge. "How can you even consider leaving me? After what we've been through together! And what makes you so certain I belong here, anyway? I belong with you; we'll go to California. They'll never find us there. You haven't even bought a truck—"

"—I gots bus fare. Neeley, please—"

"—*Don't!* Don't you even think about it!"

Gideon pulled an envelope out of his pocket and handed it to me. "You need to look at this. I saved it for years—"

"—No! I don't want to look at *anything!*!" I sprinted back to the cabin, slammed the door shut, and raced upstairs to the loft, collapsing onto my bed. I sure as hello hoped Gideon felt my frustration as intensely as I felt his. Switching on the radio, somebody sang *I'll be home for Christmas* as if their heart were breaking wide open. And in that moment, I understood the source of Gideon's weariness and sorrow over the past few weeks. Where was home for him? As much as I yearned for The Sanctum to be his home, nobody had invited him to stay forever. And I never once considered that Gideon would leave me. I had to take care of him. Although I loved The Sanctum and the people on it, my place was with Gideon.

I moved to the window, resting my head on my folded arms. Outside, a perfect Christmas snow fell, a sharp contrast to the storm brewing inside me. Hearing Gideon talk quietly with Sidabee and Baylor on the porch, their voices a distant echo, I stared at purple mountains, their rims fading into an inky blue sky with shining stars like glittery ornaments. For the moment, I didn't want to think about *anything*. All I wanted was for Christmas to be over.

Everybody had gone to sleep, but I felt edgy—unsettled, like there was something important I needed to do. As if trapped in one of those terrible dreams where you try to scream, but nothing comes out. At midnight, I crawled out of bed and tippy-toed downstairs to sit in front of the fire, surprised to see Gideon there, his hands in his pockets, his heart on his sleeve. I startled him out of his thoughts.

"Merry Christmas," he said.

"Hmm. Merry Christmas." The glow from the hearth lit up our faces in orange and gold. We sat quietly for a moment, but it didn't last. Desperate, I had to try again. "You can't leave." I bit back fresh tears. "You can't leave me here without you."

"I won't make it through the winter, Neeley. The Klan, the sheriff, they looking for me." His voice turned flat and toneless. "I'm heading north. The coal mines in West Virginia. They always needing men. They'll take an ol' man like me and throw him down a mine shaft if he'll bend his back to dig coal."

"I'm going, too. You can't stop me." Firm and filled with a determination I didn't know I had, I wasn't letting him win this argument.

Gideon shook his head slowly, in time to a distant clock. "You staying put. You belong on this farm. This be a fine place. But it don't belong to me. There's not enough work here, drain these folks-a money they don't need to spend. These're good people. Salt of the earth, for sho'. But they not *my* people. I gots to find my place with what time God give me. You hear me good. You be fine, now. In a couple-a years—"

"—In a couple of years we could all be—*anything* can happen."

He leaned over and planted a kiss on the top of my head and then rested his black, leathery paw on my shoulder. "We can write. Telephone. I'll visit every Christmas. But you have a future. Here on The Sanctum."

"So do you. Baylor's a lawyer; he can represent you. I'm not afraid of the Klan."

He chuckled. "Yes, 'um. That be true enough. You probably the only girl ever went head-to-head with Catfish Cole. But your sweet courage won't save me. You know what they do to a colored man once they gots a bone to pick. Mistah Baylor, I'm sho' he a fine lawyer, but I doubt I gots much-a chance against an all-white-mens jury. I gots to go, and that's final."

I choked back my tears. Gideon made all the sense in the world, but I didn't want to believe it.

"Please, now. Take this envelope," he said.

I took hold of the torn and yellowed envelope, cracked with age, and folded over twice. I rubbed my thumb over its tattered edge. Stuffing it inside my robe pocket, I refused to read it.

"When you ready, you open it."

I sighed. "When are you leaving?"

"After the new year."

There was nothing left to say. I skulked up to bed, leaving Gideon alone with his thoughts. I didn't want to look at whatever was in the envelope.

Ever.

As the cold first light of day brushed across my face, I remembered it was Christmas morning. But something felt different beyond Gideon's bombshell announcement and my lay-it-on-thick, never-ending drama. There was no typical morning chatter. The cabin's awakening sounds at sunup had fallen into an eerie, uncommon silence. It was quiet—unusually quiet.

I stumbled to the window and wiped away the frost with the heel of my hand. Rubbing my eyeglasses clean with the hem of my pajama shirt, I watched snowflakes trickling from skies overcast in thick Confederate gray. A *real* little red bird flew to a snow-covered branch on the tall, bare maple tree outside my window. Its bright red feathers stood out against the white backdrop as if posing for me to appreciate him, as God would want. I tapped the window to get his attention, but he flew away. Like the red bird, I decided to ignore Gideon's ridiculous announcement and pretend I never uttered one ugly word in response. *That'll show him.*

White smoke spiraled out of the smokehouse chimney. A breeze in the crisp morning air moved leafless branches of nearby trees. From my perch, I craned my neck to see the wolves. Their snouts raised, twitching, detecting the tantalizing scents of hams and turkeys; it was a small blessing—a brief yet welcome distraction from my thoughts.

My taste buds rapidly woke to the scents of Aiyanna's bacon and coffee floating into the loft. After some hesitation, I forced myself to go to the kitchen, bypassing the great room, hoping to avoid Gideon. But there he stood by the stove, bright and shiny, all teeth and smiles, holding out my favorite blue mug. Surprise, annoyance, and a hint of affection—an overwhelming combination of emotions swirled around my head as I took the mug from him.

"Good coffee this morning. Have some. Gots cinnamon in it. Miz Sidabee's waiting for you to open your stocking. They all waiting." A pan of Gideon's sticky buns sat on the counter, ready to pop into the oven; apparently, they had delayed breakfast because of me.

"Thanks." I sipped at the coffee and burnt my tongue, but I didn't let him know. Holding my breath, I touched my heart, feeling it hammer in my chest. My eyes, wide with alarm, darted from corner to corner, searching for an escape from a day that was supposed to be filled with joy. I strained to not break down and bawl on Christmas. All that I did while keeping myself rigidly still and my tears at bay.

"Let's have a good day and forget about our talk last night. For now," he said.

"Okay." It was a timid reply to how I actually felt.

Gideon followed me into the great room, where I became the center of attention. It still felt strange to be fussed over so much. Opening the gifts inside the bulging sock gave me a strong sense of what real families did on Christmas.

My stocking contained all sorts of things; a small plastic disc where you try to get the silver balls into the eye holes of the clown; pencils for drawing and for school; a book of crossword puzzles; tubes of ChapStick; a Teen magazine; a journal with a privacy key; oodles of butterscotch candy, my favorite; clear nail polish, of which Sidabee said I could graduate to color later. Hair barrettes like Sidabee's, a book of quotes from famous people, a carved wooden flute like Aiyanna's, and a pocket-sized New Testament with my name printed in gold on the front. My fingertips traced the letters stamped into the Bible's leather cover. A confirmation of my real name—*Neeley Rae Morrigan*. A declaration that I was no longer a McPherson.

The adults behind me giggled like little kids, watching me open my gifts. But all I wanted, all I had fervently prayed for until the early hours, was for Gideon to utter the words I yearned to hear: *I've changed my mind. I'm staying with you.* That's all I wanted for Christmas, and didn't get.

By sundown, the solemn quiet of Christmas Day had consumed the house. The cabin smelled of a good deer roast, pine boughs, and candle wax. Later, I watched Gideon limp down the hall to his room. His rheumatism was acting up, which made me question why he thought he could dig coal.

After admiring all my presents, arranged like a string of pearls around the Christmas tree, I returned to the kitchen and discovered Sidabee sitting at the table, engrossed in her sketching, as usual. She drew while Aiyanna playfully drizzled a line of green detergent on the supper dishes, and I grabbed a towel. It was the one time of day Aiyanna and I got to chit-chat. Laugh. Gossip. Except that evening felt different—not because of Gideon, but something else entirely. Perhaps because it was Christmas or perhaps because of something I couldn't quite put my finger on.

Curiously, Aiyanna had *nothing* to say except to hum a tune I didn't know, all while Sidabee jabbered on about her expanding waistline, Eleanor Shelton's new hairdo, Hadassa, Robeena, and Jule's matching hats, and Jesse. She asked me what I thought about Jesse like she was my eighth-grade best friend. What could I say other than *he was nice.*

Sidabee's arm flowed across her drawing paper with its usual flare. Charcoal in hand, she threw occasional glances my way as if to snap mental pictures of me to use as inspiration. Her hand then resumed its fluid motion, gliding effortlessly—smooth as a trickling creek. She appeared to work without a serious thought, free to chat and laugh. I pulled the moment close to my heart, wondering if my mother and father had any unique talents.

But the conversation took an unexpected turn and drifted toward several of her old school friends when she was my age. Despite Sidabee's earlier reluctance to discuss her past, she now shared details—like her favorite color, a vibrant pink, and her desire to visit Saskatchewan, a word she found oddly pleasing to say. She confessed her love for peaches and her distaste for the grainy grit of pears. It was a new experience, this casual, frilly exchange of words with Sidabee. She talked and talked about silly stuff, unimportant pieces of her past, as if we had known each other all our lives, and I couldn't help but wonder what other secrets she kept on the pages of that sketchbook.

As I turned my back to Sidabee to dry more dishes, her voice suddenly flooded the air, loosening the tight hold I kept on my feelings toward her. She spoke non-stop, her words rushing like a rapid river, while I stole a glimpse or two of her drawing, finding it strangely familiar. For the moment, she seemed completely unaware of my presence, absorbed in a world of words, as if compensating for her weeks of silence.

Aiyanna finished washing up, nodded to Sidabee, and slipped away quietly. I don't recall how much time passed after that. I rubbed the dishtowel over each plate and bowl until they were bone dry, putting each piece away with precision and extending my time in the kitchen as she talked on. Unexpectedly, I felt her hands turning me from the pile of dishes to face her. It was a gentle, yet firm touch, and I sensed the warmth of her palms on my shoulders, as if trying to convey something, this time *without* words.

"Why aren't you listening to me, Neeley?"

"I'm sorry. What'd you say?"

"I asked you, what do you remember about your parents?"

The question stunned me, shattering my heart into tiny pieces. I snapped, answering her question as close to anger as possible without completely falling apart. "Why do *you care* all of a sudden!?" I was beyond hurt and confused. Squeezing my eyes shut, I pushed her away, not wanting her to see the neglected part of me that had survived my parents' deaths. The abused and damaged part that had been slowly dying for over eight years. But her presence vanished. The sound of her shoes echoed down the hallway, followed by her bedroom door creaking shut. Opening my eyes, I immediately regretted what I'd said, but there it lay on the table, what she had left behind.

I staggered to the nearest chair and sat, hardly believing what I had done. My hand trembled, turning Sidabee's sketchpad around, afraid yet needing to see what she had drawn. I stared hard at the picture for several minutes until the ice wall surrounding my hardened soul began to melt and drip from my eyes, leaving dime-sized water spots on the page. It was a charcoal drawing of my mother's face, more lifelike than my fading memory of her— so perfect, like a photograph.

Sidabee's handwriting glared up at me, neatly printed words across the bottom of the page. That's when I knew God had never moved from the driver's seat.

For Neeley, the soul of Elizabeth and Martin.

I tore the picture from the pad and bolted upstairs to find Gideon's envelope. After pulling it out of my robe pocket, my hands shook so badly that I had to sit on them for a whole minute. I unfolded the fragile envelope slowly and saw someone had addressed it to Elizabeth Morrigan in Summerfield, with a return address that read simply Bakersville, North Carolina, the postmark—December 3, 1951, a couple of weeks after my parents died. Tucked inside was a folded sheet of drawing paper curled at the edges, and I knew Sidabee had sent it to my mother.

As I opened it, the truth wrapped around me like a giant spider web. No matter how I tried, I couldn't pull myself from it. A smudgy sketch of a wolf's head filled the page—a wolf with a crown of thorns on its head—The Wild Christ. Nothing else. No letter. No words. Nothing.

Gideon had slipped up the stairs so quietly that I hadn't heard him—not until he bent over and gently touched the drawing I held in my hands. I looked up into his sad eyes. He had set me free. He had given me one last Christmas gift—the gift of truth.

"How long have you had this?" I asked.

"It arrived in Mistah Pudge mailbox not long after your parents' funeral."

"Who is Sidabee?"

Gideon squatted to look at me straight on. In the second it took for him to smile, the bottom fell out of my world, and the person I believed Sidabee to be—suddenly vanished.

"Miz Sidabee is your momma's sistah. She your aunt."

"My mother had a sister? How long have you known?"

"When we arrived and saw that big totem pole. At first, I thought it jus' be a fluke, so's I waited. When Hotah uncovered that Wild Christ painting, it tore me up inside, the Lawd answering mah prayers. I wasn't quite sho' who Miz Sidabee was 'til last night, Christmas Eve, when I spoke to her and Mister Baylor out on the porch. I did the right thing. Bringing you here."

Determined to breathe and not faint again, I hesitated. Holding the aged and yellowed drawing paper tight, I choked back a sob. "Does Pudge know about this? About Sidabee and this place?"

"Miz Sidabee, she explain everything. But Mistah Pudge never knew 'bout that envelope. I hid it from your grandfather, knowing it was a sign. That maybe I was to give it to you someday. Then, when we decided to leave Summerfield, I 'membered it after reading 'bout Bakersville in the newspaper. I dug it out of its hiding place and knew where we had to go. Miz Sidabee sent it to your momma for a reason. You gots to get the rest-a the story from your aunt. She be waiting for you downstairs."

Gideon stood and turned to leave. But then I felt his hand on my shoulder. "Miz Sidabee also drew your momma, I see."

I nodded.

"Seems she gave you the best Christmas present ever. A new family."

I remained motionless, fearing if I moved, I'd wake up and find myself back in my drab and gloomy bedroom in Summerfield. But it wasn't a dream; it was undeniably real.

I listened to Gideon's footsteps descending the loft stairs, each a painful reminder of his soon departure. With his whole heart and unwavering determination, he had made the grim decision to leave Pudge, no matter what it cost him. He had set my feet on a path before I had an inkling of what awaited me at the journey's end. But Gideon knew. From the moment he first held me, a five-year-old orphan sitting on his knee, he knew that his life was a set of events leading him to this pivotal moment. He knew because his life's mission was ensuring my safety, security, and the chance to be loved by someone other than himself. And once again, I turned the thrill of discovering the truth into sadness, a bitter acceptance of having to spend the rest of my life without my parents *and* Gideon.

CHAPTER TWENTY-SEVEN

I entered Sidabee's bedroom without bothering to knock. Overpowering scents of lavender, cigars, and pine filled the room. I didn't bother switching on the lamp. She wasn't there.

I found a footstool in front of the fireplace and sat, but the fire had gone out, leaving the room chilly. I held the envelope in my hands, turning it over and over, reluctant to open it again.

I'd seen her room during my first nickel tour, but I must have been too drunk on her beauty to get a good look at it. It seemed different somehow. Normally, I would've acted all googley-eyed in her and Baylor's private room. But not that day. I didn't want to think about what they did in that big bed. Or the possibility of them seeing each other naked in there. My face flushed hot.

I reached for my necklace, finding comfort in that I hadn't taken it off. Voices echoed through the cabin and then faded away. Within seconds, dainty footsteps clicked on the hallway floor. Sidabee steps. I stood, my hands sweating in the cold room and my tongue swelling in my mouth. *It's time. It's time to spill our big, dirty secrets across this pretty rug. Damn it, anyhow.*

Obviously surprised to see me in her room, uninvited, she stood there, staring at me. I briefly considered a quick escape and bolting past her, but I wanted to know. I had to know. I watched her close the door, which creaked out an eerie pitch that said, *let's do this.* She didn't utter a word, and she didn't need to. My hands shook, holding out the envelope and reading the return address written in her handwriting. "Bakersville, North Carolina."

To my amazement, blue tears glimmered on her eye rims, one spilling down her cheek. That solitary tear melted my remaining ice wall in the dimly lit room. Yet, I stayed rooted in place, my emotions a whirlwind inside me. Her gaze shifted from my face to the envelope that had sent my world into a tailspin.

"Gideon had this," I said. "Why did you send it to my mother?"

"In case she didn't receive the first drawing I mailed," Sidabee answered softly, her eyes fixed on the envelope. "But she received the first one, I'm sure of it. I have to believe they were on their way here the day they died. I'm thankful Gideon intercepted the second one. It brought *you* here." Pulling off her eyeglasses, she raised her head, and our eyes met.

I blinked first. "Did you send more?"

"No. Just two."

She stepped toward me, but I moved back and away from her.

"Neeley, please try to understand; let me explain—"

"—All this time, you knew who I was?"

She trapped me in a corner and tenderly swept away the curls sticking to my eyelashes. "I think I recognized you at first sight, but I dismissed it as impossible. There's no way you could appear here after so many years. I convinced myself it was mere coincidence, sharing a last name with my sister. After all, Morrigan is not an uncommon name in this state. Baylor and I knew other Morrigans in school. Several families nearby bear that surname. And of course, I had never met Gideon. He told us your grandfather pulled him out of the tobacco fields to work solely on the farm. And then, after your parents' funeral, to also take care of you."

Tears gathered in my throat. "No, I heard you talking to Baylor. You called me a con artist. A liar. Why didn't you just ask me!?"

"Oh, Neeley. I'm so—so horribly sorry you heard that. It was guilt. My guilt stopped me from asking you. I wasn't ready to know the truth. *To everything, there is a season and a time to every purpose under the Heaven.* And Baylor didn't want to bombard Gideon with questions that might've scared him away, taking you with him. In the end, it was Gideon who came to Baylor and me with the truth. There's so much to tell—"

"—Yeah? Well, I've got a few things to tell you, too."

"Neeley, it's not like you think. We had no clue Elizabeth and Martin had died until—"

"—Well, *fine!* But why didn't you come to get me when you found out?" I shouted. "Do you have any idea what I've gone through?" I collapsed hard to my knees. "Why didn't somebody come get me!?" *How could I forgive her?* Ripped from my mother and flung screaming into the cruel demands of a grandfather who hated my existence—*she knew*, and yet she left me there.

Sidabee gestured for me to join her on the footstool. Despite the weight of my anger and the air thickening in my throat, I leaned into her arms, fighting the urge to despise her. For the names she called me. For not coming for me. For keeping me at arm's length. But I felt her heartbeat on my cheek, her arms wrapped around me, soothing me. And then her voice broke, holding back more tears. "We are all guilty, Neeley. All of us. For not coming for you. But there *is* much you need to understand. Aiyanna has seen the scars on your back and legs. I didn't want to face it. I *couldn't* face it—this twist of fate."

Her hands continued caressing me as I pressed against her, letting out eight years of pain. She didn't pull back like she usually did. Instead, she soaked up my tears like a giant dishtowel, cradling me and running her hands over my head and back. My crying stopped to the point of uncontrollable hiccups as she seemingly pulled a tissue out of thin air and dried my face.

"Gideon told us what happened at the Greensboro Woolworths, how you stood up to the manager and later to your grandfather and the sheriff. He told us how wonderful you are and how you faced the Klan alone. And the price you paid for it."

An unusual quiet rippled through the room, sinking into dusk's softness. I sensed a long-dreaded truth expanding from someplace in the center of me. I needed to put the world in motion again, but I couldn't find the words. I felt suspended in the silence, clinging to Sidabee as if she were a log in some lake where my feet no longer touched bottom. My voice had dwindled to nothing, and I pressed my palm flat against my chest, checking once again for my heartbeat.

Perhaps another minute passed, maybe two. But I wiped away new tears with both hands, shoved my matted hair behind my ears, and figured, well, if she understood what I was about to say, maybe I could start looking at my whole face in the mornings, not just my forehead or the part I was scrubbing. I could find some good things to say about myself. I could even stand to say my own name.

I uncurled myself from her chest and allowed the reality of what I had done to pour out of my mouth. "But did Gideon tell you it's my fault your sister is dead?" I said it straight out, like I was talking to the wall, without thought or emotion. The words rushed out of me like a mudslide, filling the room with the swamp of truth, and I was drowning in it—incapable of stopping my tongue from spitting out every horrible thing I could say about myself. "I didn't mean to, but I did it. I killed my parents. Both of them. I flat-out killed them."

"Neeley—"

"—I was five. They'd had a huge fight with Pudge; he pulled a gun, and we left in a hurry. It was snowing, but I begged my father to put me on his lap. Sometimes, he did that, letting me pretend to drive. But I drove us straight into a truck, and the car flipped over and over—and over..." My voice trailed off. Pulling away from Sidabee, I wilted to the floor on my knees once again, my face in my hands. "I did it. I killed my mother. My father."

Powerless to stop the cold, accusing voice inside my head, I said the words that smashed the last of my broken heart, laid it raw and bleeding as if confessing my sins before God on Judgment Day, barely aware of the words that followed. "I *deserved* every beating, every whipping, every time he raised his belt, I deserved it. I *deserved* it."

Sobbing my heart clean out of my chest, I didn't realize Sidabee had collapsed beside me until she took my head in her hands and peeled off my eyeglasses. She put her lips to my cheeks, kissing away the tears that mingled with her own. Smoothing the hair out of my eyes, she was breathing hard. Her voice broke. "Neeley, Neeley, you stop this. Stop. My God. That's not a burden for even an animal to bear. You were five. It was an accident."

I was dizzy; my head wobbled and buzzed with *what-ifs*.

"Listen to me," she said. "You didn't kill them. Bad things happen that we have no control over. It happened, but you had nothing, *nothing* to do with your father not controlling his car. It wasn't your fault. Nobody is blaming you—but you." She drew me closer. "Dear, sweet, Neeley. We want you here; this is your home now. Hotah and Aiyanna have repeatedly told me of their fondness for you. They love you. I think you already know what Baylor thinks of you. He loves you, precious. And I love you. *I love you*, Neeley."

It was the first honest smile I had seen on her face. Dazed by her words, I wrapped my arms around her waist and buried my face into her neck. "I love you back." For the longest time, we sat like that—quiet, holding tight to each other, until my nose began to run, and I found myself sniffling, dabbing my cheeks with a soggy tissue.

Sidabee gave her head a shake. "Well, now. I'm feeling the pregnancy woozies. Let's take a break and talk more later, shall we?"

I was about to stand with her when something stopped me. Perhaps it was the quiet, a deep calm I didn't want to leave or disturb. "Do you mind if I sit in here a while?"

"Of course not," she said. "Stay as long as you like. I'll dig into the Christmas cookies and meet you later by the fire."

Overcome by the events of the past few hours, I stayed perched on the footstool long after Sidabee had left the room. The hands of a nearby clock ticked away the seconds and minutes until the aroma of cigar smoke, the flickering light and crackle from an evening fire, and the faint yet familiar voices in the great room pushed me to my feet. In my desire to halt the relentless march of time, I took deliberate, small steps down the long, cold hallway, wiping tears from my face and soaking up the sights, sounds, and smells of the cabin and its inhabitants.

Entering the room, I expected everybody to stare at me, but nobody did. Sidabee held a cookie to her pale lips, sitting in the middle of the sofa beside Baylor, who patted her back with one hand and rested a cigar on the right pointer finger of his other. Aiyanna hovered near the fire, pouring brandy into several glasses shaped like little bowls. At the same time, Gideon and Hotah seemed caught up in a card game and a conversation I couldn't quite hear over the howling of distant wolves—except for two chillingly familiar words to many Southern men of color. *Lynch mob.* It made me shudder even with the soft strumming of guitar music from the stereo's record player.

But as I walked past Two-Toes and Elvis curled up near Hotah's chair, a small table in front of a floor-to-ceiling window drew me in. On top sat an antique lamp, a tattered Bible, and a small, silver-gilded box. I had opened it weeks before and knew it held black-and-white photographs with curling edges. But I never cared to look at them until that moment.

I dug into the box, searching for pictures of my mother and thinking about how difficult it is sometimes to tell the truth. But the truth comes out as it always does, craving the light—demanding it, in fact—needing it like we need the sun. Like an innocent prisoner, it escapes the sturdiest, most skillfully told lies—even those clouded with half-truths or secrets hidden deep in the grave.

"Neeley?"

I felt her standing there, but I kept flipping through the pictures like a deck of cards. "I want to see any you have of her or my father," I said.

"I have a few." I ignored the light touch of her hand on my shoulder. "I've missed Elizabeth more than you can imagine. We were close," she said as if by saying those words, everything was suddenly hunky-dory.

I refused to look at her. "I'm wondering how you managed to forget her if you were so close because *I* certainly never could, and I was only five."

"I never forgot my sister." She paused like she didn't know what to say next. "Look, Neeley—I—I know your grandfather was mean to you—"

"—Mean to me?" My head snapped up to meet her eyes. I shoved the pictures back into the box and slammed the lid. *"You* have no idea."

Aiyanna appeared from nowhere, handing Sidabee a cup of tea. "Show her," she said and then walked away.

Sidabee sighed deeply, placed her tea on a side table, and slowly twisted her body, lifting the back of her sweater and lowering the waistband of her pants. Horrific scars, worse than my own, puffed up blue and white across her lower back. The shock hit me full force, and I shivered to my toes.

"These scars cover my body," she said.

Setting the box on the table, I let go of my anger, at least for the moment. "Tell me," I said. "I want to know how you came to this place."

Sidabee circled behind me, motioning me to sit beside her on a nearby settee. "Your grandmother married Bainbridge when Elizabeth, your mother, was ten. Elizabeth's biological father died in a farming accident, which happened often back then."

I felt the blood drain from my face. "Pudge isn't my grandfather?"

"Not really. There's no blood between you. You could say Elizabeth was my half-sister, but we didn't think of ourselves that way."

Sidabee continued like she was finally letting go of the secret she had protected for years—a secret that had come to an end. "I was born five months after Momma married my father, the man you call Pudge. Like most single women who find themself pregnant, she felt she had no choice. That she had to marry him."

The truth put me in a headlock. I sat riveted to every word.

"From the time I was little, he whipped me bloody while Momma pounded her fists on the other side of a locked door, threatening to call the police, which she never did because my father was lifelong friends with the local force, and most of *them* beat on their wives and kids," she sighed. "But every month or so, my father took his belt to me, and then he'd turn on Momma. But never Elizabeth. Because Elizabeth was not his daughter, he left her alone. Anyway, that's what we thought. We didn't know for sure why he never touched her, but it didn't matter. We were thankful for it. He'd take a casual slap at her occasionally, throwing her out of the way when she tried to protect me or Momma, but that was the extent."

"Then why me if I wasn't his real granddaughter?"

"That's a mystery. We had hoped and prayed he *wasn't* hurting you. I'm guessing he beat you because there was no one left to take out his meanness on." Sidabee pulled a clean handkerchief from her pocket and sighed the most profound sigh I'd ever heard. "From when I was old enough to remember, I held his big fat Bible to my chest while he belted me. Over the years, Bainbridge grew worse as his drinking got worse."

"And then, shortly before Elizabeth's twenty-third birthday, she ran off and married Martin. Within days after their marriage, the Army drafted Martin and sent him to basic training. Elizabeth discovered she was pregnant only a week before they sent Martin overseas. She had no choice but to stay with Momma on the farm."

"It was November 1st and raining hard. I had just passed *my* thirteenth birthday. My father forced me to go back to church with Elizabeth. I had quit for a while, but that's how Bainbridge hid his meanness by keeping his family in the good graces of the congregation. Elizabeth and I attended service that morning without Momma because she said she was sick. As I recall, Elizabeth's back was giving her fits. Nine months pregnant with you, she said you had about kicked her insides black and blue."

Sidabee smiled then. I couldn't help but return it, anxious for her to continue.

"I remember arriving home from Sunday school, searching every room, and not finding Momma. When I asked my father where she had gone, he was drunk as usual and said, 'I don't know, I don't care. Out in the barn, I guess.' Momma never went to the barn unless it was for a good reason. She didn't like the mules. They scared her. But when Bainbridge passed out in his bed that night, I hurled myself outside to find her. She stood inside a horse stall, waiting for me with my packed bags. She drove me to the Winston-Salem bus station and the next day told my father I had run away."

Sidabee sipped her tea and squeezed my hand. "I had to get away from him; I had to. Elizabeth wouldn't leave because of Martin, but mostly because she was ready to deliver you any day. Elizabeth had—pregnancy complications and couldn't travel or leave the doctor familiar with her case." Sidabee's eyes scanned the room. "Are you understanding this so far?"

"Yes," I said. "Please. Tell me the rest."

"Momma had told me the MacLennans were her friends long before she married Bainbridge. She sent me away, hoping and praying for the best where Elizabeth and Martin were concerned. Still, Elizabeth begged Momma to tell her where I had gone, but she wouldn't chance it. And then one day, Momma secretly telephoned me here. Swearing me to secrecy about my whereabouts, she arranged for me to contact my sister shortly before you were born. It wasn't that we didn't trust Elizabeth, but one slip-up and my father would've come after me. Or so we thought. Anyway, on a planned Saturday morning, Elizabeth walked to the phone booth at the Summerfield filling station. But Bainbridge had followed Elizabeth into town, snatched the phone from her, and said to me, 'I wish you were dead, Sidabee. Don't ever call here again or come back, or you will be. I'll kill you, and then, I swear, I'll kill your mother.' Those were the last words my father said to me. He terrified me; I was just a young girl, the same age as you are now." Tears welled up in Sidabee's eyes. "And that was also the last time I ever heard Elizabeth's voice."

"As you can see, I was blessed to end up here. And, of course, Baylor's parents took me in. Five years later, I married their son."

My head throbbed. "I knew he was evil," I said, wishing I had never heard the name Bainbridge McPherson. "Sidabee, I—I never had a clue you existed. I had begged Pudge to tell me about my parents and my grandmother. But he refused. He never said a word about my family. Nothing."

Sidabee clasped her long, slender fingers together. "No. I'm sure he didn't. Why would he? I had to devise a way to inform Elizabeth of my location so they could move here upon Martin's return. I sketched the wolf and mailed it to her, aware that she was always the one to take the mail out of the box. But as time passed without a word from them, Baylor's father made inquiries and discovered that at the end of Martin's stint in the army, he sustained injuries—shot in the leg and hip. He spent over a year and a half in and out of army hospitals. Eventually, the doctors discharged him as you approached your fifth birthday. I knew my sister would try to find us, so I sent the second drawing. The one Gideon kept hidden."

I crossed my arms and squeezed myself to stop shaking. "I didn't know my father well."

Sidabee's brow lifted. "He was a good soldier. A decent man who loved you deeply. You meant everything to Elizabeth and certainly your father since he was an only child, and his parents were deceased."

I nodded, unable to say anything at all. I wanted my guilty stains gone.

Sidabee gently touched my arm. "Neeley, what happened to them wasn't your fault," she reassured me. Tenderly, she brushed my hair away from my face with her fingertips. "Remember how scared you were living with your grandfather? I was once a child like you, living under that same roof. Deep in my heart, I feared that one day, intentionally or not, he would kill me. It's why Momma sent me here. But even now, I live in terror of him."

She let out a sigh, filled with remorse I could hear—and feel. "After your parents passed away, I desperately wanted to rescue you from his clutches. Yet to see him again—I couldn't—I couldn't do it. And then, I couldn't face you. Not even when Aiyanna spoke of your scars. Truly, there is no life lived without regret. Ours was not coming for you. It was wrong, Neeley, and I ask for your forgiveness. Please, forgive all of us."

Numbed by her words, I had nothing to say. I wasn't sure how I felt. Sitting next to her—quiet again—I tried to take it all in. She had pulled a photograph out of her pocket and held it in her hand—a woman standing next to a rose trellis, like our rose trellis back in Summerfield. After a few minutes, she handed it to me. "This is my mother," she said. "Your grandmother."

I took it from her hand like a rare and expensive gem. It was my first glimpse of the grandmother I had never known—never even seen a picture of.

"My goodness," Sidabee said hoarsely. "This could be a photograph of you. Maybe that's why he abused you. Because you look so much like her."

"How did my grandmother die?"

Sidabee stood and walked to the windows, holding tight to the ledge. "Gideon says you believe your grandfather murdered her."

"Didn't he?"

"The only thing he killed, Neeley, was her spirit."

I blinked. "What—do you mean?"

"Many times, my father had threatened to kill Momma if she so much as *thought* about leaving him. But the day you were born, Bainbridge had beaten Momma badly and then drank himself into unconsciousness. She never even got to go the maternity ward to see you, or say goodbye to Eliazbeth. Momma left him in the middle of the night. Not a soul knew she had deserted my father. He told everyone that she died. In the end, Elizabeth and Martin didn't make it here, and we believed we couldn't take you away from him. Otherwise, he would've found Momma."

"What—what are you saying?"

"We had to protect her. My father would've killed her. Neither she nor I could ever return to Summerfield or any place close to it."

"*She's alive?* Are you saying my grandmother is alive?"

"She is. Maeve McPherson is alive, and she's anxious to meet you."

I looked at Gideon, who had stopped playing cards with Hotah, and then back at Sidabee. "All these years living with Pudge," I said, shaking my head. "All these years, my grandmother was right here. Why is she so anxious now? Thirteen years is a long time to wait."

"You bet it is!"

I spun around. There she stood. An older version of myself who seemed to have appeared from nowhere. Curling my hands into fists, I strained to imagine her thoughts as she faced me for the first time. Silence filled the room as ever-present as air, and my vision narrowed to the last time Pudge swung his belt at my small body, with no regard as to where it landed. Long-buried pain bubbled to the surface; remorse, grief, and anger warred inside me, and I strained with all my might to wrap my mind around the fact that my grandmother was really and truly alive.

"Neeley," she said.

Dragged back to the present, I looked at the picture in my hand and then at her. "It's you," I said.

Chapter Twenty-Eight

I would have recognized her anywhere. Her striking green eyes sparkled behind eyeglasses shaped like mine. But it was her red hair that drew me to her. At the age when most women put their hair in a bun, she chose to wear hers in a single long braid trailing to the middle of her back and streaked with gray, but beautifully streaked. She was thin as a blade, too thin, maybe. Silver earrings dangled down the sides of her neck where copper ringlets had sprung free—again, like mine. She had draped a blue shawl over one shoulder and tied it at the opposite hip over a white blouse and a straight wool skirt that brushed the tops of her black boots. She wore lipstick, red.

I opened my mouth to speak, but the words vanished before they took shape. I felt her drawing me in, speaking what sounded like the language of Hotah and Aiyanna. Words, strange syllables, and phrases I didn't understand.

She reached for me. "I have waited for this moment all my life. Welcome home, child."

Her fingers felt so slight and feeble that I hardly dared squeeze them. I remembered my baptism in the Haw River, the joy rushing over me, the flood of God's overwhelming love; and for a moment, her touch felt similar to rising from that cold river. "Pudge said you were dead. There was a funeral. A gravestone and everything."

"That sounds like Bainbridge—too proud to admit his wife had left him. Grant Dooley was the county coroner and his beer-drinking buddy back then. I'm sure they concocted some story to explain my disappearance." She sighed a deep and strangely labored sigh. "Sidabee needed me. I had to go to her. She was so young."

I nodded slightly, clenching my eyes shut. Numbness crept over my entire body that time. *Oh God, this can't be happening.*

"Elizabeth and Martin were bringing you here."

I wanted her to stop talking, but I opened my eyes and squeaked out my words. "I'm—I'm so sorry they died—"

She held up her hand. "What's past is past. I have kept you in my heart and prayed for your deliverance from the day you were born."

"The little cabin on the hillside. I'm guessing it's yours?" I asked, soft in my bitterness. The words hid my mounting anger. My heart raced; my pulse jumped beneath my skin.

Sidabee moved swiftly to my grandmother's side and answered for her. "Yes, it is." I assumed she led both of us to the sofa so nobody would faint.

My grandmother's skin appeared as delicate as an eggshell, and the faint blue veins on her face and hands spoke of her fragility. Her voice was no more than a whisper when, as soon as we both sat, she said, "Let me look at you."

Her cool fingers gently cupped my cheek and glided over my neck. The scent of her freshly starched blouse was that of my mother. She pulled me close, her cheek to mine, and held it there a second before leaning back to examine me further, when from the corner of my eye, I noticed Gideon stand at the card table, dropping his gin rummy cards, and holding tight to his chair.

"*Margaret?* That you?" he asked. "I wasn't sure, I mean—I hardly recognized you."

My grandmother turned to see Gideon's stunned face, but I think the rest of us froze solid. "Gideon." She caressed his name like a silk scarf. "Yes, it has been many years."

Gideon chuckled softly. "It *is* you, then."

"It's me," she blinked, or perhaps she batted her eyelashes; it was hard to tell. "My name is Maeve, not Margaret."

Gideon stepped closer, and I thought he was about to keel over. "As Neeley grew up, I 'spected, but never knew fuh sho'. So. That was your secret? You were Mistah Pudge wife?"

"I was."

"I s'pose I understand now. Why you disappeared. You was trapped."

"I was trapped."

"I—I have missed you every day since—since that last day. I thought you'd run off, 'cause-a me being—me being a Negro, and jus' a poor one at that. I never knew you was his wife." Gideon shook his head slowly. "Now you here. Not Margaret, but Maeve. Maeve McPherson." His deep sigh floated across the room like a tire going flat. "Law."

My grandmother stood and swept a smile around the room, silently reassuring us. Then she faced Gideon as if time and her sheer will had somehow transported them into a private place. "That's right. It's why I removed every picture of me out of that house before I left him. I didn't want you to know. I didn't want anyone to know I'd fallen—fallen in love with you." Her fingers flickered over her mouth as if waiting for Gideon's reaction. But he offered no comment. No smile. I was satisfied with his silence. She had deserted both of us.

"My regrets seem to be piling up with every passing minute. I'm sorry, Gideon. So truly sorry." Her voice, tinged with deep-seated grief, suddenly grew more heartbreaking with each tiny step she took toward him. "Before Neeley's birth, I saw Bainbridge discussing with you the possibility of moving into the shed to tend to the farm's mules and horses. I knew if you accepted his offer, our paths would cross at the house. I heard he employed you after I left him—to tend the farm. And then, after Elizabeth's passing, to also take care of the house and Neeley." She nodded. "God placed you in my granddaughter's life to watch over her. For that, I am ever grateful."

I figured my grandmother would have the rest of her life to explain what attracted her to Pudge, but the affair with Gideon was a story that could not wait another day. And, from the look on everybody's faces, we all wanted to know. The Book of Revelation had flipped open, its seals broken, and the truth poured out all over The Sanctum. All in one day. Gideon and my grandmother had turned our lives inside out.

The first day of January brought the gentle tap of ice and snow on our windows, a reminder of the continuing winter and the isolation of the mountaintop we lived on. The outside world was but a distant echo; its prejudices and evils didn't exist on The Sanctum, and that gave me hope—hope that Gideon had found a reason to stay.

For me, time finally stood still. The family gathered in the evenings, captivated by the timeless tale of Margaret and Gideon—two star-crossed lovers who had lost each other in the circumstances of their lives. A story even William Shakespeare himself would have proudly penned. I lived on the meat of it for days—the thrill and the sorrow. So did my new aunt. It was news to her, too.

Maeve, known to Gideon as Margaret, had spent her entire life in Summerfield. Her dowry included her father's horse and tobacco farm, the farm Pudge ended up with. Once a symbol of her family's wealth and status, it fell into disrepair in my grandfather's hands.

Every year, a new crop of migrant workers arrived during the tobacco harvest. In approximately the thirty-seventh year of his life, Gideon showed up in Summerfield, looking for work. Pudge, newly married to my grandmother, hired him for a dollar a day to work in the fields. Twenty-five years later, he had long been my grandfather's best tobacco picker.

In the spring of 1946, the year I was born, my grandmother and Lila Goodeve met Gideon when the Wayside Baptist Church raised money for the Appalachian Unfortunate Negro Children's Fund. The Women's Committee elected Lila to present the donation to the local colored church in a gesture of goodwill on Easter Sunday, and Maeve, Lila's best friend, tagged along.

Gideon sat in the congregation. *On the fifth row from the front, he said. I will never forget the moment I laid eyes on Margaret. Spellbound by her, I tole mahsef' 'n God, if I can't have her, I never want another.* When the service ended, he made a beeline for my grandmother, pretending to bump into her in the parking lot. *Excuse me, ma'am,* he said. *I see your car's tire is almost flat. My name's Gideon.*

M—Margaret, she said.

"I couldn't tell him my real name," she explained. "Everybody in town knew me."

Gideon winked at her. "You never tole me your last name, either."

My grandmother sighed. "I believed our relationship would go no further than the county line we crossed those times we spent—" She stopped. Her face flushed red, and I felt her embarrassment. "—The nights we spent in my car, talking until dawn." She looked at me and Sidabee, her head held high, as if she didn't need our approval for her past actions, just our understanding. "I lied to Bainbridge and told him I had to check on my sick aunt who lived at Wrightsville Beach. Gideon and I, well, it was the most magical time of my life," she sighed.

I watched them as their eyes met. The magic was still there.

"Three days and two nights. We took all the back roads and stayed away from people and towns. I thought I'd end it once we returned to Summerfield, but I couldn't. I was in love with him. We continued to meet secretly, twice a week."

"All that time, she never tole me her real name or that she had two daughters and was 'bout to be a grandmomma."

Gideon looked at me and smiled but quickly lowered his chin to his chest, his smile—gone. "I had no car to follow her, find out where she lived. Nobody knew I was seeing her. Nobody. It was as dangerous for me as for her. The law says, *it's unlawful for a white person to marry anyone except another white person.* 'Course, I didn't know she already married. Onliest thing I knew—I was in love with a red-headed woman named Margaret. A woman who entered a room and filled it like perfume. And that she lived close by. I 'spected she was married but had no way to find out. Coloreds and white people didn't associate anymore then than they do now. I dreamed tho'. I dreamed someday we'd go to Chicago, someplace folks be more accepting. But it wasn't to be."

"Gideon is right. Our affair lasted from spring until autumn. Only six months. 1946. The year you were born, Neeley. Until the day I saw Bainbridge speaking to Gideon about employment. Life with Bainbridge had rapidly grown worse. Once I sent Sidabee to Bakersville and Elizabeth gave birth to Neeley, I left Bainbridge. I had to. But poor Elizabeth, she had to suffer through my fictitious funeral. And then I heard the news. That she and Martin had died and the court awarded Neeley into her grandfather's custody."

My grandmother tugged a handkerchief out from beneath the cuff of her sleeve and dabbed at her tears. "I simply lost myself for a while. I moved out to the cabin where I live now. It's quiet there. Peaceful."

The room grew as hushed as a balmy June day. Hotah reached for Aiyanna's hand as if grateful they were of the same race and that their marriage was not up for challenge. Baylor popped a match with his thumb. Lighting his cigar with big billowy puffs, he winked at Gideon, who returned his smile, nodding, relaying a secret code only men knew. I buried my face in Two-Toes fur, my arms slipping around his thick neck. The peace in the room felt as if we could reach out and hold it. Sidabee laid her head on her mother's shoulder. "Happy New Year, everybody," she said. Her words as soft as a lullaby, she placed her hand on the small mound of baby under her sweater. "1960. Wonder what the next decade will bring?"

"Can I do that for you?" She had followed me everywhere for days. Maeve, as I had decided to call her, folded clean tea towels at the kitchen table and watched my every move.

"Oh, no. I'm fine." After making toast for myself, I mixed the Ovaltine into my milk. "I have to put a dishtowel underneath it; Aiyanna likes to keep rings off the countertops."

Sidabee had asked Maeve to stay a while in the open guest room at the big cabin so I could become accustomed to having a grandmother around. She agreed. Also, I was sure my grandmother wanted to be near Gideon. But that morning, I had dragged myself out of bed. Questions still hung inside me, not wanting to come out or go back down. Like swallowing an aspirin, which gets lodged halfway, and that bitter taste creeps up in your mouth. On top of that, I'd lost my necklace. I laid awake half the night worrying.

Maeve sipped at her hot tea, leaving a tattoo of her red lips on Aiyanna's tea cup. Her fingers reminded me of the backbones of chickens with walnuts for knuckles. "Something on your mind, dear?"

"I can't find the necklace that Hotah and Aiyanna gave me for Christmas," I said.

"Where do you think you misplaced it?"

"I don't know. I had it on yesterday. I spent the day in the pups' pen and helped Hotah cut and carry wood. Hotah said it was a necklace like the Cherokees wear to a fire dance. I loved it. I've worn it every day since Christmas Eve. But I believe it's lost forever in the snow."

"Consumed by the snow, like the three Hebrew boys—consumed by the fiery furnace," she said and sighed. And then she smiled, which, for some reason, grated on my last nerve. "One day is not forever. It'll turn up."

I nodded. *Maybe. Then again, it might rest on the ground's frozen crust until the snow melts a hundred years in the future, only to be found by another girl.* "It all comes back to snow and cold," I said finally. "It keeps taking things from me."

"Only if you allow it." Her voice sounded matter-of-fact. Like *big deal*; it's just a necklace. I could no longer swallow my bitter pill; I had to spit it out.

I set my glass of Ovaltine on the table. "*Allow* it? I don't know about you, but I don't have that kind of power."

"What I mean is—"

"—I don't care what you mean. *Allow* it? Do you mean like I shouldn't have *allowed* my grandfather to beat the shit out of me every time I looked at him sideways or said something he didn't like? Where were you while I was *allowing* him to beat me bloody? I still can't get over it—that you never even once tried to take me away from him. Or did you *allow* yourself to forget I existed so you could save *your own hide!*?" My breath coiled in fierce, short puffs from my nostrils. I felt my nails digging into my skin until I placed my palms flat on the table to steady myself. But I shook so badly the Ovaltine vibrated in my glass.

Maeve rose slowly. Her eyelids fluttered as she looked away from me, her hand moving about her mouth. I thought she might cry.

I chewed at my lip, my tears flowing hard and fast. Outside the window, a flock of crows flew past. Their ceaseless *caw-caws* filled the dead air, scolding and warning me that the resentful tone in my voice might stay like that forever if I *allowed* it. I could dig my grave, *allow* myself to slip off into that place meant for sinners, where the worm never dies, or *allow* my spitefulness to take over, turning me from sweet to sour with a flick of my tongue.

"I will keep an eye out for your necklace, and you should too," Maeve said, wrapping her shawl around her shoulders. She slipped out the back door without a sound, leaving only her perfumy scent behind.

Standing there like a pillar of salt, my spirit wholly emptied out; I struggled not to breathe it in.

CHAPTER TWENTY-NINE

Aiyanna said that Sidabee and Baylor had set off early for Boone on business, and would likely to be away for the night. I spent the rest of the foggy morning with the wolf pups, but afterward, the fog remained resistant to the sun and refused to budge, much like my attitude toward Maeve.

Water droplets speckled my eyeglasses as I walked back to the cabin. I thought about the folks who liked fog—the enchanting part, the mysterious allure of it in places they'd traveled to, like London, Casablanca, and Timbuktu. I'd never liked fog. It conjured images of dank, ancient castles, lurking vampires, and goosebumps that suddenly broke out on my neck, along with a sinister creepiness bleeding out of the ground and into my boots. But my heart stopped as Hotah appeared out of the fog. I slipped, nearly tumbling backward, and would've fallen on my rump if he had not caught me with his massive hands.

"Thick as gut-paste," he said, shaking his head, ignoring my startled look.

"I couldn't see you."

"Mountain fog. It is my old friend. How about we have a cup of coffee?"

Hotah retreated to the cabin, fading into the blanket of white, and I quickened my pace to stay within arm's reach, trailing him up the hill and the back porch. Entering the warm kitchen was a welcome relief, and I could finally see my hand in front of my face. Two wet wolves followed us inside, staking their claim near the fire, while the aroma of hot coffee wafted from the stove.

I ran my hand through my damp hair and opened my mouth to speak, but the telephone rang. I picked it up. "MacLennan residence."

Silence.

"Nobody there?" Hotah asked.

I shook my head.

"Hmm," he grunted, his voice a low rumble. We sat in the morning's stillness, facing each other across the table, sipping coffee and saying nothing.

Finally, Hotah smiled a quick curve of thin, dry lips. "Have you seen the eagle since your arrival?"

I recalled an eagle screeching over my head the day Raven died, chastising me. "Yes, I've seen it."

"Do you know what eagles do when they fly?"

"I don't know. Hunt for food? Poop on cars?"

Again, a grunt. "They do a lot if you pay attention. An eagle will ride the currents for hours, flying thousands of feet high, then dive from the sky as if they've lost their wings, zeroing in on its prey. What does that teach you?"

"I don't know," I said. Again.

"It teaches you that if you want to hunt, you must watch patiently, sometimes from great distances. Do you know who taught me that?"

I shook my head because, of course, I had no idea what he was getting at.

Hotah's mouth set into a determined line. "My grandfather. His name was Haroldo Wohali—means powerful eagle. He was a Cherokee chief. He often sent me into the woods or a meadow and said, 'Sit still, young Hotah, watch, and then come and tell me what you saw.'"

I leaned back in my chair, still pondering the point of Hotah's story.

"When I returned home and told my grandfather I saw an eagle flying overhead, he would ask, 'How long did it soar on the wind currents? Did you spot its nest? Where did you see it?' He shared tales of the eagle and its significance to the Cherokee." Hotah's words spilled out like baby chicks tumbling from an incubator. "My grandfather only spoke when he had something to teach me."

"Smart grandpa," I said.

"Yes, he was. He sometimes led me to the bank of a stream or a river with my eyes closed. Then he would ask, 'How deep is it?' I would listen. If the water ran shallow, the rocks whispered close to the surface. But I knew we had better find a boat if silence reigned over the river. That is how we knew where to cross—by listening to the water talk."

"He taught you that?" I asked.

"It is not unusual for Cherokee children to learn from their elders. We learn even when we play. My grandfather taught me the language of the wolf." Hotah sucked on his teeth for a minute, then breathed out heavily. "All of nature sends messages from the Great Creator. I attended a white man's school, but it was my grandfather who taught me to pay attention to the world and every creature on it. He talked to wolves. He understood them. Sometimes, I would follow him into the woods and hear him speak in their tongue."

"He talked to wolves? Sounded like a wolf?"

"Not quite. He felt their energy and rolled his voice in his throat in short bursts of whistles or noises using his tongue and teeth. He taught me what each sound meant: the growls, howls, yips, whines, and yelps. Wolves rely on many forms of communication. They also use their lips, eyes, and tail. The yawn of a wolf does not always mean he is tired. Sometimes, it means he is tense, and you must be careful near that wolf."

And then he paused so long I thought he had finished talking. But in the next second, he said, "I would like to ask you, Little Red Bird, what did *your* grandfather teach you?"

My sight blurred. I had to take off my eyeglasses and rub my eyes. The question came out of nowhere. It took several minutes to think about an honest answer. "To drive. He taught me to drive."

Hotah raised one eyebrow, his face pokerlike. "Did he teach you anything else?"

"No. Nothing."

"Your greatest weakness, Little Red Bird, is that you do not know how to see or listen, because no one has properly taught you.

And now, you have closed your ears to your grandmother because of mistakes she made a long time ago, and has since regretted many times over. You are wrong in your unforgiveness. God has forgiven her by bringing you here. God, the Great Creator, has placed knowledge in everything, but you have much to learn. He has given you a gift, and yet you refuse it."

Hotah looked at me long and hard as tears pooled in my eyes.

"My grandfather also taught me the mind will destroy what the heart does not break. You have imagined the worst about your grandmother, but she is old; her years are not long for this earth. She is knowledgeable. It would be a shame to waste your time together because you cannot bring yourself to listen to her. You have lost your way, Little Red Bird. Your grandmother can teach you many things if you do not harden your heart. To live a full life, you must learn to forgive, especially those worthy of it."

Tears dripped down my face, splattering on the table. "I don't mean to be a bad person. I don't mean to hurt anybody." I wanted to hug Hotah and cry on his shoulder.

"Do you want to try again?"

"Yes, but I hurt her. Don't you see? I end up hurting everybody, even Gideon. Everybody I love, I hurt." Sobbing, I soon realized Hotah was not about to pity me.

He *slammed* his fist on the table, and I jumped. "Have you ever heard of what happened on the Trail of Tears?"

I nodded as the words lodged in my throat. "White men took you from your land."

"Took us? They did not haul us away in trucks, wagons, or even on horseback. What kind of teachers do you have these days? *Took us?* Is that what you call killing thousands of men, women, and children by forcing us out at gunpoint and burning our homes? They marched us off *our* land *on foot* to a desolate place hundreds of miles away, where we died from starvation and disease."

Hotah's eyes flickered like two bonfires. "They violated many tribes, not only the Cherokee. They *took* what did not belong to them, not caring we had hunted, raised children, and grown old on the land for centuries. They did not care about our traditions and beliefs. They did not consider the sick and elderly among us or that we had buried our ancestors beneath the ground they built their towns on. Little Red Bird, your trail of tears is nothing compared to mine and my people or Gideon and his people. I have had to forgive to survive. Rivers don't run backward, and neither should you. You must forgive your grandmother and move forward to survive."

I nodded again. "Can you take me to her cabin?"

He looked across the table with his lined, tired face, then stood and pushed in his chair. "Come. Aiyanna is waiting for us in the truck."

We drove through soupy early afternoon fog in a blanket of silence. Winter had dipped to its deepest point, and the day faded fast toward twilight. Hastened by the fog, darkness promised to arrive by five o'clock. From the wolves' pens, the smaller cabin seemed farther away than it actually was. A ten-minute ride in Hotah's truck brought me to a miniature replica of the cabin I had walked out of only moments before.

Aiyanna opened the truck door to let me out, but Hotah's hand on my shoulder stopped me, and I sensed his concern that I understood he had meant only to teach me, and not to scold me. "Inside each of us, two wolves wage battle," he said. "One, fueled by rage, malice, and vengeance, it roams a thorny, bloodstained terrain, finding no contentment. The other walks in harmony with the earth and embodies a serene spirit; his powerful legs move with purpose. He is at peace."

Stunned silence was my only response.

"You have felt these wolves," he said.

I nodded. I *had* felt them. Heard them, in fact. "Hotah?" My reflection in Hotah's eyes stared back at me. "Which wolf will win this battle inside me?"

He sat with his hands gripping the steering wheel of the idling truck. "The one you welcome at your heart's door, Little Red Bird."

I scooted out of the truck and watched them drive away over the snow and rut-covered path to the road, and I wondered—how much hardship a body had to endure for that kind of wisdom.

Climbing the porch steps alone, I wiped the mist from my eyeglasses and brushed snow off my coat, imagining daffodil and hyacinth bulbs sleeping in the dormant flowerbeds. Greeted by several rocking chairs strewn over the wide porch, I saw myself sitting in one, drinking lemonade while my grandmother catnapped in another. But as I stepped toward the door, winter's wind shoved more fog across the mountain, blowing a vicious gust that stung my face.

No knocking was necessary; the door swung open. Her furrowed brow muscles rose when she saw me. Sunken cheeks and pale skin spoke to her lifetime of endured hardships, and new brown spots dotted her gnarled hands—hands lost in the mass of hair she smoothed back from her forehead. Arthritic hands. Hands born to yank cow teats, scrub floors, snap pole beans, and hide her face from the passing slap of a drunken husband.

Her purple cardigan, left unbuttoned over a cream-colored blouse, appeared soft but threadbare from the years it spent wrapped around her. The Indian beads circling her bird-like neck matched her brightly colored earrings dangling against colorless skin. But her stooped shoulders spoke of secrets and burdens she had long carried, along with the weight of my last words to her.

I let my next word come out as soft and effortlessly as a spit bubble. "Grandmother?"

Red, wet eyes stared at me strangely, and then she smiled, a smile that didn't quite reach her eyes. She wasn't wearing her usual lipstick, and I saw myself in her eyeglasses, a reflection of her younger self.

"You doing okay?" I asked, knowing full well she wasn't.

"I'm fine now. Come in, child. Shake off the chill."

It shouldn't have surprised me when I saw Gideon sitting comfortably at her kitchen table, but it did. He sat there, smiling and picking at his teeth with a toothpick. "She still makes the best roast beef sandwiches. Yes, 'um, I never had none better. Gots them little hot pickles mixed in with the mayonnaise. You should try one, Neeley."

I turned up my smile a notch. "I'd love one."

"Well. Make yourself at home," she said. "It'll only take a minute."

While my grandmother prepared my sandwich, I wandered around her front room. With two fireplaces on either side, the cabin reminded me of an antique store I had visited in Greensboro. "Your home is beautiful," I said, hoping I didn't sound foolish.

Perched high on a beam across the middle of the ceiling, a stuffed owl glared at me. Indian artifacts hung across the walls, along with Sidabee's paintings. Someone had nailed buckskins into the river rock over the fireplace mantels. I smelled furniture wax everywhere. My hands glided over the rocking chair's deep-red velvet cushion and a matching velvet sofa. Crisp white panels hung beneath velvet-corded drapes. It was one big velvet living room.

Fringed throw rugs covered wide plank floors, and fancy glassware sat on shelves and in cabinets throughout the cabin. But it was the ornate-framed photographs of Sidabee and my mother as little girls I stared at. Then I noticed a drop-leaf table where elaborately carved pipes appeared displayed but broken. Someone had arranged them on a fancy doily.

"We don't attach the stems to the bowls," she said, suddenly behind me. "They're supposed to be kept separate except when smoked."

"Do you smoke these, too?"

My grandmother's smile surprised me. "Something I do occasionally since coming here," she said.

I nodded, not knowing what to say next.

But then Gideon's reassuring voice echoed from the kitchen, covering me like a quilt. "Neeley. Your sandwich is ready."

Her kitchen was exactly as it should've been. Copper pots and pans hung from a brick arch over the stove. Canned fruits and vegetables, salt pork, and hefty tins of flour, sugar, and salt filled her large pantry. An apron hung from a brass hook on the wall, and red rose china lined the plate rails above a sideboard table next to the Hoosier cabinet. She had displayed a collection of salt and pepper shakers in all shapes and sizes on the windowsills. And Gideon, relaxed at her kitchen table, grinned like a cat chewing on a cage full of canaries. I wanted to ask him if he still planned to go to West Virginia, but I already knew his answer. He wasn't ready to mine coal. At least not for a while. Klan or no Klan.

From the moment I walked into her cabin, my grandmother seemed uneasy—until I said, "I was going to call you Maeve, but I've decided not to."

"That's fine, Neeley—"

"—I'm calling you Grandmother because you are. You're the grandest person I've ever met—besides Gideon, of course."

It broke the ice, along with years of cold and snow that had encased our hearts like ancient wolves trapped in a glacier. A faint gleam of something special twinkled in her eyes as she reached for me, her frail hug lasting only seconds before she said, "Thank you, darlin'."

Sitting at the table with Gideon, we all smiled at once. Gideon reached out and placed his large, leathery hand on my shoulder. He slid the back of his other hand across the table, fingers up like a cup, and my grandmother filled it with both of her small hands. He looked back at me, holding tight to both of us, and said, "Something you needs to remember, Neeley. There's no lost love in this world you can't find if you search long and hard enough."

"Have you always searched for her?" I asked.

Grandmother spoke first. Her lips parted, and she gave Gideon a nod and a half-grin, keeping her eyes locked on his. "No. It was impossible for him—to search for me. To even know where to start."

The tingling of their affection pulsed from my heart to my fingertips. The moment they shared lasted but a mere second or two. I didn't know then how privileged I was to be a part of it. I'll never forget Gideon's warm smile at my grandmother's next remark, "I think somehow you knew we would find each other again."

"Maybe so," he said. "Maybe so."

We talked into the evening as though it had always been that way, the three of us—together. As though nothing would ever put any of us in harm's way again. As though we could make plans to travel the world if we wanted. As though our lives had just begun, and living on The Sanctum would protect us, keep us safe, and life would go on as it was supposed to be. As it should've been. We talked about Baylor and Sidabee's baby, working the land, and tending the wolves as if the outside world existed on another planet. As though God had planted another Garden of Eden, and *we* were the new Adams and Eves.

Gideon and I decided to walk back to the big cabin, a decision we soon regretted. The ten-minute drive was more than a half hour walk. My hands were so numb when I stepped inside that I could barely lift the phone when it rang. Once again, there was no voice on the other end. "It's weird," I muttered. "The phone has rung for two days, yet nobody's there. I hope it's not Baylor or Sidabee trying to contact us." The mystery of the silent calls left me with a growing sense of worry.

"I'm sure they fine. The wind must've blown down the lines again," Gideon said. "You get some sleep."

Dragging myself to bed, I'd barely pulled off my clothes and crawled under the covers before my eyes grew heavy. I fell asleep, questioning how American Indians of the past century survived without the warmth and safety of cabins like those on The Sanctum.

The family's whisper-thin voices drifted up to my room along with the morning smells of breakfast. Baylor and Sidabee had arrived home safely. Lying in bed, I heard Hotah ask, "What time did you arrive?"

"We left Boone at four, got home at dawn," Baylor replied, his voice scratchy.

Wrapping myself in a robe, I crept downstairs and found Gideon in front of the fire. Pressing his right hand against the oak mantel, it faded into the dark wood, intensifying my urge to grab his disappearing hand and never let go.

I slumped onto the sofa beside Baylor, who cradled his mug of hot coffee. He leaned in with his usual, "Good morning, sleepyhead."

Two-Toes paced the rug, stepping over Elvis. Elvis had spread out at Aiyanna's feet with his muzzle on crossed paws. Slivers of white reflected the light at the rims of Two-Toes' eyes while both wolves seemed to strain to make some canine sense of the world. Twitching and sniffing the air, they appeared restless—a sure sign something was amiss.

Without warning, a thick darkness descended on me. Like thousands of crows flying fast over The Sanctum, it fluttered in, over, and all through me, casting the cold shadows of a reckoning. Instantly fearful, I couldn't move from Baylor's side. Not until Sidabee insisted I sit next to her.

"We've got something we need to tell you," she said.

"Is the baby okay?" I asked.

My aunt slipped her arm around my shoulders, pulling me into her. "The baby is fine." In her hand, she crumpled a piece of paper. Hotah and Aiyanna remained silent, sitting in their usual chairs. Sidabee took a deep breath. "We received a letter from the Guilford County Sheriff."

Suddenly, every crack from the fire was a rifle shot, each sigh a moan. My stomach churned with the flutter of nervous birds, bees, and butterflies in mere moments. "What does it say?" The voice was mine, yet it sounded foreign. I couldn't bear another bad thing, but I felt my heart might stop with whatever was in that letter.

"There's been a car accident, and the authorities are contacting the next of kin," Baylor said.

"Who is that?" I asked quietly.

"You," he replied.

A dizzy, spinning nausea started in the pit of my stomach. *Pudge.* "He knows I'm here? But—but he doesn't own a car. He drives a truck."

Baylor shrugged. "Maybe this is his way of telling us he's found you. We're making calls now—to inquire about the accident."

"Law, I don't gots one nice thing to say 'bout Mistah Pudge, but I don't wish him death 'fore he get his heart right with his Maker," Gideon said.

Only Gideon would think about Pudge's soul at a time like this. I wanted him dead. From the first time he took his Bible belt to my legs, I'd wanted it.

"I don't think it's too serious of an accident," said Baylor. "Otherwise, they wouldn't have only sent a letter. They would've shown up on our doorstep. My guess is they're waiting for our response."

"I think we should keep this between ourselves, not involve Momma yet." Sidabee kept her arm tight around my shoulders. My trembling had just started, and I knew she felt it. "Don't worry, Neeley. He can't take you, not without a fight from us. We've hired an attorney in Boone to help with that."

"That's why you went to Boone?"

Baylor smiled. "Yes, and for advice on how to get out from under Buchanan's demands to vacate our land. If there's a loophole, I intend to find it. After feeding the wolves this morning, Hotah and I will head to Bakersville. Sidabee, the best way to keep your mother out of this is to ensure she stays put. We'll drive Aiyanna over to spend the day with her while Gideon handles Hotah's chores in the barn. Collin is already on it, making calls from his phone at the hardware store since ours is out of service again. We'll uncover what we can about the accident. For now, let's hold off on worrying until we have some answers."

Sitting in the morning's chill, I squeezed my eyes shut so tight they ached. A horrifying image of Pudge seized me by the neck. I saw him dragging me to his truck and hightailing it back to Summerfield, where no one would hear from me again. The Devil had slithered into my Eden. A snake named Bainbridge McPherson, and although nobody had said as much, I was sure he was bringing the Klan with him.

CHAPTER THIRTY

After lunch, Baylor and Hotah drove to Bakersville to use Collin's telephone and stop by the courthouse, leaving Aiyanna at Grandmother's cabin with a pile of mending to occupy them both. Gideon ambled toward the barn as Sidabee started a load of laundry. But I finished for her, hanging overalls and work shirts in the bathhouse. As the sun dipped below the horizon, I pulled back the muslin curtains for a look outside. Sidabee had gone to rest in her room while I ran up to the loft and grabbed my lucky rabbit's foot. By then, I was into my fifth prayer for the day. Unable to fully surrender myself to my faith, I could likewise not turn my back on prayer, just in case. Wrapping the tiny chain around my index finger, I heard a car door slam.

Answering a knock at the door wasn't something I ever thought about. Like scratching an itch, I just did it. So, when I heard someone knocking at the front door, I didn't wait for Sidabee—I answered it.

Dirk Buchanan stood on the other side of the screen door, looking like a well-dressed, slicked-back politician. His eyes glittered like cracked ice, and he spoke like he'd been preaching on a soapbox somewhere in New York or one of those Yankee states.

"Well, hello, little lady. Anybody home besides you?"

The sound of a rifle being cocked echoed through the great room behind me. I whirled around to see Sidabee adjusting her eyeglasses, uneasy-like, yet gripping the gun as if she'd hunted deer and shot at men like Mister Buchanan all her life. She kicked open the screen door and stepped out on the porch as our visitor cautiously backed down the steps, palms up, retreating across the snow.

His face reflected a lifetime of coveting everything he couldn't get and a haunting hint of revenge. The exact revenge that sparked in Pudge's eyes the last time I looked at him in the barn with Gideon's rag stuffed in his mouth, his eyes wide in the dark.

I followed Sidabee outside, watching her shift the rifle a little, adjust her grip, and steady her stance.

"Why are you here?" she asked.

He tipped his hat before moistening his lips with a thin tongue. "Nice 30-30 lever action rifle you got there, Missus MacLennan. You hunting deer?"

"No. Only trespassers. I'm asking you just once more: why are you here!?"

"How about an invitation inside to talk and I'll tell you. A cup of coffee, maybe?"

A loud *huh* ripped from my aunt's delicate throat. "The only drink you'll get from me is blood. When I shoot you in the head."

Twirling his hat casually with a harsh snort of laughter, he never took his gaze away from Sidabee or her rifle. "That's not very hospitable of you," Mister Buchanan said, setting his hat back on his head. His hands clenched into fists.

Sidabee answered him swiftly. "If it's hospitality you want, you best go home. As usual, I'm sure your wife doesn't know where you are."

He bristled. "Now, that's not fair."

Sidabee had hit his weak spot.

"Fair? Ask your wife if it's fair you spend so much time at the widow Gentry's house."

Buchanan's smile lessened to something cold and threatening—definitely his weak spot. "Can't you and I talk—civil, like friends? That's not asking too much, is it?"

The first shot sprayed loose gravel and mud across the toes of his gleaming black boots. Although I jumped in surprise, my only thought was the time he'd probably spent polishing and spit-shining those boots.

"I'm not your friend," she said.

"Now, Missus MacLennan—"

The second bullet hit the ground where the snow had melted between his feet. I almost giggled.

"You've been shooting cans off fence posts again, I see." Mister Buchanan chuckled, still trying to ease the tension.

"I'd rather shoot an extra hole in your ass. Get off my property!"

My head snapped toward my aunt. I couldn't believe she'd said that.

"In a few days, it won't *be* your property," he said, "and I'll be back with the sheriff and a court order to move you out."

I guessed the third shot would've killed him had he not dodged it. That time, he laughed, nervous-like, but he choked on that laugh when she stopped to reload. By then, I realized she meant to kill him if he didn't leave at that second. My hands ached from gripping the porch post as if I'd spent the day swinging from a tree limb high in the air.

"Let me explain; I think we can settle this equitably."

She lifted the rifle. "You've got three seconds to get in your car and leave."

"Missus MacLennan—"

"—One—" Sidabee glanced upwards for a moment, as if sending up a quick prayer. Then she squeezed her left eye closed.

"—Listen to me, we need to talk—"

"—Two—" Her fingers curled tighter around the barrel.

"—C'mon. Let's be sensible about this—"

"—Thr—" The word evaporated into thin air behind the blast that slammed into him that time, its echo repeating across the snow.

Popping his wide eyes to Sidabee's, his face draining of color, he stumbled back into the fence, his alarm clear and unmistakable. His face went bone white, and he frowned, confused and in pain. He glanced at his shoulder, then back at my aunt again. "You shot me."

I stared in disbelief, my eyes wide with shock. "You shot him," I said.

But she didn't lower her rifle. She blinked, swallowed, and said, "I told you to get off The Sanctum."

"I need to talk to you!" He pulled a neatly folded handkerchief from his breast pocket and pressed it against the wound, never taking his eyes off Sidabee.

"Needing isn't getting, Mister Buchanan." Stepping off the porch, she shook strands of hair back from her face. "Next shot goes through your head. Then I'll drag you inside and say you broke into my house!"

His handkerchief did a poor job of sopping up the blood. It flowed over his hand and down his sleeve as he leaned against the fence.

"You listen to me, now. I've got a deal for you." His lips turned upward in a slow grin.

Sidabee didn't look convinced. Instead, she tightened her death grip on the gun. "I don't make deals."

"What if I told you I know who the girl is and that nigger you got sleeping in the cabin?"

"So what?"

Mister Buchanan dared to look away from her only to glare at me. His smug smile made me want to shoot him myself. He had to know she could easily take him down with one more shot, but it seemed he was a betting man.

"So—that nigger is wanted by the law. I've spoken with the girl's grandfather." He turned his glare back to Sidabee. "Of course, you know I belong to a particular social order, which I understand her grandfather now belongs to, as well. They're headed here. In fact, they're only an hour or so away. You don't want to start a racial ruckus in Bakersville, do you? You sign the papers I got in my pocket, agree to vacate your property peacefully, and I'll keep that Guilford County vigilante group from waltzing up here tonight and burning a big cross in your front yard. That old nigger can get a head start and leave now. The girl, too. Or, you can vacate your property later, of which you'll have no choice anyway, but I won't give a damn what happens to any of you."

The shock wave of his words sent me whirling. My stomach dipped and shifted, causing an even odder reaction in my knees. I lifted my head to look at Sidabee—and instantly regretted it. She cocked the rifle again, ready to blow Mister Buchanan to kingdom come. The porch floor beneath me spun in slow circles. I shook my head to clear it, but that made everything worse. The ground spun faster, and my stomach threatened to revolt at any second.

"Neeley—sit!" Sidabee's guarded but concerned voice seemed a hundred miles away. "Are you sick?"

I gripped the porch rail tighter with each breath growing more labored than the last. Sidabee shot him; she'd actually shot him—the land developer. The man who had led Pudge and the Ku Klux Klan to The Sanctum—*they were on their way*. I was spinning.

Mister Buchanan staggered forward. "Choice is yours, Missus MacLennan."

Sidabee motioned with her gun for him to leave. "Leave, Dirk! Now. Baylor is due back in minutes," she said, her voice at a half-croak, half-whisper.

"Better be smart about this, or there'll be more bloodshed than from just my shoulder."

My aunt squared her shoulders and stiffened. She hiked her chin. "We're not leaving here. Not today, not tomorrow, not ever. You hear me? Not ever!"

"You better think hard about that. You can pack up and leave peacefully, or the sheriff will do it for you. Your time is almost up, anyway." His face paled. The blood from his wound soaked his jacket sleeve. "Is that your final answer?"

Sidabee glanced at me and then back at Mister Buchanan, her voice booming with confidence and a warning of her own: "If something happens to my family or any person on this farm, everyone will know you instigated it. *You'll* go to jail. You think hard on that, Dirk!"

"Don't be so sure," he said, taking a step toward us and then another. "The whole town knows some damn savage scalped that poor woman outside of Bakersville. I say it's time to blow the lid off this place!" He grunted in pain. "You people up here are crazy. No one's gonna believe a bunch of crazies who worship in a barn with red-skinned devils and no-account niggers!"

Something inside him snapped. With his throaty growl and twisted face, he closed the gap between us in a flash, clamping his bloody fingers around Sidabee's coat collar. With his uninjured arm, he jerked my aunt up, lifting her off her heels. The rifle fell into the snow.

I flew at him, pounding my fists on his back. "Don't you touch her! Leave her alone!"

Sidabee fought hard, kicking and swinging her frail arms, hitting Mister Buchanan on his face, neck, wounded arm, whatever she could reach to break his hold. But the man was a tank, even when injured.

And then I saw Gideon, running toward us with a pitchfork, the wolves bounding ahead of him. Mister Buchanan saw them, too. He dropped Sidabee into the snow and bolted to his car. The wolves sprung to the top of his fancy Plymouth, snarling, growling, snapping at his face through the windshield, ready to rip into his throat. Gideon yelled, "Yah!" but the wolves had no intention of halting their attack. It took Mister Buchanan only seconds to start his car, spin his tires in the snow and gravel, and speed away with Elvis and Two-Toes at a fast clip behind him.

"That evil *fool!*" Gideon yelled. "You hurt Miz Sidabee? I heard the shots and came quick as I could."

"I'm shaken a bit, but fine. Neeley? Are you hurt?"

I had no voice, no words, nothing. I felt as if the world twirled beneath me once again, and I wanted to throw up and pass out at the same time. Squeezing my eyes shut and walking in circles, I pressed my hands hard against my hammering skull, struggling to relieve the sickening pressure, hoping against hope the last twenty minutes were all a horrible dream. I was spinning again. *Pudge and the Klan—on their way to The Sanctum.*

Gideon led me inside to the kitchen table to collect my wits. I slumped in the chair while he sat next to me and Sidabee poured glasses of cold water for all of us. Leaning back, rubbing his nose with the knuckles of one hand, Gideon looked at me with a half-smile. I smelled his warm, dusty scent of hay and chicken feed. Watched the sweat trickle down the deep crevices in his face to collect in his beard.

All at once, the back of my neck prickled. Staring into his tired eyes, I grabbed his arm. "We have to go. Now!"

He stood and slapped his thigh with his hat before shoving it on his head. "Neeley," he said, "I gots to help Miz Sidabee. Besides, we gots nowhere *to* go and no way to get there even iffen we did. We gone be fine. Whatever happen, we *both* gone be fine. You jus' do as you're tole. And stay safe. I sees you soon."

But inside my head, I saw the terrifying flash of Catfish Cole's sinister smile, smelled his barbeque breath, and felt his hand on my shoulder as I watched Gideon walk out the door.

I had no idea how much time had passed when I heard Sidabee rushing from room to room, locking windows and pulling blinds. Then I panicked.

Like it or not, Gideon and I had to get away. And quick. I pitched my rabbit's foot into the trash bin. It was a severed foot from a dead rabbit, for crying out loud. That rabbit sure wasn't lucky. How stupid I had been to hold on to something so ridiculous for so long. I had to hurry upstairs and pack.

I bolted past Sidabee in the hallway.

"Where do you think you're going?" she asked.

"The Klan is coming; didn't you hear Mister Buchanan?" I had thrown everything I brought into my mother's beat-up suitcase, leaving Sidabee's boots and Blossom's dress in the wardrobe.

"Neeley, you can't go. Not now. You're family. We can't lose you again."

My voice broke. "That letter the sheriff sent was a trick. A plan to flush me out of hiding. Don't you see? They're coming after Gideon, too. I'm not stupid. I watch TV. I've seen what they do to Negroes. I know the Grand Dragon; I've looked into his eyes. I don't care about myself, but I won't let Gideon leave without me. Ever! And he has to go. NOW!"

Sidabee's lips turned pale as her cheeks when she grabbed my arms. "Listen to me! You and Gideon have to face this head-on, and there's no better place to do that than here." Her hands trembled. "Besides, Buchanan could be lying about everything."

I pulled away, aware of the headlights in the driveway. "Where's Gideon?"

Sidabee sat on a chair near the front door, reloading. "He's still down at the barn, I told him where Hotah keeps his guns." She peeked out the window. "Looks like Baylor and Hotah are back. Good, because it's already dark." Looking at me, she took a deep breath. "At least Aiyanna's with Momma. They both know how to shoot straight; they'll be far safer there. If something happens, I want you to lock yourself in the bathhouse."

"I'm not leaving you or Gideon!"

"Oh yes, you will, young lady. You'll do as I say. Take Elvis and Two-Toes with you."

The wolves panted at my feet, following me since Sidabee let them into the cabin. Their attack on Mister Buchanan had left them restless and pacing. Sidabee glanced out the window again, then her head snapped back to me, wild-eyed. She rushed to the phone. "I still can't get a dial tone." She hung up and tried to switch on a lamp. "Power's out, too."

"What's happening?"

Sidabee's breath caught in her throat. "It's not Baylor and Hotah in the driveway. Whoever it is, there's a bunch of them. They're parked by the totem pole with their headlights on." Sidabee retrieved her gun, cocked it, and anchored herself by the window.

I grabbed the phone and held it to my ear, stabbing the receiver switch up and down. "Nothing. *Nothing!* It's dead."

"It's the Klan. They're gathering in the yard," Sidabee said.

I ran to a different window and watched. Shouldering rifles, the Klan stood motionless in the moonlight for an eerie moment, their hoods like white flames against the night sky, watching the cabin for any sign of us. Within seconds, they disappeared into the dark like phantoms. Elvis and Two-Toes stood at the door, showing their teeth and growling low. "Do you want me to let them outside?"

"No! Those men will shoot them. Have the wolves follow you into the bathhouse, bolt the door, and stay there!"

My insides churned like a flushing toilet. "I led them here. It's my fault. *My fault.*"

"Stop it, Neeley," Sidabee said without breaking her gaze to the outside. "Now get to the bathhouse like I said."

I whistled, and both wolves reluctantly followed. I led them inside the bathhouse and closed the door behind me as I slipped back out. The wolves howled and scratched on the door, knowing I had trapped them inside. Rushing to Sidabee, I stopped to recheck the phone. *Nothing.*

"Neeley, I told you to stay with the wolves. Go now! I'll figure out a way to contact the police. I'll use smoke signals if I have—" Sidabee stopped cold at her next glance out the window.

I yanked open the draperies. In the barnyard, blazing torches lit the darkness. A hooded Klan club member clutched Gideon around the throat like a prize cow.

"Gideon!"

I started for the door, but Sidabee put a stranglehold on my arm.

"They've got Gideon!" I shouted. Peering around the edge of the drapery, I watched as the Klan hoisted a cross taller than the totem pole into the air. It appeared as though it had grown out of the ground. They secured it with long chains and lowered their torches to the bottom. The flames lapped the wooden cross and spread toward the sky while flashes of white fire lit up the yard. Glued to the sight, I felt waves of terror and panic hurl into my throat like vomit.

Sidabee clicked off the gun's safety. "Neeley, I said *get* in the damn bathhouse!"

"No! You need my help!"

She looked over at the heavy oak armoire. "Then help me get this thing in front of the door!"

"I'll push the heavy end," I said, feeling like we were suddenly one and going to somehow win against the Klan.

With the front door secured, we returned to our posts. The Klan pranced like ghosts in the snow. Sidabee and I stood on both sides of the window for what seemed like hours, hiding in the shadows, watching. They stood in a circle around the burning cross, doing God only knew what to Gideon, and started firing their rifles and guns into the air. When Gideon disappeared into the darkness, I twisted out of Sidabee's grasp on my leg, arm, or shirt several times before she shouted, "Neeley! I can't shoot and hold on to you at the same time!"

On and on, dragon tongues of fire licked the night sky as the colossal cross burned, and I hoped and prayed everybody in Bakersville saw it. But then I felt the blood drain from my face as if a hand had tightened around my throat.

The only man without a robe or a hood stomped toward the gate and stood at the exact spot where Sidabee had shot Mister Buchanan straight through the shoulder. The unmistakable shape of my grandfather. Sidabee saw him, too, and in moments, her expression transformed from panic into a mixture of torment and tears.

Satan had risen from the pit.

CHAPTER THIRTY-ONE

"**N**eeley! I know you're in there! Get your ass out here! If you don't, they're gonna string Gideon up." Pudge slammed the gate behind him.

Sidabee pulled me away from the window and shoved me into a chair. "You stay put!"

I wrenched from her firm grip. "No! I *have* to save Gideon! Don't you understand? Don't you know who that is?"

"Of course I do! Don't *you* understand? He'll take you away, Neeley, leaving the Klan to kill Gideon and maybe the rest of us. If you go out there—if you leave with him now, we're *all* as good as dead!"

Without warning, muffled voices seeped beneath the door like a thick fog, swirling around my head and threatening to suffocate me. But it was the sinister voice of Mister Buchanan thundering across the porch that sent me scrambling. "Don't torch the place; I just bought it! Get the girl!" The front door exploded in a heartbeat, scattering fragments of wood, glass, and hardware across the polished floor. A man-sized figure dressed in sheets burst through the wreckage, further obliterating the armoire and knocking Sidabee to the floor in a single blow, flinging her gun into the shadows.

Outside, gunshots pierced the night. Suddenly, everything unfolded at once. My heartbeat thundered in my ears as I instinctively turned away from the spray of flying glass. Smoke and the echo of gunfire filled the great room, prompting me to crawl desperately on my hands and knees, seeking refuge behind the piano that stood near the back wall and a window.

Knees to my chest, shrinking in terror, I sobbed, watching hooded figures in the yard open fire. They shot into the air, shouting foul curses and celebrating their victory. I thought my heart would stop as more Klan men raced through the front door, their shapes hazy in the faint, smoke-filled light. Moving fast, they invaded every room in the cabin until one towering figure seized Sidabee within seconds. "Where's the girl!?" he shouted.

I knew the voice. Sheriff Troyer from Summerfield. I caught the shape and movement of his massive stomach as he bound Sidabee's arms and silenced her screams by tying a rag around her head and over her mouth. I screamed into my fists . . . "Sidabee!" She twisted and struggled, only to be pulled and dragged back into the shadows.

I remained pressed against the wall for what felt like forever, holding my breath, tears flowing, and hoping no one heard the roar of my pounding heart. The voices of vigilantes moved through the room, searching for me as their shadows picked their way through the cabin in a maze of darkness, overturning furniture, heaving anything in their path. Familiar accents—people I knew from my old life in Summerfield, their hostile words swirled around me. Men from my church and town.

Through the haze, the outline of another man grabbed Sidabee by her hair and pulled her across the floor but quickly reacted to something behind him, letting go of her. As Sidabee crawled away, I lost sight of her but heard the growls of Two-Toes and Elvis. They'd gotten out! The man shouted, "Wolves!" The wolves chased him out into the snow as his screams mixed with the rest of the Klan outside, who had never stopped shooting their guns into the air and hollering like drunken cowboys.

Sudden moonlight lit up the panic inside the great room. Or maybe it was a flash of lightning, I wasn't sure, but the inky profiles dashing through the door appeared dreamlike and brilliant, like a distant star. At first, I thought it was more of the Klan, but these figures blasted into the cabin at an unnatural speed, their voices eerily unfamiliar and distinctly strange. I barely breathed at what sounded like war cries filling the air. The Klan inside the house bolted out, spilling into the night air like rats fleeing a burning tobacco barn.

In the next second, my head snapped sideways, and I stared into cold black eyes piercing the darkness like coals in a fire.

Trembling at his glare, I shrank farther back into the corner. Swiftly, he seized my ankles and dragged me outside as if I were weightless. I kicked him hard, though, and he let go. Falling onto the damp porch, I sat stunned until bullets whizzed through the air, blowing out more windows over my head and smacking into the porch posts with sickening thuds, ripping them into shards of wet, thick splinters that covered my hair like straw. I flinched as another bullet cracked past my head, but screamed bloody murder when the same rough hands gripped me by my armpits, lifting me once more and hoisting me over his shoulder as if I were but a sack of grits.

Blood rushed to my head. Breathing in the animal scent of the man's damp leather coat, I tried kicking and twisting myself free of him, but he clenched my legs to his chest. Strong and fast, he carried me at a jolting run, his bony shoulder pressing into my stomach. I screamed again and beat my fists against his back of steel, but that's when my hands grabbed hold of his hair that hung down his back. Weak in his grip, I felt far younger than my thirteen years. Raising my bouncing head to view the madness, I saw only fire from the cross slowly burning itself out, leaving the shapes of hooded men moving against the darkness.

Clutching my legs so tight they ached, this mysterious man carted me to the barn as if I were nothing. I had little doubt he would throw me to the ground like pig slop. Instead, he took hold of my waist and gently set me beside a bound Sidabee, stopping only a second to stare at me before disappearing into the night.

Outside the barn, the thud of footsteps scattered as men's voices echoed across the yard, heightened by gunfire and the odd sound of war whoops slicing through the air. The wind whistled through the barn's crevices as I hastily untied Sidabee's bound hands and removed the rag wound around her head. Her eyes brimming with panic and her breathing rapid and shallow, she reached for me like a scared kitten. We clung to one another, listening to the raging war outside, knowing we were powerless to stop it.

The man with the long hair had saved both of us. *Who was he?* Distracted by more yelling and shouting, I heard someone holler, "Let's get out of here! These people are a crazy bunch of goddamn wild Indians!" That's when the barn doors rolled wide open. As taillights faded in the distance, I gasped at the sight of trucks and cars flying away from The Sanctum as fast as their tires could spin beneath them on the ice and snow. But there, in the light from the burning cross, Pudge's shadow filled the doorway, rifle in hand, his wide body blocking any escape.

"Neeley!" His rusty voice croaked my name as if his fat hand had jerked it from his throat.

A gun fired. Pudge collapsed and fell face down into the mud.

Behind him, the clouds broke into the brilliance of a full moon, illuminating the silhouette of my grandmother, her body rigid, covered in snow with a smoking shotgun in her arms.

Numb at the sight of Pudge, I knew if he weren't dead, he would be soon. Sidabee stepped over him as if he didn't exist, rushing into Baylor's arms, who had come running as fast as a bobcat after a rabbit, making shallow tracks in the deep snow. His frantic eyes searched Sidabee's, and I heard her say, "I'm fine, no pains. Baby's okay, I believe."

Aiyanna laid her hands on top of my grandmother's still outstretched arms, frozen into shooting position, her fingers gripping the gun like she'd shot the Devil himself. With a gentle push, Aiyanna aided Grandmother in lowering the gun and walking her away from the sight of Pudge to sit in the barn on a straw bale out of the cold.

I tried to imagine the two of them trudging over a mile through the snow, watching the burning cross, terrified at what they might find once they arrived.

But God didn't make Hotah's giant bear-like body for running. He arrived at the barn out of breath, his habitual lack of expression changing to one of relief at the sight of Aiyanna. "We passed the Klan on the road," he said, panting. "We saw the cross burning—"

"—Where's Gideon?" I shouted. My voice rose with each word spoken. "Has anybody seen him!?"

Sidabee held up her hand. "Do you hear that?"

"What?" I didn't want to hear anything except Gideon's voice.

A wild howling; an agonized wailing, as if from fear. The call of the wolves ascended to a screaming pitch. Baylor reached inside a cabinet and grabbed flashlights off a shelf. "He must be near the pens!"

Aiyanna stood to reload the rifle, but my grandmother hollered, "Let's not stand around here. *Find him!*"

I bolted out of the barn behind Hotah, Sidabee, and Baylor, and it occurred to me we had left Pudge either dead or dying in the mud, and nobody seemed to care.

Hotah's flashlight picked up something in the snow. *Blood.*

Ahead, Sidabee looked back at me over her shoulder. "Stop, Neeley! Don't come any closer."

Not that I listened. I rushed past her to catch up with Baylor, who arrived first at a thick oak tree. A rope hung slack around it. Frantically, I peered into the darkness, imagining the worst. I winced as the beam of Baylor's flashlight swept across my face, landing at the base of the tree and in a pool of blood. We all saw it, as well as the hundreds of footprints that pocked the snow.

Baylor searched in every direction, illuminating the area and my grandmother, who had made the trek to the tree. Exhausted, she crouched down like a fear-frozen rabbit. Her panicked voice echoed across the hillside. *"Find him."*

Aiyanna wrapped a blanket around her, lifting Grandmother to sit on a fallen log. "I'll stay here with her, Hotah. You go with Baylor!"

The wolves paced and jumped at the wire pens as if desperate to get out and help. Aware of the fear coiling in my stomach, I staggered, wanting to retch. Sidabee sensed my panic somehow and pulled me into her arms. But standing near the pens, I felt nothing but a silent scream climb in my throat. The moments seemed like hours until I heard Baylor call out, "He's not in any of the pens!"

I shrieked his name into the frigid night's blackness, *"Gideon!"* But the wolves kept pacing, stopping only to howl.

Drained of strength, Sidabee collapsed to the snowy ground, speaking in a voice that seemed to come from a long way off. "Maybe he managed to get into the cabin," she said.

"Then why are the wolves going crazy?" Even *I* sensed they weren't acting normal.

Baylor walked out of Blackfoot's pen, out of breath. "Let's think for a second."

Hotah shook his head. "If they threw him into a pen, the wolves would've led me to him. He's not in any of them."

There was no noise but the dying wind and the whine of wolves.

I took off sprinting to the cabin, with Sidabee and Baylor behind me. Peering through a broken kitchen window, I saw no sign of Gideon. Someone had ripped off the back door from its iron hinges, and I stepped over splintered wood, getting my first good look inside. A chilled congestion settled in my chest, yet sweat poured off me like a pig in July. It appeared as if a bomb had exploded.

I rushed to Gideon's room. It was locked. Pounding on the door to no response, I felt Baylor pull me back to kick it open. The room was empty. I backed out and bumped into the kitchen wall. "Where could he be? Do you think they took him?"

Baylor searched the rest of the cabin as my legs gave way and my bottom reached the cold linoleum. Hunched over, with my head on my knees, paralyzed by horror, I was too grief-stricken to move. Sidabee crumpled like a paper cup beside me.

"I always celebrated Gideon's birthday on February 1st." My throat felt so dry, my voice so hoarse. "We should have a party. Invite everybody. He loved that caramel cake at Christmas; do you think Blossom will bake it for him?" I had put an iron grip on certainty to keep it from turning me to stone.

"Sure, honey. We'll have caramel cake," Sidabee said.

Baylor returned and covered us with a blanket. "He's not in here."

I had no tears, just uncontrollable shaking. I swallowed hard. "I'm sorry about your cabin."

"Cabins can be rebuilt." Baylor sighed.

The sky had fallen on me. The swell of more grief tore at my insides. "He's hurt," I sobbed. "I can feel it. We have to find him." *Please, God*, I prayed, *help me. Help me find him.*

The soft whining of wolves pulled me to my feet. "The bathhouse!" Our eyes locked—Sidabee's wide with fear—and we stood paralyzed, sharing the same thought: wolves attacked the man who seized Sidabee, so how were Elvis and Two-Toes still locked in the bathhouse? I dashed to the closed door.

Sidabee's voice sounded as cracked and shattered as I felt, her fear echoing mine. "Let them out! They'll lead us to Gideon if he's still on The Sanctum!"

I felt a flicker of hope as the wolves bound out of the cabin into the snow. But I grabbed Baylor's arm, pulling him to a stop. "Where are you going?"

He balled his hand into a fist. "My father's old truck."

We raced to the barn, our breaths ragged, sweat streaming down our faces. I paused briefly to see Grandmother and Aiyanna, huddled together, gazing at Pudge's body in the mud. Baylor gestured to Hotah, "Get the crowbar."

Two-Toes howled in the distance; I knew his whine. He had headed toward the truck. While Baylor and Hotah rooted through a toolbox, I wasn't willing to wait a moment longer.

Sidabee must have seen the look in my eyes. "Neeley, please, stay in the barn with your grandmother."

"No!" I bolted like a startled horse. At the slope under a large elm tree, the driver's side rose slightly higher than the passenger's. Pitch blackness hid the interior; I couldn't see, but I pulled and tugged with all my might, determined to open the locked or rusted-shut door.

Hot on my heels, Sidabee had rushed to the passenger door, and I heard its piercing creak as she screamed, "Neeley, stay there!"

In a fast second, I ran around the truck bed to where she stood, grabbed her arm, and spun her out of my way. "*Gideon—*"

CHAPTER THIRTY-TWO

Gideon lay slumped to one side, without his coat, bleeding profusely, his shirt torn to shreds. His head, badly beaten, rested on the seat, with one hand tucked beneath his cheek. Almost unrecognizable, he twitched as I grasped the waistband of his trousers. Groaning, I mustered all my strength to drag him out. "Gideon! Wake up—please, wake up," I pleaded. He didn't respond. I tugged and pulled at his shoulders, frantically searching for Sidabee to help me, only to see her tumble to the ground, doubled over.

When Baylor arrived at the truck, I fell into the snow, clasping my hands behind my head struggling for air. Baylor pried open the driver's door with his crowbar while Hotah pulled me into his chest, guiding me to Sidabee. Collapsed in the snow near a wolf pen, she had vomited and sat wiping her mouth with her sleeve, breathing in rapid, shallow gasps, her tears carving icy paths down her cheeks. Looking at me with eyes that mirrored my grief, she spoke words I barely heard. "I'm so sorry, Neeley."

"Stay here," I said.

I dashed back to the truck and found Baylor feeling for Gideon's pulse. Curled like a baby, he had not moved or opened his eyes. When Baylor pulled him out, limp and lifeless, his body buckled into a heap, and I shuddered. "Noooooo. *Gideon*." My hands and coat covered in his blood, I vowed right there beside him to make the Klan suffer for what they did. I wanted to beat them all bloody. "Wake up. Gideon, no. Please, wake *up!*"

They had whipped his back; the Klan had crushed him like road-kill, splitting the left side of his face from cheek to chin and laid it open to the bone. Hotah and Baylor carefully placed Gideon on a blanket, and I hurriedly covered him with my coat. "Gideon, please wake up and talk to me," I pleaded. As I ran my hands over his forehead, familiar, large snowflakes gently fell to the ground.

And then he wiggled his fingers, so I knew he hadn't reached Heaven yet. I gently wiped blood from his mouth with my shirt, and for the first time, I kissed the top of his head. "Oh, Gideon, *you* are my grandfather. No one else." Strangely, I realized that his hair wasn't coarse and wiry. It was as soft as rabbit fur, and all those years, I hadn't known.

A rasping sound erupted from his throat. I took his blue-veined hands in mine. They trembled as I gently squeezed his fingers. He made that noise in his throat again, and I looked up at Baylor. "Please, help him."

Straining to talk, Gideon's lips parted, and his hands jerked. He grunted and slowly opened his swollen eyes, just a crack, staring at me like he was peering right inside my head. Pressing words through his teeth and a mouthful of blood, his voice barely a whisper— "I loves you—Neeley girl. I loves you—your whole life."

My tears mixed into the deep and bloody slash on his face. "And I'll love you for the rest of it," I said, gripping his hands and kissing the uncut side of his face, feeling his beard graze my chin. As his hands relaxed, I searched his eyes once more before he looked away, and I was sure I saw tears.

A silent scream rolled into my throat, and I raised my head. Hotah stared at me with pleading eyes, sending me a message he could not speak.

But when Baylor pulled me toward him, I fought like a wounded animal. "Let me be. Leave me alone! I'm staying with Gideon!" I wailed like someone had doused me with gasoline and set me on fire. The pain started in the soles of my feet and worked its way through me until I howled like the wolves. My fists bounced off Baylor's shoulders as he lifted me off Gideon's body and started toward the barn with me cradled against him like a baby.

Baylor sat on a straw bale, rocking me slowly, holding me close while I cried my heart clean out of my chest. "Neeley," he said softly.

And then I felt Sidabee crouch beside us, caressing my face and hands, stroking my hair. "Scream, Neeley. Scream as loud as you want to."

And I did. I moaned and wailed, panted and cried until I had no oxygen left in my lungs, until my shoulders shook, and my breathing grew shallow. The pain and shock of losing him had rubbed me raw. Cold, my body felt boneless, brittle, used up. I knew what no one had the courage to tell me. My Gideon was dead.

It had all come back to snow and cold.

Hours later, surrounded by family gathered in the patched-up great room for the night, I stared at everything and nothing, unable to speak. Sidabee's feeble smile did not soothe the pain in my chest. When she slid the back of her finger over my cheek, I felt nothing but numbness as I shivered violently in the cold room.

Hotah arrived after midnight with Doctor Shelton, who pulled a needle out of his black bag and shot me in the hip. I don't think anybody slept except me. I spent the night leaning against Sidabee first and then Baylor, dreaming, twitching, and succumbing to the relief of sleep.

The soft rush of the wind outside, sneaking through the crevices in the boarded-up windows, the steady ticking of the clock on the wall, and the comforting crackle of a fire—sounds as familiar as my heartbeat—roused me at the break of dawn. Baylor, snoring in an even rhythm against the wall, looked as ragged as Festus from Gunsmoke. In a daze, I struggled to upright myself until the reality of Gideon's death hit me as simply as the *plunk* of a pebble dropping into a muddy puddle. Leaning back against Sidabee, I stared into the fire.

At high noon, Aiyanna dressed in her finest tunic and ceremonial moccasins. She'd braided beads and a long feather into her hair and mine, placed a silver and onyx stone necklace around her slender throat, then set about taking care of Gideon's body, dressing him in his Sunday clothes.

I gazed at him for one unending moment, recalling the days I followed at his heels like a stray pup, asking a gazillion questions; I adored him, my small hand constantly seeking his giant one. He wasn't supposed to die. Ever.

I pressed my lips to his bruised, swollen cheeks for the last time, then stood in silent vigil as Hotah, with the utmost respect, wrapped Gideon's body in a soft cotton sheet. Over that, he placed a deer hide, securing it with rawhide laces to form a sturdy bundle. Aiyanna shared that the Cherokee, in centuries past, erected strong burial scaffolds high enough to protect the remains of the deceased from predators. But instead, Hotah and Baylor with reverence and gentle hands, laid Gideon on a wooden table and carried him to the quiet and cool barn, a place of honor and rest.

Aiyanna embraced me several times throughout the afternoon. Together, we offered prayers into the early evening. Hotah remained absent from the great room; Aiyanna said his grief was too great. His arms dripped with tiny droplets of blood where he had marked his flesh to express his sorrow and mourning over the loss of his friend. A part of their tradition, Aiyanna explained.

Later, I joined Hotah outside. "Wakan Tanka," he whispered repeatedly, his eyes wet with tears. It pained me to see Hotah lift his face to the clear sky. "Please accept the soul of Gideon, the elder, into Your Heavens." He stood in the yard for hours, praying and chanting, undisturbed. As numbness replaced the cold in my bones, I crept back inside the cabin where Sidabee told me she had received a call from the funeral home; they were coming to prepare him for burial, free of charge.

Standing at a broken window, I watched the ambulance, flanked by two police cars, drive slowly to the barn. When Sidabee and I walked out the front door and down the stone path, Collin met us halfway, his head slightly bowed.

"We're taking the deceased to the funeral home," Collin said. "My condolences, Miss Neeley."

I nodded, then buried my face into Sidabee's shoulder.

Baylor said the ambulance and police procession through Bakersville to the funeral home proved more effective than any newspaper headline. A single glance at the convoy sent the townspeople into a tizzy. Their explosive gossip, we heard, landed in newspapers all the way to the White House. The Klan had killed another Negro, without a trial, in cold blood, right under President Eisenhower's nose.

Tupperware containers poured in from everywhere. I'd never seen so much food together at once. Each had a card or note attached: *Our deepest sympathies.* Aiyanna and Sidabee crammed the sorry-for-Neeley dishes into the Frigidaire, root cellar, and pantry. Looking at the dozens of casseroles and salads covered in aluminum foil and wax paper, I felt thankful, yet wanting none of it. No Jell-O mold, cake, or even a ham stabbed with cherries, pineapple slices, and toothpicks delivered the slightest bit of condolences.

The following morning, I stood by a window, gazing out at the barnyard where the Klan had gathered around the burning cross, gripping Gideon by the neck. It often seemed like a terrible nightmare I was desperate to wake from. But watching the funeral home car returning Gideon's body to The Sanctum, it felt as if the horrifying event had unfolded only an hour ago.

Grandmother requested Gideon be laid to rest in the MacLennan cemetery near the old stone wall. The totem pole Hotah and Gideon had crafted together, a gift they presented to Baylor and Sidabee at Christmas, stood tall next to the gravesite. The sight of it, visible from my loft window, offered a bitter but sweet comfort.

Gideon was a man of simplicity. Only a handful of words needed to be spoken over him, perhaps a scripture or two— and maybe Sidabee could sing a church hymn. Beyond that, my request for no formal funeral service seemed right. Few, if any, of the locals knew Gideon. It wasn't necessary. So, it shocked me when the whole town of Bakersville showed up for the burial. Cars and trucks filled with both Negroes and Whites, dressed in their Sunday best, arrived and gathered near the grave.

I walked outside into crystallized snow from the night's frost. An achingly clear blue sky glimmered above us the day we buried Gideon. He would've loved the sky that day.

A hushed crowd watched as Sidabee and Baylor ushered me to the grave. Breaking the silence, Sidabee opened Gideon's worn hymnal and began to sing. Soon, all the mourners sang loud, sorrowful songs, wept, and called the Lord their Shepherd. In the low, slanting light, I stood amidst the swaying bodies, my heart heavy with the weight of his absence, wondering how to survive without him.

Never had I seen a more impressive burial than Gideon's. High on a Blue Ridge mountaintop, they lowered his casket into a deep hole dug by volunteers. I stepped to the open grave with a handful of dirt, sprinkling it over the wooden coffin in its resting place.

"Ashes to ashes . . . dust to dust . . ." Baylor's few words said all that needed to be said. At that moment, while dirt flowed freely from my hand, I experienced the most desperate desire to fall into the grave with him. *Oh, Gideon. Please. Come back.*

Two-Toes and Elvis, on a leash, nudging through the crowd with Hotah, consoled me the most. They sat near the grave where I stood long after everybody returned to the cabin. Watching Collin and Jesse shovel cold, loose dirt over the casket, I didn't want to think about Gideon down in that wintry ground. I turned toward what was left of the day's sun, hoping it might dry my tear-soaked face.

A breeze picked up, and my nose caught the reek of the chicken coops and damp earth. I thought about the days growing longer and that soon, the fields would bloom with chickweed, confederate jasmine, bloodroot, and violets. It wouldn't be long until harvest, canning season, and the first snow again. Time had become my enemy, and as much as I wanted to, I couldn't stop it.

I don't remember how I got back to the cabin, but the next thing I knew, I was mingling quietly with folks from town, most of whom I'd never met until that day. The funeral guests, nodding as I walked by and imagining what to make of me, ate from the smorgasbord laid out in the great room, spilling coffee on furniture, dropping crumbs on the floor, and finishing the last of our cider supply. They spoke in low, shocked tones as if none of them were to blame. And when I'd had enough, I excused myself to hide from the stares of strangers. And to wonder.

Would Gideon be dead if it weren't for him bringing me here?

Holding on to him as long as possible, I spent the night recalling his broad, freckled face, his soft chuckle, the slight limp in his walk, and how he swayed when he prayed. Instead of sleeping in my loft bed, I laid on the floor in Gideon's room, restless, fidgeting in the itchy black funeral dress Doctor Shelton's wife had dug up for me at the last minute. A long sigh came from somewhere inside my hurting heart. For all of Gideon's Christian religion, he had died in the worst way possible for a Negro man to die.

The sweetness of his memory engulfed me with the familiar sorrow of remembering my parents. Yet, oddly, the loss offered a small amount of comfort. Gideon's smile was gone forever, but he was now beyond harm's reach. Still, I felt hopeless and deeply discouraged, descending into a stunned depression where I stayed for a long time, trying my best not to be angry with God, and in the trying, hearing Gideon's voice inside my head as he once told me—*girl, gettin' mad at God jus' takes too much time and energy to get over.*

A week later, my soul still bled, struggling to heal itself. I walked around as if I were incapable of the slightest emotion. I knew as much as anybody about grief, and I had a right smart mess of it to do again. I glanced at my Timex, picturing Gideon's smile and the pure joy in his eyes when he gave it to me on Christmas Eve. It's how I needed to remember him.

Eventually, everybody in town set their tongues to talking about Mister Buchanan and his threats against The Sanctum. He couldn't take the heat. We heard he packed up his wife, two sons, tiny house, and bandaged shoulder and moved back to New York City. *One less bigot in the South*, my grandmother said. But my nightmare was far from over.

I had avoided Sidabee's bedroom for days. In fact, I refused to go near the hallway that led to it.

After carrying Gideon to the house, Hotah and Baylor had rolled Pudge out of the mud and onto a wagon, where they believed him to be dead. When Aiyanna hosed off the mud, she saw him flinch, so they carried his massive body to the closest bedroom, Sidabee and Baylor's. They summoned Doctor Shelton, who said transporting him to a hospital or back to Guilford County would kill him.

Sidabee confessed she preferred that rather than allow her father to die in her marriage bed. But Baylor refused. "After he has passed on, we, at least, will rest in the knowledge we did our duty as Christians. Until then, Doctor Shelton will stay with us to care for the patient, and we will continue to mourn Gideon's death."

It wasn't fair. Gideon lay in the cold ground, while Pudge lay at Hell's door on Sidabee's rosebud sheets.

When the Bakersville Sheriff investigated the incident, there wasn't a question as to the fact that a mob of cutthroats, led by Bainbridge McPherson and Catfish Cole, had run amuck over The Sanctum, shooting off guns and terrorizing its residents. "No doubt someone shot Mister McPherson from a stray bullet," said the sheriff.

"No doubt," said Sidabee.

I turned my attention to my grandmother, who had taken to her bed. She had lost Gideon once again. I sat for hours, telling her stories about him—nothing about how badly Pudge mistreated him, but good stories of his courage and thoughtfulness to me and others. I wanted her to know what he was like as I grew up and how his kindness had saved my life. I talked about him as if he were still with us, sitting at her kitchen table, waiting for another roast beef sandwich.

While watching her sleep, it came to me then that I needed Pudge to live. His flaking, putrid body had decayed in Sidabee's four-poster bed long enough. In fact, I wanted him well enough to stand trial and spend the rest of his life in the prison he meant for Gideon. The time had come for him to face me.

CHAPTER THIRTY-THREE

Doctor Shelton reported that my grandfather recognized death and sensed the dark shadows of its approach as he fought to breathe. An infection had set in, unleashing waves of agony that beat on him, sapping his remaining strength. Trapped there, he had refused to talk, and I assumed he wanted death to claim him. To get it over with. But I was told he struggled to get up from time to time, growing weaker with each attempt to free himself from us. Drifting in and out of consciousness, he offered only piercing glares at Doctor Shelton or Jesse whenever one brought him medicine or changed his bandage.

The first time I entered Sidabee and Baylor's bedroom, I found Jesse sitting in a chair, reading by Pudge's bedside. Since the night of the uprising, Jesse had silently watched me from a distance, giving me space to grieve. When he stood, his kind, dark eyes smiled. Somehow, he knew a storm brewed inside me because he rested his hand on my shoulder and said, "Do you need me to stay?"

I shook my head, ignoring the tiny ache in my chest and swallowing back the bitter taste in my mouth.

"He has asked for you."

I gave Jesse a slight reassuring smile as he left the room.

Sunlight leaked in and around the edges of the curtains, long cracks of light falling in spiraling patterns across the furniture in the gloomy room. I tried to see Pudge's face hidden in the shadows. Sidabee's bedroom had lost her lavender scent and the spicey aroma of Baylor's cigar smoke. An antiseptic smell mixed with a sour stench hit me as I stepped closer to where Pudge lingered near death. I had prayed for him to die for so long, but I felt only an extraordinary and disturbing sadness.

Pudge's head swayed and sweat on his pillow. His wet, yellow eyes had bulged to the size of chicken eggs. He gritted his teeth and stifled his groans when he saw me. "I want to—go home," he said, his voice hoarse and labored. I turned to leave the room, but Aiyanna and Sidabee walked in with a tea made of catnip and vervain to reduce his fever.

Aiyanna felt his brow, then gently lifted and cradled his head in one arm and tilted a cup to his lips with the other. "In the name of all that is holy, we will not help you die, sir. We will leave that to our Heavenly Father."

With the cup to his lips, Pudge let out a hideous grunt of pain between clenched teeth. "So many regrets," he said.

Sidabee glared at him. "What did you say?"

"God—will not forgive—what I've done, but—" I saw him shudder as he drew in a sharp breath.

I broke the quiet with a blinding fury that roared through every cell in my body. "Don't you *dare!* Don't you *dare* ask Sidabee or me to forgive you! Don't you goddamn dare!"

I flew out of the room to Gideon's bed, throwing myself onto where he had slept so soundly only days before. I had buried my best friend, and the man who came to kill him lay only a few feet away, wanting forgiveness. I didn't understand the mercies of God then, and I'm not sure I understand them now, but I know God doesn't always fill us in on His plans for good reason. I had no choice. I had to trust God knew what He was doing, allowing Pudge to live a few more days.

Sidabee's cereal had turned soggy, her coffee cold. She shoved them aside and leaned on the table, elbows propped up. Her eyes looked sore, as if she'd had cried all night. While I finished my breakfast, she hid her face in her hands, surrendering it seemed, to a decade of bitter and tormenting memories. Tears seeped through her fingers, trickling down her wrists, and she stayed like that, weeping, until countless sobs appeared to chill her to the bone. I sat in silence, watching her shiver, listening as she bellowed toward her room, toward the father she despised. And then she prayed silently, lips moving, eyes tightly closed. In a second of defiance, Sidabee sat up straight, her back rigid, nostrils wide, and her look one of relief rather than defeat.

The sun had come out. She wiped her eyes, blew her nose, and stood to kiss my forehead. *"Many are the afflictions of the righteous,"* she said, *"but the Lord delivers us from them all. It's almost over for Mother, me, and for you, Neeley. He can never hurt us again."* I think she finally came to terms with it. With all of it.

The mood in the cabin remained somber and quiet. I took meals to Grandmother who discovered Pudge had survived, only to lay dying in her daughter's bedroom. Aiyanna kept me busy with housework and repairs to the cabin. But every evening, I stretched out on Gideon's little bed in the cozy room near the kitchen, disturbed by my own memories of Pudge talking about *Jew boys*, *niggers*, and *shit-for-brains* women. I had seen the evil of racism. I had lived with it my whole life—saw its pain in Hotah's eyes.

The Cherokee ghosts on The Sanctum had saved us the night the Klan came. If my suspicions were correct, they had formed a war party in the spirit world and entered through a window of time down by the totem pole where I had seen the little Indian girl. They didn't have to save me and Sidabee, two white women whose ancestors might have run them off their land, but they did. They saved us.

Too bad for Pudge. His white-hooded ghosts had deserted him.

After feeding the wolves with Hotah one morning, I decided it was time to see Pudge again. I wanted him to know he had not only failed me, but he had also failed in every aspect of his pitiful life. It seemed the flames of Hell were waiting for him, and I needed him to know why. I was out for blood. But as I peered into the bedroom, I found Doc Shelton sitting in the corner and my grandmother standing at the foot of his bed.

"Bainbridge," she said.

Clearly in pain, Pudge opened his eyes. "You've been here—on this farm—all this time?"

"Why didn't you leave Neeley and Gideon alone?" With as much loathing as I had ever heard from her, my grandmother's question demanded an answer.

He clenched his teeth, and his breathing grew wheezy. "The farm is in trust to her—remember? You shut me out—when you refused to put—the land—in my name, and then you deserted me," Pudge said. "You deserted me, and then put the farm in Neeley's name. A baby you never even saw. I needed her. I couldn't even sell the farm without her. You—did that to me. Why did you leave me, Maeve? I promised you I'd change."

My grandmother held tight to the four-poster bed, nearly buckling at the knees. "I had memorized every one of your promises by heart. I would *never* have given you my father's land. *Never.*" Struggling to stand and finish what she had come to say, my grandmother appeared to fight her own battle of personal restraint. "I want to know something, Bainbridge. I know you buried me, but how did you explain away Sidabee?"

Pudge closed his eyes, seemingly unable to look at my grandmother. "I forced—Elizabeth to say Sidabee had gone to live up north—with friends and that she died from diabetes. Everybody knew *you* were a diabetic—it wasn't a hard lie to believe. I never wanted Neeley—to know about Sidabee or to go looking for her. I figured if she found Sidabee—she'd find you. If she knew the truth, I'd lose the farm—I'd lose everything. In my mind, you *were* dead, *both* of you." His eyes fluttered. "Where is—where is Neeley? Please, I need to talk to her."

I saw the look Grandmother passed to Pudge. She wished him dead even more than I did. I felt a tightening that started in my shoulders, rolled down my arms, and curled my hands into fists.

Grandmother let go of the bed and stepped back. "I pray God forgive you for the atrocities you have heaped upon this family," she said, each word cut from a block of ice. "But I never will." When she saw me, my grandmother walked toward me and pulled me into her arms. "He wants to talk to you."

"Okay," I whispered. I waited until Doctor Shelton stuck a needle into Pudge's flabby arm.

"Take your time, dear," Doctor Shelton said. "He's not long for this world." Watching the good doctor follow my grandmother out of the room, I hoped he was right.

I stood there, looking at Pudge, feeling nothing. His jowls hung loose from his cheeks, and under his chin, the skin sagged as if someone had scooped out his meanness. His hair had turned grayer, and his entire body appeared the color of school paste. The corners of his mouth and eyes curved downward. His outside may have changed, but I clung tight to my belief that he hadn't reformed a bit on the inside. Not in the slightest. Pudge's terrifying and stone-cold heart remained visible to God and everybody. At the end of his life, he had not been able to hide a single sin. What a fool.

Caked with dirt and sweat, Pudge's stench had oozed into the rest of the cabin. It amazed me that Sidabee put up with it. Sitting by his bed, I watched him roll his head from side to side. It wasn't long before he discovered me sitting there. "I hope God turns up the heat in Hell today," I said.

"Neeley," he whispered, his chicken eyes popping wide, "My feet. My feet are hot."

I shrugged. "I suppose Hell is an awful place. You ready for it?"

"Uncover them—please."

I pulled the sheet off his chalky-white feet that looked and smelled like dead fish attached to his veiny legs.

"Thank you," he said.

I stumbled. His *thank you* about knocked me over, but I kept my distance, attempting to read his grubby face and darting eyes. "How did you find us?" I asked.

"A newspaper. Under your mattress. You had circled The Bakersville article. I—I'm sorry." He spit out the last two words like they tasted of vinegar.

I shook my head. "What are you sorry for? Tell me."

"You—know." His breaths became short and labored.

"No. I want you to *tell* me. Tell me what you've done that you're sorry for."

His voice grew weak. "I did *everything* wrong, and I'm sorry. You reminded me of Maeve. You look like her."

"Saying you're sorry doesn't change a thing. It doesn't change you *or* me or bring Gideon back. *Damn you.* If there's a bottomless pit or a lake of fire and brimstone, I hope—I hope—" My chin quivered. "I hope you land in it. Today! *Damn you.*" I had to hear myself say the words to know I meant them.

Seeing dark circles under his swollen eyes that looked like bruises felt strangely gratifying. He groaned and coughed, struggling to speak above a whisper. "Well—you may get your wish." But his stare bore a hole through me until, a heartbeat later, he broke eye contact. "I'm still sorry," he said, and I shivered at his response.

I frowned, not understanding. It wasn't like Pudge. To apologize.

"What day is it?" he asked, the words scraping his dry throat. As if reading his thoughts, I offered him a sip of water, and he greedily took it in until he'd had his fill.

"It's Saturday, I think. You've laid here for two weeks."

"Two weeks," he repeated.

"You've lost a lot of blood," I added, my voice trembling.

"Please, may I speak to Sidabee?" he asked softly.

"She and Baylor have gone to Bakersville, and I—" I hesitated when I couldn't swallow around the rock in my throat. "I'm in charge."

Pudge nodded. "I guess this is the way it's supposed to be."

He couldn't finish, couldn't make himself relive the nightmare he'd put us through—yet he knew he could never escape it, even at the hour of his death.

"Tell my daughter—I'm sorry," he said, his raspy throat gurgling. "I didn't kill your grandmother. But I drove her away. I searched—everywhere. When I realized—not even Elizabeth knew where Maeve and Sidabee had gone—I buried them. I buried—the truth. To muzzle the gossip."

He coughed loud and for several minutes. I had nothing to say to him that didn't include swear words, so I held my tongue.

"Please—listen closely. Maeve put the farm in trust—to you. Your grandmother was to remain—as your guardian. I didn't know that—until one day I—I had a question about my tax bill. My lawyer, Judd Hastings, wrote me. Told me what Maeve had done. I had Judd petition the court to appoint *me* as guardian, but the judge refused. There was no legal death certificate for your grandmother. That didn't matter anyway. The land was to be turned over to you on your eighteenth birthday, regardless of who was guardian. Judd couldn't make it—mine. I—I didn't want you to have it." He coughed again, spitting up spoonfuls of blood.

I held a wet cloth to his mouth until he stopped. "I don't know what all that means, Pudge," I said rather sarcastically.

"Call—Judd. He'll explain." He coughed again, his voice hoarse and full of phlegm. I wanted him to stop talking. "About Gideon," he said. "I know you cared for each other. Call my lawyer; he'll make sure—you're taken care of."

I wanted to scream in his face for the years he beat on me at the drop of a hat, and for ripping Gideon from my life. Instead, I sat in the dim light, imagining the sting of death. What it felt like to have your soul dragged to Hell by a stinging tentacle.

Pudge had turned his face toward the door. "Neeley," he said. I stood, and when I placed my fingertips on his cheek to turn his face to me, warm tears rolled over my fingernails. "Neeley— why do you let wolves roam through this house at all hours?" He gazed past me, staring at the wall. "Look at 'em, standing there."

I turned, thinking Two-Toes had slipped in. Or maybe Hotah had walked in with Elvis. But there was nothing. Only a gloomy room that smelled of exhaustion lit by embers in a dying fire.

I looked back at my grandfather and squeaked out the words. "There are no wolves in here, Pudge."

With dry eyes and a sense of detachment, I watched him in the silent, dim room. He spoke in short, labored whispers, making no sense, as if his words bore the weight of his guilt and regret. His eyes never opened again, but his distorted face reflected the torture of unresolved and unconfessed sins. Sometime later, Aiyanna beckoned me out of the room. "Let him pass alone," she said. As the family gathered that evening, each silent second ticked by slowly, waiting for Pudge to wither and turn into a corpse.

At dawn, I felt compelled to see my grandfather one last time. Nearing the room, my eyes burned, and I held my breath as the sour milk stench almost stopped me in my tracks. Opening the door, I found Baylor collecting a basin of bloody rags and soiled clothes, attempting to clean the room. Pudge's skin looked wrinkled and mushy as if he had soaked in water—overnight. His hair clumped in dirty strands from his fall into the mud, and his massive body appeared like a pile of raw bread dough spreading across greasy sheets. Sitting near the bed, I was grateful his eyes were closed, but his head had tilted back, parting his chapped and swollen lips. In that chilly and solemn moment, there was no mourning to be done. I felt nothing but relief.

Baylor cleared his throat. "Neeley?"

I looked up from my chair. "Yes?"

"Our local sheriff is on his way here. Since Pudge is from Summerfield, we should transport the body there for burial."

I nodded. "I'm not going back there."

"I know. A Missus Vivian Crumley, a neighbor, has agreed to handle the arrangements."

I watched as they carried Pudge's body out the door on a stretcher, covered with a large black blanket, and sliding him into an ambulance.

Cars full of onlookers and reporters from as far away as Raleigh had gathered outside the closed gates of The Sanctum for days, snapping pictures and hollering for somebody to come talk to them. When the Bakersville Sheriff arrived, he glanced back over the roof of his cruiser. "Don't those damn people have anything better to do?" He motioned to his deputy. "Get rid of 'em," he mumbled. "Damn reporters. I hope that Reverend King knows what he's stirred up." He pulled out a pencil and a small notebook. "Who here is next of kin?"

"I am," I said. Who else would claim him? I had hoped some unknown relative would show up and take responsibility for his affairs. Still, I knew Pudge was an only child who produced no children other than Sidabee. Of course, the old rumor was that he had sired a couple of offspring nobody knew about. But that was only Summerfield gossip.

Which, I supposed, left Sidabee. Except she wanted nothing to do with him, his dead body, or his burial. She'd seldom stepped foot in her own bedroom the whole time he lay dying. She and Baylor had moved into the guest room and planned to stay there. Hotah and Baylor, as well as many volunteers, had repaired the damaged cabin and property, and I heard Sidabee say they would burn every stick of her bedroom furniture, the mattress, and even the wall hangings as soon as the coroner removed the body.

But nobody was as glad as me to watch the hearse barrel away from The Sanctum that windy January day. What had connected Pudge and me felt like shackles. There was no blood between us. Only lies. He *never did* say he loved me. Not once. He never even noticed my scar was gone. He only asked me to forgive him in hopes it might keep his sin-sick soul out of Hell. But I wasn't about to forgive him. Maybe someday. Maybe someday I'd *have* to forgive him to keep *my* soul from nearing the hinges on Hell's back door.

I discovered Pudge had enlisted the Klan's help to find me, promising to deliver Gideon into their hands. With that, he succeeded. But in the small town of Summerfield, people liked to talk. Already agitated after many of their men returned home wounded from the uprising, the townsfolk more than likely cursed the day they met my grandfather.

I like to think the misguided in Summerfield dropped out of the Klan. Baylor heard federal police had arrested Catfish Cole and moved him to a jail in Raleigh to stand trial for killing Negroes throughout the Carolinas, which included the cold-blooded murder of Gideon Jackson.

James W. Cole was no longer a dragon—or a pastor. The Wayside Baptist congregation sent me a letter of apology. It also detailed their plans to demolish, rebuild, and rename the church. Within the week, we heard that a judge had dismissed Sheriff Henry Troyer from his duties, having him arrested and confined to a Guilford County cell to face trial for conspiracy to commit murder. This discovery made me smile, and I thought, had Pudge lived, he and the sheriff could've shared a cell. I would have liked to have seen that.

I soon understood that Pudge had never satisfied the tongue wager's curiosity after he claimed to send Sidabee away, bury his wife, and then pretend to grieve over my mother's automobile accident and funeral. The town never knew the truth; they only *thought* they did. To drown out the rumors, Pudge turned to drink, showing his resentment for raising me in ways only the Devil himself would enjoy. The man I believed was my grandfather had used me, hoping to keep the farm and collect sympathy from the town. He failed.

No doubt about it, my painful past had made me a walking target. My parents' death left me stunted. But Gideon, a man of quiet courage, made me go on, leading by example and not knowing it. His abiding love, so pure and so unconditional, had watched over me day and night. As much as I'd loved him, he had loved me more. Still. Images from the last moments of Gideon's life twisted into my dreams. Every morning, tight, painful knots coiled inside my gut.

Watching January pass from my bed, I drifted in and out of sleep for hours, feeling like the Creature from the Black Lagoon. All I did was concentrate on getting through the day, smothering the memory of Gideon's beat-up face that exploded to the surface like a mole tunneling through the dirt.

Doctor Shelton looked in on me some. But finally, Aiyanna and Grandmother, tired of traipsing up the steps to feed me, dragged me down to the great room, propped me up on the sofa, and covered me with a quilt.

The great room had turned chilly and dark, a soft-gray color. The fire had gone out. Or maybe it was me. My stomach ached. My arms and legs hurt. The weight of every horrible memory I wanted to forget refused to budge from my pounding head.

Somewhere amidst my grief, I heard pots and pans clanging, dishes rattling back and forth, and the sound of my grandmother's voice, sweet and tender, singing an old song Gideon had sung to me many times during the trials of our lives. The words echoed from a sore spot in my heart. *"There is a balm in Gilead, to make the wounded whole, there is a balm in Gilead, to heal a sin-sick soul."*

It wasn't long before Grandmother appeared with a cup of tea and a plate of ginger cookies. After a few sips and a nibble or two, I laid my head in her lap as she sang what Lila Goodeve had told me months before was her favorite song: *"Reach out and touch the Lord . . ."* Maybe that was hope enough. Closing my eyes, feeling her fingers in my curls and the soft pull of her hands through my hair, I fell into a deep and dreamless sleep.

I sat on the porch the first day of February with the chilled air misty but pure once more. It was Gideon's birthday. While I took in the view, the smell of earth and rain wrapped around me like a life quilt. The hills behind the cabin, shades of gray, purple, and blue, combined into all the colors of a black eye. The beauty of my surroundings swept over the open spaces and rose on waves of foggy rims to the deeper blues of the more distant ridges. But the mountains were merely the backdrop to something bigger, a home to the people and the wolves who claimed them. As words from the Pioneer's Creed circled my head . . . *only the strong survived*, the tightness in me suddenly loosened like cutting a rope.

That winter, I learned more than a few secrets about telling the truth. You can bury the truth, but you can't kill it. Baylor preached that the truth sets us free. Gideon died for the truth. I say the power of life and death is in the tongue, and the blood we spill for it. But life and death are temporary; the truth goes on forever.

When shepherds quarrel, the wolf has a winning game.
~ German Proverb

Chapter Thirty-Four

Sidabee's face softened, and her smile grew brighter with the passing days, her baby blossoming under her clothes. I joined her in the evenings, drawing and learning her craft. She said I was *quite good* and had framed two of my drawings to hang in the great room. She sketched a likeness of Gideon I loved, and I asked her if I could hang it in his room over his bed. That way, when I went there, as I often did, I could imagine him huffing at me, *I'm not sitting up here in Heaven blaming you. Law, girl, get on with your life.*

Life—what a curious word. When I thought long and hard about it, I realized life's most significant gift to us is freedom—the freedom to choose. Pudge's choices cost him his life. But then, there is redemption, which turns our adversities into advantages and the worst of our choices into blessings for us and for others—despite ourselves.

God undoubtedly blessed us the morning Baylor brought home the February 2nd copy of the *Greensboro Record*. The headlines leaped off the page.

Woolworths Made Target
for Demonstration Here

A group of 20 Negro students from A&T College occupied luncheon counter seats, without being served, at the downtown F.W. Woolworth Co. store late this morning—starting what they declared would be a growing movement. The group declared double that number would occur at the counters tomorrow. Employees of Woolworths did not serve the group, and they sat from 10:30 a.m. until noon. White customers continued to sit and get service. Clarence Harris,

Woolworths manager, replied, "No comment," to all questions concerning the "sit-down"... and about what he planned to do. Today's 20-man action followed an appearance at 4:30 p.m. yesterday of four freshmen from Scott Hall at A&T who sat down and stayed without service until the store closed at 5:30 p.m.

I smiled. The movement had started. Gideon would've loved it. The same Woolworths that refused to serve him, the same Woolworths manager who had accused him of stealing and lying. Even Hotah smiled. "Good news," he said. "It is beginning."

It, indeed, was the beginning of good news.

Baylor contacted Mister Judd Hastings, Esquire, who called us back several times to let us know he had worked things out about the farm in Summerfield. Since Grandmother was alive and not dead, as everybody thought, technically, the farm still belonged to her.

Within days, Grandmother sold at auction the two hundred acres, which included the house, contents, and livestock. The money went into a college fund for me, a building fund for a new church on The Sanctum, and paying off my aunt and uncle's bank loans.

Baylor and Sidabee's new bedroom once again smelled of special-occasion perfume and cigars. But before they turned their old bedroom into a nursery, the one Pudge had died in, Hotah gutted it to the studs and performed a smudging ceremony to cleanse the room of negative energy and to restore harmony to The Sanctum, after which Baylor recited the 91st Psalm.

Although nothing prepared me for Sidabee's surprise. She had invited Sara to spend the night—with me! My first honest-to-goodness sleep-over. I found a record player and five bottles of the latest nail polish shades in my loft room to mark the special event. Sara brought her 45s, and we danced in the loft, painted our fingernails, and tacked up pictures of Bobby Darin, The

Everly Brothers, and Ricky Nelson from one side of the room to the other. I didn't fall asleep until sometime after midnight.

In the morning, when I finally cracked open my eyes, Sara was already gone, and Aiyanna stood at the foot of my bed. "Today is a special day, Little Red Bird," she said. "Do not ask questions. Today, you will celebrate the dawn of your womanhood, as many of us have done. A special gift awaits you."

"What—"

"—Ah! Do not ask questions," she said.

All I could do was grin and go with it. Nothing on The Sanctum surprised me anymore.

A pair of beaded moccasins and a long, soft leather dress with fringe along the sleeves lay on my bed. Aiyanna and Sidabee didn't speak as they dressed me, brushed my hair, and led me to the barn.

No one had set up the barn for church. It was dark inside, as Sidabee and Aiyanna ushered me through and out the other side to the fire pit, where Grandmother stood, holding one of her ornate pipes.

Aiyanna took the pipe and told me to sit before the fire. "This is a special occasion," she said. "Many believe a powerful good can come from the respectful and proper use of the pipe, but only if regarded as a spiritual instrument by the pipe holder, whatever her lineage or race. In the past, American Indians suffered from those who came upon our red path only to convert, destroy, and replace it. But the MacLennan family respects our ways, and we respect theirs, so we have married the two. Do you understand and agree, Little Red Bird?"

I nodded, noticing we were all female. It seemed no one invited the men to this event.

To the left of me sat Blossom and Sara, and to the right, Grandmother and Sidabee crossed their legs in front of the fire. A few of the women from the barn church sat in the circle, holding a drum, a feather, or their Bible to their chest.

The drums beat slowly, and the ceremony began when Aiyanna loaded a small amount of tobacco into the pipe. Holding it firmly by the bowl in the palm of her hand with the stem pointed outward, she faced east, south, west, and north, sprinkling tobacco on the ground at each turn. Inserting more tobacco, she prayed, touched the pipe bowl to the earth at her feet, and then pointed it at the sky. Turning to me, she smiled. "Do not be afraid, Little Red Bird. The smoke stands for truth: truthful words, truthful deeds, and a truthful spirit. Do not inhale the tobacco. Only take it into your mouth, hold it briefly, and blow it out in one long breath. Then we shall see what awaits you."

I did as I was told.

My head started spinning almost at once. Traveling fast down a tunnel of blinking lights, my body felt like a bullet shot from a gun. Dumped out on the other side of the tunnel into grayness, I watched the fog swirl around me so thick it frightened me at first. Looking behind and below me, there was nothing. Nothing but thick, soupy fog. I thought maybe I was dreaming, but the sensation was like nothing I had ever experienced, and suddenly I felt warm and relaxed. But in a split second, the fog carried me to the front of Baylor and Sidabee's cabin, where it parted yet hovered close.

I stood outside, looking through the porch window. Men in suits and ties and women in party dresses held drinks, talking and laughing, while a few couples gathered around a Christmas tree that towered inside the great room. People milled about, filling their plates from the large rectangular dining table covered with bowls of food and a large turkey. The table was well-lit from the chandelier and decorated with a centerpiece of pine and poinsettia plants.

I recognized the barn church congregation and some folks from town. But when Aiyanna walked past the window where I stood, I gasped. Holding a baby against her shoulder, Aiyanna paced back and forth with a little bounce in her step, as if trying to get the baby to fall asleep or burp. The infant, wrapped in a tiny Indian blanket, shot out its little fist, and I stared at its curly red hair. Sidabee sat near the table with a countenance of pure joy that bubbled in her laugh and shone in her eyes. A small boy of about four or five slid off her lap onto the floor, only to be picked up by Hotah and handed to Baylor.

I brushed tears from my eyes when Sidabee reached for the baby in Aiyanna's arms, stood and walked to the other side of the room. There, she situated herself in an oversized chair away from the guests, opened her blouse, and kissed the infant's tiny hand while it turned its small head onto her breast.

A few of the guests suddenly pointed toward the stairs, and what I saw next dropped me to my knees. I saw myself in the most beautiful dress, almost floating down the loft steps. Someone had fixed my hair, pulling it up into a grown-up style, and I wasn't wearing my eyeglasses. Jesse waited at the bottom step, smiling up at me. Everybody applauded, the sound reaching me through the window. Baylor raised a glass and spoke—muffled faint murmurs in the mist.

In my excitement, I had to hear him, and I moved to the door. I had to go through that instant, and as I placed my hand on the knob and turned it, the fog moved in and I felt myself spinning again. Within seconds, I opened my eyes to find myself at the fire circle with Grandmother's pipe in my lap, and my arrowhead necklace, which I thought was gone forever, hanging around my neck.

Hotah's giant thermometer read fifty degrees.

Underneath a vast cobalt-blue sky, the clouds mirrored the color of smoke, creating a vibrant picture of balmy days to come. God had adorned the bare, gray maples and elms behind The Sanctum with tight red buds, a sign of the impending spring. From a distance, patches of dense woods painted the hillsides closest to us in a blush of raw pink. Sprinkles of the first spring flowers huddled over the fields. Warmer air, like a long-lost friend, circled me, whispering the coming end of winter.

I shifted my boots in the snow, packing it under my feet. Time became dense and thick, and I reveled in the end-of-February thaw that was nothing short of magnificent. It was a pleasant day after weeks of temperatures hovering around freezing. Although I didn't find as much warmth in the bright sky as I had hoped for, the sunshine sifted through the clouds and trees, elevating my mood.

Grandmother had found my necklace near the boulder, almost at the exact spot where I had discovered the arrowhead. It was as if the stone had made its way back home. I made a silent vow never to lose it again. From that day on, I decided to wear my necklace only on Sundays, the day I knew I'd see Jesse.

Dark eyes fringed with black lashes stared back at me. A tuft of pitch-black hair hung below his wool cap, his scarf streamed out behind him, and his leather-gloved hands were wrapped tightly around his Bible. Despite dingy jeans with ancient stains, he smelled of soap and laundry detergent, a smell memory I cherished.

I paid no mind to our tiny congregation standing about; instead, my attention zeroed in on Jesse walking beside me. When we opened the barn door, it groaned and creaked from the cold. Hotah had already built a fire in the stove. I hoped they wouldn't build the new church for a long time, as I had come to love Sunday morning services in a barn.

Sara and I caught a case of the giggles until Grandmother gave me the eye to quiet down. It felt good. Getting the *eye* from her. God and Gideon had given me a family.

When church ended, Jesse asked Baylor if he and I could go for a walk. Jesse was proper that way. We walked to a hillside on The Sanctum I had never seen. A place where frozen rhododendron leaves, wrapped tight as beeswax candles, hung with the rigid formality of the thick velvet curtains in my grandmother's cabin. Patches of ground gleamed in the sunlight, and I was sweating in my coat as we strolled along an ice-rimmed stream.

There was no sound for several moments except the muted crunch of my rubber boots sliding against billions of ice crystals. Much of the snow had melted, but large patches spread over the hills and meadows like white spots on a black cow. A breeze no stronger than a breath danced over the warming earth, rustling spring growth and stirring life on the mountain from winter's sleep.

Finding a place to sit in the sugar-like crystals that frosted the dormant winter grass, I ignored the cold seeping through my coat.

Jesse sat still beside me, staring at the sky and watching a cloud twist on a wave of wind.

"It's so pretty," I said quietly, my eyes too on the sky.

"You're pretty," he said.

I smiled. "I'm talking about the clouds, silly. But they're like so many things in life—here one second, gone the next."

"I'm not going anywhere," he said, "except to medical school one day. But I'll always live here. This is my home. I hope it's your home as well."

I felt a chilled breeze against my neck. My hair tossed about, escaping my new wool hat. As Jesse stood and grabbed my hand, I felt like a young woman in love with life for the first time. He smiled, pulling me to my feet. His eyes never left mine. "I love your eyeglasses; I love your red, red hair," he said. "I love—you, Neeley McPherson, Morrigan, or whatever your name is. I think I will always love you."

My knees gave out, and I fell into the snow again. "Really?" A blush warmed my cheeks.

Jesse took off his gloves and helped me to my feet—again. Tiny diamond glints of ice sifted to the ground beneath me. "Really," he laughed.

I slipped my chilled hand into his. Jesse's fingers closed around mine, and I felt the heat of his skin. My hands grew unusually warm as we strolled through the woods, our fingers entwined, talking like old friends.

"Did you know," said Jesse, "the name Morrigan is a figure from Irish mythology who appears to have been a goddess, taking the form of a wolf?"

"You're kidding, right?"

"Not at all. See, Neeley, even *your* father had a connection to wolves."

As we stepped around bare trees, rocks, and pine boughs, I untangled myself from the clutches of the past. The fire-hardened chains of every memory surrounding Pudge were the last things I wanted to remember that day. "Do you dream dreams or have visions?" I asked. "Have you—have you ever seen the future?"

He hesitated as we stopped along the path. "I dream, sure. But I've never had a vision or the privilege of seeing the future."

"I have," I said.

He grinned and took in a deep breath, studying me again. "You have?"

I nodded and returned his grin.

"Will I marry?" he asked.

"Yes."

"Do you know who?"

"Yes." I giggled.

"Well—?"

"I'll tell you. Later."

"Why not now?"

"God sits in my driver's seat," I said, pointing to the sky. "He'll let me know when."

Jesse smiled again; we needed no words. He kissed me instead—my first honest-to-goodness kiss. I felt the pressure of his lips, the thrill of his face brushing against mine. Is there any love purer than the love of a first kiss? His lips were moist and warm, and neither of us felt embarrassment for it.

A new growth of grass swayed in the breeze near us. Jesse motioned with his arm in a broad sweep with the horizon. "Let's pretend a few years have passed," he said, pointing to the cleared pastures before us. "Can you imagine a great harvest of trees on that piece of land?"

My eyes closed against the last of the winter sky. His face touched mine again, and his breath was soft in my ear as he spoke. "Acres and acres of Christmas trees," he said. "Our trees. Yours and mine."

"Our trees?" I asked, opening my eyes.

"Beautiful enough for even the White House."

"Our trees," I whispered. I believe that's when the last snowflake of the season touched my cheek and slid down my neck.

Respect the elders
Track the young
Cooperate with the pack
Play when you can
Hunt when you must
Rest in between
Share your affections
Voice your feelings
Leave your mark

~ Wolf Credo

CHAPTER THIRTY-FIVE

The icy season has passed. Our breaths, once visible in the chilled air, now blend unseen in the warm breezes overtaking The Sanctum. This morning, the wolves are quiet. The Blue Ridge Mountains, anchored firmly in the earth's crust, stretch as far as the eye can see and awaken to the miracles of spring. As temperatures rise, the white landscape, once frozen and fragile, is replaced with the brush strokes of God. New growth coils upward toward greener pastures and golden sunlight.

But I will cherish the blankets of ice and snow covering The Sanctum in winter because Gideon brought me to this place in the coldest of seasons. Now, only death can take me from it. It's part of me. It is my home.

Standing at the window in my loft room, I press my scarless forehead against the cool glass—a contrast to the heat of my thoughts. The taste of Jesse's lips lingers on my mouth. I won't say anything about the kiss—not yet. But I think about it every morning when I raise my favorite blue mug to my lips. That kiss comes to me, pure and unwavering, often throughout the day.

In the evenings, my family gathers in the great room below me, as is their custom. Hotah and Aiyanna, with their strange hair and clothes and liquid-brown eyes, sit near the fire, sip their nightly coffee, and chat in a blend of Cherokee and English; Elvis and

Two-Toes are always nearby. Sidabee has temporarily set aside her charcoal pencils and paints and has taken to knitting everything from hats to baby booties. Baylor still fiddles with the TV, coaxing it to work while puffing on his cigar, the smoke spiraling up to the loft. Grandmother drops in occasionally with some contribution for supper and to catch up on the day's activities.

I like to listen to the conversations below and smell the hot coffee, the leather, and the wood. Years from now, and until I meet the Apostle Peter at the Pearly Gates, those aromas will remind me of this beautiful cabin and each family member.

I keep Sidabee's sketch of my mother in my loft room, framed on the wall above my bookshelves. Although Sidabee's paintings hang in the homes of many of the region's most prominent citizens, I treasure this piece of her work the most.

Baylor took it upon himself to continue my lessons until school starts again in the fall, and I have become an A student, as there is no reason to hide anymore. He taught me *agape*, an ancient Greek word—means the love of God. That kind of deep, abiding love flows in and out of every living creature on this mountain.

People have told me they feel an actual tingle when they walk through the front door and see the painting of The Wild Christ. Still others say there's some kind of magic around here—I don't know anything about magic. But what I do know is that The Sanctum is alive. The land is saturated with history and the hereafter. It's not haunted. It's simply a place where the spirits of the past coexist peacefully with those in the present—a bridge where the two meet.

As for me, I will no longer dwell on my Summerfield past. I have no fond memories there except for the howling dogs at the edge of the woods. The origin of my life is nestled among them and at Gideon's feet. To me, it was a battlefield where I fought my way through tangled masses of bigotry and intolerance to get to this place of sanctuary, hoping for something good to happen. And it has.

I still wake in the night to wolves howling in the distance. But at moments like this, when everything is quiet and peaceful, I think of those who love me. I am in awe of their suffering and strength. And I will never abandon the memories of my parents or of Gideon. His face appears to me in the flames of a Sunday bonfire, in the spring leaves of a poplar tree, in the curves of a passing cloud. Strange to see a Negro man's face in a white cloud. He will be my angel forever. Of that, I am sure. For I believe in Heaven. I believe it in my bones and my blood and that one day—I will see him again.

I can testify, after everything that occurred during the awful winter of 1960, the memory of it still clinging to me like heavy mountain snow, I harbor nothing but sorrow for those who embrace hatred and bitterness and bigotry in their hearts. What soothes my soul these days is the compassion and agape love I feel toward every four-legged creature that ever roamed these cold mountains.

One thing I've learned is that God doesn't own a clock. With Him, the hours, minutes, and seconds don't exist. He does things in His own sweet time. I think for those of us who believe in Him, living day-to-day involves a lot of scary twists and turns. Sometimes, it requires a mountain of faith. Because, like Gideon said, the rain falls on the just and unjust. God doesn't guarantee us a good life, only a good afterlife—if we believe.

For now, the Great Creator has handed me a second chance, and I plan to latch on. I have no intention of pushing His hand away. He has set me apart from any girl living in the Blue Ridge and watches over me from the corner of His eye. He has blessed me with a double portion—a wolf pack family of my own and all the love that comes with them. They are the face and voice of God inside me.

The End

A Word from the Author

As I embarked on this story over a decade ago, little did I know of the fierce passion that would overtake me in writing *The Sanctum*. To include the paranormal and spirituality from different points of view, I focused first on a young girl with a head full of fuzzy red curls who called herself Neeley.

This skinny, orphaned thirteen-year-old who wore thick eyeglasses and hand-me-down dresses captivated me from page one. Placing my redheaded girl on a tobacco farm in 1959 and in the caring hands of an elderly African-American male, a rugged individual who wasn't afraid of his gentle side, I quickly fell in love with the characters as the novel wrote itself, dragging my heart behind it.

History is a crucial element of the narrative, and with *The Sanctum*, I hope to transport your mind and pierce your heart, addressing the many atrocities we face today. For years, overt prejudice festered within my family. My southern grandparents wholeheartedly supported segregation. The Civil Rights Movement changed many hearts in a new generation, yet the battle against the scourge of racism endures to this day.

I have lived near the small town of Summerfield, North Carolina, for over twenty years. Horse and tobacco farms have saturated this picturesque area for decades and still dot the landscape. It is here I discovered James W. Cole (1924-1967), an ordained minister at the Wayside Baptist Church. In 1958, he toured as a tent evangelist, broadcasting a Sunday morning radio program. He also became an active member of the Knights of the Ku Klux Klan and, eventually, the Grand Dragon of North and South Carolina. The man intrigued and appalled me, making his mark as a true antagonist within these pages.

The International Civil Rights Center and Museum, located in the restored F.W. Woolworth Co. building in downtown Greensboro, North Carolina, is an iconic department store written into history and this story.

Further study of the Civil Rights Movement demanded I consider rights for all people. My great-grandmother was a full-blooded Cherokee, according to our family historian. Researching the Trail of Tears brought the story full circle for me.

And finally, the wolf appeared—a fascinating animal. The wolf represents family and order. It is a subtle character, but a voice to be reckoned with. I continue to be mesmerized by wolves, and having studied them, I discovered some folks who loved the animal enough to create wolf sanctuaries. Having spent time on a sanctuary near Bakersville in the Blue Ridge Mountains, I vividly recall the day I sat staring at a sign near the entrance that read, *The Wolf Sanctum*.

From that moment, I called my novel in progress, *The Sanctum*.

~ Pamela King Cable

Other Books by this Author

The Televenge Trilogy

Andie Oliver is a devout young woman dedicated to God, her husband Joe, and the influential televangelist Calvin Artury—a Godfather in a Mafia of holy men. As Joe immerses himself in the megachurch ministry team, sinking deeper into its corruption, Andie determines to free him from the Reverend's control and far-reaching influence. To uncover murders and long-hidden secrets, she sacrifices everything, including her children. In a valiant fight for her life and the lives of her family, Andie confronts the very definition of sin and shakes the Christian evangelical world to its core. Evading ruthless adversaries who will protect Reverend Artury at all costs, Andie Oliver battles the dark side of televangelism and those who have made a mockery of the church.

Televenge
Book One of the *Televenge* trilogy

Avenge Us All
Book Two of the *Televenge* trilogy

Vengeance Is Mine
Book Three of the *Televenge* trilogy

Southern Fried Women
A collection of Southern gothic short stories

For more information or to purchase, go to:
GracelynRose.com

www.ingramcontent.com/pod-product-compliance
Lightning Source LLC
Chambersburg PA
CBHW020235010826
48973CB00006B/1516